The

Retribution

Symphony

Josh Knox

© 2020

Chapters

0

Felix

Depeche Mode, Never Let Me Down Again is the best song about cocaine anyone has ever written.

Some kid at school once told me that and I couldn't agree more. But, when you think about it, cocaine, snow, the Teufel, has plenty of its own dedicated love songs, theme songs, if you will, but methamphetamine doesn't have a dedicated, theme song does it? Or not at least one which is well-known?

Nor does MDMA? I don't think? I'm not sure, but, nonetheless, shouldn't all uppers have a theme? Like, a dedicated anthem? Something to play in the background when you use them with your friends. Like a boxer's entrance music, to welcome the experience that's coming?

They all deserve proper respect. Proper homage.

Now, don't get me wrong, I'm no junkie, your humble narrator, but I do appreciate the powerful effects drugs can have in terms of boosting human performance.

Of… elevating our potential.

Of expanding the limits of our bodies and minds.

I don't really use any downers. I see no point in them. I like to be in control. I drink alcohol for the sake of appearances and I enjoy being inebriated as much as the next person, but, uppers… uppers are the key to my success.

Cocaine, methamphetamines, xanthines, Theophylline, MDMA, norepinephrine reuptake inhibitors, Serotonin–norepinephrine reuptake inhibitors, Tricyclic antidepressants, cigarettes, caffeine, whatever's available, I'll take it.

Live life at the very limit.

Live life at the edge of your potential.

Otherwise, why bother?

Why am I thinking about this right now, you might ask? Well, it's because the swirling blend of adrenaline, fear, excitement and rage surging through my veins at this very second feels like absolutely every single upper imaginable concentrated into one overwhelming hit I've just taken and yet, still nothing like that at all.

I'm faced with almost certain death and it is a magical experience.

Three people stand in a semi-circle around me in the well-lit living room of a large, two-storey, terraced house in East London, at, what I'm guessing is sometime between 10pm and midnight.

My back is facing a television where whatever was playing before this current scene manifested has been paused and a daunting close up of an animated rabbit with bulging eyes is staring inquisitively out of the screen into the room before him.

That rabbit, if he could see us from out of that screen would see me, a tired and beaten warrior, (I added the warrior part for dramatic effect), in standard goth-issue black trench coat and black military boots, kind of hunched, or leaning, rather, over the shoulders of a skinny Muslim guy with close-cropped hair, who is shirtless, but wearing brown boots and blue jeans, a gangster wannabe who's kneeling on the floor at my feet, helplessly, mumbling to himself nonsensically, contemplating Lucifer only knows what right now.

The rabbit would see a five-inch SOG Seal Pup Elite combat knife shoved just deep enough into the throat of this blubbering thug that withdrawal of the blade now would allow him to walk away, for the wound to heal up and for him to continue his life and yet only the smallest of thrusts further into the flesh would end that life abruptly. The rabbit would see me, covered in sweat and blood, panting like an old dog and yet pulsing with energy, more than willing to do *either* with that blade right now.

The rabbit could also not look past the aforementioned three other people crowding the room... all with their eyes keenly fixed upon the theatrics before them.

As I survey the room, much as that little cute rabbit might, an impressive array of emotions is on display in the audience, ranging from curiosity, to panic, to hope, to anger and undoubtedly a good dose of fear thrown in there for good measure.

Two machetes and a big-arse kitchen knife are drawn on me at the moment. The owners of the weapons are standing in the classic semi-amateur stance of unskilled fighters who have learned only through watching movies and playing video games. Wannabe gangsters. Waiting for an opportunity.

Waiting for a signal.

Real gangsters don't hesitate.

1 Dimitri

Felix

Trees and bushes rush past in a whirlwind of colour. An endless blur of greens and browns and dry yellows. Infinite forest. The faint sound of birds chirping intermittently breaks through over the drone of the car's engine for a moment, then is gone in an instant as we continue to zoom along.

Any moment now we'll crash.

I'm silently praying for it.

More and more trees and even more bushes blur alongside us.

A white sports car recklessly overtakes us, speeding. It races off ahead out of sight.   *An opportunity missed.*

More trees zoom past. More green. More blur.

The windows are rolled right down to let in fresh some air, some relief from the sweltering summer heat. I'm praying for something to happen.

Anything.

The sun bakes down relentlessly. The wind rushing in from outside presses my sunglasses into my face. Beads of sweat roll down my back. And yet, I feel nothing. I feel nothing except empty.

Please, let something happen. Let us hit a deer, run over an old woman, explode in a ball of flames, let Chinese jets fly overhead and begin an invasion of the country. Just… something.

Trees blur past. Waves of heat cascade through the car. We race on. Nothingness. Emptiness.

A bus approaches from ahead. I watch it move steadily towards us with anticipation. Perhaps this is it? What will it take? The driver to lose control? Some kind of distraction? I close my eyes and imagine the bus driver's hand slipping on wheel, just enough to clip the front of our car... we're not likely to survive at this speed, no way, I brace for it, I can see the driver through the front window, a grim expression on his face, here we go...

Please...

The bus cruises past and we carry on, unscathed.

Nothing.

Emptiness.

More trees, more heat, more blur

More of that hollow echo.

How did it come to this? Why am I here?

What happened to the person I was supposed to become? How did I lose it all so rapidly? How did I fall away from it? Lose grip of life?

Physically, I'm there. On the bus, on the train, at my job, at the grocery store. I'm *technically* there, but yet, I am definitely not *there*, if you know what I mean.

The world moves around me in a drone of activity... People talking, moving about from place to place, engaging with each other.

The world happens around me. I know it does. I read the news, none of it matters, just words on a page, photographs on a screen to me, all of this, everything I see and hear, it all just occurs. And so do I.

I occur, but not as part of it, not like these other people do.

I occur within the world, yet without the world.

I'm becoming increasingly detached from life, from all of this. This was not what I expected my life to be.

Wake up, shower, dress, work, come home, cook, eat, watch mind-numbing rubbish on television, then sleep. Wake up, repeat.

A few interesting events thrown in here and there, a film at the cinema, a holiday overseas, a walk along the Thames, sure, just to break things up. But still, these fleeting moments are quickly swallowed up by the numbing expanse of everyday life.

I'm twenty-five years old. I need more out of life than this. What am I facing? Another 40 years of this absurd monotony and then I die? This is the end of 2010, soon to be 2011, this is the western world. I have choices. But what am I funnelled into? A lifetime of consumption and time wasting.

But, there is hope. My generation fights back. Millennials they call us. The lost boys of the century.

We want something more.

And what I want is out.

If this is all life has to offer, then that's it. I've had enough. I need anything to relieve the boredom.

Even death. Sweet, sweet death. The forever sleep. I'll take *that* over *this*.

And yet, here I am, for now, melting in the backseat of a worn-out Mercedes-Benz which is probably as old as I am. As worn out too. Kind of fitting really. This car and I could share some stories.

Life takes you both to places you try very hard to get to, and to places you try very hard to avoid. In those instances we have limited choice, except for how we react. For some people, it will destroy them, for some, it helps them grow, evolve, for the rest... well, for us, we give up a little bit of our soul to survive and then, we carry on. A little bit less than we were before, but still wiser for the event. It's as simple and as depressing as that.

The world outside the window continues to blurs by, a faint smell of pine wood drifts through, but it's overwhelmed by the nauseating smell of melting rubber coming from somewhere as the heat bears down. Sweat rolls down my nose and my sunglasses begin to slide down. It's too hot to move so I just tilt my head back, roll down the window again and lean into the wind, letting the force of the breeze keep them in place. I can't decide what I want.

The road is empty now, no hazards, nothing.

Just the grim blur of forest.

I consider reaching forward and snapping the driver's neck in one violent move, just like they do in films, snapping his neck and sending us all hurtling towards uncertain consequences, but certain excitement.

We slow down, I watch the driver changing gears, the blur slows, the trees and bushes begin to take shape again. The breeze is less, greasy Wayfarers slip off my face onto my lap, an oily layer of sweat coats the bottom of the frames.

The heat is unimaginable. It seems to drain all my energy. I can't even move to pick the sweaty sunglasses up. The sun beams into my eyes.

I feel dizzy.

I feel nothing.

I sigh.

The heat is overwhelming.

The signs along the road begin to highlight our final destination. We are approaching the airport.

This trip is over. Done. Back to reality soon. A fortnight spent in New Zealand, purposefully distracting myself from the realities of my life. A fortnight over too quickly.

It's too hot to speak inside this car. All of us are silent. I know that Connie will be thinking of something meaningful to say later on, some words to wish me a safe journey home etc... but, I hope at the time she says nothing, that the words don't come.

I just want to be here forever. I don't want to get on that fucking plane.

Once we park the car the three of us trudge along to the departures gate. Silent. It's too hot to speak. Our footsteps heavy like the marching of weary soldiers as waves of heat rise up of off the gravel of the airport car park.

Sweat leaks from the middle of my back. My chin begins to itch. It's either an insect or a bead of sweat. Nonetheless, I've no energy to check. Fuck it. Ignore it. My shirt is so damp it hugs me like cling film. Disgusting.

A bug buzzes around my ear. I trudge on and ignore it. By now I'm too hot and too exhausted to even wish for some kind of chaos, like some King Kong type monster grabbing my plane out of the sky and snapping the whole thing in half as I take off. Right now, I can't even summon the energy to care.

A faint sound of waves crashing hits my ears. I'm so delirious from the heat that it could easily be my imagination. Then again, even a mirage of water would be welcomed right now.

Imagination versus user experience.

Imagination versus reality.

The noise begins to echo in my ears, faint at first, like listening to someone's heartbeat through their chest, louder and louder, becoming more distinct. More real.

I must be suffering heat stroke. But as we enter the airport terminal, I'm confronted by a giant waterfall, with water cascading down the side and making waves that crash over the base.

I stop and stare at that waterfall.

The water crashing down from above and eventually becoming one with the water below seems like a perfect analogy to life – after flowing down the river of growing up, we set out with such high expectations, at the top of the water fall beautiful and elegant, and then, in what seems like no time at all, we plummet, crashing down, and we hit hard on the bottom, we become nothing, simply one little drop in the pool of dirty water known as life. An ugly, undignified nothingness, amongst an ugly and undignified world.

Colin speaks suddenly, the first words any of us have managed in what seems like hours, the shock of hearing his voice makes it seem unusual, not his own. It snaps me out of my trance, "finally, we're here", he says. We all nod, nothing else needs to be said just yet.

Finally, is right, I think to myself. Lucifer... I need a drink.

As I cool down inside the air-conditioned airport the world starts coming alive around me again. I worry about my iPhone in my pocket, if the damp from my sweat has been damaging the electronics. What on earth has been happening inside this sweat pocket? Disgusting.

I feel filthy. I feel nothing else.

Do I even wish I did?

After a few minutes more of death marching through the busy terminal and a few uneventful moments spent checking in, I find myself standing at the departure gates, ready to proceed through the dignity destroying process known as Customs & Security...

It's time to say goodbye to Colin and Connie, I'll miss them both. It's been two years since they left London, and I'd not seen them since. An invitation out to their wedding was a long overdue excuse to get out of London. I needed the break, I was burning out at work and the thought of escaping to the other side of the world for a couple of weeks was too enticing to turn down.

And here I go, back to reality. Lucifer... I need a fucking drink.

Colin smiles at me and begins to say something, I cut him off before the words come out, "it's been an absolute pleasure," I say, giving him a hug, "thank you both so much for inviting me," I add as I give Connie a quick hug as well. "Also, I really appreciate the ride to the airport."

"You are most welcome, mate, it's been far too long since we saw you. You're always welcome here!"

"And we can't wait to come visit you in London," Colin adds with a smile.

I nod, we say our goodbye's, and I turn away and walk towards Customs & Security.

A welcome breeze from a nearby human using a magazine as a fan strikes my face, blowing my hair across my chin and into my mouth. I'm proud of my long hairstyle, I keep it chin-length, but its well-kempt. You can get away with longer hair as a guy in the office these days, so long as it's in a creative profession, or something like tech. Only a few years ago and that would be a big no-no. Times are changing.

Despite the heat today, no doubt I'm looking good. You might think I'm proud of my job too, working in architecture. Making good money. Life on track. Less drugs, less alcohol than before. Acting like a grown up, feeling more mature. More independent... On paper, my life is perfect, great flat, great friends, great job. But that's the problem. This is not what I imagined for myself. It's a continuous emptiness. The infinite empty. Life was not supposed to be this.... meaningless.

I spent so long trying to grow up, to be an adult and do all the adult things I'm expected to do. I even, can you believe, considered raising a child or two at one stage or another. Oh, shit, how things can change...

How could I bring my own flesh and blood into a world as fucked as this? It would be a punishment. How could I do that them?

What benefit would that serve? I can't even find my own happiness, let alone devote years to encouraging the happiness of my spawn.

I keep feeling this... this... boredom, this dissatisfaction. This... disappointment, with all the world around me, from the worst parts to the very best, it's all just... not what it was supposed to be.

Everything is the same.

Every day is exactly the same.

Days roll into weeks, weeks to months and blah, blah, blah you know what I mean. Years roll by and there you are. Like a rock in a river. Unchanged. Everything else moving forward. Everything except you.

Nothing. I feel nothing.

The most wonderful experiences, the things I used to take great pleasure in doing, now seem mandatory, like part of a ritual.

Go to the cinema, watch a film with friends, sit out on the balcony and drink all night with my favourite music playing, go to a pub and try random craft beers I've never seen before or ever will again... these are the things I do in my spare time. But... to what end?

All of it lacks joy, lacks authenticity and lacks taste.

Life lacks taste.

Nothing. Nothing, means anything anymore.

I need something. I need something else.

Life cannot carry on like this. I was born for something better. A life more... extreme. Something that gets the heart pumping. Something that makes you feel alive and reminds you that death awaits around every corner. Always.

Hell, I've dreamed of living that life. I tasted it 3 years ago during an encounter Tommy and I had with a few blacks one night in Camden.

We were leaving a club in the lock market at about 2am and we unwittingly walked through some dispute between 4 black dudes in the middle of the street and Tommy got clocked by some dude who was apparently raging at anyone any anything that moved. Anyway, Tommy lunged back at this guy and before we knew it the middle of the road was full of black guys all swinging fists at each other, and Tommy and I included, anyway, we both managed to throw a couple of good punches at guys which I suspect were from both sides of this dispute before I spotted one of them pull out a knife and Tommy and I made a run for it. As we sprinted off down the street police cars screamed past us, lights flashing and sirens blaring. The fight, that we'd kicked off, continued to rage on behind us.

I never felt more alive than I did that night 3 years ago. Never since.

I need something. I need some*one*, perhaps?

I need excitement. Whatever.

Cooled down now and with music in my ears I make my way through security - no drama to be had this time - and begin walking the long trek through endless swathes of overpriced alcohol and under-priced cigarettes towards the departure gates. I take a deep breath of thick, ambient, heavily conditioned air and, adjusting the satchel on my shoulder, veer at a pace towards the my gates.

I know what I need to do.

I need to take a massive risk. I've tasted the normal life. I've lived it properly. Three years since graduation, three years, a haze. Another thirty-five, forty years of this? Then what? Retirement? The golf course? The bridge club? The old humans' home? The death bed? No, thank you, please Lucifer, no! I was not made for this. Its unnatural.

I've tried hard to live this life as it was expected of me.

People talk about families and houses and long-term investments, long-term stuff. Hell, if I told you honestly, long-term for me is about five years ahead at any time. Making plans beyond that seems ludicrous to me. Some people can do it, but I am not some people.

Many times I've caught myself praying for something to happen, anything dramatic. To break The Haze.

Sometimes I'll be standing on the train platform, watching the train approaching, wondering how quickly I would die if just took a quick leap in front right at the last minute.... And then, whoosh, the train passes and the moment is lost, as its brakes come and on everything sudden slows down to a snail's pace... It's a metaphor for my life and the missed opportunities slowing down to this emptiness I wander aimlessly around in now.

I am nothing.

I feel nothing.

I contribute nothing.

I've lost the will to carry on down this path.

I need to get out, escape, this big, empty void. The rat race. I need out more than perhaps I am willing to admit. And I cannot do it alone. The urgency is evident, escape now, or just forever sleep.

The dull music coming from speakers in the departure lounge stops and a voice begins mumbling something unintelligible, half drowned out by the drone of humans around me and half by the awful sound quality of the intercom itself.

I reach my departure gate with 15 minutes to spare and I consider getting a snack or a vodka. Or both. I'm sweating from the heat outside and the march to get here, and a sensible person would take their coat off or perhaps put some shorts on, but, as we all know, fashion overrides comfort and I know I look good right now. Plus, I've never owned a pair of shorts in my life, so the point is mute. I will stand here, fashionable and fucking sweating.

I take out my phone and switch my music to some angry death metal. A rush of energy fills my body, seemingly from nowhere, but we all know it's from the music. The music spurs me on. My body can sense alcohol ahead and knowing it's coming seems to calm it down.

I need a drink or three, I need a boost.

How fucking long do I have to wait here in this waiting room?

How fucking long do I have to wait here in this fucking life?

Approaching the bar I catch my reflection in the window and the sadness washes over me again.

I see a gaunt face staring back, a vampire-looking creature that would do anything and everything to feel... something special.

What a powerful and also pathetic way to be...

I need that drink.

Every step forward I take towards the bar seems slower and slower, like the brakes are being slowly applied to my world.

But I fight through it.

What point does all of this have?

A few drinks later I'm sitting alone on the edge of a cold metal bench when the humans start boarding the plane. The sun has begun to set and my music has taken a darker tone.

Alice In Chains, Rain When I Die, comes on. I let it play.

Goodbye, New Zealand – a land as far from home as you can get.

Yet, I could never leave my mind behind. I can't escape that.

No, unfortunately, the old haunting thoughts remain with me no matter what.

The distraction has been lovely, but the way out of the black hole, is through.

I have to face it all.

The only sure way to leave your mind behind is with drugs. The only way.

But for now, my options are limited.

I decide that in order to alleviate the blanketing depression, just for the night, since I don't have access to any chemical assistance, and I have 24 hours of travel ahead of me, I need to get good and proper wrecked. Yes. I'll buy the plane out of alcohol. I'll drink it dry, as best I can.

Felix

I'm sitting in the semi-darkness of a dimly-lit economy class cabin. The only passenger still awake on a twelve-hour flight, the last stretch of the journey after a four-hour stopover in a crowded Shanghai airport and before that an eleven-hour flight from my original location.

The most exciting part of the whole journey was my discovery that there are designated smoking rooms in the Shanghai terminal. Inside the fucking airport! Inside which dirty 'sometimes smokers' like me as well as filthy 'all-the-times smokers' like most others, can stand about and rabidly inhale concentrated nicotine as though those little death-sticks were somehow little life-sticks and none of us could live without them.

The remainder of the stopover was dull. The terminal smelt like a petrol station forecourt. The free internet didn't work. The paid internet didn't work. My fucking mobile phone didn't work in that fucking country. I had no local currency to buy any of the random shit they were selling in the too-brightly-lit and too-colourfully-dizzying stores either. So, all in all, it's been a long, tiresome and disappointing journey.

On this plane right now, I finish my somethinth cup of wine and watch contemplatively as frost forms on the window beside me. The sunrise from up this high is a beautiful shade of orange. I twirl the empty plastic wine cup in between my bony fingers.

What the Hell should I do with my life?

How did it come to this?

How the Hell can I get myself back on track?

How can I find happiness?

I've thought myself too deep.

I'm gone in too far and now I'm tainted.

Got my regular thoughts all dirty from the really bad ones down deep.

How can I do this? How can I get myself out of this hole?

I take a deep breath and crush the plastic cup in my hand.

How, Felix?

You know how… Because that is what you do. You morph, you change, you evolve. Oh, yes, you do. It's time for another Spring in your life. It's time to evolve and advance.

"Excuse me, sir," a flight attendant looms above me, leaning in all wide-eyed and fake-smiled.

"Hi," I reply, holding back any enthusiasm deliberately. My earphones are still in and I take them out of my ears reluctantly. Anyone who is going to disturb the serenely dark ballads of Lana Del Rey better have a fucking wicked reason… I look up expectantly, this time with a fake smile around my pursed lips.

"Would you mind fastening your seatbelt please, sir? We're going to experience some turbulence."

For some reason these words linger for longer than they should. 'You have no idea what turbulence is, love,' I think to myself, then find myself staring away out the window at nothing.

I shake off the hopelessness and glance around exaggeratedly at the seven other passengers in my range of sight and consider the hundreds of others in this metal tube along with us. "What about these people sleeping?" I ask her, nodding my head in the direction of an overweight Chinese couple sleeping with little red eye masks on their faces across the aisle from me.

"I'll take care of them," miss-cannot-blink replies, following up with an even faker smile and I'm already bored of this interaction. Although, I must say she seems enthusiastic about her job. Far too enthusiastic to not be functioning on some lovely drugs. Xanax or Valium, I'd guess. Something in that category of numb. Something to keep up the 'happy, happy', keep up the hours of fakeness. She's wearing glasses so despite her wide-eyed staring, it's hard to see how dilated her pupils really are. Am I jealous of her apparent high? Yes, yes I do.

I don't know what she means by 'take care of them', and as I lean back and close my eyes I fantasise a scene where the attendant rips her clothes off down to her underwear and then massacres every single sleeping passenger with only a plastic airplane knife in a highly sexual, yes, orgiastic bloodbath. The final moments involving her rubbing the blood of her victims all over her well-toned body and then pouring blood down her throat from the neck of a freshly decapitated head. My imagination goes wild... it goes wild and where does it go? Straight to a flood of violence...

"Sir?"

I snap back to 'reality' with what I can only hope is an obvious scowl, but I nod in submission as I buckle my seatbelt. Such a good boy you are, Felix.

The attendant carries on down the aisle behind me and the turbulence she promised never eventuates.

Lana Del Rey returns to my current experience of life and I sigh in contentment.

"If you call for me, you know I'll run. I'll run to you."

London calls for me now. It's time to go home. Enough time has passed. A fortnight of fuckery. Two weeks of drifting and thinking. Where will this life take me?

No answers yet.

I let all the bad thoughts drift right back in.

I let the darkness envelope me and take me wherever it wants to.

I embrace the moment.

An epiphany is coming.

Where did we go wrong?

What direction do we have?

A generation of political correctness has left us ungoverned and unguided by our parents, by our teachers, Hell, by all authority figures.

Now, we just act. We struggle. We're still children in our 20's and 30's these days.

We're still children.

Lost children.

Who leads us? Our parents surely have no idea.

Politicians? Fuck me, politicians are no longer trusted. Probably in general that has always been the case, but our generation had it thrust in our faces when, as children we watched President Bill Clinton lie to the world about his affair with Monica Lewinsky. Then when the truth came to light, the avalanche of debauchery and corruption was exposed and Billy Boy was forced to admit he was a lying, cheating, sex fiend. The President of the United States, a sex fiend. A liar.

We're a generation that grew up in a world where we knew that even the person holding the highest position is just a poisoned as the rest of us.

Our distrust in politicians was solidified, you could say it reached boiling point when as teenagers the United States Government conspired to stage the infamous false flag operation on the 11th of September 2001. Again, lies to the citizens world straight from the government. Blatantly lying to us to benefit themselves and those around them. Fuck us, right? Fuck the people.

The trust never came back. And it never will.

Just like religion, trust in government has had its day.

Rightly, we lost faith in religion, but we've replaced the church pew with the television screen, the words of god with a bag of crisps and the ten commandments with 10% off. Our generation don't worship gods, we worship consumption and distraction.

Instead of each of us becoming our own gods, we turned (or were turned) into an army of mindless consumers, Hell bent on pursuing the relentless acquisition of materials. Of possessions.

We should've replaced religion with nothing. But, we've had to fill the void. It could've been with a lifestyle based on freedom and enlightenment, of a perfect balance between individuality and community. A new beginning. Yet we're a generation left lost and disconnected. A generation left weak and powerless.

A life made for living, exploring and enjoying has become a life spent either working or distracting ourselves.

If we aren't at work, we're watching television, playing video games, we're on social media, staring into our mobile phones like zombies while the world moves on around us.

We're lost.

No direction.

No trust in our leaders.

No faith.

Nothing to live for.

I rest my head against the glass of the plane window.

Frustrated and deep in thought. The coolness of the glass is soothing.

I fall asleep and I don't wake until the plane landing back in London.

I take a black cab back to my flat in Mile End and dump my luggage in the hallway as I arrive.

Pulling a packet of Parliaments from my pocket I open the balcony door and step out into the evening air. The sun is setting and its rush hour. I can see and hear humans swarming about in the streets below, frantic, rushing home, rushing back to their pointless lives.

I reflect on my own life. I reflect on the lives of an entire generation.

We are frustrated. Lost. Hungry. Thirsty. For something.

A generation with a void.

A generation with a thirst.

Thirsty, yes. But for what? Fulfilment? … No, it's not as simple as that. Not for us. What do *we* thirst for?

Danger.

For the thrill of the unknown.

For the wild.

We thirst for all the things that are absent from our lives. Out of reach. Abstract to us in our modern age.

We thirst for the primal.

For that rawness that connects us to the world as the animals that we are.

Look what we have become.

Man. No longer the hunted. But no longer the hunter.

Life has become a distorted bubble of civilisation where we are sheltered from the reality. The hollowness of our own lives. The pointless nature of everyday existence.

Each morning our alarm sounds. Screaming at us to get up. We struggle. It's always a struggle. Even after those nights you dedicate to getting to sleep early so you can catch up on sleep lost. It never seems to work.

Always tired.

Everything always hard… uphill.

We wake, then what? Breakfast? Usually skipped. Too much time spent snoozing, hitting that lovely snooze button on our phones…. No time. We are always in a rush.

Life is hectic, sweaty and frustrated. We're desperate to catch the next train, the next bus, the quicker lane on the motorway. Desperate. Desperate to get to work. To our jobs. Never enough time. No time.

No… we just relentlessly deal with life, the consuming beast that we loathe the most. Desperate to get to where we 'need to be'…. Fuck, we're so desperate that most of us are in full panic mode if our journey is somehow delayed, train trouble, traffic jam, missing our bus. Meltdowns and tantrums all around!

For fucks sake.

How desperate have we become? And why? It's pathetic.

Then when we do arrive at work, we're flustered, tired, definitely still tired.

No breakfast, of course there was no time for that and certainly no time to think of it right now. Time now is only to be spent checking email. Praying that nothing has arrived into that little list of limitless shit that will ruin your day. No big drama. No client demanding something urgent. No boss upset over some work you've done, or not done… We stare at that inbox praying that that list of terror is, just *this* morning, at least for *now*, just, all okay.

Then what? The day drags on.

A day broken up only by a series of seemingly random interactions with colleagues.

Oh look, I'm in the kitchen building a coffee and the HR manager Mavis walks in.

"Mavis."

"Hello Felix."

"How are you?"

"Oh, I'm good thank you. How are you?"

"Good. All good."

Insert awkward silence here…

"So, it's getting cold isn't it?

"Oh, yes, it's going to be a cold winter I think."

Meaningless words on and on and on...

You all know how the rest of this conversation goes. You have it every single day. You have it over and again with your respective Mavis's, John's and Ashley's and et al.... a series of seemingly random interactions occurring within a closed workspace with a finite number of people and a fixed number of locations for congregation. The aforementioned kitchens, the printers, the stationary rooms, the bathrooms, the corridors...

Randomness is absent. As is variation. As is interest.

Take the conversations you have during these interactions and I bet you could copy and paste them into any day of the week, probably with any colleague and you'd never know the difference.

Its meaningless. We don't know these people. We almost certainly didn't choose to work with them, and, well, vice versa. We don't know them, and they don't know us.

And thank absolute fuck for that.

Because them knowing us, the stressed-out, problem-ridden, lonely, self-hating, depressed, empty, desperate, tired people we are truly are, well, knowing that, the detachment, the hollowness, the uselessness of conversation would become all too material.

They don't know us, and we don't know them.

Thank fuck for that.

We've got enough stresses, problems, emptiness, etc. etc.. in our own lives, we don't need yours too, thank you very much.

We don't know people and people don't know us, because we choose not to.

Because life is easier that way.

Because life is safer that way.

Because knowing ourselves is hard enough.

I'm twenty-five years old and I don't *me* well enough, how can I know you?

The day drags on. The afternoon clock-watching begins. The counting of the hours, the minutes, the seconds until it is acceptable for you to escape. For you to slide quietly out the door hoping your exit is not noticed or questioned by too many. Sliding quietly out to "freedom". Out to your life. To the final stretch of today's journey. Then the desperate, frantic, rush home.

Then it begins again, desperate for the next train, the next bus, the next lane on the motorway. No time to waste now. Most of our day wasted most of it in the office. It's dark already, night-time soon, get yourself safe. Get yourself home. Have a drink. Have a rig. You've got no time. Not enough time.

No time for what though?

No time for *what*?

Do we ever ask ourselves that as we laze on the sofa? Fed, drink in our hand, zoning out on Netflix or whatever, force-feeding our mind distractions from the television? No time for what?

No answers come and we don't care.

Then the sleepiness begins to set in. The tiredness catches up. A hesitant glance at the clock tells us that we should really have gone to bed an hour ago. Probably two. But we have no time, no time. We might as well squeeze in another episode, one last drink.

Then the sleepiness becomes overwhelming. And so too do the regrets, all the wasted opportunities. All the wasted time.

Better to sleep. Yes. One more drink and then sleep it off.

Tomorrow is another day. I'll do that thing to change everything tomorrow.

Yes... tomorrow.

I'm not depressed, I'm just tired.

….

I can't go on like this.

It will kill me.

2 Edvard

Felix

Back in London, I return to the office, but something in me has changed.

The days' drift into each other. I am ever so aware that I am the cliché rushing to the office each day, drinking myself to sleep at night and convincing myself that I'm not depressed, that I'm simply 'tired.'

My pride is shedding away. I am losing grip of who I really am.

Perhaps I am evolving.

Perhaps I am dying.

I lurk about the streets of London in a haze.

I sit at my desk in the office staring at my computer, nothing matters anymore.

I've been back for a week now and every day another part of my mind seems to be disconnecting itself from reality.

I find myself noticing and considering random things I wouldn't have noticed or stopped to consider before.

The first day returned to London I watched a middle-aged man tripping out on the pathway alongside the canal in Mile End park, reaching up to touch the leaves of an overhanging tree and mumbling to himself that they are precious space leaves from the next galaxy. Perhaps they are, perhaps we're the ones seeing it wrong and he's seeing the truth. Who knows?

Next is the angry black man (why do they all look so angry and aggressive? Look as though life is permanent nuisance?), the angry black man marching down the steps from the bridge, marching along, looking seemingly regular enough, until he gets a bit closer and you notice all his teeth are missing and he's pissed himself. And as you look away in disgust you hear him mumbling something to a nearby squirrel and realise he's asking it for "spar changes" from a fucking squirrel at 7am on a Monday. Welcome to London.

This morning on my way to the office I saw a father arguing with an ill-disciplined son outside a police station in central London. Yet, despite how petulant the son was, as he was smoking rigs in a feigned-casual manner and arguing back fiercely, I could still clearly see the underlying submission, the acceptance of the father as the highest authority. Despite his comparative youth, his physical superiority, I could see it was the psychological superiority that would win at the end of the day. The father figure would win the argument. Even in that brief moment as I marched by, I could see the defeat in the son's eyes. No matter how long he argued on, he'd already lost. Why? Because he will never overcome the fear.

The fear.

Because it's fear that drives humans, fear that drives all animals.

Everything we do is based on fear. Every. Single. Thing.

I could list every human action you can think of, and explain how fear drives us to do it. But you now it's true, so I won't waste my time or yours. Just think of this - why does our body breathe? For fear of death. Our body does this because it fears the alternative...

On my way home a guy falls asleep on the tube, in the process dropping his dinner all over the floor, a box of fried chicken and chips, the noise barely wakes him up before he grunts and falls back to sleep, head swaying from side to side as the train carriage hurtles us passengers to our destinations. Perhaps this guy has the right idea? Perhaps 'fuck it', 'fuck what anyone else thinks' is the answer… 'I'll stuff my face full of deep-fried shit, drop it all over the floor and then comatose out in front of you. Fuck it. Who cares?'

Fuckinell… I shake my head. Imagine if we were all like that? Imagine if we all lived like animals…

No… some of us have to be civilised. To keep humanity moving forward…

I'm sick of this.

"Satan, if you are watching, please give me something. Please slap me out of this state," I say aloud. No one in the train hears me.

I laugh to myself at how ridiculous I'm being right now, but I feel such fucking rage.

Rage is the only way to describe it.

It's been building inside of me for months now. It started slowly at first. I just noticed myself being more upset about things, more involved in small shit that pissed me off. It's been growing like a virus inside of me, to the point where I'm actively seeking opportunities to vent, to let off steam. Seeking any opportunity the universe will give me to like, fucking shove some rude mother fucker off a train carriage onto the platform for some kind of shitty behaviour. To just, have an excuse to get physical... anything will do. It's a furious storm inside me that needs to be unleashed.

I hate myself.

I hate myself.

The rage I feel within, the rage I wish to direct at everyone around me, is really, honestly, all directed towards myself. I fucking hate what I have become.

I fucking hate who I am.

I'm so massively disappointed in the decisions I've made in my life.

I need to escape this path or I need to kill myself.

What else can I do?

...

I've called out for something to change for what seems like forever, never expecting anything would really happen. Never expecting my prayers would be answered.

And then?

Well...

Friday changed everything.

...

Be careful what you wish for.

Felix

The day started like any other. The usual fucking bullshit routine. Everything a rush. Filthy, rude humans on the tube. Shoving and complaining. I get jostled around along with the masses and swear under my breath. I get tube hands within seconds of touching the pole and I stand there with that awful thought all

Londoner's get of wondering how many other humans have already touched this exact fucking spot today with their sweaty, unwashed hands…

I listened to Wagner on my journey in to the office, drowning out the bullshit around me as best I could. Train was held at Bank Station; someone pulled the passenger alarm at Holborn for whatever reason. Great. The Central Line, the heat, the sardine squeeze. The same commute, over and over again. Expected. Hated. Needed.

I marched at pace from Bond Street Station to the office in Berkeley Square, a sweaty mess, running late, socks damp and shirt sticking to my back. It made no difference; the bosses were later than I was. My rushing was in vain. Typical.

Still sweating while making coffee in the office kitchen as soon as I arrived, Donnie walked in, didn't say a word, didn't even smile. I ignored it, did what I needed to do and then walked back to my desk. Despite him being my boss and sitting right next to me, over the last three weeks we've hardly spoken a word to each other and that's fine by me. I'd be happy to never speak to that cunt again in my life.

But still, three weeks of tension has been building. I know it's coming, I know the hammer will drop at some point. The fucking snarky comment from him will arrive. The questioning of my work. My intelligence. My purpose in being here. My purpose in being alive! It will come… It is well overdue. It has to come.

Perhaps I even want it to.

Perhaps I fucking *need* it to.

Bring it, you fucking arsehole. Give me that excuse.

Anyway, I remember sitting there that afternoon, thinking to myself, Donnie you giant fucking cunt, today is really not the day to be confronting me.

I could feel the rage surging inside me. I could feel my body vibrate and tingle. My hands were trembling. I wasn't ready to be back at work. I'd had such a great time in New Zealand, and yet, here I was, another week back in the grind and already I was forgetting my holiday.

The rage, both at myself and at Donnie was twisting away inside me.

Yet that sixth sense we all have told me that today was not the day. Today was not the fucking day that some shit or another should kick off and I end up kicking back so much harder in return that the small part of me that actually cares, really worries for those around. On that day, it will get nasty. I know that for sure.

But a good kick off is exactly what I need to relieve this tension.

Anyway, I was sensible took deep breath, distracted myself and carried on.

I drifted in and out of paying attention to my work. Things happened upon my screen, keys got pressed on my keyboard and my mouse clicked away like clockwork, yet I was simply acting on autopilot. Years now this endless shit has gone on, spreadsheets, reports, presentations, conference calls, strategy changes at the last minute, demanding clients, incompetent bosses, typical fucking bullshit. Again, and again. Some people can handle this... It's driving me crazy.

The sketches I make, the designs I draw up mean nothing to me. These days, I'm just ticking the boxes.

My life…

Monotonous.

Repetitive.

Mindless.

Empty.

I'm nothing more than cog in the machine, making other people wealthy while I churn away and wear myself out.

The pressure building up simply has to be released. One way or another. I have so much pent up rage…

If I don't snap out of this soon, my casual jokes about stalking the office with a pump action shotgun, dumping shell after shell of lead into my colleagues, blood and paper flying everywhere, computer screens exploding, screams drowned out by deafening blast after deafening blast, this whole scenario would become not just a joke, not just a dream but a glorious reality.

There is a pressure point and the gauge just keeps on climbing. Its past dangerous. We're critical now.

I was ready that day. Ready as I ever have been. Ready for anything. Whatever. Fuck it. Ready to die. Ready to run. Ready to cry.

I just don't care anymore. I need to unleash this rage and direct it right at those who fucking deserve it. Like a room full of gas just waiting for tiny spark to set it free and bring down the whole building, I just need any excuse to explode.

I recall waiting, at my desk, festering in my own fury and silently praying to Lucifer below that this fucking giant cunt beside me would say something to fuck me off. Something arrogant, something patronising.

I was on the edge. Waiting.

Day dreaming. Mentally rehearsing.

I'd stand over him, grab him by his shirt collar and pull him in closer to me, he'd gasp in shock, his hands rushing to my wrist to pull himself free, but he'd be too late. I'd rain down punches on him like a storm cloud from Hell. Raining down across his face, aiming for all the softest bits first. Knuckles into nose, blood gushing from nostrils, knuckles into eye socket, tears welling up, knuckles into fingers of blocking hands. I'd be raining down with both fists next, like a wild man, seemingly out of control yet perfectly aware of what I was doing. Donnie would've covered himself in a foetal position by this point, so I'd aim for the exposed bits, wild animal noises escaping my throat, spit flying everywhere, knuckles against neck, ears, throat, chest, chin. Wailing down, like King Kong, licking the blood off the back off my freshly split knuckles, some of it my own, most of it his. Growling and panting. All the rage flowing out these fists of mine.

Once I'd satisfied the urge, I'd hold them up in front of his cowering face, showing him the weapons I'd used to dish out this punishment. Never again would that arrogant cunt ever treat anyone like a piece of shit.

Even the fantasy of carrying out such action sent a flood of serotonin coursing through me. But reality was thrust back into my face when my phone rang and startled me out of my glorious fantasy. I recall picking it up with a particularly heavy sigh that I hoped didn't go unnoticed by those around me.

By 6:00pm I'd finished work, we always leave early (on-time as far as I am concerned) on Fridays, and I was making my way to Shoreditch. My flatmates and I were going out for drinks, Tommy was celebrating a promotion at work, and well, any excuse to drink is a good one for me at the moment.

On the way to the pub, as I walked from Liverpool Street station, I watched from across the street as some old guy, drunk as fuck, to be sure, attempts to cycle home with his groceries. Twice he wobbles and crashes over, cans of soup and god knows what else rolling about the road. He picked himself back up, swearing and muttering under his breath, collecting his supplies in a spectacle of staggering and groaning before he finally wobbled off into the distance, leaving a can of soup rolling about on the road.

I don't quite know how I felt about it, amused, I suppose. Jealous, perhaps. This guy really didn't give two fucks. Life wasn't getting him down. It made me want to drink even more though. I was thinking to myself how despite how pathetic this old man is, I still envy what I imagine is the simplicity of his life. Mine seems so full of unnecessary complications and grafting away to keep pace with the world around me.

Outside the pub I'd phoned Tommy to check how far away he was. He told me his short cut turned into a long cut and he'd be late. Typical Tommy.

Tony was already there when I arrived and I bought us a drink at the bar before settling at a table. Tony and I slipped into our usual bullshit conversations. This time it was something about homeless people. Something along the lines of what homeless people talk about when you see them chatting to one another on the streets? Do they discuss how many cigarette butts they found today? The best spots to find cardboard boxes to fold into mattresses? Tips on practising their desperate expressions for the tourists? It was a fucking great question and we discussed the matter in depth until Tommy arrived a short while later and got a round for the three of us.

A few drinks later and I wasn't really paying attention to the guys. I caught bits and pieces of the conversation, most of it I found a bit cliché, some of it didn't make any sense out of context, but I was getting drunk and context was swiftly losing its importance. I was distracted. Tommy and Tony appeared to be discussing some deep shit every time I glanced over at them and it was a bit much to be honest.

"Let people judge you for who you are. If they like it, great, if they don't, then, to Hell with them. I am what I am. If you don't like it, well, there's the door. No one's forcing you to be around me," Tommy explained loudly at one point. Too serious for me.

I sat there and did my best to absorb these words while sipping my beer, the room fading in and out of focus. Usually I would've jumped at an opportunity to voice my opinion on this. But that night, I just didn't seem to have the enthusiasm.

The pub got busier and busier and the conversation was harder to hear. Not that I really cared.

The last thing I remember was "like, I always wonder, looking for a place to sit and seeing a park bench left empty on a busy day. What does everyone else know that I don't? Why isn't anyone else sitting there?", Tommy, again. Nursing my ever-warming beer, I tuned out completely at this point and tried to think of something happy. A nice memory, like fucking while listening to death metal at 3am followed by sending girls staggering in a post orgasmic haze from my room. Properly bent and sent.

Back when I had the time.

Back when I had the enthusiasm.

I remember I'd looked over to Tommy and Tony, still talking away heatedly. I remember thinking of my family and how I was losing all sense of emotional connection with them, and with everyone else too, for that matter. It was a heavy thought that I really didn't want to deal with.

"Let's get the fuck out of here," I'd said at about this point. Unexpectedly alert again and desperate to distract my mind from these bad thoughts.

Tony didn't seem to hear me, but Tommy stopped talking and answered something like "what? Why?"

"We just got here," added Tony.

Fuck off, Tony, I was thinking to myself, not looking him, focusing on Tommy. I'd much rather have been at home, with a drink in my hand and listening to my own music, not the shit playing in that pub.

Tony insisted on one last round and half an hour later, I was finally sitting in the back of a black Volkswagen CC, heading home, telling Tommy to turn up the music he was playing on the stereo. Tony, sitting in the passenger seat and frantically and, well, drunkenly, messaging someone said "no, hold on, I need to make a phone call. Laura just tried to call me. What if something's wrong?"

"Laura's got you by the balls, mate, that's what's wrong," Tommy quite rightly said, trying to make eye contact with me in the rear-view mirror, a big grin on his stubble covered face.

I just nodded back in reply, not interested in the joke, "just get us back home... Tony, you should listen to Tommy, stop trying to get in her panties, she's playing you. She's trouble, mate. Proper trouble," my words of wisdom were falling on deaf ears, no doubt.

"Hold up, we're nearly there anyway."

Tony sighed in response and avoided eye contact with me for the rest of the trip home.

"Turn up the fucking Slayer," I repeated, leaning forward to reach into the front and grab the dial.

"Alright, fucker," Tommy said, slapping my arm away. I watched him turn the dial and let Tom Araya's voice tear into our souls. Tommy stepped on the accelerator and I felt some degree of calm as we drew close to our flat in Plaistow.

We lived together in a small flat, just the three of us. We all shared similar interests, similar mindsets. We had a common belief in leading lifestyles based on true liberal principles. That's right, liberal, but I mean that in the most pure sense of the word. I'm no Socialist, that's for sure. I mean liberal, as in, freedom of the individual. Libertarianism some call it. Fundamentally, we all believed that each of us are our own gods. There is no higher power in existence than each person's own mind. We lived our own lives with complete freedom, hindered only by our respect for those around us.

We were all smart guys. Well-educated, from good backgrounds etc.... Tommy had a commerce degree and had started working as a real estate agent for a big-name firm in the city. Tony was a nurse, studying still, but working part time at the Royal London Hospital.

I, of course, was doing my thing as an architect. Designing structures of pure art that some construction company would inevitably tear to shreds in a series of cost-saving exercises, leaving my designs a shadow of their potential glory. Typical.

Anyway, back to that night, we pulled into our street at about 11pm, it was dark but warm enough to be outside late, a typical July evening in London. Never quite the summer we all deserve. but the one we always need at the time.

The three of us rented your typical 4 bedroom terraced house towards the end of the street. We'd lived there together for some time now and that place was as much a part of our friendship as any of the three of us. It was like, one of the crew, I suppose.

As we pulled up outside that night, I remember getting an uneasy feeling in my stomach, that kind of queasiness you feel right before an examination at school, or when you're fighting with your girlfriend and you think she might be about to bring up those messages to "other girls" on your phone that you know that she knows that you know she knows about. Don't try and tell me that you don't know what I mean…

Anyway, the lights were on inside the house, but only upstairs. Now, this was unusual as none of us had a habit of leaving the lights on upstairs, usually it was the living rooms lights, if anything. But, hey, as you do, you never really think too much about it in these moments, do you? Hindsight makes us all experts, but the immediacy of life often makes us fools.

Tommy parked a few houses down across the road from our place in the closest available spot and turned off the ignition. The night was still and the air was fresh. Tony jumped out of the passenger seat first and I took a moment to grab my satchel, making certain that the little bag of snow I'd bought earlier in the day way still there. Safe and sound. I was looking forward to getting stuck into that tomorrow. So, with my fingers reassuringly tapping the little bag and Tommy casually closing the driver's door and yawning loudly, all seemed well.

I turned to say something to Tony, but, I can't remember what, because it was at that moment that all Hell broke loose.

I can't recall whether I heard Tony cry out first or the yell of a shadowy stranger as he appeared suddenly at our front door step, just a few metres from Tony.

Now, I have to say, and I hope you understand, the entire scene happened in a surreal pendulum of ultra-fast movement as well as painstaking slow motion. So, allow me to summarise, which is essentially as good as my memory will offer me.

So, within moments of that shadowy figure emerging, a group of Arab youths spilled out through our front door like maggots out of a dead cow's eye socket. The reality of what was happening struck all three of us guys at the same time.

These fucking cunts had been in our goddamn house. Burgling the fucking place, and we'd come home and caught them in the act. Now they were pissed off, scared, aggressive, and who knows what else... probably high.

They saw us, yelled some shit to each other and then marched towards us like they owned the place. Like they owned the whole fucking street. Egging each other on and cocky as fuck. I counted at least six them. All young, like early twenties. All wearing hoodies, gloves and couple were wearing backpacks filled with stuff from our flat.

The whole scene was a circus of "bruv, bruv, bruv" and "fucking knock these clowns out, Kamal." That kind of thing. So, hostile and with the element of surprise now firmly on their side, the fuckers were on us like flies on meat.

I instinctively looked over to Tony and Tommy who were frozen in place between me and the gang. Tony managed to yell out something indistinguishable and Tommy, always the calm one, raised his arms up and began to speak, presumably saying something to diffuse the situation, but it was only seconds before one of the bastards grabbed him by the collar of his coat and shoved him backwards into the side of the car.

The next few seconds were a vicious blur of commotion.

I stood stunned, registering only the sounds of trainers hitting the footpath heavily, screaming and shouting all around me, the grunts of someone struggling to breathe behind me, the hollow smack of someone to my right being kicked in the stomach as they lay on their side.

The next moment a hand had grabbed my arm and it snapped me out of my trance. As I moved to look around, I saw the shiny steel of a large knife being pulled out and someone yelling "stab him up, bruv, stab him up."

The next thing I know I'd struggled free of the hand grabbing my wrist, lashing out with my satchel, instincts, I suppose, and I remember catching a glimpse of Tony running and screaming for help down the street.

I kept thinking; I hope someone comes out soon! Where is everyone? Why is no one helping us?

We were outnumbered, outmatched and helpless and these fuckers were now coming at me at this point. I had my eye on the one with the knife who was darting toward me at a pace.

I only had a split second to escape. I didn't even think about it. I just threw my satchel as hard as I could at the nearest arsehole and then turned and ran, faster than I ever thought I could. I just fucking ran. Adrenaline coursing through me, giving me super speed for a short time. Nothing else mattered but escape. Pride was irrelevant.

As I reached the alleyway that leads to the park, my chosen safe harbour, I remembering hearing the sound of these cunts in close pursuit. I could hear them breathing heavily and I swear I could feel their breath on the back of my neck. At least three of them were chasing me down. If they caught me, I'd be dead.

The dampness of the air felt thick in my lungs and my breath steamed out around me as I fled. Without thinking of it, I watched myself as I dove over a broken fence as high as my waist and kept running into the darkness of the park, not stopping to look back over my shoulder. At this point, my body was doing its own thing. My mind was to slow to keep up. I ran until I couldn't hear the footsteps charging after me anymore.

I'm not sure how long I waited in the park, in the shadows…

Scared and helpless.

Scared and useless.

But eventually I heard police sirens and after a little while I knew it was safe to venture back out.

I cautiously made my way back to the house and every little sound I heard along the way jolted me like an electric shock, sending panic coursing through my veins. I was terrified.

Back in our street, the whole neighbourhood had finally decided to come out. Not to help us of course, but to perv at the whole spectacle, now that it was someone else's problem and not theirs. Now I feel so annoyed by this, but at the time, I just felt so embarrassed slinking back there after running away like a little girl. But, what could I do?

There were at least three police cars and two ambulances at the scene. The blue lights flashing sporadically up and down the street just added to the surreal feeling of the whole event and pushed me to the verge of vomiting. The hardest part was the walk of shame I had to take along the middle of the road, all the way down to the cordoned off area outside my house. A hundred pairs of eyes judging me. A hundred hushed voices murmuring about what a coward I was. For fucks sake… They were right.

All I recall of the next bit was being told by a police offer that Tommy had been stabbed in the stomach and in the chest and behind him the scene of a paramedic putting pressure on Tommy's torso and another rushing towards her with a bag of equipment.

I couldn't properly comprehend the whole thing and all I wanted was for it all to stop. I needed it to stop. I needed to breathe.

Tony was sitting there, hugging his knees on the steps of our flat, with two police officers stooping above him asking all kinds of questions. He didn't appear to be answering, he was just staring at the footpath behind them. His eyes were glassy and vacant.

I remember standing there wondering what the Hell just happened. Questioning if it was real and trembling uncontrollably as the shock began to set in.

The reality of what had happened took a while to sink in.

We'd been targeted, I guess. These street rats must've thought we were all out for the night. They obviously thought they had a bit more time than they did.

Fucking cunts.

Tony didn't look at me when walked back to the scene. Perhaps he did see me there at some point, but I didn't look over at him to see. I couldn't bear to face him.

The night dissolved into questions and questions and phone calls after phone calls and telling the same useless story to concerned friends and relatives. The same sequence of events told enough times I couldn't tell if it was the truth or not anymore. It was just the facts.

I did my best to tell them I was okay, that it was going to be okay. I didn't even recognise my voice by the end of it. By the end of the night it was someone else possessing my body doing the reassuring and I was just another listener on the call.

After a while I just let the police and the support team take over my life.

I completely switched off and went into autopilot. I'm not sure I ever switched back on to manual mode.

Tony and I spent that night in some hotel in Stratford that the police set us up with. Our flat was a crime scene and we couldn't go back in for at least a few days apparently.

No sleep was had that night.

Only fear and sweat.

....

Tommy didn't make it.

He died just before dawn from the chest wound.

The police came to the hotel and told us the next afternoon. Hours after he passed away. Fucking, hours. That bothers me now more than it did at the time. But, to be fair, I was already detaching myself from reality by then. It could have been a year after he died, I wouldn't have cared. It wouldn't have mattered. Tommy was gone and nothing would ever be the same again.

After the funeral Tony moved back to Cambridge and I moved into a new flat, on my own this time. Tony and I never, ever, had a conversation where we spoke about what happened. We just skirted around it the few times we hung out after the incident. I felt like it was never the right moment to bring it up. And then within a couple of weeks we'd both moved out and that was that. He probably felt the same way as I did... nothing to say... no words to change the reality.

In fact, Tony hardly spoke a word after that night. It changed him beyond all recognition. I feel like we're drifting apart. Quicker than you might expect. I suppose seeing each other is too much of a reminder of what happened.

I suppose it changed me too. It must have. It's only been just over a month, yet it feels like Tommy has already been gone for years. We were so close and without him around every hour feels like a week and every week like a year. In an instant I can still see the scar on his chin which made his beard grow in a strange pattern in one spot. I can still feel the roughness of his hands when we shook, callouses from lifting weights without gloves. I still hear his raspy voice repeating snippets of long-lost conversations as though he was here in the room right next to me.

During the month since his death Christmas came and went, it was the most miserable thing I have ever been through. I sat through a three-day family Christmas session where every single member of my family tiptoed around the murder and didn't say a fucking word. In fact, they basically did their best avoid talking to me altogether to avoid any awkwardness in case they said anything that reminded me of the fact that my best friend was just murdered right in front of me.

They said nothing.

Not even an obligatory 'we're so sorry'... Fucking useless.

I realise that most people just don't know how to deal with these kinds of situations.

I didn't want to talk about it, but I did want them to want me to talk about it. I wanted them at the very least to try to get me to talk.

And I got nothing.

Fucking useless.

I spent those three days over Christmas and Boxing Day sitting around the lounge watching rubbish television and drinking mulled wine and whiskey from waking up until I couldn't feel my cheeks any longer and I'd passed out in exhaustion on my favourite worn-out brown chair in the corner.

As soon as the time came when the extended family started dispersing from my parents' house, I swiftly packed my bags and avoiding any fanfare, waved goodbye to my mother and father from a cab in the driveway as I made my escape.

My mother sent me a message a few minutes later asking me to come back and stay for New Year's. Fuck. That.

New Year's Eve I spent alone in my new flat, drinking a bottle of absinthe I'd brought back from Prague last year and snorting a couple grams of snow off the screen of an iPad my mother gave me for Christmas. I distinctly recall that my soundtrack for that evening was Alice In Chains and it was a superb choice. It always is.

The next few days were a blur of snow, cigarettes and emptying of my liquor cabinet.

I listened to music. I sketched random shit in sketch books. I lay on the floor of my living room staring at the carpet beside me and ceiling above me, thinking about absolutely nothing at all.

I passed the time.

At one point I ventured outside for supplies. I went to an off licence on Burdett Road, to buy some alcohol and some meat.

When I was there, I asked for a bottle of Russian Standard and realised the guy behind the counter was drunk as fuck. He was some Indian guy who'd clearly been getting wrecked on his own supply. He stank of piss and beer and he could barely speak any actual words. Just breathing hot beer breath wrapped around mumbled noises.

When he eventually worked out what I wanted he reached back behind the counter and lifted a bottle off the shelf which he proceeded to immediately drop onto the floor at his feet. By some kind of miracle, it didn't smash and, flustered and apologetic, this guy manages to get the bottle into a blue plastic bag after a few failed attempts and a lot more heavy breathing.

I was also a bit fucked, so, to be fair, I couldn't care less. The whole spectacle was amusing but by then I just wanted to open that fucking bottle and get that alcohol in my veins.

Anyway, he bagged up the meat sticks I bought too and then handed me over the bag, smiling and wishing me a good night, then turned his attention to the customers behind me. Since I was also drunk and high it took me a hot minute to realise that he had completely forgotten to charge me for the goods. And, of course, I thought to myself, just go with it. Fuck it. As I left the store I heard him slurring away some conversation with another customer and I disappeared off into the night with my bounty. My only venture outdoors was a complete win.

Anyway, fast forward to now.... Today is the 8th of January 2011, four weeks to the day since Tommy was killed and the police have been unable to find the cunts who did this to him. To us... These cunts killed Tommy and the police called me this morning to tell me they do not "have any credible leads at this stage". Fucking useless. So here we are.

It makes me shake with anger just thinking about it.

The fact that my friend, my closest friend, was murdered in front of me and I was unable to anything about it, is bad enough, but the fact that the cunts who did this may go unpunished is more than I am willing to accept.

No. No. No.

Tommy deserves more than that.

I think back on that night and it turns my vision red with anger, but for some reason it also floods me with exhilaration. As though the only time I ever felt alive was in that very moment. When I was staring death in the face, only then did I truly feel alive.

I ran, sure, but who wouldn't?

No, what my mind goes back to was that superhuman feeling we get that is only ever provided only by adrenaline. That feeling of absolute connection with every part of your body. Like you are in complete control. Able to get every last ounce of work out of every single fibre and vessel. Yet at the same time feeling like nothing more than a demon, possessing a host.

It's almost as though every day since then has been more and more of a disappointment. Every day taking me further from that simple feeling of just being alive. I feel more and more dead with every day that passes now. There is no end to this descent in sight.

But that moment... In the moment....

The thrill.

The excitement.

The adrenaline that surging through your body when faced with danger is a high that no other drug can possibly give you. Adrenaline is your own personal upper, tailored entirely to you. Nothing can compare.

Fuck, I crave it. I need something...

I need to feel alive again.

Felix

I have a dream that keeps recurring. It's a little bit different every time, but the main idea remains the same. I'm back in New Zealand, just before all this madness took place. I'm on a beach. It's a beach party with thousands of people. Three of four DJ's playing on stages set along the beachfront. People drinking and dancing. A hot summers day. You can picture it... Earphones are in I'm choosing my favourite Slipknot track, turning the volume up and making my way down the rocks onto the sand as a cool breeze washes over my body, providing fleeting relief from the scorching heat.

I like being here, I like the party scene and the chaos... I like to watch. But I don't like to be involved.

In this dream the goal seems to be finding a spot near the stage that I can watch the party, listen to my own music and just be left alone.

As I walk, my music stops playing suddenly. Not that I could really hear in my dream anyway... But it is at this moment I realise that something is not quite right. It's dark now, and most of the beachgoers have gradually moved towards the main stage, meaning I'm pretty far away from any people. Pretty well isolated down this end of the beach. A sense of dread comes across. Vulnerable thoughts race through my mind, like a series of lightning bolts striking me.

I am alone.

Isolated.

As far as I can tell my senses realise before my brain can catch up that something is not right at all.

Then the Sober Fear rises.

At about this point each time my music suddenly roars back into life. The sound blasting at me what seems like twice as loud as it was before.

I tense up and as I reach into my pocket to take out my iPhone and turn the volume down, I see someone move out of the darkness towards me. I stop in my tracks. Something tells me this is not a good situation.

This is not a friend.

This is a threat.

The dream is always like this.

And every time it reaches this point, the Fear is worse.

I always turn the volume off on Slipknot completely and try my best to act calm, show no fear. I examine the situation quickly - we're alone down here, me and this threat. I'm standing on a rock about a metre off the ground, this person is standing on the beach, wearing a blue baseball cap, pulled down over his face, about four metres in front of me. Watching me watching him.

I have to make a move. Show no fear.

Walk on past him.

Be alert, but confident.

Fuck. The fear is real.

I jump down from the rock with all intention to keep on moving back towards the main stage, pretending not even to be concerned about blue cap guy, just concerned with getting back to the party.

I am determined to keep on moving, but I see this mother fucker make a move the second I land on the beach.

In the moment of instability caused upon landing on the sand, he moves towards me in just one or two long strides. In the dreams, the distance he covers each time makes perfect sense.

In this dream state it's all a bit surreal and hard to tell what is happening, but I know its bad news.

"You alright, mate?" I ask him, in the most angry voice I can muster at the time, but it always sounds so weak. Thinking about it now, I'm not even sure I actually say anything at all.

The next thing I know he appears right next to me. He's about a foot taller than me, a skinny, Maori dude in his early twenties.

"Nah, bro," he spits at me, "I need your phone and your wallet... you know how this goes," he finishes.

And here I am, being mugged on a fucking beach in peaceful New Zealand and little old me came here to get away from this kind of shit. From the random London stabbings and muggings, to the gang fights on the streets to the delinquent youth roaming about aimlessly intimidating people and stealing property. This kind of shit is common place in London. It is out of fucking control. But I did not expect this in New Zealand too. No way.

The Maori guy reaches into his pocket and of course I know exactly what is coming.

Each time, at this point, I have a moment of clarity. A moment of self-awareness which rises up, or is triggered from somewhere deep within. A moment in which I realise that I will not submit to this cunt. That I will not give him phone, nor wallet, nor my dignity. If he wants them, he'll have to take them. Prove himself.

In dream world, this all seems entirely reasonable. I can do anything.

As he pulls out the knife from his pocket, I make my own move. I lunge towards him, grabbing his wrist with my left hand and beating him in the nose with my right, catching him completely by surprise.

With my hand on his wrist, he struggles to stab me, clutching the knife tighter as he tries to wriggle out my grip. He's strong, much stronger than me. I don't have room for error. We stumble around and I punch him square in the balls, a low move, I know... No man should ever hit another man in the balls, but when you're fighting for your life, well... you're fighting for your life.

The fucker keels over forwards and there's me trying not to lose grip on his wrist, doing my best to pull his arm down, shaking it, trying to get him to drop the blade. At this point, each time, his fist comes at me from my right, I'm too slow and he smashes me across the chin and Lucifer, I swear the world stops spinning for a moment. He hits me good. But fortunately, the adrenaline or dream equivalent is kicking in by now. My earphones fall out from my ears and drop to the sand below. Nothing else matters right now except for staying alive.

Rage takes over me, a real heavy rage, like the rage of a lifetime of frustration all built up. A lifetime of being taken for granted. Of being overlooked. Of being the odd one out. Of listing out everything I didn't get... A raging fire of wild thirst that needs to be quenched.

At this point I let out a growl and begin punching this fucker over and over. I'm punching his hands and his arms as he tries to protect himself, but eventually I land a few good ones on his head and face, and I keep going. Growling now. Raging. Punching over and over until I begin to feel his hand losing the grip on the knife. His attempts at blocking and his struggle against me becomes weaker and less effective. I keep throwing punches. Landing more and more and now I'm screaming. No, I'm laughing. I'm fucking laughing. And I'm loving it. The burn of the rage fuels me. And fuck, it feels great.

Eventually I land a heavy blow to his throat and he drops the knife, raising up groggy hands to his throat. I let his right arm go and now I'm free to finish him off with both fists free.

I don't hesitate. The cunt barely has his hands up to his throat before I'm on top of him, punching his face over and over, with both fists, blood everywhere, his teeth coming loose now. I can feel his teeth bending inward from the impact of my fists. Soon I'll cave them in.

I don't stop. I never do. I don't know how long I continue for before I stop punching him and just stand there laughing.

I roll backwards off him. At this point he isn't moving anymore.

My breathing is always heavy.

I look down my hands, covered in thick, dark blood. Much of it is my own. My knuckles are split, my ring finger looks broken, but I can't feel the pain.

I only feel pure energy pulsing through me.

Pure, unrestrained, energy.

I'm lit up like lightning has struck me.

Alive.

I take a moment to sit there and catch my breath. How long it takes, I have no idea.

Nothing matters right now. Only this powerful feeling I have.

Eventually the world begins to seep back into focus. The sound of the ocean exists once more, mixed with the bass of the music from down the beach, the sounds of laughter and drunken antics of humans.

I stand up slowly. It always seems to take forever to get myself back upright and steady.

My body moves in slow motion. I don't even look over at the unmoving thing at my feet, instead I scan the beach instead for my phone, fallen from my pocket in the midst of the encounter. Once found, I put my earphones back in. It seems like the right thing to do. Put my music on. Carry on. Right?

As I look back down toward the main stage it's no longer a main stage down there but a small car driving away down the dunes, racing further and further from me.

The guy in front has disappeared and instead cockroaches, by the thousands, begin to scuttle out of the water towards me. Just before they reach my feet, I wake up in a cold sweat.

Every. Fuckin. Time.

3 Edward

Felix

I went back to work for a few days shortly after the incident, but I just couldn't focus on anything. It was useless. So, I've taken bereavement leave, or what I like to call sanity leave. My bosses were very eager to give me the time off and as far as I can tell, this sanity leave is indefinite. My boss never clarified when he expected me to return. He just said "take as much time as you need, Felix."

And so, I am.

During my first sanity week off, I moved to a new flat in Mile End, a one bedroom new-build. And since then have otherwise distracted myself with Netflix and drugs and porn and alcohol and whatever else made the days shorter.

Despite friends and family insisting I go visit them and get away from it all, I have no plans for travel. No plans to leave London. No plans for anything at all.

No plans.

No future.

I just want to drift. To go about my life without the rush. Without the desperation. To walk like a human being amongst a group of strangers, not like an aggressive starving animal hunting its' prey. Not like a guy in a suit in a hurry to rush his life away.

I just want to sit in a park. Stare at the squirrels. Watch the world go by through a café window.

I just want to drift. To not be constrained by someone else's schedule. Someone else's demands.

I want to wake up when my body decides to.

I want freedom.

I want to tune out from the news, from television and billboards. From social media. From life.

I'm a slave.

I'm a slave.

And, I know it.

You know it.

We're all slaves.

We're all slaves.

Going back to my old life, my life before the incident seems impossible. The more I reflect on things, the more abstract it becomes. Is that how I want to spend my life?

Another forty years of that nine-to-six monotony, then bin me off into retirement and obscurity until I wither up and die as nothing else than one less human to compete with for earth's resources? No.

The beauty of this current disconnection is that it allows me time to contemplate.

To consider my next move.

I have a thirst.

I have an itch.

I've taken quite a liking to strolling about aimlessly on my own. Feeling the rhythm of the city under my feet. Focussing on the movement of the people. Watching them. Knowing they are oblivious to the thoughts going on in my head and taking great satisfaction from these little secret conversations I have with myself. The little games I play.

Every time I walk through this city there seems to be a new skyscraper piercing the skyline. They are everywhere, a dime-a-dozen an American tourist might say. But the wicked fantasy-like colossus we will call the Shard, is by far set to be my favourite. The way it will penetrate the skyline, looming above us, all-imposing and yet remaining so inviting and innocent, appeals to my admittedly warped mind. I wish I could see its completion.

I wish I could see its completion?

I repeat those words in my head.

What the fuck, Felix? Why would you say 'you wish you could?'

I walk up to a shop window and look at my reflection in the glass.

I see a youthful guy, jet black hair, yellow eyes and a face almost constantly fixed with a sly grin. He's wearing a long black trench coat, the same one he's owned for years, a white shirt under a blood red tie, a black waist coat, a black jacket, with black trousers and a pair of black brogues.

I look good. I stand out, for sure, but I like that, this is London, anything goes so you

have to go that little bit further.

I've lurked about in various corners of planet Earth, visited many cities, but all I can say is there's nothing like good ol' London town and there is also nothing good about ol' London town.

The streets are as dirty as they have ever been, covered in spittle, empty food wrappers clinging to bushes for dear life against the breeze, bags of rubbish lie stacked up in alleyways, spilling out onto the footpath for days and days. London, we love you, like the filthy whore that you are.

I keep on walking and pass some random guy, properly mental, with the whole shifty eyes, laughing away at everything, and talking to himself thing going on. Fingernails all chipped away and what's left of them are attached to blackened fingers clutching a cigarette, and he sidles up beside me at the pedestrian crossing near the Lyceum Theatre and says "oooo, mate, oooo, look, god damn, sexy, there's Emma Watson, over there," pointing at two girls walking together across the street, neither of which, I see, are in fact Emma Watson. "Fuck. Oh my god, Emma Watson, so beautiful," the nutcase carries on as I smile politely in his direction and look away.

"Hey, hey, Emma!" he yells out.

The two girls don't even notice. The mad bastard then starts blowing kisses across the road at the girls and then says to me again, "wow. Mama mia!"

Fortunately, the pedestrian signal turns green and he begins ambling off in the direction of St Paul's Cathedral, I cross slowly and then dodge traffic to cross to the other side of the road. I am in no mood for someone else's madness today.

A heavy rain has recently ceased falling and the air still feels damp and thick. It's a familiar sensation. Nonetheless, the fact that it's the end of January and cold as fuck here doesn't help the situation at all. My fingers are so frigid that I'm struggling to make them retrieve a cigarette from my pocket and light the fucker.

My first priority, after lighting this fucking cigarette of course, is to source some snow. Only then can I possibly carry on with my day. It's 7:37pm, I've not slept since I woke up yesterday afternoon and I've no interest in starting any sleep-related activity right now. No time for that kind of behaviour. Besides, these days I don't sleep at night. At night the world comes alive. Why would I miss out being part of that? Cities are lit up in grids of bright yellow lights and buildings with windows like little glowing teeth, with neon signs and other light displays there for all to see. Glorious. A hundred little red lights swarming their way off into the distance and a hundred white lights streaming towards me are just car lights to most, nothing interesting, but for me, they are part of what makes each night a wondrous experience.

I love night. The glow of the moon on the grass, the way that the darkness covers everything in clean, neat shadows. All the filth and disorder are hidden from view. Only in darkness is real purity found. That pure dark and that kind of serene quiet which washes over the environment. Even in the most dense and noisiest cities, there's a noticeable change when the sun goes down. The night is more peaceful. The night is made for people like me. When the sun sets the world becomes ours until it rises once more. Then the masses of regular humans can have it back for a while.

I have a number, a contact for a guy in Greenwich who can hook me up with some snow, £60 a gram, apparently. I walk to the nearest train station and get on the DLR towards Greenwich. The carriage is pretty empty, just me, a guy in a suit look like he's heading home from work and a couple of homeless people making out in the end. The two of them snogging each other is accompanied by all kinds of animal noises that I really don't need to hear. I turn up the volume in my earphones and close my eyes, letting the swaying of the carriage soothe me as *Satie's Gnossiennes No.1, Lent*, pours into my brain. I focus my attention on the task ahead.

Get snow.

Get high.

Get out and about…

Get aggressive.

Feel something…

Tonight, I'll stalk the streets, the alleyways, the council estates. I will stalk where danger lies.

Tonight, I fear no one.

Tonight, I am the one to fear.

Tonight, I am the hunter.

I don't care what happens.

I don't care if I get mugged, if I get stabbed, if I get raped, whatever. I just want to feel something. Anything.

If I die, so be it. I'll go out with a bang.

I'm sure I'll die feeling more alive than I ever have before. The sheer poetry of that thought resonates with me.

I'm sick of this life.

This empty, nothingness.

I know I'm depressed, and I know that this is a fucked-up way to think, and I know that this is a waste of a good life, but this is *my* life. I choose what I do with it.

I eventually arrive at the location and meet the dealer, jumping into his car and making the exchange with the typical smile and fist bump, it's all over in about thirty seconds and I'm back on my way back to the train station.

Now I need to decide where to start. I'm not looking for trouble, I'm a warning against it. Don't fuck with me and I won't fuck with you.

When walking in open territory, bother no one. If someone bothers you, ask him to stop. If he does not stop, destroy him.

My mind is clear, more clear than perhaps ever before.

I open one of the baggies I bought, crushing some of the nugget snow with my thumbnail and then corner it with my credit card. Then I'm sniffing in that beautiful rush that's loud and pretty obvious as I stroll the high street of Greenwich. But tonight, I don't even care who sees me.

There's only one thing I need in my life from now on. No more acquiring stupid material possessions or aspiring for that next rung on the fucking ladder. All I need is to quench my thirst for danger. That feeling that I have supressed for so long. That longing for... something different. I think I know what it is. I feel the thirst for that shot of adrenaline that comes when the fight or flight response kicks in and takes over. I thirst for this moment, this split second when I'll choose the red pill, disconnect from the matrix, jump down the rabbit hole, stand and fight. I felt this moment when those arseholes jumped us and killed Tommy. I feel that moment in my dreams when I'm fighting on the beach. I feel alive then and I feel dead now.

As I march back towards the DLR station, like a sign from Lucifer himself, a situation presents itself, an opportunity for me to put my money where my mouth is.

Test yourself, Felix. Is this you, or an fantasy of you?

As I march my way along the alleyway towards the DLR, I come across a very solidly-built black teenage guy harassing a young black girl as she tries to walk to the train station. Now, this is London, and I know that most people wouldn't risk getting involved. They'd try to rationalise, 'he's not physically abusing her, he's just shouting about and following her'. They'd tell themselves 'for all I know it's her boyfriend or brother. Hell, she could even be the one at fault here and he's acting entirely reasonably in being upset' etc. etc...

Yeah, perhaps... but, let's be honest, probably, *not* right?

This kind of typical *polite, turn a blind eye*, reaction is to be expected from most British people. It's typical *bullshit* as far as I'm concerned.

Without much deliberation, I decide to make a move.

As expected, the adrenaline quickly begins to flow. Muscles are tensing and vision sharpening. All the good stuff. I double my pace and close in on the scene in front of me.

I'm not sure exactly what I'm going to do, but, fuck it, I'll improvise. I don't care. The aggression is real. That's all that matters. This is all too perfect.

There's a brief moment where I suspect I've missed my opportunity. The shouting stops and the girl turns and walks away. I'm on the verge of slowing down to reassess the situation, but in that same moment the fucking guy reaches for the girl's handbag and shoves her hard backwards as she pulls it out of his reach, I decide to intervene, no matter what. Fuck it.

I dash up to the two, making sure the sounds of my combat boots on the concrete are echoing out as loud as possible in the night. That's right, you big fucker, someone dangerous is coming…

The shit-head turns around and looks over at me, sizing me up, glaring at me, expecting me to be just another a fearful citizen and just pass on by ignoring the situation. But I continue marching right at him, my eyes locked on his. There's a moment of shock that registers and then he quickly replaces it with aggression.

"Yo, what you wan't, bruv? This ain't your bizniss. It's wif me and ma girl."

"Leave her alone," my voice is deep and steady.

"Bruv, why the fuck would I do that?"

"Because if you continue to harass her, I'll have to stop you."

"Haha. You? Fuck off, bruv."

"Seriously, mate. Leave her alone. Walk away."

"You think you can stop me, bruv? Haha."

"Well. I promise you I'll try. You don't know me. I don't know you. You haven't seen me fight. Neither of us have any idea what we are in for here. And sure, you might win. You might fucking kick my arse. But then again, you might not. Either way, won't go down without a fight, that I can guarantee you." The clarity in my words is serene. It's as though my brain is working as efficiently as a computer in this moment. The words ring out loud and clear, it sounds like another person, not me at all. And all of it is completely true. I carry on, "and even you, despite being bigger than me, won't get out of a confrontation with me without a decent amount of damage. So, it's up to you. Is it really worth it? Because I'll certainly stand my ground any day. I've nothing to lose. No one would expect me to win. You are the one with the most at stake here."

"Fuck off, bruv." He's fuming. But he's thinking.

I stare at him, unblinking, ready to grab this cunt by the throat and choke the life out of him if I have to.

"Fuck that shit, bitch ain't worth it." He's thought well.

"Good choice," I say, nodding with my chin.

"Bruv, if I see you round here, my boys are gonna fuck you up."

"Why, because you can't do it yourself?"

A pulse of adrenaline ripples through my body as I notice his right arm twitch and for a moment, I expect him to strike.

"Fuck off, white boy!" he yells and throws his hands up in the air wildly, as if shrugging off the whole situation.

He realises that this just isn't worth it. That I will actually be a fucking problem for him if he carries on. A problem he can't be bothered with.

The big fucker turns around kicks over a rubbish bin as he storms off back down the alleyway that leads to the main road.

The girl thanks me, telling me she's worried for my safety, that her boyfriend is real dangerous guy etc… I ignore her and walk on towards the station. This situation really had almost nothing to do with this girl. It was more a matter of principle. It was even more a matter of me proving something to myself.

She follows me to the station and continues to try to speak to me.

I ignore her. I zone her out. Like a mosquito flying away.

This is *my* moment.

I relish the feeling.

I relish life right now.

As I walk with this not unattractive black girl two steps behind me I see two figures standing in the shadows off to my left. The two of them clearly watching me, but as I turn to face them, they're gone, and all I see is an old skip covered in graffiti, I must be losing my mind.

Once inside the empty station the girl gives up and takes a train heading east. I board a train heading west, I don't bother to say goodbye. I simply don't care.

The Felix walking these London streets is a very different Felix than this city used to know. This Felix is stepping up. It's make or break time. Only perfection will do. There is absolutely no room for average anymore. He is evolving.

I have a thirst under the surface.

It's been waiting to be quenched for so, so long.

I have an itch.

It's been there waiting to be scratched. Irritating. Nagging at me for what feels like forever.

A thirst waiting to be quenched for my whole life.

I'm ready.

That night. That night with those fuckers attacking us. That woke something in me. Set alight a fire which is now raging inside me.

The kindling was always there, just waiting for something to light it off.

And Hell, it feels so good, that fire. Almost hypnotic... no, it's definitely hypnotic.

And in that moment, staring across at that motherless fuck just a few moments ago, I was awake. I'd snapped myself out of the haze. I felt alive.

I felt the fire burning and I was ready to face anything. To do anything. To die.... to *live*...

I continue to roam the streets until the sun comes up and the humans come out.

I am seriously at risk of losing my shit in this state.

Felix

The next afternoon, I wake up and curse at myself for being so foolish, I'd tossed and turned for hours wondering what might've happened if that black dude had properly kicked things off, if he'd come at me. What? I would've been stabbed, or worse... fucking killed... for some random girl, on some random street... for *what*?

The real Felix will always make a stand, and put himself in danger in *certain* situations. Well, to be honest, never really physical danger. Not like this. Not like last night.

For fucks sake.

Last night, that was a moment of anger. The rage swelled in me and whilst it felt wonderful, I know that it's pointless for me to just go out onto the streets and vent my rage against all the many shitheads out there. Eventually, one of them will kill me and that will be that. It would be utterly pointless. Nothing would be achieved except my satisfying my own ego for that small moment, then I'd just be another statistic.

I'd rather do something bigger.

Something impactful.

I'd rather make a proper difference in this shitty city. But, fuck, I really don't know what I could do... But then while part of me wants to make this city a better place to live in for everyone, another part of me wonders why this feels as though it falls on my shoulders alone.

Why am I the only one who really seems to care?

A few days later a couple of old friends of mine invite me for drinks in Soho, and since I've not been out on the town in over a month, I decide I won't make an excuse on this occasion and I'll actually go.

I join them and a group of four others and we begin our trawl through Soho. I'm relatively silent, not much to say really. The guys understand what I've been through and I suppose they are all unsure how to behave around me and what to say. So, they buy me drinks, make small talk and basically leave me alone.

A few hours later and we've made our way into a club recommended to us by a drunk guy we met working behind the counter at a chicken shop, who we also happened to meet inside said club about 5 minutes after we arrived, much to our surprise and confusion. I suspect he followed us there.

Nonetheless, tonight, the shadows have come for me and I'm embracing them already.

Empty. In a room literally packed to the rafters with humans, I stand there, feeling nothing but *empty*.

Disconnected to it all.

Nothing makes sense to me anymore.

Has it ever?

How could I ever go back to the way things were?

I look down from the balcony, watching a girl, roughly my age, perhaps a bit younger, black hair, very pretty, tight blue jeans and a white vest - she's dancing, swaying back and forth. Dipping her shoulders left to right and bobbing her head roughly in time with the thundering, no, the booming, hip-hop re-mixes the DJ is blasting out into the room.

She takes a sip of her drink, something red, a girly drink with a straw and too much ice and she smiles at her friend. A larger girl, with a very pretty face, who leans over and whispers something in her ear. The black-haired girl laughs, puts down her drink on the table in front of them and they both start dancing vigorously. The smiles on their faces are real. It's a real moment of joy and connection between two friends. A moment that I just don't seem to relate to any longer. It seems so... distant.

The music thumps on and on, relentlessly.

Two girls dance side by side on the stage near the DJ and they have my full my attention.

The way they move, beads of sweat running down their temples, bodies grinding against each other. The suggestive movements. Sensual. Sexual. Primal. I should be aroused. Interested. I'm not a faggot. I should be loving this.

I *should* be.

A group of guys near the stage down there are ogling the dancers, commenting to one another. I know the kind of dirty comments they are making.

I used to make them myself.

When I used to care.

When I used to feel… something.

And now?

Empty.

I feel nothing now. This is all just nothing to me.

Not a single sexual thought or anything of that nature comes to my mind. No blood rushing to my dick. No emotion of any kind seems to come.

The only thing I feel is lonely.

Frozen in my own mind, like a clock that stopped ticking a long time ago.

My heart races from the snow in my bloodstream.

I look away from the two dancing girls just as they kiss one another. I hear a couple of lads behind me yell, "oh yeah, look at those bitches!"

Typical.

I stare down at the palms of my hands for a moment. The club lights flashing all over them reflecting off the thin layer of cocaine sweat oozing out with each heartbeat.

What the fuck am I doing here?

I turn back to the black-haired girl down there in the blue jeans. She's stopped kissing her friend and it now sipping a fresh drink that has appeared from nowhere and dancing again, one hand up in the air while she holds her glass. This time I notice something different. This time I look into her eyes, and I see the Sadness.

The Sadness.

You know the one.

It can come and take hold of us for any number of reasons, but for her, you can tell it's the sadness of a girl who's been unexpectedly hurt. A girl who loved someone too much and who didn't get loved the same back.

And it is fresh.

Its fresh and it still brings her to tears if she thinks about it too long.

You know how sometimes you just know. How sometimes you can look into someone's eyes and without rational explanation you just know what they are feeling and why.

I can see it. The way she moves, somewhat reluctantly, forcefully, hesitantly, thinking, thinking too much.

Those are the eyes of someone who has given herself over to the bad thoughts. She probably came out here tonight to distract herself from it all, but the thing about the Sadness is, it will hunt you down no matter where you go and no matter how fast you run…

Now she won't give too much of herself away. Always a few steps ahead. Guarding herself. For better or for worse, she'll go home alone tonight.

I feel her pain. I feel her sadness. I feel, looking down from this balcony right now, lording it over the dancefloor, like a god emperor, in a room teeming with overwhelming sound, lights and movement. A god emperor. All seeing, all knowing. But the more time passes since Tommy was killed, the less I see and the less I want to know.

I see the girl with the black hair and the blue jeans and I feel the sadness in those eyes reflecting the sadness in my own. I pray she doesn't look upwards and see me. She doesn't deserve that. She is out having a good time, trying her best to forget it all.

No one needs to see that.

Hell, I can hardly bear to look at myself in the mirror any more. It's haunting, my face. Like a mask on a sack of meat.

I turn my back on the black-haired girl in the blue jeans. The voices of my friends around me drone on, hardly audible through the pounding bass.

I look over at them, but no one looks back.

I feel relieved and then make my way downstairs towards the exit.

Satisfactorily drunk. Unsatisfactorily still sober.

As I make my way down the stairs the room tilts a little bit and I lose balance. I try to remember the last time I ate anything. I have no idea. It seems like a lifetime ago since food had any flavour, so why bother?

My face and my fingers feel numb.

I wander through a sea of humans, politely manoeuvring them around as I forge a path to the front doors.

Tonight's experiment has been a success. The one thing I've realised is that the harder I try to pretend everything is okay, the harder I try to fit in again, the more obvious it becomes that I simply do not belong here anymore.

Like struggling in a mental quicksand, my thoughts only make my reality worse.

Something has to change.

As I move out into the fresh cold air of the night, a sense of absolute relief dominates. The booming, pounding music fades and the fresh night air fills my lungs. Like a sweet reward after a mission accomplished.

The world around me seems slightly more worldly again and some kind of unexplainable wrongs seem righted.

The loneliness is heavy, but the acceptable is growing.

If I can shrug myself out of this Hell-mind perhaps I can live a life again. Perhaps. Perhaps something close to that of a normal human. Oblivious. Content.

But, I suspect not.

I miss Tommy, and yet as the days go on it feels like our entire friendship was just my imagination. Like a film I watched or a book I read a long time ago. Realistic, but not *real*.

With every day that passes now the old Felix too seems less real, less tangible. Like a fading memory and more like a story I've heard third hand a long time ago.

Tommy was my best friend and without him, without someone who understood me and was always there for me, meaningless has found new meaning.

I light a cigarette and decide to walk the way home from the club, ignoring taxi drivers circling around like sharks and dodging the hordes of drunken idiots sprawling across the footpaths.

Walking is the only thing I can do to keep my mind from turning on itself.

Felix

Bow Church, the next stop on the DLR. I alight, focusing on the music in my earphones doing its best to distract me from my surroundings. It's one of those days.

I stop outside the station and light a cigarette, a filthy fucking habit that part of me wishes I could avoid. But only a small part. I enjoy it and to be honest, the chances of me living long enough to get lung cancer or something are fucking slim.

The thick, pungent cigarette helps slice through the haze I'm in today, at least for a few minutes. Cigarettes and Mozart, one of life's great combinations.

I stare at an old lady outside the station who's mouthing off at a bus driver, some drama about a bag of oranges. Some typical old black lady drama that all we Londoners just learn to ignore.

I wander off. Aimlessly.

Just walking.

Saturday morning.

Late February.

Nothing else to do.

Roaming the streets of East London, if you pay enough attention, you can always easily be repulsed by the dirtiness of the footpaths, the rundown storefronts, the shabbiness of the people around and the general lack of care these people seem to have for their environment. For the place they fucking live. Their own neighbourhood.

It's the areas filled with middle eastern and Indian shops that are the worst. Their third-world villageness continuing to infect London like a cancer on her beautiful body.

Import the third world, become the third world…

My mobile vibrates and I check to see who's calling. It's my mother. Fuck. I really don't have the energy to speak with her right now, so I walk on and let it vibrate away in my hand until she gives up.

I wander into a random corner shop and buy myself a packet of Marlborough Gold's since I'm almost out, and a can of Red Bull. I down the Red Bull in seconds, like a professional outside the store and then light a fresh cigarette.

The sky is a classic London grey today and there's no breeze at all. If you took away all the people from this scene, literally nothing would be moving.

If I focus for long enough, I can remove the people and the cars from my view for a brief moment.

Serenity in shittiness.

I spot a junkie sitting on a set of steps outside a long-since closed shoe store further up the street. He's filled a paper bag with what can only be glue or perhaps paint and he's sitting there 'huffing'. I scan the guy, partially interested, more out of boredom than anything else. He's wearing a purple vest with some faded brand logo on it that's no longer discernible, a pair of oversized and very scruffy dark green cargo trousers and a pair off suspiciously new looking trainers which he almost certainly stole recently. His skin is all dirty with dark patches of grime botching his arms in various places. Grease stains on his clothing blend into grease stains on his skin until you can't even tell where the filth begins and ends. He doesn't even notice me as I walk over to him. He takes another deep huff from his glue bag and leans back in a dazed pleasure, muttering to himself.

This isn't exactly a nice area of the city, not well landscaped, no name-brand fashion stores, no nice restaurants, but that isn't the point. This is the part of the city where I live, Mile End. If this part of the city is ever going to drag itself out of the pit, we can't have fuckers like this sprawled all over the streets. Degrading the place. Degrading us all. This fucking junkie doesn't belong here...

It's this kind of disgrace that just makes East London even more shit than it needs to be. It could be a nice place. It really could. But then you get this scum bringing the whole thing down.

I'm trying not to get worked up, but I can't help myself.

I approach this piece of shit and stand over him.

I've no idea what move I am going to make next. I feel a kind of anger, or disappointment, or something. Probably just disappointment, I think to myself.

But with who?

The junkie looks up at me, his eyes glassed over as fuck and a thread off drool hanging out of his mouth, "got ne' change, mate?" he asks, slowly extending a shaking hand towards me.

At that moment I realise I could probably stomp this piece of shit to death here on the street and no one would even notice he was gone. Probably has no family, no real friends. He's a useless waste of space and I'd be doing the community a favour.

People should not mistake a sustained period of psychological stability for someone being cured of insanity.

At that very moment, fortunately (for whom?), I notice a pair of uniformed police officers walking in my direction. I panic and think for a second they are coming for me, but I realise they aren't, they are just joking amongst themselves, not even paying attention to me as I loom threateningly over this pathetic creature beneath me. A male and a female police officer. And, well, I have to stop for a second and check this female police officer out. She's absolutely gorgeous. It's a marvel, female police officers in London. They are above average on the Fuckable scale, for some, as yet unexplained reason.

This one walking my way is model-quality. Slim, blonde, sharp features. Her body, I bet, is absolutely incredible, but its hidden under the bulky and unflattering met uniform – still, I have a vivid imagination.

As the pair draw closer, I have to break my stare. Not wanting to draw attention to myself, I start walking past them, stealing a last fleeting glance of her as we pass by, less than a metre apart. God. She's a fucking hot cop. I must say. If someone is going to arrest me for something, I hope it's her.

I finish another cigarette as I keep walking and I then turn right and make my way into Victoria Park, it would be nice to get some fresher air and see some semblance of nature for a change.

To give you an idea, the weather is *not so miserable* today, well, by London standards anyway. The sky is filled with heavy looking clouds and everything is cast in that classic London-grey, but it's not raining, at least.

I march on, Mozart is changed to Tool, is changed to Nine Inch Nails, is changed to Korn, as I ride the musical rollercoaster.

I walk past graffiti on the side of an estate agents building which reads 'We Are Everywhere'. For some reason it gives me the chills and I can't help but wonder who wrote that and what they really meant.

I distract myself by lighting another cigarette.

My boots crunch twigs and dry leaves underneath me as I enter the park, I can't hear the satisfying crunch due to the music in my ears, but I can feel it and it makes me feel like a giant stomping away on cities far below.

The park is relatively empty today. I guess it's about 4:30pm. A girl on rollerblades cruises past me and a couple holding hands talk excitedly as they walk ahead of me. In the quiet as the Korn song in my earphones ends and changes track, I hear the couple speak words in a language I don't recognise and don't want to.

I pass them by purposefully without a purpose, making my way straight towards the middle of Victoria Park.

Why?

I've no idea. I'm just bored and probably depressed.

Cyclists race past me too close for comfort, it annoys me, but what can I do? By the time I turn around they're long gone.

I change the music to *Alice in Chains, Rooster,* for some reason it seems to fit the atmosphere today.

A group of Chinese students sitting on the grass to my left begin to pack up their picnic, filling Tesco bags with empty beer bottles and crisp packets.

I march on.

No end in sight.

No purpose.

My mind, unsettlingly clear. Unsettlingly empty.

No demons today. Just the lonesome void inside my mind.

To be honest, the demons are better. At least they give me a distraction from the nothingness.

But right now, for whatever reason, I feel just fine without them.

I take a deep breath and stand up a bit straighter, pushing my chest out a bit more.

I feel calm.

A little French bulldog runs past me, pausing only for a moment to sniff my boot then, disinterested, he trots on by.

I feel a strange sensation come across me, like a moment of revelation is coming.

It's odd how you can spot them coming sometimes. Like a natural warning alarm sounds out in your body, forcing you to pay attention to what is coming next.

And I do.

And it's a moment neither you nor I will ever forget.

I wander along the bridge leading from the canal into the heart of Victoria Park and as I put my phone back into my pocket after changing my soundtrack to *Pearl Jam, Fuckin Up*, I do a double-take as I see a young Muslim guy in a brown leather jacket storm across the pathway ahead of me from right to left, making his way aggressively through a crowd of Korean students.

I freeze for a moment and I almost trip up as my legs stop working.

I see a side profile of face that I've come across before.

A face that is etched into my memory like a tattoo on my mind.

I see the face of the first fucking cockroach bastard that exited our flat that night that Tommy was killed.

I see the eyes of a mother fucking shithead that got away with murdering my best mate.

My heart feels as though it skips beats for eternity.

I'm not even walking anymore, I'm just gliding along.

The music in my ears goes silent and the park around me becomes coloured only in black and white.

This is the cunt.

This is one of those fucking cunts.

He's right there.

He's right, there.

He storms on and I find myself completely fixated.

Stunned.

Immobilised and useless.

Fear surges in me.

Hatred surges right behind.

The hatred feels stronger.

I have no idea at all what to do in this moment. I pull the earphones out my ears and let them fall to my side, hanging there on their cable.

The cunt storms on along the path and heads out of view.

Something primal inside me takes over and overrides the fear.

I find myself moving again. Following him. Moving hastily to catch up.

He moves on at a steady and predictable pace which makes it easy for me to keep up but tricky for me to avoid being noticed as I trail behind but I'm anxious that he'll turn and see me and I'm not sure what I'll do if he does.

It doesn't really matter in this moment.

I realise that I'm holding my breath so I make a point of exhaling slowly.

'Out for ten seconds, in for seven', I repeat in my head as I breath accordingly.

I try to maintain a distance of around twenty metres behind him.

Clarity seeps in and I do my best to act like I'm walking somewhere for a purpose, like I know where I'm going, confidently just strolling along at my own pace. I try to reassure myself that if he does look back, he may not recognise me anyway. I tell myself things like; I'm not dressed as I was that night, I'm not wearing a suit, my hair is not slicked back, I don't look like the corporate Felix, quite the opposite in fact, black trench coat, military boots and chin-length hair loose and blowing in the breeze around me.

Surely, he wouldn't recognise me.

Surely not?

I manage to convince myself this is true and I don't wimp out, turn around and walk away.

Nonetheless, I panic at every unexpected movement he makes and when he pauses for a moment to take his phone out of his pocket, I almost have a heart attack and end up abandoning this crazy deed altogether. But I compose myself as he carries on walking, distracted now by talking on his phone which makes me feel slightly more relaxed. He's too far ahead for me to hear what he's saying but as we move on, I catch a couple of words and he sounds pissed off which immediately washes away the relief I'd been feeling moments before.

What the fuck am I doing?

I'm following around a violent criminal who's already attacked me once before, it's getting dark outside and the further I walk the less familiar I am with this neighbourhood, and the likelihood of me running into trouble grows exponentially. I must be fucking mad.

After a while, this prick ahead of me takes a sharp turn and makes his way towards a large council block. I slow down and take stock of my surroundings. It's quickly getting dark outside now and the street lights shine bright overhead. I watch as this cunt trods towards a set of stairs in the middle of the generic-looking council block and I realise that I didn't really think this through very well. What the fuck do I do now?

I've followed him to, well, wherever this is… it may not even be his home, it could a friends/ a girlfriends? His dealers? Hell knows.

Fuck.

I walk slower, still keeping to the footpath like a regular human, and consider my options.

I watch out of the corner of my eye as he disappears up the stairs and for a moment I think I've wasted my time completely. I consider heading home. This is best, Felix. It's dark, getting cold and I'm staring at a council block in the middle of south Hackney. Not the place I really want to be.

I realise it would be too obvious if turned around right at this moment and just walked back in the direction I came from, who knows who is watching me right now? So, I press on and decide I'll check my phone for directions to get the fuck out of here once I'm on the next block, but just as I reach the end of the council estate, I see figure in a brown leather jacket emerge on the third-floor walkway, pull a key of out his pocket and open the first door on his left.

I got you, you motherless fucking cunt...

Excitement!

I stop in mid-step and can't help but stare. I'm sure my mouth is wide open and I probably look like a damn crack head, but I don't care.

Mission accomplished, Felix. You found of those fuckers that killed Tommy. The cops couldn't even find them...

Now I'm not sure what I'm going to do. I'm too excited to make a proper decision right now.

The one thing I do know is that if I stand here staring for a moment longer, I'll surely be noticed.

A moment of panic hits me.

I try to think clearly.

Now I know where one of these fuckers' lives.

Now I know where one of these fuckers' lives.

The words repeat over in my head as though the functioning part of my brain is doing its very best to get through the haze and convince the panicked part to be sensible and snap back into action.

This place may not be where he lives, fair enough, but the purposeful way he marched across the carpark and up to that flat tells me that he knows this place well. That he's very comfortable here. And he has keys….

I can find him here.

At least this one cunt.

At least *this* motherless fuck.

All the pain and suffering he's caused to not only me, not only Tommy, but I'm sure countless other innocent people have suffered at the hands of this fucking cunt. This fucking cunt and a million just like him. There is a chance for me to amend that. Or at least try.

Rage begins to build momentum inside me.

I remember how helpless I felt at that moment when they attacked me. How worthless and small I was...

How could they get away with this?

How could they be allowed to get away with this?

No. No. No.

Fuck. Fuck. Fucking pieces of shit cunts!

I feel my fists clenching and my fingernails digging into the palms of my hands.

Fucking, fucks sake.

There's no possible way I'm going to stand for this.

No way am I going to let this just go. Let these fuckers just carry on while the police and everyone else close the fucking case and ignore it.

I have to do something. Anything…

I've got nothing to fucking lose.

Nothing.

I fucking hate myself enough as it is.

I fucking loathe my boring life and every little part of it.

Every day is exactly the same.

Please do not touch me.

I am soaked in darkness…

Fuck.

No way can I go on like this…. I have nothing.

I am nothing.

Every day I repeat the same routine.

Just drifting along.

I'm sick of it.

It's time to do something about it.

It's time to do something with my life.

Something to be remembered for.

Something noticeable.

Make a fucking difference in this world.

Make even one small part of it better.

I have nothing to lose, because I lost myself a long time ago…

I put my earphones back in my ears and hear *Marilyn Manson, Lunchbox* playing. My phone is just doing its own thing, playing whatever it likes now.

I take deep breath as a flood of anger makes my skin tingle.

In a moment of total clarity, I know exactly what I will do...

I will take down these fucking street rat cunts that did this.

I'll wander the streets and hunt them down like the filthy little vermin they are.

I won't bother going to the useless police or anything like that. They have already proven themselves useless.

At best, they'd arrest one or two of them, they'd put them on an expensive trial, at the taxpayers expense of course, and with no guarantee they'd get convicted. I'd have to testify and make myself a target. Even if they were convicted, this useless justice system in the UK would probably allow them back out on the streets in just a few years to do it all again. And in prison, well, they'd just be in there with their mates, wouldn't they? Again... all at the taxpayers' expense...

Do you know how much it costs you, as a taxpayer to keep a single prisoner in prison for a year?

Around £40,000.

£40,000!

That is more than the average salary in the UK. Absolutely absurd.

Do you know what the cost of a single bullet is?

Around £0.10.

Ten pence....

Do the fucking math...

What are we doing?

The statistics don't lie – they are just fact. Around 60% of prisoners in this United Kingdom of ours are previous offenders. Meaning they've been convicted of some other crime at some point... at least once.

60%...

Once you are on the spectrum, your chances of rehabilitation diminish rapidly.

I'm not going to let these fuckers get away with the light touch justice in this ridiculously politically correct self-defeating nation.

Fuck them.

They need to be taught a lesson.

And all the fear has been washed away from my soul.

All of it.

I have nothing to lose.

If I die in the process, well, fuck it, what a way to go. It certainly won't be dull and it certainly won't go unnoticed.

I'm a mad mother fucker, I know, but if I succeed, if I do this properly... the world will be a better place for it and people will one day thank me.

And you know what, even if they don't, Tony will. Tommy's family will. And that is enough for me.

Fuck these shithead cunts.

There is no allowance for blind forgiveness. An eye must be taken for an eye. Anything less is blatant weakness in front of your enemies and such weakness must be avoided at all costs.

Tommy always believed that the greatest sin a person can commit is to be apathetic. To not care, to find excuses to not do what we know we really should. For if we don't care about what happens in the world around us, then we aren't part of that world at all, we simply happen to exist within it. That isn't life, he said. Living is coexisting. Coexisting with all those around us. Living is acting in harmony with the world around us. Acting in harmony and also acting to *maintain* that harmony. When that harmony is disrupted, only an equal disruption can restore it to order.

An eye for an eye.

Balance.

Societal harmony depends on it.

And so do I. In his name, but also in my own.

Most people wouldn't be going to the lengths I intend to go to, most people would find some way of moving on. But it's important, it's part of our shared valued system. We were wronged, and so, we must restore the harmony.

No room for forgiveness. No room for apathy.

I'm going to kill the guys who did this to us. I'm going to kill every single one of those fuckers and in doing so clean up at least a small part of this shitty fucking city.

4 Elisabetta

Felix

The wind begins to pick up and I feel the bitter cold biting at my ears. I know that I can't wait around here for too long without looking rather suspicious, and to be honest, this neighbourhood makes me nervous enough that I just want to get out of here as soon as I can. I'm silently praying that this cunt comes back outside soon. I guess I've got around five more minutes at most before I'll have to leave, and then I'll have to chance coming back here tomorrow to wait again.

Loitering around this council block on the off chance that I'll see the guy I need to see pop out may seem like a completely ridiculous idea to you, and you are right. That is exactly what it is.

I pull out a cigarette and fumble around in my coat pocket for a lighter. I'm leaning over the cigarette and cupping it with my hand to fend off the wind when I see movement in the area of the guy's doorway just as my cigarette lights up.

Boom. Fucking go, Felix.

Light floods out the doorway of his flat as the douchebag exits. He's changed into a dark green puffer jacket, black Adidas tracksuit bottoms and white trainers. He pulls the door shut behind him and then dashes back towards the stairwell. I stomp my unsmoked cigarette out on the ground to avoid drawing his attention and slink back into the darkness behind me.

A young couple walk past, barely paying me any mind as they chatter away about what they plan for dinner. It's properly dark now, even though its only around 5:30pm.

I watch as this prick exits the stairwell on the ground floor, now he has his hood pulled over and hands in pockets, sauntering away, back in the direction we came from earlier.

He doesn't even glance my way, and I'm glad he's wearing the hood, which should reduce his peripheral vision and make it harder for him to see me following him. I can't tell from here if he is listening to any music, but if he is, that would be even better.

As I move discreetly, fifteen or twenty metres behind him, I find myself more and more convicted in my idea to track these fuckers down. The thought crosses my mind of just taking this guy down right now, right here on the street in a moment when no one is looking and I have no doubt it would provide me with some degree of satisfaction. But I also know that afterwards I would quickly regret that this cunt would be the only one to suffer. If I just took him down right now, the others would scatter and I would probably be caught within hours. The game would be up and proper retribution would not have been delivered.

The more sensible side of me knows that since absolutely no planning has gone into this mission right now the chances of me fucking this up and being caught are extremely high.

No, no. no, Felix.

This is right thing to do, find these boys. Find as many of them as you can and then you can work out what to do next. Perhaps, I'll throw a fucking Molotov cocktail into their group as they stand on the street or drive a car right through or something? When the time is right, I'll work it out.

Felix, just find these guys and take the information to the police.

No.

I know that that would be useless.

The cunt up ahead of me pauses for a moment before he crosses the street and as he looks both ways he glances in my direction and my fucking heart skips a beat. Did he see me?

Yes, he did! Oh, fuck!

Panic hits me hard and my palms ooze with sweat.

I look away and pretend to be walking in the other direction.

Fortunately, he pays me no more attention and presses on ahead. He doesn't recognise me at all. I let out a long breath, cross the road and increase my pace to keep up.

Fuck…

I feel my heart beating faster with anticipation and possibly excitement.

Felix, you are crazy.

I may be crazy but I haven't felt this excited about anything for a Hell of a long time. I have nothing left to lose, really. I don't give a fuck about my job, I don't ever want to go back to that. I don't want to waste my days away in front of a computer pretending I give a good god damn about any of it. About any of that old life… I've gone too far.

Violent thoughts race through my head. I'm going to take these fucking cunts head on and I don't care if I go down in the process, just knowing that I tried something is good enough.

I keep my pace up with this cunt. We walk in unison. Like a puppy following its master.

The wind picks up again and a flurry of leaves swirl around on the path in front of me. I count four other people walking on the same street as us this evening. Four innocent and unsuspecting souls. More would be better. The busier the street is, the less likely I am to be spotted. But, what can I do?

Regardless, I still don't feel as though I stand out too much. I'm just a guy walking along the street. Anyway, if this guy notices me following him, I'll just veer off and head home. At least I know where he lives, I can always come back another day and try again.

It's okay. I tell myself. It's okay. You are safe. He isn't expecting anything like this. You are just a guy walking the same way as him on a street that's all. No need to worry.

I tell myself this, but I don't really believe it. Given that I know these guys are capable of murder, I'm understandably on edge. I wish I had a drink right now to take the edge off, help me act less tense. But, alas, I have nothing.

The shithead ahead of me stops at a set of lights and waits for a break in the traffic to cross. I slow down, not wanting to catch up to him before he has a chance to move on.

This scene makes me even more tense. Argh, come on, Felix. Get yourself together. Act calm.

My breath steams out in front of me in quick waves and I feel like I'm overheating despite the cold.

Calm down, Felix.

The arsehole ahead pulls out his mobile and stares at the screen.

At this moment I feel small something tapping on my nose and hands and I panic, thinking that something awful has happened, totally irrationally of course, but, nonetheless in this very abnormal situation, the mind wanders to all kinds of places.

Turns out it is raindrops. Small drops are smacking down on me as I pause and watch this fucker stop to tie his shoelace. I pretend to check my phone for a moment and then I see him jog across the road with his hands in the pockets of his jacket.

I follow him, dodging a BMW and a lorry as I do so. He keeps on jogging and I worry that I'll lose him. I can only reasonably jog behind him for so long before it becomes far too obvious that I'm following him.

He rounds one last corner and then slows down to a trot and then eventually back to a brisk walk. I'm praying he's about to stop.

The rain starts pelting down harder now and I can feel my trousers becoming damp, my hair clinging to my cheeks.

Please be stopping soon, you cunt.

He does.

He makes a sharp left and walks past a low brick fence up to the front door of an average-looking two-story terraced house.

There's nothing more I can do. I'm not sure what I intended to do next. I hadn't thought this far ahead in the hour since I found this guy.

I finally break off the hunt and cross the street slowly, dissolving myself into the shadows and all the while acting as though I'm still on my own journey to someplace else.

Light washes into the street as the front door of this house opens and I see two young Arab guys at the door shaking hands with the green jacket guy as he enters and out of the corner of my eye, I see him slam the door shut behind him.

Bingo.

Those must be his mates. I don't recognise them at first. But, these guys, either are the guys who killed Tommy, or they must be connected to the guys who did. Even if I find out nothing else, I'm one big step closer to justice.

In my final act I take note of the house number, 6, as I stoop down to tie my laces and then I'm up again and off down the street. That's enough for tonight. I've done well.

Excitement overwhelms me.

Adrenaline flows and the rush I get from this mission accomplished is like a hit of the best drug ever.

Fuck.

This, my friends, is living.

This, is truly being alive.

My walk home turns into a jog and I take note of the street name as I leave it and make my way in the direction of what I believe is Hackney Central Overground Station.

Felix

The next morning, I wake early. I could hardly sleep from the excitement of last night. I tossed and turned all night and tried my best to tell my brain to calm down. But obviously, it didn't work. It never does, does it? At one point I got up and grabbed a scrap of paper and pen and wrote down a few notes. Just so I wouldn't forget.

A few ideas...

I make myself a cup of coffee and put on some *Elisabetta de Gambarini*. I have a lot of work to do.

The heating in my flat takes a while to get cracking so I lean on the radiator in the kitchen and reflect on things.

This is going to be very dangerous and the sensible part of my brain tells me I shouldn't do this. *Just walk away from it.*

But the thrill I got last night was too much. I need to feel it again.

Fuck, I felt like a secret agent! I felt like I was starring in my own little film.

I take another sip of coffee and make my way to the living room window. I hear voices from outside but they are too muffled to make out the words. Not that I care anyway, it's just nice to know that there are other humans around and that everything is real. I haven't lost my mind.

In that moment last night, more important than anything else, I felt alive. I felt like in those moments, my life actually meant something. That I had some kind of purpose. Hunting humans. Even right now, right this minute, I know where at least one, possible two of the cunts who killed Tommy live! Fuckinell. That is incredible. In less than 24 hours I've done more than the police did in 24 days!

I know, I could take this information to them right now, let them investigate and take these guys down. Off the streets. But, let's be honest. What's the best possible outcome I could hope for? That the one guy who stabbed Tommy goes down for a few years and is out in half that time? While the rest of them get off with a slap on the wrist and are back out on the streets looking for me like a pack of rabid hyenas? Come on...

I like Boris, he seems like a good lad, but he's really not pressing the Met to do their job properly. The streets are dangerous, and they really shouldn't be.

An ambulance rushes past outside and derails my train of thought. I listen as the sirens fade off down the street and around the corner. My mind wanders to wondering what madness has taken place just now that requires an ambulance. My thoughts don't go to the statistically most likely scenario of an accident in the home. No, they go right to a stabbing, a murder, a gang fight, a rape... This is what I suspect. My mind used to be balanced. I feel that balance becoming increasingly elusive.

The worst-case scenario if I take this information to the police? They 'investigate' but can't prove anything or come up with anything solid at all and so give up. Unfortunately, this is the likely scenario. And to be honest, any outcome that lies between the two described above is as good as useless.

In any and all scenarios from here on out, given the fact that I'll certainly need to testify as witness, I'll have one huge goddamn target on my chest, you can be sure of that.

Neither scenario involving the police appeals to me at all.

This is the only way you'll get closure, Felix, do it. Take them down yourself.

I find myself staring off at a smudge on the corner of the kitchen bench and snap myself back.

No, Felix, this is suicide. Just leave it alone.

....

Fuck.

Let's be sensible.

Come on, Felix, be smart.

The first thing I need to do here is get some names. I need names and I need faces. I think there were six, perhaps seven guys there that night, but I have no idea how many in their little gang in total. I need more details.

But how?

I can't possibly stake out the house or the flat, no way in Hell. That would be far too risky. No.

No. No, I have to be smart…

I pace around my living room and drift in and out of paying attention to the background music.

Come on, Felix. Where is your lightbulb moment?

My mobile vibrates on the table next to my laptop and I move to stand over it to see who it is messaging me.

My Mother. Classic.

Her message reads 'Is now a good time to call?'

No, now is not at all a good time for a call.

I ignore the message without hesitation and think to myself, a few months ago I would've phoned her right away and had a good old chat, but now, I can't even begin to imagine having a normal conversation with her. This is yet another sign of my withdrawal from society at large. I am aware of this.

I put down my coffee mug and take a seat at the table in front of my laptop.

How do I get names?

Come on, Felix…

I drift into the music for a moment. *Elisabetta* keeps on playing and the upbeat tempo contrasts sharply with the dark thoughts swirling in my mind. I dive deeper into the purity of the sound.

Then it comes! Like a gift from the gods.

Bingo. I know exactly how!

Mail. Fucking. Mail.

I'll take some letters from the rubbish bags left in the front of the house on Horton Road and hopefully that will give me something to work with. Once I've got a name, I can use Facebook to put a face to it, and see make sure it's one of the cunts from that night. This is excellent. It's fucking genius.

From there on I can also use Facebook to find the others! Check his friends list, see if the profiles of his friends spark any memory of the cunts there that night, and piece it all together from there.

I'm standing up, my hands are trembling and I'm impressed with myself. This is a long-shot, but it's fucking exciting.

No doubt it'll be difficult, but damn... I really am like some kind of secret agent here. A fucking detective. Detective Felix.

I've got to be careful that I don't get recognised. In day to day life I stand out a bit too much I think, longish black hair, usually stomping about in boots and a black mac, not exactly the most conspicuous character, so my first stop today needs to be Stratford shopping centre. I need a new wardrobe from some of those cheap fucking market shops. A hunting wardrobe. Loads of cheap, generic clothing Enough for me to wear a completely different outfit every time I'm out hunting for these pricks.

I make myself another coffee, shower and then head out.

By the time I return back to my flat I've spent a few hundred quid on a whole load of random stuff that in normal circumstances I'd never, ever, allow myself to be seen dead in. But this shit will do. Cheap and nasty. Loads of colours. Absolutely nothing like the rest of my wardrobe.

I can throw all of this shit away as I'm done with it.

Once I'm home I jump online to find out when the next rubbish collection day is for Horton Road. Looks like it's Wednesday, two days from now, so I need to go there late the night before and grab a bag, I can only grab one, so it'll be luck of the draw. No way I can wander around the streets with two or three rubbish bags without looking pretty damn conspicuous. Even one will make me look like a mental homeless bum, but I'll have to deal with that.

Felix

Tuesday night. Dressed like a regular fuckwit. Yellow hoodie, blue jeans and white trainers, with grey wool gloves.

I couldn't bear to look at myself in the mirror for longer than I needed to. I've never dressed like this in my entire fucking life. I dress with style, I dress dark, I dress smart. Corporate Goth, decorating myself in only blacks, whites, greys and reds.

These blue jeans alone are enough to fill me with a tonne of self-hate, let alone the yellow hoodie. But... sacrifices must be made.

I put on a pair of tortoise shell glasses with non-prescription lenses, you know the kind, hipster junk, like some kind of fuckin Clark Kent cunt. Some arseholes even wear these without lenses in them, just the fucking frames... Disgusting... Yet, here I am.

I decided the best time to set out was between 10pm and 12pm, any earlier than that and the family may not have put to trash out yet, any later than that, and the streets are likely to be too empty, making me stand out like a sore thumb roaming about with a stolen rubbish bag from someone's property. It's a weak rationale, but it's the best I've got. So, let's rock n roll.

After a line of snow and a shot of tequila, I make my way outside into the streets of the wild, wild East. Although I feel uncomfortable walking around in this ridiculous gear, I have to say, as I move through Mile End, for perhaps the first time ever I get the impression that I'm assimilating rather well. No one seems to be paying me any attention at all, which is unusual for me, I have to say. There is something to be said for dressing like an average cuck.

I feel like a ghost.

A fucking ninja.

A short while later and I am turning left onto Horton Road. Time: 10:45pm. A lone old lady walks towards me on the same side of the street and she is the only soul I can see. This is promising. I slow my pace and wait until she's passed before doing proper scan of the street.

All seems relatively quiet. About a third of the houses still have lights on inside which seems about right and so I make my way steadily towards number 6.

I have to do this next bit very quickly and I have to act as natural as I possibly can.

Despite the nerves, I feel confident. The only reasons for me not following through on this, are, one, there are no rubbish bags out there, or two, someone from the house is hanging about and could spot me.

Otherwise, I have to do it. No turning back now.

I make my way along the opposite side of the street so I can get a better view of the house. As I get closer, I do a quick scan around and listen out for any signs of life.

Nothing.

Now is the time.

My heart skips a beat or two and I notice that I'm biting hard on my lower lip. I try to stop but I can't.

Forget about it, Felix. Press on. Cross the street.

My palms are sweating profusely inside these gloves and a bead of cold sweat runs across my forehead. I wipe it off with the back of my hand and take the last few steps up to the front of the house.

Fucking Hell. Felix. Be swift!

The curtains are drawn in a darkened living room and the only lights I see are in the upstairs rooms.

Adrenaline surges and sharpens me up and I'm completely focussed on the task at hand. Not a single other thought could enter my mind right now. I'm wholly focussed on one thing only. It's incredible the way the human body works...

With one last glance around and a deep breath I lean over the low brick fence and open the lid of the green rubbish bin. Inside are at least two black rubbish bags.

Lucifer, the smell... I breathe out through my nostrils to push the fetid odour out.

Go on, Felix, take it!

I grab the top bag, yank it out in one clean motion and close the lid again as quietly as I can.

Then I march, and I mean fucking *march*, further down the street and around the corner. I simply have to move now. With the bag knocking against my leg and my heart beating sporadically I make my way to a small row of shops, where I proceed into the shadows around the back, drop the bag and take a long-needed breath of oxygen. Was I holding my breath the entire time? Surely not...

Oh, my fucking Hell.

My heart hammers away like a maniac.

I think my nuts crawled up inside me when I rounded the corner back there and a car cruised past at the exact same moment, headlights glaring in my face and bearing down on me. I can only wonder what the passengers thought of me scurrying along the road with a fucking rubbish bag in my hand, hood pulled over in the darkness of the night.

Well, actually, they probably thought, "oh, classic London…"

I move on from this and get to business. No time to waste. I make quick work of ripping open the black bag and pouring its contents out onto the damp concrete.

A few more cars cruise past out on the street in front of the shops and my heart skips a beat with every single one.

I hear faint voices from inside the corner shop I'm lurking behind and I swear if I wasn't so tense right now, I'd shit my pants.

The ensuing scramble around in the filth, the egg shells, empty chicken packets, food scraps, plastic bottles, tissues… fucking Hell, is worse than I could've ever imagined. I come close to dry retching a number of times as I move about snotty tissues, what appears to be vomited up noodles and too many questionable blooded bandages, until I finally find the shit I'm looking for. I'm looking for anything that resembles anything official, or any fucking envelope at all. And under an empty Chinese takeaway box, I find papers.

Gold.

I fucking strike gold.

I find two letters, a bank statement and what appears to be a letter from an estate agency.

Bingo.

I have one last dig around in the awful mess to see if there is anything else, but this is it.

Fucking Hell. Please, Lucifer, let there be something useful in here!

I stuff the soiled papers into my hoodie pocket, pull the hood down a bit more over my forehead and then with hands in pockets, holding my treasure tightly, I march myself out onto the street and off down towards home.

Mission (hopefully) accomplished.

Felix

The moment I arrive home I feel a sweet wave of relief wash over me. I fucking made it to safety. My heart still pounds like crazy and I fix myself an extra strong vodka and tonic immediately, without even stopping to take off my shoes or jacket. Fuck it. I need the drink.

I gulp down the first one, basically inhaling it, and then pour myself another. As I wait for my breathing to slow to a normal pace, I turn some music on, *Mozart's Menuetto II; Trio I; Trio II from Serenade No. 9 in D, Posthorn*, and let it soothe my nerves.

Right, Felix. Let's do this. Fuck, I hope you have some treasure here. If you don't, you'll be waiting at least a whole week until the next rubbish collection day, even longer if anything goes wrong.

I lay down a couple of plastic shopping bags on the table and then, putting my gloves back on, proceed to empty the contents of my pockets.

Ketchup (I presume) stains everything, as well as tea? And some kind of pasta? I gag but hold myself steady. Fortunately, the address on the envelope and the estate agent letter inside read clearly a female's name, but the bank statement reads 'Abid Majid'. I don't know much about Muslim names, but this sounds male to me.

Right. So, this could be the winner. Fantastic!

I take a moment to finish my second vodka and then decide I need to change out of these clothes and shower all this muck off before I carry on.

I do just that, in an excited rush and five minutes later I'm back at the table, vodka (number four, now?) in hand and my laptop open in front of me.

Felix, before you rush into this, you need to think. How traceable is what you are about to do? Any searches you make from your own Facebook account will be stored somewhere in some server for ever and ever, and if the police or anyone else, MI5, whoever, wanted to find a connection to anyone who did anything to Abid in future, this would be a route they would logically go down and it would lead them directly to you.

No. No. No. Come on. Be smart.

I pause with my fingers hovering over the keyboard. No searching from my own account. Fortunately, I have a VPN program that I use to stream films so I can scramble my IP address making it unlikely a general search on Google would be traced back to me with any degree of ease. If at all.

I get up again, open the nearest window, grab a packet of cigarettes and my zippo and sit back down, lighting up a Marlboro Gold and fingering the side of my laptop nervously.

Here we go. No turning back. VPN on.

I type this cunts name into the Google search bar and add the word 'London' to help narrow down the thousands of fuckers there must be out there with the same name.

Boom.

Up comes at least six decent results. Three Facebook profiles, some kind of high school football profile from the mid-2000's and then a few more spurious results as employees from random companies, but the Facebook profiles are the ones I really want. They're the most likely.

This is going well.

I jump onto my Facebook profile and double-check that I'm fully logged out and then just for good measure I erase my all of my browsing history and delete all cookies and saved passwords and everything else I can get rid of. Next, I turn off the laptop, finish my cigarette, then turn it back on, and, satisfied I'm now safe searching, type this fuckers name again and click through to the first Facebook profile in the list.

The profile picture is a bit hard to work out, it looks like a middle-aged man and his younger, fatter, wife.

Nope.

The next one in the list is a guy in his late twenties with no shirt on, standing in what can only be a gay bar in Soho. Highly unlikely and I don't recognise his face at all.

The third one is the golden ticket. Welcome to the fucking chocolate factory, bitch.

I pause for a happy moment. I can feel my cheeks tense with a smile. Muscles that haven't been properly flexed for some time. I light another cigarette, take another gulp of my somethingth drink of the day and take stock of my success.

A young, slim, Arab guy in his mid-twenties who looks, well, he looks like an absolute cocky arrogant little cunt. You just know them when you see them. He's posing in a vest taking a selfie in the mirror at a gym (even Mile End gym, perhaps?), showing off his very average physique, and of course he's filtered the picture to make his little muscles seem more impressive than they actually are. Classic, douchebag...

The remarkable thing is that as I stare at him, there's an instant recognition in me. I know that I've met this mother fucker before without doubt. *Fuck, this is exciting!* Even though it was night time and even though it all happened so quickly, I recognise him still. It's his jawline that gives him away, those sharp lines and the over-groomed 5 o'clock shadow beneath beady, cunty little eyes is unmistakable.

I finish vodka number x and lean back in my chair. I've got you, you absolute cock-sucking motherless fuck.

A mixture of emotions swirls through me. First delight and then a myriad of other sensations cascades around, before the rage sets in and takes over all. As the rage rises up I grit my teeth. If I had this cunt in front of me right now, I'd throttle him, poke his eyeballs out with my thumbs and skullfuck him death. Nothing could stop me.

I let the rage run its course and I watch as my hands tremble like someone suffering from Parkinson's Disease before the cool, calculated part of my mind eventually regains control.

I've got one, I can't believe I've actually got one!

There's no stopping me now. Nothing at all will stop me from following through on this. I have nothing left to lose. I have to try to take these bastards down. If for nothing else than my own satisfaction. My own sanity.

If I die in the process, I'll die in the name of Tommy and I'll die happy.

Back to work. I set up a fake Facebook account using a random Gmail address I make up on the spot and once I'm logged in, I can see Abid's profile in a bit more detail. He has most of his personal details Private, but I can see his friends list and from there I can start to piece together his little gang.

I find the green hoodie guy who I already know lives on Frampton Park Road pretty easily, Qusay Hamza Zubeidi.

From memory there were six or seven guys there that night, so my list is not going to be easy to put together. I spend the next two hours going through Facebook profile after Facebook profile looking for young Arab guys linked in some way to each other (particularly Abid) who fit the profile of what I remember, young, early twenties or late teens, and I cull all the ones who don't live in London or just don't look the part.

By noon my list is fourteen. Fourteen fucking guys who seem to be closely connected. Only five of them are clearly Abid's friends as I've seen them in a few photographs together. The faces also look familiar and so, I'm suspecting these cunts are part of his little gang. The others, are... questionable. They all begin to look the same to me. More research will be required.

At 12:19pm I print out an A4 sized photograph of all fourteen fuckwits and write their names along the top. The picture quality varies and staring at the array of potential killers in front of me I'm somewhat downbeat at my prospects of actually identifying all of them. But this is where I have to start. I've got to start somewhere.

I yawn and my back aches from leaning over the laptop for so long.

It's raining and I didn't even notice it had started. I've left the windows and the balcony doors open and the curtains are getting damp and the breeze coming through is moist and sticky.

I need a nap.

The music changes to *Richard Wagner - Götterdämmerung - Siegfried's Funeral March,* and it's really not what I need right now.

I get up and change it to something completely different, *Slayer, Angel of Death,* it seems more fitting.

Sitting back down, cigarette balanced between pursed lips, I realise that there is one very obvious link I've uncovered amongst all this Facebook stalking which is absolutely worth investigating, and may be the key to it all. Mile End gym.

Mile End fucking, leisure centre.

One of these guys I've found, a familiar looking young guy, Hani Hussein, works at the gym, and not only that, but the gyms pops up in more than a few of the profiles of these fourteen guys. Mile End gym. It isn't far from my flat. I haven't been to the gym in over a year, but I'm thinking I should renew my membership down there and see if I can recognise a few faces.

It's as good of a place as any to start.

Cunts like this tend to be very close-knit, hanging out in their little cliques as often as possible, usually on street corners harassing girls or standing about in cul-du-sacs talking shit. In general, these Muslims are much more cliquey than white boys tend to be, so there is a pretty good chance these boys go the gym together.

If I can find just one of these fuckers in there and I can hopefully find out who else is in the gang, who's the leader and one-by one track them all down to where they live. This is the plan.

I'll be able to start planning Retribution.

I may never know which one of them actually stabbed Tommy, but that doesn't matter. I hold them all responsible and they shall all be punished accordingly.

An ambulance rushes past outside, snapping me back to reality and I realise that I'm completely exhausted. No death metal can keep me awake. I yawn, stub out my half-smoked cigarette and rubs my eyes. My whole body feels heavy. There is nothing more for me to do right now.

Felix, you've outdone yourself.

I climb back to bed and finally sleep a restless sleep.

Felix

The next afternoon I'm dressing myself in regular human clothing again, snorting about a third of a gram of snow and then making my way outside into the cold and the rain.

It's just after 1pm and I figure, as I know that most of my snow dealers (and thus my closest connection to the underworld), are operational from about 1pm onwards, I figure these fuckers are probably on a similar schedule and so my best bet is to head to the gym now and renew my membership, but mostly scout the place, hoping that these degenerates, just like the other degenerates in this city, are starting their day around this time and heading to the gym about this time before they head out and cause trouble.

It's fucking spurious, I know, but it's the only thing I can think of which makes any sense, short of just spending an entire day in the gym hoping they come in.

At the moment there is literally no other way I can think of to do this.

And so, I make my merry way over the Mile End gym and head into the membership office. Once I've sorted the membership out, I head into the main part of the gym and set myself up near the back on one the treadmills where I have a good view of the whole gym, in particular the weights section, where I'm quite sure the boys spend most of their time.

The place is fucking empty, and despite knowing how fucking weak this whole idea is, I'm still really disappointed when I see not a single young Arab guy in the weights section. Only a couple of older Pakistani men and a jacked up black dude that looks a bit like a short Wesley Snipes.

So, I do this for four days in a row. Four fucking days in a row, hanging about the gym at the same time for two-three hours at a time – seriously - while waiting to spot just one of the cunts on my shit list.

When that doesn't work, I decide to try a different time of day. I have to mix it up, so I ask when is the busiest time in gym, the cute girl on the desk tells me it's between 6am and 8am, and then again at the end of the night 8pm-10pm.

I almost ask her when Hani is working his shifts here, but I realise that would absolutely fucking insane and fortunately I stop myself before the words can escape.

Careful, Felix. You fuckin maniac.

Three nights later, close to deciding to give up and change tactics entirely, I strike pay dirt as four Arab boys enter the gym and stride past me as I sit sweating on the shoulder press. My heart skips a beat and I almost have a full-blown panic attack as Abid saunters past within a metre of me, looking every bit the leader of the pack.

I look away quickly. Desperate not to draw his attention by staring for too long.

My heart pounds as I look out the corner of my eye at him.

Holy fuck, I broke into your rubbish bin, stole your rubbish and hunted you down. You mother fuckers. I know where you live.

Fuck.

Felix you've done it.

I try not to stare but it's hard not to, there he is right there. Setting himself up on the bench press.

The other three all seem familiar and they all look rough as fuck. I'm pretty certain I have all their pictures printed out in my list. Almost certainly. That tall skinny one, definitely.

Thursday night, 8:33pm, and these boys are finally here in the gym.

Abid, Qusay, I've got you two fuckers lined up, now, I need to add your three shitty little mates to my list.

Emotion mix? Relief, excitement, fear, happiness, anxiety... a heavy dose of anxiety.

I do my best to act natural and carry on with my workout while I calm my nerves.

And this, friends, is how your humble narrator tracked down all seven of Abid's little fucking gang of cunts.

It didn't take me long to realise that their routine was relatively consistent. It turns out they meet at the gym Thursdays and Fridays at about 8:30pm. It also turns out that Hani works at the gym Friday's and when he finishes his shift at 9pm he usually joins them for a training session.

The crew was a slightly different composition each time, but after a few weeks, I realised the common theme was, Abid (always Abid, he was always there), and I narrowed down the rotating list of boys he'd be training with to six others. This 'main' crew included Hani, and of course Qusay.

From there, it was a pretty simple exercise of following each of these pricks home, one by one. The only complication, Abid and two of the others, Kamal Hasan and Ali al-Tikriti, drive to and from the gym, which made it impossible in the first instance to follow them. But then I got the idea of simply hiring my own fucking car that I could use to follow the cunts around.

It took me two months to whittle down a network of fourteen cunts to the seven motherless fucks I'm sure were there the night Tommy was killed and to work out exactly where each of them live, and also work out some semblance of their routines.

I've found it amazing how oblivious people can be to being followed or to being watched by others. It's understandable, the distractions of life are immense, from staring at our mobile phones as we walk around, to listening to music as way of drowning out the outside world, not to mention the overwhelming busyness of living in a city such as London, where we simply can't pay attention to everything, we simply can't absorb all the information around us, even if we wanted to.

And so, for someone like me who is determined to follow, determined to watch and who is also especially careful to disguise himself, the whole process just got easier and easier as I became more confident and more comfortable with my hunting.

Two months. Seven cunts.

Seven lives mapped out. Seven lives destined to end.

The thrill of the hunt has been like nothing I have ever experienced in my life.

But I remain torn.

A lonely and ever-weakening part of me still calls out from the corner of hopelessness for me to pull back from the brink. I lie on my bed with a vodka and tonic in hand fidgeting with a cushion and this sad, lonely rational part of me attempts to make its voice heard.

Right now, I could stop. I could just drop all of this. No harm has been done. Not by me. No serious laws broken (except for stealing a rubbish bag). I could, right now, just take all this information to the police, hand everything over to them and make myself available to testify as witness in court. Let the authorities take these fuckers down.

But… as we know, dear friends, that would be a death sentence for *me* and not for *them*. The British justice system is broken. I'd be exposing myself to all kinds of questioning from the police – how did I get all this information? Why have I waited so long to tell the police? etc. etc… it would be obvious I've had some kind vendetta in mind.

No. There is simply no other choice.

Nothing else would satisfy me anyway.

I want to be the one who delivers justice.

I want to be the one who puts things right.

I want revenge for Tommy.

I need to do this. I have nothing else now. Nothing else matters.

I'll take my time. No need to rush this and fuck it up. It's too important to risk a single mistake. If this is the last thing that Felix does, and it may well be, then so be it. If I try and I fail, I will die happy knowing I did my best for Tommy.

But I won't fail.

I won't.

I'll give myself over to the hunt, completely.

I'll become a lone wolf feeding only on rage.

5 George

Felix

A thick fog covers the windows of my living room as I pull back the dark-grey velvet curtains to glimpse the outside world. A dull light shines up at me from a nearby lamppost, but mostly I can see only the heavy darkness outside. The night is silent and almost completely still. *Delibe's Flower Duet*, is playing through the tall speakers which stand either side of the living room television. Outside the temperature has dropped considerably. Classic London springtime. I can feel the cold struggling to get at me through the glass. The wind outside is faint, barely strong enough to rustle the handful of leaves I hear scraping along the ground below.

3:30am, early Monday morning. The whole world is your playground at this hour. At this hour anything goes for those of us who dare to venture out while the rest slumber. If only the rest knew what us creatures of the night really got up to after they tune out. After they close their doors, close their eyes and close their minds...

Better they don't.

I let out a deep sigh.

I want to smoke a cigarette, but I know that will only make me more anxious.

My heart races.

...Patience Felix... You'll be out there soon enough... Tonight it begins...

I've spent the last three months formulating my plans and rehearsing the coming executions. I quit my awful job, I never went back in after the bereavement break they forced upon me. Instead, I spent week after week following these cunts around, working out where each one of them lived and planning exactly how I am going to kill every single one of them. Seven cunts over seven nights.

I know who they are.

I know where to find them.

I know exactly how they will die and in what order.

I know more about these mother fuckers' last days on earth than they do. It's such an incredibly powerful concept when you think about. To know when another person will die. To know that they are living their last days alive, and they don't even realise it.

The power is in my hands.

Literally.

The gym at Mile End was a great place to start tracking them, and once I'd gotten started it was like I went from putting together a 10,000-piece puzzle with no picture for guidance, to holding the box right there in my hand.

I worked out that the main hangout spot for these cunts, the main gathering place for these goons, is around St Thomas Square near London Fields.

All sevens of these fuckers live between Victoria Park and Dalston Junction.

It wasn't hard at all to track these fuckers down; they meet at the square every fucking day and then eventually they head off either alone or in small groups together. They're so wrapped up in their own bullshit that following them around proved less dangerous than I'd initially anticipated.

During this whole time, the scariest moment came at one point when I was following behind one of these guys and they turned around sharply and walked back directly towards me on Haggerston Road. I panicked as he stared right at me and I almost lost it and ran. I was completely flustered, but at the last minute, as he got close, I had a moment of courage and stood my ground. It turned out to be the right decision as the fucker just marched on past me without a further glance, I suppose he 'd forgotten something he had to go back for. I remember him passing so close to me the belt on my trench coat flapped in the wind and brushed across his thigh. The cold sweat of fear oozed out of me and in order to avoid arousing further suspicion, I took my phone of out my pocket, and faked a call from my boss about some work bullshit, walked right on down the street, without even lifting my head, let alone a glance backwards. When I was out of sight I almost fainted from a combination of holding my breath and the fact that my heart was beating so hard I thought it would climb out of my chest and go run off on its own to somewhere much safer.

Delibe's Flower Duet finishes and *Pizzicato Polka*, starts playing. But this is really not what I need right now and I change it up completely by putting on some *Soundgarden, Blow Up the Outside World*. Much more suited to my current mood.

The last few weeks have been rushing by whilst I've been finalising the actions of the week I have ahead of me. I've been mentally rehearsing what I need to do. I've been working in the early hours of the morning. In the late hours of the afternoon. In the midst of a shower when I have to jump out with shampoo still in hair to furiously scratch down notes on any paper and any pen I can grab. A full night of sleep seems like an alien concept to me.

I have become a ghost to society, catching moments of sleep during the day when I can, spending my nights pacing up and down my flat amending and refining plans. Preparing myself, mentally and physically.

I enjoy this lifestyle. The night is quieter, better for concentrating.

The deeper I've gone into the preparation, the more I've found myself detached from the world.

You are evolving, Felix.

I've truly gone underground and withdrawn myself completely. I barely look at my mobile phone. No social media. No Facebook. None of this kind of shit. No contact. Just pure focus.

And you know what? The deeper down the rabbit hole I've gone, the more I've realised how achievable all of this really is. How actually feasible my fucking plan can be.

But, I've also realised that a part of myself is truly non-existent. Something is truly missing. Something that most people have, is simply not there.

The thing inside most people that holds them back from carrying out the worst fantasies that enter their minds. The thing that restrains them. That barrier, for lack of a better description, is not there inside me. You might say it's what makes us human. But as far as I'm concerned, it's the part of the human mind that separates the strongest from the rest. It's the part of the mind which stops one human from killing another human. I don't have that. I know I can kill.

And I will.

It is as simple as that.

These people deserve to die. The world will be safer without them.

And I have nothing left to lose.

I stretch my back out and roll my shoulders, trying to keep my muscles fluid despite the weariness that is constantly lingering.

I think back to a moment when I was at primary school and a group of boys were bullying a friend of mine, Georgie. We must have been about eight or nine years old and it was lunchtime on a hot summer's day. They'd followed us around the back of some of the classrooms, alongside the swimming pool and when they knew that no one could see the four of us, they set upon him.

It was remarkable, there was an obvious complete lack of appreciation for the fact that I, his mate, was right there, right next to him. They simply went for him and completely ignored me.

Now, as a bit of back story, which might help, my mother was a teacher at that school. I'd grown up under the protection of having my mother as one of the staff at the school I went to. No matter how naughty I was, no matter what the situation, I became untouchable. None of my teachers were willing to properly punish the son of their colleague, of their friend. And so, I got away with a lot. I learnt very young that it's most certainly not what you know, but who you know. That old adage, is indeed true.

Anyway, the boys that were attacking Georgie knew who my mother was, and knew that to some degree, on some, unspoken level, I was not to be touched. They grabbed Georgie by the back of his shirt and flung him against the fence that separated the pathway from the pool. He let out a pathetic scream. A scream that only encouraged these fuckers. The largest and ugliest of this group threw a few amateur punches at Georgie, only one of them connected properly, but it was enough. Blood began to flow from his lip and I stood there, paralysed and dumb, shocked at the scene in front of me.

Georgie yelled out for them to stop, but the three of them, backs towards me like I didn't exist, began to lay into him as he struggled to stand himself back up.

At that moment, something inside me was triggered. I remember the next few moments, but I don't remember them as though it was me, I remember them now as though I'm retelling a story told by someone else. I was not in control of my body.

I remember calculating in split seconds that any attempt I made to pull those boys off Georgie would be futile, I was outnumbered and out-muscled.

The memories fade over time but I recall finding the caretakers storage cupboard to my right and much to my relief watched as the door flung open as I tugged the handle in desperation.

Inside I grabbed the first tool/ weapon I could find. It was an outdoor broom with a wooden handle and black bristles.

With the boys circling Georgie, by now cowering in the foetal position and whose screams had become whimpers, I steadied the broom in my hand and moved forwards.

None of the boys saw me coming.

I remember swinging that broom with all the strength I had into the back of one of them and then the rest is a real blur. I can only recall Georgie pulling himself to his feet beside me as I swung that broom side to side towards the three boys, who all stared back at me, backing away with a satisfying blend of confusion and fear in their eyes.

Georgie got to his feet and the last thing I remember is telling him to run, as I dropped the broom to my feet and did the same.

I can't even remember what came of that whole episode, but I know for sure that no teachers or anyone else in a position of authority ever found out. The only thing that changed for us was that those boys left Georgie alone from that point, and you better believe they never came anywhere near me.

Why this memory crops up right now, I'm not sure. But it seems fitting. There's a part of Felix, no matter how selfish he might seem, that is totally selfless. The arrogant side of me sees this as a weakness. The rationale side of me is turning this into a strength.

The nearest other person awake in my vicinity is in the flat directly above mine. He's a twenty-nine-year-old cafe owner who's currently preparing a bowl of instant noodles before he leaves for work. Through the open window in the kitchen I can hear him moving around faintly above me. The deathly silence of the night outside us exacerbating the sounds of a plastic noodle packet being ripped open and water beginning to boil on a stove top. He's awake, yet, he's oblivious. For all intents and purposes, I'm completely alone and most certainly unwatched. My movements tonight, as with most nights, will go wholly unnoticed.

The only real light in this room comes from my laptop which is switched on behind me and sitting on the glass dining table. Its screen casts off a strange blue glow and creates curious shadows on the walls around me, bathing the room in a cool beautiful darkness. It is peaceful. I prefer to think in the dark. It helps me focus. It's calming, therapeutic, and... mine.

I'm in an unusual state right now. Physically I'm well-rested, energised and 'pumped' but intellectually, I'm totalled exhausted. I slept most of yesterday and woke up just after midnight this morning in order to review the mission details, to ensure that any last-minute preparations could be made and all double and triple checking could take place. I've been intently reviewing the details at my laptop non-stop since then.

So far, I've had two cups of coffee, a couple of Marlboro Gold's and a banana since I woke and its high time I consumed 'lunch'. I've a lot to accomplish today and have to ensure I have sufficient energy. A light meal with some slow-burning energy, low in refined sugar and with a just enough fat to line my stomach to keep me feeling full.

I laugh to myself. Come on, Felix, how about just a shot of vodka and another cigarette?

I let the curtain fall back over the windows and make my way over to the kitchen, glancing quickly at my mobile phone to double-check the time. One hour and twenty-seven minutes until I need to leave the flat. Plenty of time. The trip I need to take will be short, between twenty and thirty minutes depending on the availability of black cabs. At this time of day, traffic shouldn't be an issue. I'll need to be at the final location no later than 05:30am which will give me time to get in position and be ready to complete the mission by 05:40am at the latest.

I can feel my heart racing and the excitement of the coming events almost derails my train of thought. I take a deep breath and try my best to resist grinning like a naughty child. I've waited so long for this day... A tidal wave of retribution is imminent.

I'm already dressed for the mission tonight and thorough preparation has gone into sourcing all the clothing I'll wear over the coming week. Nothing has been left to chance. No possibilities have been overlooked. This is what I was born for. This is my nature. Precision and professionalism. Perfection. Death perfection.

Don't get me wrong, the risk I'm taking is immense. I have no misconceptions about how risky this is and I'm well aware that this could - and probably will - go horribly wrong at any point and that will be that. That would be the end of Felix and his intentions, ill or otherwise. It could all end tonight. Sure. I could fuck things up royally within a few hours and then it'd all be over. Who knows? Who, the fuck, knows?

Well, actually, we all will shortly, friends.

I as I pass the television to my right, I catch a glimpse of my reflection in the blank screen. A small, yet muscular body dressed in black Converse trainers with black trim, black rip-proof tights worn over the top of a pair of dark grey thermal tights, a plain black long sleeve t-shirt with a crew-neck collar worn over a dark grey thermal long-sleeve t-shirt and a very dark grey hooded sweatshirt over the top of both. A pair of brand-new black leather gloves is sitting on the dining table, still inside the plastic bag they were purchased in. Beside that is an unopened box of generic disposable black surgical gloves. The thickest kind I could find.

In a non-descript black backpack I bought from Primark perched next to the dining table, I've put a thin blue windbreaker, a green V-neck pullover, a pair of light blue jeans, a yellow scarf and a red woollen jacket with the bright yellow 'Royal Mail' logo printed on the back. Also inside the bag are two wigs, one short and blonde, the other, shoulder-length in light brown, a pair of gold wire-rimmed glasses with plain lenses, a small music player with earphones, a 500ml bottle of water, a roll of duct tape, a small plastic spray bottle filled with 500ml of the strongest bleach I could find, a pair of police issue handcuffs and a .455 calibre Colt 1911 British Service Model pistol with a seven-round standard detachable box magazine. This old pistol as well as a pump action shotgun were left to me by my father who was a bit of an enthusiast back in his day. I've no idea how he got hold of the pistol, as he was only licensed to own the shotgun. It may have been an old WWII leftover. Possibly my grandfathers? I'm not sure. Nonetheless, it's going to prove particularly useful for today. Today must be successful. There is absolutely no room for error. A gun is the best way forward for the first move I take. I have to take down at least one of these cunts and a gun will make sure I do.

The Colt 1911 is one of the most common pistols in the western world, having been widely used in western militaries since 1911. Thus, seeing action in two world wars, the Cold War, The Korean War, the Vietnam war and countless other military conflicts. Not to mention its particularly wide use by anyone from police forces, to security services, to sports shooters, to hardened criminals. It's reliable, deadly and slim, which means it's great for concealed carry. Great for executions.

The .455 cartridges which I've carefully cleaned with bleach before loading the seven round detachable box magazine with are old stock, which is the biggest risk I face with using this pistol. If for some reason the ammunition doesn't work, I'll have to resort to the combat knife sheathed and strapped to my inner leg. But I have to remain confident that the ammunition will do its job, despite having sat in storage for decades. It's been kept dry and there are no signs of corrosion at all, and, to be fair, I only need one of these rounds to work in order to get the job done.

.455 ammunition is renowned for having more stopping power than the .45 rounds which were commonly used in the U.S. issue of this pistol. The .455 packs that little bit of extra punch, without adding much to the kickback of the Colt 1911.

At first, I didn't quite like the way the Colt 1911 felt. Too thin and awkwardly shaped to fit in my hand comfortably. The barrel is also relatively long and I felt this pulled the gun towards the ground, so I was constantly tipping it up to get it straight. But, in order to get used to it, I carried it around for ages. Walking about with it in my flat. Practicing targeting random items, like the kettle or the microwave. Watching films and quick-drawing it on certain characters I'd chosen, just to get a feel for the gun and the way it moved in my hands. Now, it's like an extension of my body. To say I've become accustomed to it just wouldn't suffice. I love this weapon and it will be sad to see it go forever in just a few hours. But this is how it must be. Once it's fulfilled its purpose, it needs to go.

I stow the pistol in my backpack rather than in a pocket, a holster or tucked into my belt, as I intend to ditch the whole backpack and all its contents at once if my plans happen to go awry.

All the items I've prepared for the coming events were carefully chosen and purchased with dirty ol' hard cash at various stores across London over the last couple of months. The items were purchased, where possible, from stores that I carefully selected due to their lack of surveillance cameras and lack of general busyness. I leave nothing to chance. I can't afford to.

Currently, my hair, which has gotten even longer in the last months, is held back behind my ears with bobby pins, and my eyes, although naturally a yellowy brown, are tonight a dark green due to the contact lenses I'm wearing.

Despite my usual gothic appearance, in this outfit, for all intents and purposes I'd blend into a crowd with ease. You wouldn't notice me on the street more than you would any other person walking by. I've realised that there are all manner of ways to change the appearance of *one* person into the appearance of *many*.

For the coming week I've arranged numerous changes of clothes and disguises involving wigs, glasses, sunglasses, bandages, fake scars and piercings. Some of which I'm sure I won't even end up using, however, I prefer to be over-prepared.

Although, on that note, I still find myself absolutely averse to complicating one's actions in life. In any circumstance. It's not the way I was raised. "Simplicity and accuracy Felix. Simplicity and accuracy, are the keys to success in life," my father used to say.

As a teenager I used to sit with him outside in our backyard, each with a beer in hand and a BBQ going beside us, discussing the problems of the world and our solutions to them. Such great memories. Despite my age, I always felt as though my father listened to me, respected what I had to say and took my opinions on board.

My father was an automotive mechanic. He worked in a non-descript workshop in Angel for many years. I used to go there and spend time with him as a child. I'd sit in his little office, surrounded by greasy car parts and greasier nude girl calendars on the walls. Everything in the workshop seemed to have a thick layer of grease covering it, even unturned pages of the sales ledger in the office seemed to somehow be already coated with a specific filth. Memories of that time in my life, I'll never forget. At lunchtime on the days I was visiting, we'd walk to the chip shop down the road and buy far too much fish and chips for the two of us to finish, but this never mattered as the other guys in the workshop would always be keen to help us finish off when we reached our limit.

My father used to tell me all about the things he'd seen in his life. How he'd seen the city change. Change from something which was part of the United Kingdom, part of England, into something… "else", as he described it. He told me of his frustrations seeing decent hardworking people like him being left to fend for themselves against criminals as the crime rate rose and rose. He left no doubt in my mind that something was terribly wrong. It became obvious that there seemed to be no real punishment for those who hurt others. Just a 'slap on the wrist' as they say, and the older I got, the worse I realised this problem was.

My father died a couple of years ago from a heart attack. I was told it runs in the family. He wasn't a smoker, a drug user, or anything like that. He had a healthy diet, he drank moderately. But, as happens, the universe just decided that his time had come, regardless of all his good intentions.

My mother and I never really got along. She re-married and my father fought tooth and nail to get custody of me as a child. He loved me with all his heart, and I loved him back. He always tried his best with me. I must admit that his parenting wasn't always perfect, shit, it wasn't even sufficient if I'm being honest, but he meant well. He did his best. I know he always hoped that I'd get a good job and live a safe and comfortable life, far away from his mistakes.

Despite my father's shortcomings as a dad, he was all I had. When it truly mattered, he was there for me. Always. If I really needed him, if I was desperate, facing the abyss, he was there to pull me back. He might not have been there for the school debates or speech competitions (both of which, along with most subjects at school, I was generally rather good at) or to pick me up from school when he was supposed to. He would forget my birthdays and get my name confused with my brother, but, I learned to forgive this. He was a busy man. A solo father working hard to put food on the table.

He was there when I was really in trouble, when I needed advice. He would always make time when it really mattered. We had an understanding. I would look after myself as much as I could, but when I got stuck, when I truly couldn't solve a problem myself, he was ready to help me. I would find him next to me. Ready to instruct me. Teach me. Coach me. Warn me. And most of all protect me. I ran to him with my problems and asked for guidance. He was always there to help. Appearing in an instant when it mattered.

Parenthood at arm's length...

It was all he knew. And, I suppose it made me a stronger, more independent person.

I suppose....

My father did his best to warn me about and protect me from the world around me. I was a small child living in an average-at-best neighbourhood, in an... intense city..., where one needs to be 'on their toes' all the time. He made me wary, and it kept me safe.

I could speak about my father at great length, as he's the only person outside my closest friends who I've ever allowed myself to be vulnerable around.

My father did his best to raise a good citizen.

I believe I've taken everything I needed to know from him, and everything I've learnt from the real world, and combined the two of them. Nurture blended seamlessly with nature. This is the only way I was able to function through my many lonely years. This is the only way I could achieve some kind of balance and the only way I could clear my thoughts.

More recently, I've established a clear balance of the idealistic views of my father, and the simple reality of the society we live in.

I've embraced the reality of contemporary society earnestly, whilst not letting go of the ideals of where we could/ should be. Our family held the same views, generally.

I joked that our family motto should be 'the way forward is the way back'. We all love our history and everything that has made us who we are today.

My teenage years were spent mimicking the best of everything around me. I always had a feeling that I was destined to do something extraordinary. Something, very much 'out of the box', and I've spent many years waiting for a sign of what that was.

Finally, it has come.

I've tapped into a sleeping part of my mind and awoken the beast.

I've found my true purpose.

I need to become the archetype of perfection. I need to become a chameleon. I need to master adaptation. I need to become a symbol of consequence.

This planet earth, the country we call our home, this thing we label society, is all nothing more than dirt and water covered in animals with opposable thumbs fighting an endless battle to get ahead at the expense of others. Animals killing animals over dirt. This primal struggle has been taking place since the beginning of time. Creatures of all kind doing anything and everything they can to better other creatures to get ahead. Today it's still a primal struggle. We can pretend, in our own arrogance, that were on some elevated mission, something spiritual or supernatural... yet, a primal, animalistic struggle it still remains. A swarming mess of individuals fighting only for their own good. Animals in a pit. Cage fighting. A great big cock fight, but with no spectators except ourselves. We fight each other for no one's entertainment except our own. Who actually fights for anything righteous these days? Who really achieves anything meaningful?

Why do humans still hold onto ancient heroes, both mythical like Zeus or god, or real like Alexander the Great or Winston Churchill, with such ferocity? Why? Because no one in contemporary life comes close to matching what these heroes stood for, or so it would seem.

Basically, nobody cares anymore.

Apathy reigns supreme.

The greatest sin of them all.

We find ourselves naturally shocked when appalling things occur around the world, we watch the news and make comments on how terrible things are, and then in a flash, we move on. Back to our own concerns. We don't really care. We accept it as 'just the way things go' and move on. People need to take action if they really want change. Being upset about something means nothing. The only person affected then is you. If you really want any change to occur, these days, you have to make it happen yourself. You have to rise up and take action.

This is what I believe now more than anything else. We must defend ourselves, because the authorities that we have handed over our protection to, handed over control to, are failing in their duty to us. We are being left with no choice, but to act on our own.

My friends and I were attacked and my best friend was killed. Stabbed to death by a gang of shit-heads barely disguising themselves as humans.

They got away with it.

They fucking escaped without a single consequence. For months now, they've carried on. Lucifer only knows how many other decent citizens have suffered at their hands since then...

But they have no idea what's coming. Those fuckers…

No one does.

Justice…

Now, I realise I might be insane. Quite possibly, yes.

In all reality, the practical, reasonable and realistic side of me tells me that I am indeed.

I am insane.

In the most technical respect of the term. Yes. I am not 'sane'.

One of these things is not like the others…

I mean, I'm going to execute seven people within the next week. Seven human beings. Seven living, breathing, people, are going to be no longer living and breathing people, due my actions.

I will kill, seven human beings.

That's insanity, right? Deliberately causing that to happen? If that's not insanity, what is? …

But what if it's not? What if it's human nature to carry out such an act? What if it's built into our DNA? To take a stand? To fight? To kill?… And what does it matter? Really? Honestly? What material impact does it have upon the life of anyone unrelated to the matter if I execute of these guys? What lasting effect would it have to you regular citizens out there if I end the life of another, totally unrelated person to you…?

Who knows? Who cares? All I know is that I don't…

Insane or not, fuck it… I simply must do this…

I've been meticulous in my planning. All I know now is that these mother fuckers must be removed from society. The failings of the police force to effectively weed out these types, the failure of our communities to force them to integrate, the failure of our justice system to punish those who break the rules, both the rules of law and the rules of humanity, of common morality, are simply outrageous. These failings are simply unacceptable.

These cunts that killed Tommy have been in trouble with the law before, you can tell. Undoubtedly there've been numerous people who have suffered, violently, ruthlessly, and all too easily at hands of these fuckers. Despite that, even if they've done nothing else, for what they did to me, Tommy and Tony, they deserve to be removed from society.

Mother fuckers like these will continue to destroy and end lives until the day they die. Without a doubt. And so, the only solution is for them to be removed. Permanently. Now. No more waiting. I have to nip them in the proverbial bud. No more destruction and pain inflicted upon innocent citizens by this bunch of thugs. I won't stand for it. I can't erase what they've done in the past, but future pain and suffering must be prevented. Pre-emption. If it's good enough for the government of a nation to make pre-emptive strikes against another country on behalf of us citizens, it is good enough for us citizens to take the same action against arseholes like Abid and his mates.

The ability to prevent something terrible from occurring. This is where the real power lies. In this respect real change can take place, one can make a real difference. By taking pre-emptive action, one can make a real contribution to society.

It's time I made a contribution. I've come to realise that I've little choice but to act on behalf of my fellow citizens. As someone very wise once said, 'if you want something done right, you have to do itself yourself'. Well, in contemporary society, it would seem, if you want something done *at all*, you have to do it yourself. To Hell with the consequences.

The current leaders of our so-called 'first world nations' have, for some unexplainable reason, chosen to pander to criminals and ignore the atrocities which occur on their very streets, in their very neighbourhoods, against the very citizens they are supposed to represent. For whatever reason, far too much criminal behaviour is no longer punished as a serious matter. Lefties considers criminals as people who need 'help' and 'mentoring' in order to 'guide them through their issues' or whatever politically correct nonsense the fucking hippies in power espouse at the time. Our leaders have become afraid to appropriately punish criminal behaviour, instead they direct law enforcement efforts towards banal behaviour such as people driving their car a few miles over the speed limit or smoking a bit of weed while relaxing in a park. Our leaders don't seem to care about their citizens any longer... But then, did they ever?

In any case, at some point things used to be very different. Crime was punished, and punished properly. Penalties existed for infringing upon another person's rights, penalties which were serious deterrents. Currently, according to the BBC, between 1980 and 2011, there's been more than five-thousands murders in London, six-hundred of which were unsolved. That works out to about twenty per year.

Twenty per year over the last thirty-one years. Almost two per month.

Absolutely hopeless. And yet, I bet if I drove too fast down Pall Mall or perhaps walked down Oxford Street with a UKIP placard, I'd be arrested and prosecuted on the spot.

Mental.

The police have told me that they have 'no strong leads' in Tommy's murder.

No strong leads.

And the dismissive way in which they told me this made it clear to me that they were winding down their investigation at that point. Just another robbery gone wrong...

Fuckinell.

As I said, if you want something done at all... do it yourself.

I always kind of knew this would be the outcome, that they wouldn't catch the bastards, but of course, I hoped it wasn't true.

Since Tommy died, I have come to embrace this.

I smoke the last Marlboro Gold in the packet and consider opening a new one.

But, no. I don't need it. Tonight, I need nothing else fuelling me except for pure retribution.

Sweet, sweet, vengeance.

When they start disappearing, when bodies start showing up, the police will have to take notice. They couldn't care any less about the drugs and the violence raging in the London underworld, there realise that there is nothing they can do to stop it. As long as it's kept out of the public's eye, no one can complain.

But murder is another story. Murder hits headlines. People want answers, people want to see someone convicted. So, the police (probably reluctantly) throw resources at it. This means I need to be on top of my game.

And so, I shall be.

I've prepared well. I'm ready. I'm prepared to kill. I've become an agent-in-waiting of retribution and cleansing.

I'm the antidote to the continued erosion of society.

I am nothing.

I am everything.

I have become a ghost to society.

I have become an angel of retribution.

If I'm going to Hell, I might as well enjoy the rest of my time on earth with no rules...

Rules are made to keep the losers losing.

Rules are made by winners to keep the losers losing...

Felix

I rack up a few lines of snow, make a cup of coffee and light a cigarette as I sit back down at my computer to read over my notes one last time before I begin.

So much time has passed since I began planning my actions that all second, third or fourth thoughts are gone. There's no turning back now. I'm fully prepared to carry out my missions according to the exact plans I've established.

The first will undoubtedly be the most difficult to get through.

The first mission will be an absolute, unadulterated test of my emotional and physical capacity to take the life of another human being.

You can easily do it, Felix.

But, once the first test is passed, I'm sure the others will be easier and more systematic. Thus, I have chosen the easiest mission first. The one least likely to involve complications.

I open the folder on my laptop and click on the document labelled 'Kamal- 1'.

Sipping an ice cold can of Coke Zero, I read my notes one last time.

Name: Kamal

Appearance: Approximately 185cm tall. Close cropped hair. Slim build. Usually wearing grey baggy jeans and white sneakers, with t-shirt. Has a gold bracelet on his left arm. No particularly distinguishable features.

Address: Gayhurst Road

Time of Execution: 05:15 Monday 14 March

Location of Execution: Current residential address. Gayhurst Road.

Weapon of Execution: Colt 1911 British Service Model, cal .455 Webley Auto. 8 rounds (7 in the magazine, 1 in the chamber).

Method of Execution Initial series of 3 pistol shots to the left side of the chest from a distance of approximately 1 metre. Followed by a secondary series of 4 pistol shots to the torso from a distance of approximately 50 centimetres. Lastly, a final silenced pistol shot to the left temple, at an angle of 45 degrees towards the middle of the brain to empty the 7-round magazine.

Additional Comments: Element of surprise is key. Act swiftly and decisively.

Kamal lives in an old, classic, two-story terraced house with a dark grey trim and dark brown tiled roof. The house is unkempt and rundown, as you might expect, but it's in not a bad area altogether, most of the other houses around seem to be looked after. Kamal lives there with his girlfriend and no one else. Just two pathetic fucks.

The only real concern I have is that his girlfriend will answer the door and not Kamal. If that happens, I'll need to quickly subdue her and then go inside and find Kamal. This will very likely cost me the element of surprise, especially if he's already awake, or she screams outs and wakes him as I move in. But if I'm quick enough, I can still get to him before he realises what is happening. I can incapacitate his girlfriend and move swiftly into the bedroom and take him down before he even realises that there is a threat.

On his sleepy street before 6:00am hardly a soul stirs as far as I've seen. Kamal won't be expecting anyone to be knocking on his door at that time, but the Royal Mail costume will get him to open it. Who's going to turn down a parcel?

Over the last month I've been around there three times monitoring the street and only once has a neighbour has been outside at this hour. Some middle-aged woman collecting the early morning paper and letting a geriatric cat outside to piss. I've not seen anyone walking a dog or driving to work for example. Before 6:00am, Gayhurst Road is a ghost town.

At the front of Kamal's house is a low brick fence with a thick a hedge running along the top, alongside the footpath and right up to a relatively enclosed front porch. This is perfect. The big shabby hedge provides excellent cover during the dark pre-dawn hours for sinister activities. The motherless fuck inside that house sleeps soundly tonight, but the bastard's time has come.

I drink a glass of water and put on some Mozart in the background.

I've come so far. Yet… there is so much to do.

My view on life has changed materially.

No, you know what… I think it has just been refined. It is no different to what it always was… I've simply taken an ideal and made it into a practicality.

Felix, you are doing something purposeful with your life.

Even if I was to fail in this whole operation tonight, just knowing that I attempted to remove this filth from society would be enough for me to die happy.

But I will not fail.

I simply will not allow it.

In one hour and twenty-five minutes Kamal will be punished for his crimes and in two hours and five minutes I will be back here at my desk, satisfied and mentally rehearsing for the next execution.

Where society has failed, I will succeed.

Kamal

The fuckin' fat white boy at the burger shop fucked up my order tonight and gave me some kind of bacon burger. I ordered a mother fuckin' regular chicken burger, bruv! A fuckin' *chicken* burger. And this boy decides to get all fuckin' aggressive with me, putting filthy pig, fuckin' *bacon* strips inside my fuckin' dinner.

I didn't realise until I was biting into the fuckin' thing just now driving home. Biting into a fukin' chicken and pig burger. For fucks sake.

But, I can't be fucked going back now to complain. He's lucky I don't fuckin' stab him up. He's lucky I don't make a fuckin' point. I'm a fuckin' Muslim, bruv, I don't eat that shit!

Fuckin' white boy... I throw the burger out the window of my car and instead shovel the box of chips into my mouth.

I'm already pissed off enough from a shittiest fuckin' day ever dealing with the fuckin' idiots I work with at the gym and all I want to do is smoke the day off. That fuckin' chicken shop boy is a lucky shit tonight.

I park my car on my street and then head off back towards the shops to get some real food. It's been a fucked 24 hours, man... At some club last night, or like, early this morning, I got into a fight with some football dickhead, who thought he was a tough gangsta and kept fuckin' staring at me from the side of the room. If I'd had it my way, I'd taken the fucker out right there on the dance floor and made a fuckin' statement of it, but I ended up waiting and following him into the bathroom and kicking his arse in one of the stalls. I made sure he was bleeding before I went back out into the club, got the boys and got the fuck out of there. The music was shit anyway and the girls were all white dogs.

When I woke up this morning I spent too long on the phone arguing with Qusay about what we're going to do with the big fuckin' TV we got from this place in Clapton a few nights ago. It's a fuckin 65 Inch OLED Smart 4K Ultra HD. All the latest technology shit. I want to keep this mother fucker. I mean, bruv, I found the house, scoped it out and I took the most risks when we was busting in. It's my score. I don't know what this fuckin' thing is worth, a couple of grand perhaps? Probably could get at least a grand for it on eBay or whatever, but, man, sometimes you need some fuckin' perks. It would look great in my bedroom. Anyway, Qusay is too fuckin' straight and too fucking scared to let us keep any of the merch. He's worried that the cops will somehow come to my house find this exact fuckin' TV from that exact fuckin' house in Clapton and then somehow link it back to him. Fuckinell, bruv. I can't be fucked dealing with this kind of shit. Arguing with that pussy over a TV is fuckin' up time I could be spending on other shit, bruv. Arguing with him ain't making me any money.

Anyway, I order a kebab and eat it as I walk back to my car. Before I even get inside it, or finish my fuckin' food things manage to get even worse, which is a fuckin' amazing job to be sure. Izzat's little brother phones me to tell me that the fuckin' cops have just nabbed Izzat for carrying a fuckin' blade in Edmonton.

For fucks sake.

Turns out the cops had stopped them both, fuckin' searched them and sure enough, Izzat, the dumb fuck had a fuckin' blade on him. Now he's in the fuckin' holding cell and his brother wants me to front some cash to get him out. It's 10:45pm and I really' can't be fucked with this right now.

"Fuck no", I say, "that idiots made a fool move. I ain't going down there."

"Please, bruv, please, I ain't got no cash".

"Shit, nah. Lemme, sleep on that shit," I said, and then hung up before he could reply.

Fuckin', mother, fuck.

Once in the comfort of my bedroom I light my bong and, kicking my shoes off, sit on the edge of my bed, exhausted.

Sometimes, I wonder if it's all really worth it. Fuckin' shit, bruv. I really wonder...

As I exhale and a big plume of smoke clouds around me I begin to feel the calmness wash over me.

What the fuck am I doing, hanging with all these fuckers?

But... then I wonder what the fuck I'd actually do without these stupid cunts. No matter how fuckin' stupid they are. Izzat, Qusay. Fuck, man. Those are my boys...

It's been one of those fuckin' days.

I need to relax.

I lie back and drift into a stoned, restless sleep.

Tomorrow is another day. I'll sort my shit out then.

6 Gustav

Felix

Time to move.

I wrap a brown scarf around my neck. It's particularly cold night, a perfect cover for wearing all these layers without looking conspicuous. I can pull the scarf up around my mouth and nose to disguise my identity even more and I wouldn't get a second glance.

I pull the black gloves on tight.

I am ready.

I double-check everything I'm wearing and then lastly, I pull on a blue wool knit hat and lower it over my ears. I check through the contents of my backpack one last time. It's tightly packed and heavy, but every item inside is absolutely necessary. Satisfied, I sling it over my shoulders and take one last look in the full-length mirror...

I make an unremarkable figure, no features too distinguishable, just an average-looking guy in his mid-twenties, dressed appropriately for the temperature. I take care to ensure again that I have no identifying material in my pockets, no credit cards, mobile phone etc...

I place my front door key and flat security access card inside a small black coin purse which I leave hidden in the dirt of a large potted tree on the steps of my flat block as I make my way out of the door.

From Heath Avenue I walk for three minutes to the nearest taxi stand. I hail the first taxi in a queue of four and climb into the back seat. Black cabs are the only sensible option. I don't drive as this would be too easy to trace and public transport has too many humans and too much CCTV. It makes much more sense to use bicycles, taxis or simply to walk.

Nonetheless, it's still very important to be careful with taxis, as the more and more have CCTV inside them now and I certainly can't risk being identified. So, wearing disguises inside taxis is essential.

Just as important is the use of a number of different taxis in the journey to a single destination. I reckon that at least three separate taxi trips from one location to another should be taken in order to reach a single, specific destination. Each trip from one location taken to a completely unrelated location, and then a new taxi from that location to somewhere else unrelated and so on. For instance, tonight this first trip I'm now on will take me to Mace Street, a location two-point-five kilometres south east of my final destination.

Once I arrive at Mace Street, I'll cross through a short alleyway to the street parallel where another taxi stand is located. In the alleyway I'll take off the grey hooded sweatshirt, switch to the green v-neck pullover and stuff the sweatshirt and wool cap I'm wearing back into the backpack. Then I'll take the first taxi I spot to Northiam Street.

The second taxi trip will take me one-point-eight kilometres directly past the destination I'll eventually end up at. This time, when I get out, I'll switch to the yellow scarf, put the wool cap back on and also the pair of reading glasses, before I grab the next taxi.

The final trip will take me two blocks over from Gayhurst Road, outside an old flat complex where once again I'll change my outfit in the darkness before finally making my way to Kamal's house.

At every point the trail will go cold.

In the taxi I sit in now, I lean forward in the back seat and, avoiding eye contact with the driver by staring at the muddy floor, I ask him to take me to Northiam Street which I know will take three to four minutes' drive at this hour of the morning. I disguise my voice by speaking with a slightly foreign accent and the driver mumbles something which sounds like agreement before punching the address into his GPS and starting the journey.

As I stare at the floor of the taxi, I spot a banana peel rotting under the driver's seat, a swarm of ants labouring over it. I wonder where their nest is? Perhaps somewhere in the floor of the taxi? I find myself staring at the swarm. Pondering. Becoming one with the swarm. Losing my focus... I snap myself out of it and roll down the window for some fresh air.

The streets are relatively quiet but there is still enough light human-activity here and there for me to go unnoticed amongst it. And fortunately, the driver seems much more interested in listening to some foreign football game on his radio than engaging in small talk with me.

At every point the trail will go cold, I remind myself with a grin.

As we arrive at Northiam Street I remain silent while the driver determines the fare, £7.75, which is outrageous to be honest, but with gloved hands I hand him a £10 note I withdrew a few days ago from an ATM (again with gloved hands). Admiring the crisp newness of the note that probably hasn't yet been touched by human hands I tell him to keep the change. He attempts to turn around and thank me, but I'm out of the car before he can do so and walking swiftly, but not suspiciously, towards the alleyway directly across the street.

The night air is particularly cold and my ears and nose start to go numb as I walk. I do my best to ignore it and move forward, purposefully, listening intently for any sounds of other people in the vicinity. I can't risk looking around over my shoulders as this would be to suspicious, so I rely on my other senses to guide me.

I slow down once I reach the alleyway and as I step into it, much to my relief, I see it's empty and dark. I slow to a casual stroll and listen harder, just to be certain....

... The alleyway and streets around are devoid of human presence. I can hear a television set on in a house bordering the alleyway, but the sound is faint and clearly the television set is on the side of the house, facing away from me. I take one quick glance around to make sure I'm not being watched, then I quickly move two paces to my left into an area shadowed by a rather large oak tree looming overhead. I tug off the grey hooded sweatshirt and shove it into the bottom of the backpack, pulling out the green v-neck pullover and quickly throwing it on. If I wasn't wearing the thermals underneath, I would surely freeze out here, it's that fucking cold. I take out the blonde wig from the front pouch of the backpack and smoothing my hair back to ensure no strands will be showing, I pull it on tight.

I don't scan the area again, as that would arouse suspicion, I simply pick up the backpack again and sling it over my shoulder, walking briskly again towards the opposite end of the alleyway. Act natural. The sound of the television grows fainter until the only sound is that of my footsteps echoing. Echoing as though a giant was whipping the concrete below me with his giant-sized belt over and over. Damn it. I tell myself to walk quieter but the order is ignored.

As I reach the end of the alleyway a wave of relief followed by an unfamiliar sense of confirmation rushes over me and I feel myself smiling again. Everything is going so well. But then, of course it is, I planned it so perfectly.

Twenty metres to my left are three taxis parked with their lights on waiting for business. I move towards the nearest one and open the back door.

The second trip takes nine minutes, the maximum time I'd allowed for, and once out of the taxi, I walk around behind the tennis court shed next to London Fields and change my disguise again. Remove the brown scarf and black tights. Put on the yellow scarf, the pair of glasses and put the wool cap back on.

I walk for two minutes to the taxi stand outside the shopping complex further down the street, approaching the row of cabs from behind. Being extra careful to ensure that by some chance the taxi driver which just dropped me off up the street is definitely not the taxi I climb into.

The third trip takes ten minutes and drops me close to Forest Road. Two blocks over from Kamal's house. I walk through an empty park and change quickly behind a thick bush. I'm half-expecting to find some homeless bum sleeping there as it seems like a good, warm spot to sleep in if you are homeless scum, but it's totally clear.

I put on the blue jeans and red Royal Mail jacket over the grey tights and green pullover. I leave the glasses on and put the light brown wig on under the wool cap.

I check the time, it's 5:05am and it's a roughly two-minute walk from here to Kamal's house. Perfect.

I proceed to Gayhurst Road briskly. The streets are quieter than I'd expected. Not sure if this is a good thing or a bad thing. Less potential witnesses is always a good thing, but on the other hand when not a creature stirs, you can hear a pin drop...

As I reach Gayhurst Road the nerves start to come back and the reality of the whole situation starts to hit me.

I am here.

I am ready.

This is it. Now.

This is what I planned for, for so long.

This is the culmination of two month's planning and waiting.

The culmination of countless hours consumed with overwhelming thoughts of hatred.

This mother fucker broke my world. Now, I'm going to break him.

"I am going to break you, mother fucker," I whisper angrily. It feels good to say it aloud.

Here I am. On the cusp of it...

A cold breeze washes over my cheeks and I feel a sudden burst of anxiety catching hold of my mind.

What the fuck am I doing?

This is wrong. This is terrible. Taking someone's life is a sin!

I am about to become a killer.

I'm scared, obviously. Lucifer, they'd fucking skin me alive if they caught me, these cunts.

Fuck. Fuck. Fuck...

If they catch me before I catch them...

Ugh... All kinds of horrible thoughts flood into my mind. My heart is pounding like never before and sweat begins to pour down the back of my neck. Cold sweat... This is going to start a fucking shit storm!

... You need to do this Felix. Come on. Remind yourself. You are here for a purpose. The city needs you to act upon your plans. The world needs you to act upon your plans. You have to do this...

I need to do this.

I have to make a difference...

I need to focus right now. I can't lose momentum. I need my music.

I need something calming, but with a hint of anticipation and of destiny. I need a proper soundtrack for the scene ahead.

Bach's Toccata & Fugue in D Minor BWV 565 Fugue. The perfect choice.

I take the small iPod out of my bag and slip the earphones into my ears. Despite my best efforts, my gloved hands tremble as though I've suddenly developed Parkinson's disease and it's with some difficulty that I eventually manage to select *Bach's Fugue*.

Upon pressing play, the beautiful sounds of harmonic organs, the sixteenth notes, the overwhelming intensity and glorious story-telling rush into my ears and begin flooding through my body with incredible momentum. The massage of music starts with my brain, then works its way across my limbs and then puts me in a state of constant reverberation as it courses its way throughout my nervous system... Absolute bliss... The anxiety is receding.

I keep walking purposefully towards Kamal's house and make my way past his car parked out on the curb.

No time to waste dawdling. Move, Felix.

Without thinking I notice myself using gloved hands to pull the pentagram pendant I'm wearing out from underneath my various layers and kiss it, a gesture of respect for my fallen comrades, but also a reminder of who I am deep down. Rock and fucking roll.

Once in position, I take the Colt 1911 out of the backpack and place the backpack on the front porch, hidden from view from the street by a large empty blue plant pot. Inside the backpack I find the empty 500ml water bottle and the roll of duct tape. Kneeling down, I shove the barrel of the pistol into the opening of the bottle and then proceed to tape it on the end of the barrel with the duct tape, acting quickly, but with surprisingly steady hands. *Focus Felix*. In less than thirty seconds my makeshift silencer is complete.

My heart pounds like a bass drum in my chest as I approach his front door, yet the world around is completely quiet. Peaceful. Asleep. Just me and my increasingly menacing anticipation is disturbing the calm.

I focus on griping the pistol properly, readjusting the handle in the palm of my hand until it feels right.

I take a deep breath and let it out slowly. My heart continues to beat away to its own heavy tune...

... *You could turn back now Felix. Walk away from this. All of this. It isn't worth it. The fucking shit storm you are about to ignite. It's not too late...*

No. I need to do this. If I don't do it now, I will never be satisfied.

... *No, you do not. Walk away...*

I walk towards the door and press the buzzer.

This bastard needs to die.

The punishment of these cunts begins now, with the end of Kamal.

On the front step I position myself carefully out of view of any neighbours as best I can, standing close to the door as I wait for Kamal to open it.

One more deep breath, ten more rumbles of thunder in my chest.

This is it.

I hear heavy, sleepy footsteps approaching the door.

I hold the pistol with a steady arm, which surprises me given the violent beat of my heart. My entire body feels as though it is going to shake apart like and yet my arm is stea...

The clicking of the door unlocking marks the sound of no return.

I smile. This is it.

The violent thunder inside me disappears.

I am calm.

Everything is calm.

Dream-like.

Serene.

A scene of art is unveiled as Kamal opens the door. Everything pauses for a moment. I can see every detail completely.

He stands there in front of me, a tired, quizzical, yet friendly expression on his face.

As I raise the Colt and aim it at his chest, three centimetres to the left of the centre, horizontal to his armpits, his face begins to contort in slow motion. I watch as the muscles along his jaw line quiver and tense. His lips part slightly and purse back. The skin around his eyes stretches and smooths away the small lines of crow's feet as they open wide.

His eyes themselves.... his eyes... they say it all. A flash and they know his time is over. Even if his brain has not yet registered it. His eyes give him away and accept his fate in a moment of incredible assent. It's quite emotional. Touching. Beautiful. Satisfying.

Bach's Fugue continues to play quietly in my ears.

I stare into those eyes with a blank, unreadable expression on my face which I hope fills Kamal's last coherent seconds with utter confusion and terror as I squeeze the Colt 1911's trigger.

The .455 Webley Auto bullet exits the chamber at seven-hundred feet per second at the muzzle, with two-hundred and eighty-nine foot-pounds of energy, and travels through the end of the duct tape covered plastic water bottle and pierces the blue cotton of Kamal's bath robe turning threads of blue into dust, before tearing through the top layers of skin and hurtling into pure flesh, taking strands of chest hair and blue cotton along with it. The sound of the bullet entering to his body reminds me of the 'popping' noise made when you pierce a packet of vacuum sealed meat with a knife, and this popping is curiously just as loud as the sound of the pistol actually firing. The makeshift silencer letting nothing but a dull popping sound ring out on Gayhurst Road at 5:15am on a Monday morning. The only sound I'm concerned with is the hollow ringing out as the empty shell casing ejects from the pistol and arcs its way down onto the hard wood floor in his hallway

When the bullet rips into Kamal's heart, turning ventricles, atriums and valves into minced meat he lets out a gargling noise as his body and mind struggle to come to terms with the event unfolding, failing to create words, or even a real yell, just a garbled "unghhhh" as he helplessly raises his arms to defend himself. It's far too late. And his eyes know it.

I lower the aim of the pistol slightly in order to keep it directed at his heart as he begins to fall backwards in slow motion, and I squeeze the trigger again twice. Two more bullets soar out of the chamber. The second bullet connects roughly two centimetres above the spot where the first bullet entered and tears into his chest, desperately trying to reunite itself with its escaped chamber brother. The impact sends Kamal's already flailing body back further, causing the third bullet to connect much further down his chest, right where the bottom half of his left lung is. The popping, piercing of the flesh is followed by a hollow 'wheezing' sound which reminds me of someone coughing softly inside an underground cave.

Kamal's body topples backwards, arms grasping out, helplessly searching for anything to grab to stop the fall. There is nothing.

Kamal's tail bone strikes the hard polished-wood floor first, followed the rest of his frame. His blue bath robe hangs loosely around his body as though it's struggling to distance itself from him, as though it doesn't want any part of this.

Kamal looks up into my eyes as blood begins frothing out of his mouth and nostrils. His arms reach up at his sides, however they've lost all strength and quickly give up and fall back to his sides, vibrating on their own terms as his body begins its death throes.

Another gurgling noise escapes his mouth along with a mouthful of blood, sending a small spray of red up into the air which lands right back down across his twisted and exhausted face.

I move forward into the hallway of the house. Careful to only take a few steps inside to reduce the likelihood of leaving any DNA evidence such as hair or sweat. I stand to the left of Kamal, pistol held tight and slowly nudge the front door partially closed with my elbow, blocking views from potential passers-by, just in case.

As the door slowly swings back towards its frame, the room becomes considerably darker. The light of the outside world, of hope, of salvation for Kamal, diminishes. It must be very dramatic from his perspective. But this is not just about him, this is a defining moment in my life too.

The end of Kamal... and... the 'what' for me?

The beginning? Or the beginning of the end?

Kamal lets out a final garbled "ugh" and his eyes begin twitching and rolling around like apples bobbing in a barrel. A pool of thick red blood is massing on the floor underneath his torso and it's time I finished this and leave before things become too messy.

I squeeze off three more shots. Three more barely noticeable puffs of sound as the bullets exit the chamber and three more soft 'pop's as the bullets rip into his torso. Small sprays of blood shoot up into the air and linger for a moment, glistening in the early morning sun as it begins to rise outside. Beautiful little mists of scarlet hovering above a torso turned into an assortment of flesh, bone and lead. The blue bath robe is ruined, bullet holes and blood stains have rendered it as useless as Kamal himself.

I take a few short breaths.

His body is limp.

He is gone.

I kneel down next to Kamal and place the now blown-out end of the plastic water bottle against his left temple. The final touch. I angle the barrel at forty-five degrees, pointing it toward the centre of his brain. I feel myself smile again and I squeeze the trigger one last time. Kamal and a beautiful blue Gucci bath robe no longer exist. Just a pile of flesh, blood and cotton remains in this house.

Bach's Fugue in D Minor reaches its climax. I feel completely calm. Relieved. Overwhelmed with a sense of triumph and success...

... You are doing the right thing... You will succeed Felix...

I leave his corpse bleeding out there in the hallway. A message.

After collecting the seven empty shell casings, removing the Royal Mail jacket and checking myself for excessive blood splatter, I pull the front door closed the door behind me, grab my backpack and make my way back to my flat via another three taxi trips with another 3 costume variations.

The Colt 1911 I'll dismantle and disperse pieces of into various storm water drains across the city as I move about over the next twenty-four hours. The clothing, backpack and wigs I was wearing will be soaked in thick bleach, shredded into pieces, and then burnt. The reading glasses I'll clean with bleach and shove into the rubbish bag in my bathroom before dropping it down the rubbish chute in the block of flats. Not a trace will be left. At every point the trail will go cold.

A curious sense of satisfaction and overwhelming relief is decorated with heavy dread inside me.

It feels good.

It feels bad.

As the city wakes and the sun begins to rise over London, there is one mother-fucker down and six to go.

7 Hector

Felix

I suppose most people would be feeling waves of guilt and remorse right now. Feelings of dread and, or, nervousness. Haunted by a sense of impending doom. Failing that, at least some feelings of shame or reproach, surely?

I feel nothing. Just calm and, well, content. Yes, that's it. I feel content. Satisfied. Sitting here on the edge of my empty bed. *Alone, always alone....* I'm feeling calm, content and resolute.

There's nothing quite like feeling comfortable being utterly alone. Knowing that you can exist without needing a sliver of real connection to another human being. Nothing at all. Complete detachment. Complete independence. Unrestrained freedom. The feeling is something close to godly. Something close to that. No care or affection is at risk of being wasted on someone else.

Love only yourself.

Have no responsibility. No risk of loss.

You have to relinquish yourself from the weakness and constraints which come with that all-too-common trait we call empathy. What you should seek is the antithesis. The ability to think and act solely for one person. Ultimate efficiency. Utter freedom of the sort which can only be achieved at the cost of a complete severing of any emotional connection to another person.

I've asked myself on many occasion if I was born disconnected from this world, or if I grew more and more detached over time as I realised the universe around me and I were simply wholly incompatible.

I freely admit my lack of comprehension of the world around me. Most of all, I realise I lack appreciation for the norms of society and the customs within which the majority of people choose to live. Modern society certainly confuses me. Particularly when I look back at societies of old.

Perhaps a disposition such as mine would be more suited to a medieval time, an era where personal discipline and sense of order were the rule of the day. An era where those who stepped outside the bounds of the law were punished for their crimes accordingly. Punished severely and appropriately. The kind of punishment which sent a message to others considering carrying out similar behaviour.

I can only dream of this time.

A paradise lost.

Don't get me wrong, I do care for others on some level. But it's a generic kind of caring that I think many people feel. I want to make society a better place. Clean up some of the scum in this city and at the same time make a statement which will not go unnoticed by the masses. One which may inspire others.

I do want to make the planet a better place to live. But, to be honest, I don't truly know who for...

Do I strive for society to become better, safer, more structured for the other people who inhabit it? Or do I want this to be a better place simply for myself? Do I just seek personal retribution and my subconscious is trying to mask this selfishness with some kind of quasi-honourable crusade?

I've yet to solve this mystery. And perhaps it doesn't really matter either way.

In an ideal world, everyone would just leave everyone else the fuck alone. No one would be imposing anything on anyone else. Not imposing laws, rules, judgements, not a single thing. Just leave each other the fuck alone. We should be free to do what we want, as long as it doesn't negatively impact anyone else. Isn't that the ultimate society that every system on this planet is ultimately trying to drag humanity towards? A kind of society where the citizens just behave well without being forced to.

Or am I just an optimist?

When I began planning these executions, I was very strict in deciding that, one - no innocent people were to be harmed. As this would defeat the purpose of my acts, confusing the message I'm sending to both Abid and society at large. And, two - the only people to die would be the seven people on my list. These seven, well, now six, are the crucial players in Abid's demented game. These bastards, running wild across the city, are to be strategically removed. No one else needs to die to achieve my goal. And three - Abid needs to suffer. He needs to live his final days in utter fear. And his suffering needs to be slow and drawn out. I could walk into his house and stick a dozen bullets in his chest any time I liked. But that wouldn't be satisfying at all.

I want Abid to suffer as his whole world, everything he has spent his whole life working towards, is systematically ripped away from him.

I want him to suffer the whole time he knows that I'm coming for him.

Soldiers often say that when they look into the eyes of the person they are about to kill, they, that moment, can see that person's entire life in their eyes. As though they are brought closer to that person that anyone has ever been or ever will be. Intimacy beyond normal human comprehension is experienced, moments before the kill.

I don't believe this true at all. In his last moment, I saw nothing in Kamal's eyes except for fear.

Sheer fear.

Perhaps I knew enough about him already, or perhaps, I just didn't care enough.

They also say that once you have taken another person's life you are never quite the same. That something inside of you dies. That you forever feel a sense of emptiness.

When I killed Kamal, I felt nothing but a sense of accomplishment.

While taking his life, I knew that planet earth was definitely better off without him alive. I ended the life of someone who no longer deserved to live. Someone who was destroying the communities that had welcomed him and his kind into. Destroying that sense of community, that very fabric of what makes our Britain Great.

And yet. I am so far from finished.

It's no good hoping and wishing for something to happen. This only distracts you from taking action to actually make things happen.

For me, the distractions are gone. I've begun my mission. No going back.

Let the cleansing continue.

Felix

When I was a child and I was upset or stressed, the only thing which apparently calmed me down was playing classical music. So, my parents would put me in my crib and play classical music cassette tapes on a little stereo until I was soothed. This method of musical calming has continued to help soothe me even to this day. I believe it always will.

I didn't appreciate why I reacted so well to that kind of music until I began to study music at high school and found out about classical music, or baroque music. Up until then, I'd just thought of it as old people music and never paid too much attention. But something changed in me when I heard *Mozart's Symphony Number 9 I, Allegro Molto*, that piece drove something inside me wild. It was like the metal music I was listening to at the time, Slipknot, Metallica, Slayer, it had the same energy, but with beauty instead of gore. It was magic.

Aside from a love for its sound, the physical and neurological benefits are not to be overlooked or indeed understated. Firstly, in terms of productivity and cognitive function, classical music is proven to help sharpen the memory by activating the genes that help the brain process as well as store information. It's also known to help with insomnia or people in need of better rest in general. This is because most classical music has a slow tempo, regular rhythm and no lyrics which is conducive to preparing your brain and body for sleep. Lastly, the calming effect that classical music has on most people is proven to lower blood pressure over a sustained period of time and exposure to classical music. It's odd, but for me, the thing I notice most is how much it sharpens my senses.

On the other hand, there are plenty of times when being calm is not helpful at all. When being properly fucking pumped up is the way you want to be. This is where my love for metal music comes in. I've been listening to metal music for as long as I can recall. Definitely as far back as early teens and to be honest, I was probably listening to it early than that too. The scene was big in my neighbourhood and all of us kids used to roam about wearing Metallica, AC/DC, Slayer and Megadeth t-shirts. I think most metal fans start out with something relatively easily accessible they find in rock, and then slowly but surely slip into the first layer of accessible metal, like Metallica, for instance, but if you carry on into the dark and mysterious void, you'll end up going as heavy and as black as you want to. For me, metal is an outlet for aggression and in the same way that classical music helps my brain process things, metal music does this for me, but in a completely different way. I feel completely energised and clear, purposeful, when I listen to metal. It's like, a shining pathway lights in up the darkness and shows me the way forward. Nothing quite like that feeling of power and certainty. It's like a drug. It's better than a drug.

Music helps the millions of brainwaves pulsing every second in my brain work together in some kind of comprehensible rhythm. At times too much is happening inside my head at once to allow any singular strain of thoughts to realistically escape to the surface.

Overload.

Like an airport which suddenly has too many planes arriving at once and cannot cope with the situation at all. At these times I need music. I need something deep and penetrating to distract me. The kind of music which affects you from the core. Music which permeates through you and takes over your body. Music which can take you to the highest highs or the lowest lows and absolutely anywhere in between. With classical music, lyrics are not necessary. There's absolutely no need for such a crude measure of communication. The music speaks for itself. The music is so far beyond words, that nothing else matters... Bliss.

And when I need to let off some steam, go wild, the aggressive power which metal has is truly magnificent and categorically unbeatable.

Without music my brain would have overheated and boiled itself over into oblivion many years ago. As a child even. Now, I realise the importance of keeping the mind in good health.

It's difficult though, for my mind has many issues. I know that a part of me thinks too much, thinks too hard about things. I've always been a problem solver. A *doer*. Someone who sees a fault and does whatever they can do make it right again. We see a problem, and our minds run off on their own and formulate a solution, and we become laser-focussed on solving that problem. This is just the kind of people we are. I think it runs in my family.

Life for people like us can be very hard. The world around us is so broken. So far from what an ideal world should be. *And we are idealists at heart.* So far from the world we expect to live in when we are children.

We grow up, we become more aware. We realise the faults and the issues of the societies in which we have been thrust into. We realise that we are just one of many. One of many. Not special at all. A statistic, at best. That all these problems around us, the world itself, so eternally wrong, cannot be changed. That we, as humans existing on this planet, simply perpetuate the existing problems and carry on. People like me, who become aware, know that *probably* we can't change the world, we know we *probably* can't alter the path that billions of human beings are just spiralling towards and yet we still feel compelled to try. To do *something* to try and set things right.

This world we all live in is so primitive. So, so primitive. Despite how advanced or sophisticated we like to think we are, we continue to kill each other just like any other animal, only at record levels, through war, violence and murder. Not to mention all those who die through starvation, disease and inequality as a matter of course.

We continue to wipe ourselves out at a pace never seen before in nature. No other animal has been so overwhelmingly self-destructive and harmful, both to themselves and to their environment.

Humans have seemingly come so far... Yet, if you peel back the thin layer of 'civilisation', we've hardly moved on at all from being animals. We call ourselves civilised because we have electricity, we wear clothes, drive cars and live in cities. Sure, we are more technologically savvy, but having iPhones and Facebook does not make us fundamentally any more than animals. We still rape, murder, steal, hate and hurt each other to get ahead.

Humans do not exist in harmony. Certainly not in the way which nature, left to its own devices does.

Not. Even. Close.

Humans are still singular entities interacting with other singular entities. We are not a harmonious unit like an army of ants of a herd of elephants working towards a common goal. We are not civilised. We have long way to go to move on beyond primitive self-serving animals.

I know that I can't change things. Eventually my actions will be lost in the annuls of time no matter how much publicity they receive in the short term. But I can't stand to live with myself if I do nothing. My best friend's honour deserves it. My own honour demands action. And so, action I take.

If I was a selfish fucker, if Felix was a totally self-centred little shit, he'd just carry on his life and milk the most out of it that he possibly could. 'Fuck everyone else', he'd say. And so that would be his life.

But that's not who I truly am.

I'm ready and willing, and, fuck... I *already* have... put my head above the parapet and made myself a target... no... a symbol... I'm willing to do the things for my society that they are unwilling to do. The things that they shouldn't have to do. I'm that man. I love my culture and my people, more than they probably love me. More than perhaps they love each other. More than perhaps they love themselves...

But... it's important to me, and that's all that matters.

If I die trying to make their lives better, at least I'll die knowing I did something good for the masses. Whether they understand it, whether they appreciate it, whether, whatever... I don't actually care.

I'll do this for them.

I'll do this for me.

I wonder how the public at large will react if word of this gets out.

How far has our society fallen from actually punishing those who hurt us properly? How weak have we become? How brainwashed by leftist political correctness?

If I'm caught, the question will inevitably asked, "why?" "Why did he do this?" "What drove him to this?" "How do we explain this?"

And despite the obvious fact that I'm seeking vengeance for what happened to me and my friends, without doubt the media and thus society at large, will undoubtedly still try to label me a psychopath. They'll argue that unfortunately in this world people like Tommy are killed in random acts of violence all the time. They'll say that the people close to them do not *all* start going on a killing rampage shortly after. They'll pin their argument on that point and make me out to be some kind of nutjob.

They'll pull apart my lifestyle, well, what they know of it, to make me out to be crazy. Sure, I dress all in black, mostly. I listen to heavy metal, yes, I have shoulder-length jet-black hair, yes. I sometimes wear a black trench coat, yes.

Do I use a lot of drugs? Sure. But plenty of people do. Nonetheless, I understand that if I'm caught, my whole lifestyle, my drug use, my views of the world, will be ripped apart as strangers try to find a reason. A reason why someone is so completely mad that they would go on a rampage of killing people.

People are obsessed with 'reasons why'. 'He was bullied at school' 'He was sexually abused as a child', 'his father beat him' etc... etc... These are the headlines you read, am I right? These are the typical explanations given. These are the headlines you *expect* to read...

But why does there have to be a reason? A simple, accessible and familiar explanation? I guess because this makes people feel safe. It makes them feel calm and content knowing that these 'crazies' out there, these 'psychopaths,' they read about are *vastly* different from themselves and their little circle of family and friends. These animals are completely unlike them and just plain 'messed up' due to some 'obvious reason' they can pinpoint and then climb into bed holding on to the illusion that they are safe. It's important for them. They need to feel safe. They need to feel distant from this behaviour and different from the humans who carry it out.

When it comes to me, the concept of revenge won't suffice. Not when the scale and predetermination I have planned is revealed. They'll not be able to simplify my actions like they want to.

I'm giving them nothing they will find easily acceptable to hold on to.

I don't fit the stereotype that they will be expected to be presented with.

I lived a very normal life as a child. I was well educated. Happy family life. Never bullied or abused when growing up. None of the usual attributes of a serial killer. None of the usual attributes of someone who decides, who plans, and who takes action to kill other humans. None of the textbook rubbish is relevant here. No signs would have been visible to anyone. And yet, I have killed someone. Killed a fucking human being. And will kill many more. Systematically and purposefully.

I light another Marlboro Gold and open the kitchen window to let the smoke out. I sit on the kitchen bench next to the stove and use the kitchen sink as my ashtray.

Alice In Chains plays on in the background from my stereo, just playing a shuffle. The song, *Over Now*, rings out.

It's been less than 24 hours and Kamal's face is a swiftly becoming nothing more than a long-since faded memory.

When I force myself to picture his repulsive face, I feel nothing but utter serenity.

Absolute peace and tranquilly knowing he no longer walks this earth.

Indeed, I relish in the of pride knowing that I'm responsible for this.

But do I feel any haunting guilt? Not at all.

That's a useless and weak emotion to have...

I finish my cigarette and light another. After this I'll pour myself a drink and try to relax.

I'm going to kill the cunts responsible for Tommy's death.

And I will fucking enjoy doing it.

Am I crazy?

No, I am not.

Am I a psychopath?

No.

Am I a sociopath, as the world would label me?

Yes, indeed, I am.

Felix

I slide a Soviet NR 40 combat knife out of the sheath attached to my belt and adjust my gloved fingers to get a solid grip. The NR 40 combat knife was provided to the Red Army from 1940 onwards and was used as the standard combat knife for Soviet forces throughout the second world war. It's unusual in that it has an 'S' shaped hand guard which curves towards the blade on one side and back towards the handle on the other. The knife is specifically designed to be held with the blade facing toward you, perfectly aligned with Soviet knife combat training fashion at the time. The kind of knife fighting stance which is ideal for sneaking up and eliminating enemies from behind. I picked this one up at a trinket stall in a market a few nights ago from an old Hungarian man who selling all kinds of World War Two paraphernalia.

The blade in my hand glistens beautifully in the blue glow coming from my laptop and I dip a brand new cleaning cloth in a bowl of olive oil, one last time, carefully running the cloth one way down the length of the blade toward the tip. Tiny threads of cloth rise up along the edge of the blade, severed loose as oiled cloth and razor-sharp blade engage each other. This blade could not be any sharper. I've spent the best part of thirty minutes this afternoon sharpening the blade to a sweet perfection and I've been practising thrusting and stabbing motions on and off all morning. Rehearsing the coming events in my head. On my laptop sits open the document outlining the fate of Izzat.

Name: Izzat

Address: Parkholme Road.

Time of Execution: Between 00:01 and 04:00 Tuesday March 15.

Location of Execution: Current residential address. Parkholme Road.

Weapon of Execution: Soviet made NR-40 combat knife.

Method of Execution: Izzat will be executed with a single stab wound straight through the heart, followed by a twisting of the blade to ensure certain death. If there is a struggle or any sort, he will be severely wounded and unlikely to be able to resist effectively. Nonetheless, a small can of pepper-spray will be used in this instance.

Additional Comments: Target is to be executed as he sleeps. A physical confrontation is far too risky - Izzat is young and very athletic. He is also very wary from what has been observed. Sneaking up on him while he is awake would be particularly difficult. The target will be eliminated in his own bed.

If he is home, he will be home alone. He has no partner and I've never seen him bring girls to his home. If he is home. It will be just him, and me.

Izzat

I first hear about Kamal's murder while I'm standing in my bedroom eating a block of chocolate and checking my email on my phone. A message pops in from Abid reading 'U better come over 2 mine. Kamal's bin shot. He's dead bruv.'

It seems as though the initial shock wore off pretty quickly, or maybe reality just wasn't sinking in, because the next thing I know I was calmly changing into a pair of blue jeans, a green t-shirt and slipping on my boots. Listening to some Drake as I got drank some Coke in the kitchen.

A few minutes later as I walk back toward my bed to collect my phone and my house keys, my phone rings and I answer it quickly. A call from Qusay.

"Eh. Izzat. You alright, bruv?"

"Yeh. I am. Have you h..."

"Yeh, bruv. Fuckin' heard it."

"Right."

"Going to Abid's. Meet there."

"Already on the way, bruv."

As I cycle toward Abid's place soon after an unwelcome and overwhelming sense of fear washes over me out of nowhere. It feels as though the normal part of my brain is telling the rest of the brain that *this* time, you really should be worried. As though this could be the start of something awful. Sometimes my brains tells me things I don't want to know.

I don't want to believe it. No one has dared to strike at us for, like, so many years. We've had the occasional beef with some fuckin' new-cunt's-on-the-block who don't know we're the bosses, but we've always sorted that out pretty quickly. We've never had nothing of this sort. For one of us to be murdered... Fuck. This kind of shit never happens.

Kamal must've fucked someone off proper. No way this shit was like, random. Kamal's a fuckin' loose cunt. He's the one always getting into fights, always the loudest mother fucker. So, I guess, fair enough, bruv. Someone he had a go at, probably found out where he lived and got some revenge...

That means it could be anyone...

Or could it... Bruuuuuv... I remember. Fuck...

Kamal got into a fight with some fuckin' white boy the other night. Some fuckin' white boy in a club in Shoreditch or something....

Bruv... That's gotta be it?

I cycle left onto Abid's street and slow down as I wonder if that fuckin' white boy have been someone? Found out where Kamal lived, come back at him for that shit?

Fuck. Maybe. Yeah, maybe.

There are plenty of crews in this city, plenty of fuckin' dealers and boys on the street. Not usually white boys, but you never know.

Fuck, Kamal. Your loud arse fuckin' mouth got you killed, bruv…

The crews in our neighbourhood know who we are and what we're about. They know to just leave us the fuck alone. We try not to fuck with civilians on our own turf, so they have nothing to worry about. No one local is stupid enough to challenge us openly anyway. Nor would they want to.

But the more I think about it, I bet that fuckin' loud mouth cunt has got himself killed over some stupid argument with the wrong mother fucker. Probably over some fuckin' bitch too.

As I arrive at Abid's house, I see Hani and his brother Mohammed parking in Abid's driveway up ahead. We gotta work out what the fucks going on and then we gotta find that fuckin' white boy.

Abid

My chest rises and falls heavily. My palms feel clammy. There's a loud seething noise in the room, and it's coming from me. The word 'fuck' repeats itself over and over in my head. My brains swims in a murky swap. On the outside, I do my best to make sure my face looks staunch. No words are said. The room is silent except for my uncontrollable seething. I try to reign that in. *Breath slower, Ab, come on.*

I need to show strength and leadership right now, but all I feel is anger this wild rage for revenge. Rage against everything and everyone I come across. It's stupid, but it's real.

The murder of Kamal can't go unpunished. Control over both my boys and my territory has to be maintained with ruthlessness. People respect and fear our crew based on the presumption that if they cross us, they'll be lucky if they live long enough to regret it. We've earnt that respect. We're fair, we're orderly and we aren't fuckin' animals. We aren't out of control. If we were this whole fuckin' neighbourhood would be in chaos.

I light a smoke without thinking about it and then realise that I can't smoke in house, my mum will fuckin' kill me, so I stub it out in the kitchen sink and then stick the smoke in my pocket to throw it out later.

I see my boys arriving outside and I walk downstairs to let them in the front door. With the rage and frustration rising I have to restrain myself from punching a hole or six in the wall along the way. That won't help shit, and my mother would fuckin' kill me.

Once inside Izzat tells me what happened with the white boy in the club the other night and this all makes sense to me. Kamal was, unfortunately a bit reckless and to be fair, bruv, if any one of us was going to get themselves into this kind of shit, it would've been him.

I tell the boys what the cops told me. Kamal was shot in up, execution style in his hallway in the middle of the night. Cops reckon it was a professional hit. The guys even took the bullet shells with them and no one in the neighbourhood saw or heard anything. So that makes me think, yeah, must be that white boy was some fuckin' player or something. Probably Kamal fucked up and got into a fight with the son of some Russian gangster or some shit.

We move out the backyard so we can smoke and as I light up a joint I'm praying I'm right and this ain't some turf shit with one of the other crews in the neighbourhood. I mean, we all keep within our own territory and we just don't fuck with one another's business. None of the crews want to risk violence in the streets, turf wars are bad for everyone. So, another crew hitting us is pretty unlikely.

But, still, one of my boys has been murdered. This is an attack upon me as much as him. I can't let this go unpunished. I've gotta be seen to do something. For the sake of our whole crew and our whole neighbourhood.

You don't fuck with Abid's crew, bruv.

"Let's find this fuckin' white boy. Dealer, gangster son, crewboy, or not, I don't fuckin' care who is is, bruv. He's a fuckin' dead man."

I'm not sure if I believe it or not, but the important thing is, the boys do. They all nod bad in agreement and we get to work.

8 Ignaz

Felix

Izzat ad-Douri. A useless waste of space. A useless, predictable, waste of space. Tonight, he'll be hanging around with the others at the edge of London Fields until around midnight, then he'll make his way home. Always home. And always alone.

He's a bit older than the others and owns his own place, a studio flat. I've never seen him take a girl home or anything. Perhaps he's a faggot? Doesn't bother me. Doesn't really matter. So long as he's home alone tonight he can be whatever he wants to be.

I travel to Izzat's flat on Parkholme Road using two taxis and then walking the remaining distance through the dimly lit suburban streets of East London. I position myself across the street from his flat behind a thick hedge so that I'm well hidden from view from the street but still have a good view of the council block in front of me.

A short while later, at 12:41am, to be precise, a black cab pulls up outside the block and I watch as a well-built guy in his mid-twenties stagger drunkenly out of the cab. He's barely three metres away from me, so close I can see the grease shining in his close-cropped hair and the almost feel the heat radiating from the redness of his cheeks where the whiskey's taken hold.

I watch as he staggers away from the taxi, slamming the door shut before the driver slowly reverses and then pulls away down the street. The guy belches behind a clenched fist, a sound which is exacerbated by the silence of the night, and then proceeds to fumbles around for his keys. I'm fascinated as he sharpens himself up long enough to find his keys, sort them for the right key and make his way directly to the entrance walking like a sober man for at least ten steps. Moments later he's disappeared inside the block and once again the street is completely silent. The nearest sound is coming from a flat four stories up where a cheap stereo plays some hideous 90's pop music.

I take a deep breath and readjust my position again to keep the blood flowing in my lower limbs.

The final countdown is on.

I feel nothing but excitement and a gradually building confidence that not only have I planned this perfectly, that I can actually carry out the plans I've formulated.

You can do this, Felix. You know you can…

I survey the block again, counting the balconies up to Izzat's flat. Now that I see it in person, the climb looks daunting. But I'm filled with conviction.

I can do this.

I am going to fucking do this.

A few moments later a light flashes on in Izzat's bedroom. I lean back and crane my neck to see what's happening. I catch glimpses of the muscular fucker, shirtless as he moves about his bedroom. The cynical part of me says he must be on steroids… no way he can be 'that built' naturally…

Izzat disappears into the adjoining bathroom and I continue to wait. I rehearse the coming events over in my mind and then he suddenly reappears, towelling himself dry as he walks slowly back into his bedroom.

From the shadows of the hedge across the street I watch Izzat as he takes a number of garments from his wardrobe and arranges them neatly on his bed. His sense of organisation is admirable.

After finishing towelling himself, he takes a pair of black pyjama bottoms from the bed and slides them on quickly. He then takes a matching black t-shirt from his bed and pulls it over his still slightly wet torso. He has an amazing body. No doubt. Tight muscles all around and large shoulders, almost like a boxer. Definitely steroids. But nonetheless, he's built to fight. Built like a warrior. There is no way I could take him down in a physical confrontation. Surprise is the only way.

Now towelling his hair, he makes his way back into the bathroom out of sight. There's no sign of anyone else in the flat. Another night alone for Mr ad-Douri, as expected. Part of me is somewhat disappointed in him.

I watch on as he re-enters the bedroom and finally reaches for the blinds. He stares upwards as he pulls them closed, completely unaware of my ominous gaze as I stare on. The final signal is sent a few minutes later as the light goes out and his room becomes bathed in darkness. 12:58am. Now, I need to give him time to fall into a deep enough sleep. An hour should suffice. This should also ensure that most of his neighbours are also asleep or otherwise secure enough inside the block to not see my exploits.

Once again, I mentally rehearse. Envisaging my pathway up to his bedroom. Following through my steps carefully in my mind's eye. Picturing myself climbing the fence and jumping onto the wall that surrounds the block before pulling myself up to onto the first-floor balcony. Then, on to the second. And so on, finally up to Izzat's balcony.

I've estimated that the total climb will take two minutes at the most. I could do it in one minute if nothing goes wrong. All I need is a two-minute window of opportunity tonight. And I can wait here in this bush for as long as I need to. I have nowhere else more important to be. This is it.

This. Is. It.

I lean back and shake my legs to keep the blood flowing and keep them warm. Right now is a good time to relax. Clear my mind while I wait. I plug in my earphones and prop myself up against the fence running along behind these bushes. *Hector Berlioz, The Damnation of Faust,* flows sweetly into my ears and throughout my body. Beautiful.

I keep my eyes fixed on the council block. Envisaging the climb and most importantly the execution itself again and again until it's a seamless sequence of events which my mind is completely prepared for on all levels.

Finally, at 01:45am, after thirty minutes of almost complete inactivity in the block and with only one flat's lights still on at the very end of the Izzat's floor, I decide it is time to act. Now or never.

I wiggle my toes and shake my body to get the blood flowing again all over. I take my earphones out, turn my music off and check my equipment again. Everything is in order. The time is now.

I crouch up slowly and survey the area around me one last time. Peering out of the edges of the bushes checking for any pedestrians approaching from either side. The street is empty.

Taking a few deep breaths, I stand up and move swiftly out onto the footpath and then with a brisk walk, not too quickly in case my rapid movement catches someone's attention, but swift enough to avoid lingering, I cross the street and climb onto the top of the dark grey wrought iron fence that surrounds the whole council estate. Standing on the top with my feet placed carefully either side of the spikes and balancing myself by holding onto the floor of the first balcony in front of me, I take another deep breath and remind myself that I'm more than capable of scaling these balcony's above me.

.... You can do it Felix. You need to do it... Climb....

I reach up and push my body up at the same time, launching myself just high enough to get a firm grip on the railing of the first-floor balcony. The rest is too easy. I pull myself up onto the first balcony with ease and then follow the same process to reach the second. Then again to reach the third. I don't look down.

Once I land on Izzat's balcony I crouch down in the darkest, most shadowed corner and listen carefully for any signs of anyone having heard my movements.

The night is quiet.

Deadly quiet.

I take a small glass cutter out of my backpack and inch myself quietly over to the sliding door. I've practised this manoeuvre a half a dozen times with picture frames I picked up from a charity shop. It really does work just like you've seen in films.

I place the cutter approximately fifteen centimetres below the handle and lock and begin cutting the glass. Speed is the key here. Even if the sound is loud enough to wake someone, which it almost certainly isn't, if I'm quick enough, it will all be over and the night will be once again as quiet as impending death before anyone might realise what it was. I cut away a almost a complete circle approximately twenty centimetres in diameter and then take a roll of adhesive tape and carefully cut off a thirty-centimetre strip which I place across the circle I've cut into the glass and flatten out the tape carefully on either side. This is to hold the glass in place for the next step. I now run the glass cutting blade across the last section of the circle, doing my best not to let the glass piece fall through. The final step is the most dangerous and requires the most skill.

I take a tennis ball from my bag and holding it carefully I tap the centre of the circle gently. The glass circle moves slightly. I tap again and it begins to become dislodged. With a final gentle tap the circle comes loose from the rest of the pane and rests there, held in place by the strip of tape. I slowly peel the tape back and rely on its adhesiveness to hold onto the circle of glass as I pull it towards me. I realise I've been holding my breath for Lucifer only knows how long and I let it out slowly as the neat circle of glass lifts out exactly as planned.

Once the circle of glass has been removed, I place the glass cutter back into my backpack and leave the piece of cut glass on the balcony to my left before reaching up and sliding the door open slowly. I'm careful to open it only enough for me to slip in. This is the loudest part of my entrance. It was always going to be the most risky.

I slide the door open carefully, wincing as it squeaks and rumbles along its tracks. No turning back now. Satisfied its open wide enough I put the glass cutter back into its pouch, hold my breath and listen carefully, praying that the sound wasn't hardly as loud as it seemed to me. Soft breathing comes from the bedroom to my left, otherwise I hear nothing except the refrigerator humming away. I move inside delicately.

.... *You can do this Felix. This fucker deserves to die. His life is forfeit. Take it....*

The bedroom door is ajar and I move in swiftly. I need to act quickly and then be gone from here.

Izzat is sleeping on his side, with the blanket pulled up loosely around his neck.

I move to the side of his bed, still crouching. Still quiet.

I slide the Soviet NR 40 Combat Knife out of its sheath and beside his bed position myself carefully in the correct stance for killing. Legs at squatting distance apart, back arched slightly backwards and leaning off to my right so I can build up momentum. I reach over and grab hold of the blanket with my left hand. The knife's trajectory I carefully visualise, tracing its pathway with imaginary line right to Izzat's chest. Right to his heart.

Beside me, this cunt breaths a deep breath and his face twitches. He is dreaming. I hope it's something peaceful. Something I can ruin.

I take a deep breath and again ensure my posture is perfect. The time is now. *Do it, Felix.* I throw the blanket back exposing the top half of his body. With the knife's tip held approximately fifty centimetres above Izzat's heart, gripping it with both hands now I stab it downwards in a forty-five-degree angle, shifting the whole weight of my body into the thrust. I remind myself that I need to be prepared with my left hand to shove his shoulder backwards and force him to lie on his back should he jerk upwards and lash out.

The knife strikes flesh before I have time to breathe out, the tip of the blade making a popping sound as it breaks the first layers of tight flesh before tearing further, deeper, through the layers of muscles and soft tissue on its race towards the heart. Leaning over the bed, I let go with my left hand and place on Izzat's right shoulder, shoving him backwards, a perfect tandem force of stabbing and shoving is carried out to maintain the position of his body completely flat on his back. In the same movement I slide onto the bed on top of his body and straddle him in a very awkwardly sexual position.

He lets out a screeching, choking, howling kind of noise which, although unusual, would hardly be noticed by someone in the next room if there was one, let alone any of the other flats nearby. He looks up, wide awake now and eyes reveal how shocked he really is and begin to roll back into his skull. His arms rise up in a brief moment of attempted defence, but then drop back down onto the bed like a couple of banana peels tossed into a rubbish bin. All his energy seems to be sucked into nothingness. A black hole has swiftly absorbed every ounce of will his body once had. All in one short second.

Everything he thought he knew about the world has been proven so right, and so wrong. He is nothing. And, even if his mind has not yet caught up, his body has realised one crucial thing... It's over now.

Knife ruptures heart with a piercing pop.

He eyes meet mine as I straddle him. Knife embedded in heart, legs straddled either side of hips, left arm shoving limp right arm down, my eyes glaring back at his. The shock which a human body displays in such an instance is almost cartoonish, and a kind of childlike bewilderment looks up at me. Almost comical. Surreal. Sheer dismay and total confusion. I love it.

His body shudders slightly and at first, I think he's mounting some kind of hopeless defence, but it's simply his body going into the death throes. His eyes stare on into mine and his mouth opens in slow motion. A disgusting moaning, or more like croaking, kind of noise starts escaping his throat. We continue to stare right into each other's eyes. I start to panic that suddenly he's going to scream out loud and all Hell may break loose if he wakes his neighbours.

But I stay strong.

I can't let go of the pressure on his right shoulder just yet, there is still some life left in him yet.

The croaking sound continues and panic starts setting up camp in my stomach. Then the croak recedes to nothing more than a gurgle and a rush of thick steamy blood rises up out of the depths of Izzat's throat. Seeing this wave of hot blood washes my panic away and I let out a long sigh. This fucker is gone...

I take note of the beautiful blend of fear and confusion he has displayed for me tonight.

He has been reduced to nothing. A scared child. Pathetic.

He tries to speak but his mouth is filled with so much blood he simply chokes and coughs. I feel any fight in him go completely. His right arm goes soft and I release my pressure on his shoulder.

I grab the NR-40, still embedded in his heart, with both hands again and lean my face in towards his. "Fuck. You," I say, emphasising each word. He says nothing. I don't even know if he can hear me anymore. It doesn't matter anyway.

I grip the handle tighter, right hand over the left and with all my strength, I twist the blade clockwise, leaning into the movement and throwing my weight into it. Ventricles and atriums becoming minced meat as I twist and twist.

Izzat lets out a long groan I didn't think he has left in him and his body shudders again. The whole bed beneath us vibrates as his body spasms. I twist the knife again and a long stream of blood runs out of his mouth down his left cheek onto the pillowcase. He is fucked.

With both hands still gripping the blade tightly I twist the blade back the other way, anti-clockwise this time and the sound of his heart being diced to shreds is drowned out by the sound of his last breath. It's a moan which emits from the core of his body and escapes through his mouth with a kind of heavy sadness to it that I can't help but appreciate. His body expected to live on for years to come and the anger and confusion it feels at this moment of extinction culminates in one emotional release of agony and anger.

His eye's flicker. No longer staring into mine but staring off somewhere into the great distance behind me that only exists in Izzat's now dying mind. His eyes race around for a moment and then stop.

Dead.

It's all over.

His corpse stops shaking. It's all over. Blood continues to drool out of his mouth onto the pillow. Pooling along with the rest and soaking through to the bed sheets underneath.

I shove the knife down hard once more. As deep as I can get the blade into his heart, just to be sure he's gone, but his corpse gives no further reaction. I hear a faint scraping sound which must be the blade of the knife against bone. Rib cage. But otherwise, silence.

I let out a sigh of relief and sweat runs down my back. Gross. I need to be careful that none of it runs off my body and leaves a trace in this room. Time to move.

I yank the knife out of his heart and watch as blood splatters all over Izzat's chest. His black t-shirt is now a piece of contemporary art and the blade of the knife drips warm blood steadily across him, steam still rising from the fresh wound.

I take a deep, satisfied breath and steady myself. I'm drunk on the adrenaline and the room swims around me like I'm in a whirlpool. I listen closely for any sound which might suggest neighbours have heard anything.

There's nothing but the faint sound of a television set from somewhere else in the block and a lorry rumbling past outside. No time to fuck about. I survey the situation I've created. The bed is a complete mess and blood has somehow sprayed over the headboard, as well as the wall above it. The splatter has reached further afield than I expected. I notice little spots on the bedside table, the carpet beside the bed and Lucifer only knows what else…

I breathe in deeply for three seconds then out slowly for seven. My heart rate slowly returning to normal and my thought processes becoming slightly clearer. I lean over and wipe the blade of the NR-40 clean on the yellow blanket at the foot of the bed before returning it to its sheath.

From my backpack I remove the small spray bottle filled with bleach and begin to spray the scene in earnest. This bottle is larger than the one I took to Kamal's place; this one is 1 litre of supermarket-brand heavy-duty bleach mixed with a bit of water. I first spray the areas of Izzat's body that I came in contact with, his shoulder and his thighs as I straddled him, as well as his torso where my hands were at some point. Despite wearing gloves and clothing which covered all exposed skin, I can't take any chances. No. Fucking. Chances. I also spray myself, covering the entire length of my body in a nice coat of bleach before I stand back to admire my work.

Once I'm satisfied that the body lying in that bed has been doused sufficiently, I fetch the piece of glass that removed from the sliding door, toss it on the bed beside Izzat and tip out whatever is left of the bleach across the glass circle and the bed in general for good measure.

The smell of the bleach starts to give me a headache and as I put the empty bottle back into my backpack, I check the time on the stand next to Izzat's bed, 02:13am.

Turning to leave I spot a very familiar pair of sunglasses sitting on the dressing table beside me.

Mother fucker.

Mother.

Fucker.

Those are Tony's….

My mind is transported back to a thousand memories where Tony was wearing those blue mirrored aviators… Emotions start to manifest. I cut them off and stand up straight. This is not the time or the place for emotions…

Except anger.

This fucking cunt… Stole them… That night…

There is a temptation to take them, return them to their rightful owner, however the notion is fleeting. *You are a professional now, Felix. Leave them.*

I take care to check that everything is clear outside block before slipping back out onto the balcony and making my way steadily back towards the ground, balcony to balcony.

I notice a ringing in my ears as make the final jump down to the hard concrete path and I'm not certain how long the ringing has been there. I compose myself as best I can and swiftly walk towards Forest Road. But the ringing intensifies and my vision starts to blur. This is not good.

I take a right down Cumberland Close, eyeing a row of cars parked along the kerb on the opposite side. A large worn-out looking Mercedes van is parked in the middle of the row and I make my way casually towards it. There are a lot of trees, creating plenty of shadows and difficult angles for witnesses to see exactly what I'm doing. I take the NR-40 out of its sheath and then the roll of duct tape and a heavy-duty magnet. In a few short seconds I've securely taped the magnet to the knife and stuck it to the underside of the van, well out of sight. I hear a car approaching further down the street.

"Fuck," I whisper to myself.

I move swiftly along footpath, the ringing in my ears returns, louder this time, my chest thumping, hands now visibly trembling. A dark veil envelopes my mind.

What is happening?

I climb a low fence and change out of my killing gear amongst some thick bushes near a basketball court, changing into a fresh disguise before walking towards Dalston Lane to hail a cab. The ringing continues and my stomach convulses. I need to vomit.

I take out my mobile. My hands are shaking so much I have to use both hands, holding my pocket open with my left hand while I reach inside with my right. Finally, after considerable effort and holding back from vomiting I turn the screen on and select the music folder.

Within moments Handel's brilliance is coursing through me and I begin to feel calm again. Relaxed. Everything is going to be okay.

As quickly as the sun can shine bright from behind clouds on a grey day, the darkness retreats and I carry on.

9 Igor

Felix

When I was growing up, I always felt a little different than the other children, they all seemed so immature to me. Despite them being my age or a little bit older (I was usually the youngest in my class due to being moved up a year as a result of good grades) I could never properly relate to them. This wasn't to say I didn't have a lot of friends, on the contrary, I was very popular during my school years, and I remember being often the leader in circles of friends, both in the playground and for various school activities. I never joined any sports teams, although I was asked to try out for football a number of times. I always found it so pointless. Too much commitment, training evenings, matches on the weekends, having to 'fit in' with the football lads... I decided at some point early on that I would much rather spend my time elsewhere, mostly hanging with mates outside the library and playing card games or just chatting shit.

Despite my refusal to be involved in sports or the usual group activities, I was no outcast in school. I fitted in well enough.

There were always the children you know would end up somewhere in the criminal justice system. The ones who would bully other children or torture animals or just had that *blank* look in their eyes, as though nothing human existed behind them. You know the type…

I was nothing like these children. No. I was a perfectly normal boy. No hint of the overwhelming compulsion to take another human being's life such as I have now.

But I suppose life has its way of drawing out our most extreme and hidden tendencies as it goes by. As a child, you wouldn't have picked the person I would end up becoming, but we all change, even those of us with the staunchest opinions can be forced to alter them by the experiences that life thrusts upon them.

Look at me… I have become a killer.

A killer of bad people.

And some of the baddest people I know are out there right now on the streets of London. If they haven't worked it out already, it wont take long before they realise that I'm coming for them. Soon they'll begin to panic. And the mother fucker who killed Tommy. He will be last.

I'm striking those around Abid systematically, closing in on him, tightening the noose, little by little.

One by one, his little gang of cunts will fall and then so shall he. I want him to know what it's like to lose his best friends.

I want him to feel what I felt.

Energised and determined, I pull the blinds down in my bedroom and climb into bed. I fall asleep the moment my eyes close. I drift into a dreamless, restful slumber.

Balance is being restored.

Mohammed

There aren't many things which really get Abid really pissed off. He's usually calm enough, sometimes even a kind of scary-calm, even when he should be freaking out. But I'm sure when news of Izzat's killing, on the back of Kamal's made its way to Abid, no doubt he would have lost it, bruv. He's a hard fucker who hardly gives away any emotion. Just short bursts of anger. He's clever and he's like a big brother to me and Hani. He took us both under his wing when we first moved to the neighbourhood.

Abid's a good guy. He's been looking after his mum now for years since she got sick. He's gotten me out of so many situations, I can't remember them all. Hani, my younger brother, I try my best to look out for him, but Abid seems to always have us both covered so I should hardly bother. Abid, he's our hero. He's also a good friend. And I'm sure he needs me right now.

Hani and I cycle across the canal to meet Abid, Qusay and Ali in Victoria Park. Abid hands me a joint as soon as I arrive and I take a long and deep drag before passing it over to Hani.

Abid is calm. As I told Hani he'd be. But it's scary to see. He just stands there as though nothing serious has happened. It freaks me out a bit, not gonna lie.

The conversation we have is brief. I wonder why he made us cycle all the way over here, but, then again, it wasn't the kind of conversation we could have 'on the record,' over text message or phone etc…

Abid told me to get a message to all our contacts on the streets that our highest priority is to find out who the fuck it was that murdered Kamal and Izzat. We gotta know if there's any word of anyone who those guys might have pissed off recently. Gotta find out if anyone has made any even the lightest threats against them or any of our crew.

Abid tried to avoid sounding desperate but, to be honest, it was hard for him to appear as though he didn't suspect exactly what we all suspected was going on. Hard for him to pretend like some mother fuckers weren't specifically targeting all of us.

"We'll have this dealt with soon enough, boys," he said with a nod and a fake smile before waving us off.

We all pretended to believe him.

As I Hani and I cycle off to meet up with a couple of guys we know, I think on things.

One murder, one hit at us, would have been explainable. Especially Kamal, he had a lot of enemies.... But, bruv, both Kamal and Izzat, one day after each other... Very unlikely.

Those two didn't always get along either. Izzat thought of Kamal as a "lazy lunatic who should learn to keep his mouth shut." So, they didn't hang together unless we were all doing something. Which makes it unlikely they'd make the same enemy. And, now, it's looking pretty unlikely that the killer is this fuckin' white boy from the club that Kamal had a run in with either. I'm sure it ain't him. Pretty sure Abid doesn't think so anymore either. It's not that simple. But this makes the whole situation so much more concerning. Two of our boys taken out and no obvious answer as to why. Fuckinell...

As I pedal along my hand makes its way to the handle of the blade I have stashed in the back of my jeans. A little flip-knife job, just big enough to slice a cunt open deep enough so he won't never cross you again, but not so big as to be a pain to carry around.

Feeling the cold steel there within reach is reassuring. I sigh deeply, with teeth clenched, my lips puffing out. This is really fucking up our business.

I look over at Hani. Quiet little Hani. He looks back, I can see the fear in his eyes, but he's tough. He'll follow me into a fuckin' warzone if he had to. I just need to stay strong for him.

Felix

Tuesday afternoon I wake, 1:00pm. I put my mobile back down on my bedside table, roll over and stand up beside my bed. I move forward, thrust the curtains aside and open the window. Icy air rushes in and I welcome it, feeling my skin start to shrink back, the hairs on my arms rising up and goose bumps forming. I take a deep breath of cold, fresh air and embrace it as it wakes me up. Nothing like extreme cold to sharpen you up.

In the kitchen I light a cigarette perched between my lips and turn the kettle on. The sun isn't shining today, the sky is a dull London grey. Nothing but a gloomy semi-glow filters in through the blinds in the kitchen and the thick curtains looming over the living room only deepen the depressing ambiance. However, nothing can get me down this morning. As depressing as things feel, my mind is an untouchable happy island. I smile to myself and reach into the fridge for the bottle of milk. The kettle clicks off and I finish making my cup of coffee.

Pulling back the living room curtains and looking down, I see the ground is damp and the street below shows all the signs of it having rained through the morning. A car rushes by and wind blows leaves across the driver's door. The car passes by and the leaves continue to swirl for some time before finally settling on the road again. Somewhere a dog barks. Somewhere else a motorbike engine roars. I leave the curtains open and begin stretching. I'll do five minutes of yoga while my coffee cools.

A lot of chiropractors argue against early morning stretching; however, I think that most people just don't know how to do it right. I put on *Mozart's Piano Concerto #21 in C, K467.*

My mind is absolutely calm.

Tadasana.

Across the city, my next target has no idea of his fate. But he soon will.

Abid must be climbing up the walls in frustration by now.

Utthita Parsvakonasana.

I'm reminded for a moment of Tommy and the kind of guy he was. Wondering what he would think if he knew what I was doing. If he would appreciate the full glory of what I'm accomplishing in his name.

I doubt he would…

He'd probably tell me I was insane and that I should leave this to the police.

Ardha Chandrasana.

I try to shake off thoughts of Tommy, shake them off as I have done for the last few months, and it leads me to think of Abid's family. He lives with his mother. His sick mother. I've seen her once. She's in a wheelchair with an oxygen tank and everything. She looks like a nice enough lady, a law-abiding citizen. I doubt highly if she knows who Abid really is, what him and his friends really do to people. The lives they destroy.

Malasana.

Abid appears to be a well-educated guy, from a good background. He's been looked after. His mother loves him dearly from what I've seen. So why the fuck has he gotten involved in this kind of life? He could have done whatever he wanted, gone to university, gotten himself a decent job.

Parsvottanasana.

But you know what? This means nothing to me. Fuck him. Abid is a filthy fucking criminal who will die alongside those little cunts he calls his friends.

I finish my routine and shower before making another coffee, hunting down a fresh packet of cigarettes and then taking a seat in front of my laptop. The third file is for Ali. The 'brawn' of the crew, you could say. Well, only because he is fucking massive. Big, fat and disgusting to look at. A fucking NHS nightmare waiting to happen. I can only imagine how much the taxpayers will have to spend on this cunt over his lifetime. Once the diabetes takes a strong hold and his kidneys start to give up on him…

Anyway, Ali seems to be crucial to Abid's control of his territory. He is the big guard dog which Abid likes to have around to intimidate people. He's slow as fuck though and seems like a pain in the arse to deal with. The guys always seem to be waiting on Ali for one reason or another. He's slow, but big and scary still.

His death with be a sore blow to Abid and the others.

I read through my notes again and stop when I get down to my additional comments. I get up and fetch a glass of water before returning to read this part in detail.

This guy is a scumbag pervert of the worst kind. I would not be surprised at all if he he's raped someone in the past. In the 3 times I've followed him he has harassed random girls every single time. I followed him one afternoon and watched him harass 3 girls in the space of 15 minutes, even groping one girl on the tube which resulted in her slapping him, which I found particularly enjoyable to watch. He continuously displays violent and perverted tendencies towards females.

I close the notes and lean back in my chair, finishing my cigarette with one last deep inhale. Ali is a piece of shit animal and I'm going to enjoy this one very much.

Ali

Today was a pretty good day. My cousin Aziz got an early release. Six weeks sooner than planned. Not too sure why. He said it was due to his negotiation skills, but I'm pretty sure it's just because the prisons got too full again. Someone else's turn in the block, I guess.

Anyway, I don't care, it was good to see him. He told me the first thing he wanted to do when he got out was eat some fuckin' Nandos and smoke some weed, and that was pretty fuckin' fine with me.

My uncle and I picked him up from Pentoville around noon. For whatever reason he was in a really shitty mood and hardly spoke to us on the ride home. My uncle tried to make small talk but it was awkward and he gave up so we sat there in silence most of the drive. Ali's a few years older than me, but he's done two stints inside already. One for assault and this last time for dealing coke.

A few minutes ago, we arrived home at my uncle's place and a bunch of family were there waiting to meet Ali. My uncle said he felt like slapping him for being fucking rude. All he wanted to do was get high and be left alone. Fair enough, I guess. He just spent eight months inside, he should be able to do whatever he wants.

I tell the family that we're going out to get some fresh air and they don't argue. As the two of us walk down the street, I can feel the anger radiating from him. His face muscles are all tight and his eyes are all squinty. With teeth clenched he mutters "fuck all this fucking shit," to himself. Or to me. I don't care to ask him to clarify.

I keep walking in stride with him as he moves faster and faster now, more aggressively. I do my best to keep up with him more out of respect for our friendship than anything else, but I'm getting a worried. He's making seething noises and walking with his chest all puffed out.

This is awkward, I'm not sure what to say. I'd rather be anywhere but here right now. Aziz pissed off, is Aziz you don't want to be around. He's, uh, a bit of a loose cunt.

By now I'm getting pretty hungry and I want to remind him that we'd planned to get some Nando's but the moment doesn't seem right anymore. We keep moving through the crowd, I dodge people with grace while Aziz just throws his chest forward and ploughs his way through. A few frustrated expressions and groans of dismay rise from people as we march on through. Aziz doesn't appear to notice.

Then it happens.

I knew it was coming.

With fury raging from somewhere in his core, and for no apparent reason, Aziz snaps.

A young Spanish-looking guy approaching us along the crowded footpath in a yellow jacket and a sporting a totally innocent smile is in the wrong place at the wrong time, bruv.

Aziz strikes with lightning speed. He lets out a wail of pure rage as he balls his right hand into a fist and hurls it toward this guy's face. A punch as though from the flaming hand of the Devil connects with the guy's left eye socket, the momentum of his walking forward and Aziz's marching towards him exacerbating the sudden, devastating impact. Aziz's Hellish punch knocks this guy clean into the air. Feet off the ground etc. etc… The sound is simply sickening. Like a lorry ploughing into a cow on a country road. Heavy and wet. Gross.

As this guy lifts off the ground and begins his travel backwards, trajectory towards nothing but the footpath, Aziz lets out a deafening wail. No, a howl. A deafening howl of pure wrath. "I'm not going to let some fucking cunts lock me the fuck up!" he screams.

I have no idea what he's on about, I just clench my teeth and survey the area. Of the roughly thirty people in our direct proximity, I'm without doubt the most qualified and experienced to deal with this situation, the most likely to be able to act in an appropriate manner, yet, I'm so fucking stunned by this entire scene that I freeze up... He's been out of the can for, what, an hour now, and already captain shit-for-brains is doing his best to put us both back inside. Drool runs down the corner of Aziz's mouth and I find myself very, very afraid of him. I don't know what I should do.

Screams rings out from the crowd around us. I don't know whether it was the howl or the punch which set them off, but it doesn't really matter. This poor guy's body hits the footpath with an empty thud which bears no comparison to sound of the punch which proceeded. His back and shoulder hit the hardest. A crunch rings out from some unknown bones giving in to the concrete that makes me wince. I stare on with the rest of the audience. Shocked. Unable to make my brain and body engage with each other to form any kind of appropriate reaction. I am a vegetable along with the rest of the spectators around us.

The next thing I register is Aziz on the guy like a lion seizing his prey. He grabs him by his hair and yanks him back up to his feet. This is only going to get worse, bruv. The poor guy screams out and an unhealthy amount of both blood and tears are running down his cheeks. Aziz begins punching him in the face while he holds him by a handful of his hair. Strands of it tearing are out as each punch strikes his skull and the force shoves his whole head backwards. His head reminds me of a piñata being bashed over and over with a stick by a blindfolded kid, only the stick is a fist the size of a football and the piñata is some guys face.

Blood oozes from his eye sockets and nose. Blood floods out from broken splits on his lips. Screams ring out from the crowd again, until they drown out the sounds of the punching for a short while. A reprieve for my ears. My eyes are not granted the same privilege though.

As the screams die down, with almost perfect timing, almost as if he was waiting for the quiet, a nauseating crack rings out through the street as the guy's left cheek bone implodes. This is followed by a satisfyingly hiss escaping from Aziz. He's loving this. He's unloading everything. A final few strands of hair are torn from the guy's skull with small puffs of blood as they separate from his scalp. I see the skin around his cheek bone begin to sag.

Aziz lets go and the guy drops back hard onto the concrete.

Aziz stands himself up straight and dusts off his jeans. He's breathing heavily and sweat runs down his temple.

"Ya, fucking cunt," he says to the unconscious body below him, as if to justify his actions somewhat.

A police siren wails in the distance.

"Let's get the fuck out of here," I plead.

"Yeah, alright," he sighs, his breathing and his composure returning to normal at a pace which is very worrying.

Aziz bends over and wipes his blood covered hands on the unconscious guy's yellow jacket and then we both turn and run like fuck back toward the park nearby. A park where we used to play as kids, but now it's just another hideout for a couple of adult thugs.

More screams ring out from the spectators behind us as they close in on the guy and as we scamper all we can hear is a chorus of yelling being drowned out by police sirens.

If I get arrested for this fucking shit, I'll kill Aziz. I will fucking kill him. What the fuck was this about? He's a nasty piece of work we've got enough problems on our hands at the moment without this. "Abid better not find out what just happened," I say to Aziz, without daring to make eye contact.

"That's a warm up for the cunts who killed Kamal and Izzat, bruv."

On this occasion, I have no doubt he's telling the truth.

10 Isabella

Felix

It's funny how the improbability of real danger, of a real threat being posed to us, combined with an innate sense of British politeness, (even amongst absolute cunts) causes us to ignore obvious warning signs, instincts, which one should really take note of. We've grown more and more trusting of strangers around us. As time has gone by, our sense of suspicion and instinctual fear has eroded. Not by great external influence I don't think, but simply by our collective penchant to ignore the instinctual suspicion we should have of strangers. The footsteps approaching from behind you at night, the stranger in the shadows of the parking lot, the sense of suspicion you have for the person sitting behind you in a darkened cinema. These are all natural, reasonable things to be wary of, but I feel as though, for whatever reason, we have become all too accommodating. Not wanting to look panicked, or distressed. Saving face. We just assume that everything is fine and pray for the best.

But the fear we feel is there for a reason. It's a warning. Ignore it at your own peril.

Fear the unknown.

Be suspicious.

Consider everyone guilty until proven innocent.

It's what keeps the best of us alive and safe.

If Ali sees me tonight, and has any wits about him, he'll be suspicious of me, but I'm hoping I can strike hard enough and fast enough that it won't be an issue.

From my current position I can see the back door of the kebab shop where Ali works, helping out his uncle, the car park between me and the door as well as a bit of the main street over to my left. I came past here earlier today to make sure that Ali was working and then made my way back here around an hour ago, shuffling up from underneath an overpass about hundred metres back.

Shuffling because tonight I am a homeless bum. I'm dressed in a worn out brown blazer, covered in dark grease stains, a pair of dark blue denim jeans, complete with ripped cuffs, a green wool hat, a greasy grey scarf and a black t-shirt, on my feet are a very dirty pair of sneakers, the only thing not fitting this homeless-bum-chic is the pair of new black leather gloves on my hands. Everything else screams 'homeless drifter'. Screams 'ignore me'. Screams, 'it's okay to pretend as though I do not exist' Screams 'society has forgotten me, so you should too.'

The shadows surround me. Wrapping me like a blanket. The bright lights shining from the shop seem particularly intense due to the thick darkness tonight. Ali is right there inside that shop right now. He is but metres from me. Excitement builds.

The icy cold begins to pierce these worn-out layers of bum-clothing and I can feel goose bumps rising on the backs of my forearms. It's around four degrees at the moment, and it was raining this morning. The last thing I need right now is for more rain, this fucking icy wind is more than enough to make this a very uncomfortable situation for your humble narrator.

I breathe slowly into my scarf, doing my best to avoid letting any steam rise from my breath.

I don't exist down here.

I am nothing.

No one is sitting right here beside this skip.

And if they were, they wouldn't be worth noting. Just another homeless bum bedding down for the night.

Don't bat an eyelid. Don't stop to consider this pathetic creature. Keep calm and carry on.

I finger the iPod in my pocket. Not willing to risk breaking my disguise by pulling it out, I peer down into my pocket discreetly and select *Igor Stravinsky, The Firebird*, and the intensity pups into my eardrums with a sublime determination. As I sit with my back against the concrete wall running alongside the giant council estate adjacent to the car park I visualise the series of actions which I'll soon carry out. Mental rehearsal. Over and over.

Twenty-eight minutes pass and in the gap I can see out to the main road, a handful of random customers enter and exit the shop, none are Abid or his boys and none of them take any notice of me. It gets quieter and a few of the other shops out in the street begin to close.

It must be around 11pm by now and I'm sure this kebab shop will close any minute. I continue to wait, freezing, until, finally, after what feels like hours, it's game on as I spot my target exiting the shop. The heavy back door flies open with a loud thump, the hinges creaking under the weight of a mighty thrust and out strides the fat, bald, giant, Ali al-Tikriti.

Alone. Heedless. Predictable.

The bright but confined lights out back of the kebab shop reflect off his shiny head, highlighting the beads of sweat which've accumulated on his brow and I try to determine how many steps he needs to take until he reaches his moped. At this pace, I quickly calculate about twenty steps. Time to move.

I slowly rise up, taking the earphones out of my ears and stuffing them back into my pocket. The dirty brown blanket I take with me, throwing it over my shoulders as I straighten myself up and stretch my lower back.

Ali continues meandering towards his moped, totally oblivious of me. He hums a broken tune to himself and I find myself smiling at his total lack of awareness of his surroundings. His stupidity… no, simplicity, makes this all the more exciting.

I survey the area quickly. A few cars pass by out in the street in quick succession, travelling off into the night. I can hear voices from inside the block of flats behind me, laughter and singing rings out, otherwise, the streets around are quiet. The setting is perfect.

I am blessed tonight…

Ali is cursed…

I make my way toward his moped slowly, not wanting to attract his attention just yet. I'm just another homeless bum dawdling aimlessly around the streets, nothing to take note of, Ali. Don't turn to notice it. Don't acknowledge it. Ignore it…

My heart starts beating quickly and sporadically, as though a series of explosions are occurring within my chest, only contained by the thin walls of flesh comprising my heart. My body knows what's coming. It knows what it required of it now. This is it. Ali is about to be removed from this planet. Shortly, he'll no longer exist. Just a pile of flesh, blood and bones. Nothing more. His twenty-odd years of life have culminated in this moment. A death at the hands of a 'random' assailant in the filthy car park of a dirty kebab shop in a shitty corner of a shitty city. His final steps taken will be in a damp car park covered in dirt, saliva, phlegm, urine, rubbish and Lucifer only knows what else. His life and all his achievements, have come to this. This rather unremarkable end. This inglorious finish. Pathetic.

Exactly what he deserves.

Ali wobbles toward his moped like the obese slug that he is and lets out a series of mumbling noises as he fumbles for his keys in his back pocket. I approach him with bum-like speed, ambling my way to murder. He appears to take no notice of me at all. His focus exclusively on the set of keys now lying in the palm of his hand. He mumbles something to himself that I have no interest in discerning and then slowly lifts up one of the keys from the bunch with his left hand, staring at it as though it's some kind of foreign article he just withdrew from his skin with tweezers. A brilliant swirl of confusion and determination displayed across his ugly, sweaty face.

Two more cars cruise by the parking lot and carry on down the road. A minor distraction. Ali continues staring at the set of keys as I reach his proximity.

One metre away. He still takes no notice. The homeless bum outfit almost seems like a waste of time and effort now. Almost. But the real fun is coming.

"Mate. Hey, spare a bit o' change, please?" I croak, my voice echoing out pathetic and desperate in the empty parking lot. It sounds perfect. Right according to plan.

"Fuck off cunt," Ali replies, instantly, barely moving to look over his shoulder at me.

Also perfect. I love it. I smile on the inside, possibly on the outside too.

Ali turns from me slightly, tries to stick the key into his moped and lets out a Hellish belch as he does so. The stench of fried food and sugar streams past me. The sound of the belch rings out through the car park.

I hear the key slide into position and this is my cue to move.

Action time.

Go time.

This is it.

Number three.

Fuck you *all*.

No turning back.

Ali makes a move to sit on his moped and this is my moment to strike. Here we go...

I ask him again, "spare a bit o' change?" croaking my voice as best I can. I am a bum. A piece of worthless shit. Nothing to worry about. A failed human. Look down upon me with scorn.

Don't look too close though, you'll see the deceit in my eyes...

Ali turns to me again, "You still here cunt? Fuck off, fuck off!" he hisses, anger radiating from his shiny face.

I lower my eyes, my ruse is complete, everything has gone according to plan. Vindication, Felix. Vindication....

As he turns his back on me for the last time he ever will, I reach into the pocket of my blazer and carefully extract the guitar wire I've threaded through a pair of skipping rope handles. I grasp each rubber-coated plastic handle with gloved hands and move myself gracefully directly behind Ali with one side-step. With a quick glance down to ensure the guitar wire is ready, hanging freely with enough slack, I lunge forward and lasso the wire around Ali's neck. There are no more chances to check for witnesses now, this is it. No turning back. Go with it, Felix. Concentrate. Act swiftly. Act professionally. This will be fine.

Do it.

Do it.

Do it.

The guitar wire hooks around his neck precisely at the moment he moves forward to position himself on his moped and he lets out a shocked noise, albeit with a drunken delay. It's a noise which reminds me of the sound a creaking cupboard door makes in the middle of the night when you are sneaking a snack and trying not to wake your parents.

I clench my fists tighter around the good old skipping rope handles and grit my teeth as he begins to struggle. He is a giant of man. This will not be easy. He will fight. Of course, he will. I expect it. And I want him to.

His hands reach up to his throat in his initial reaction, his body's natural instinct. Desperately attempting to grasp hold of this foreign object gripping his body with deathly intent. His body knows there is a serious threat. Something is attacking it. React. Defend. Fight or flight... Fight... Of course... there is no chance of flight now.

With sweaty fingers Ali fails miserably to grasp hold of the thin guitar wire digging into his throat and I take the one and only opportunity I may have to bring him down off of his moped. I tug him back backwards and he slides off the seat. I swing my right knee backwards and then using all the momentum I can muster, just as quickly I fiercely drive my knee forward into the spine of this behemoth who is at my supposed mercy, pulling myself up off the ground in the act and using my grip around his neck as a brace. My knee strikes directly in his lower back, and the force ripples upwards through his body. A grunt is released from the depths of his lungs which would never have otherwise escaped. Ali is in considerable pain.

The fat cunt tries to turn his body around and face me, I turn with him, staying behind him. We move in a semi-circle, a dance of death, a comical scene to be sure. The wire slices his fingertips as they frantically skim along the length of the wire enveloping his neck, to no avail. My grip is too tight. The wire is already breaking through the first layers of skin and blood is beginning to rush to the affected area. I swing my knee into his spine twice more and as his brains registers the pain in his lower back his legs begin to quaver and give way. Weakness. Weakness which I have every intention of exploiting...

I lean back and settle into the strangulation. Pulling the wire ever tighter and using my body weight as leverage to bring this whole ordeal to a close. As expected, his legs completely give way and his knees bend, bloodied hands still at throat level, clutching in a frenzied fashion at his rapidly collapsing throat. His knees strike the concrete parking lot ground with a rather dense thud. Splashes of water rise up underneath him from the puddles of water accumulated during the day's rain. Another horrible noise emanates from the body of Ali fat boy. This one sounds like bear having an orgasm, a long moan which rings out loud and long. Too loud. I need to wrap this up...

I lean back further, tugging the guitar wire with all my weight and all my strength. Caught up in the satisfying moment. Not caring if his whole head rips loose with the force I use. Just wanting to finish this.

Fuck you, Ali. There are all too many reasons why you do not deserve to live. As your last breaths slip out of your carcass, please reflect on your failed life. Remember all the good times you had as you fade away. They were the best of everything. You no longer exist.

I pull so hard on the skipping rope handles I feel the layers of his flesh giving away and the wire grinding against his windpipe. I lean back as far as I can go and the back of my hat touches the ground behind me. I can feel the cold dampness of the car park ground rising up toward my skull.

Ali lets out a few more distorted garbles as I watch as my exposed wrists turn white with the intensity of my grip.

Almost too suddenly, he is finished.

He rolls over onto his left, limp.

He is gone.

His body begins to shake uncontrollably. The death throes.

I love it.

I grip tighter still on the piano wire, now lying completely on my back on the ground with this behemoth on top of me. I wrap my legs around his chest, enjoying the death throes as they permeate through his body into mine. I lay there vibrating in time with his corpse as the last bits of life shudder out of it. Interestingly there is so much heat that steam rises up from his body creating streams of white mist which could almost be mistaken for his soul escaping his dying flesh. In my head, this is exactly what is happening.

Fuck you, Ali.

You are done.

No longer will you haunt this planet.

No longer will people fear you.

No longer will you have any meaning to anyone.

You are gone, fucker.

Gone…

Qusay

I don't want to tell Abid. Fuck. No fuckin' way am I going to be the messenger on this one. Kamal's dead, Izzat's dead and now Ali's been fuckin' murdered. Killed in the fuckin' car park of that shitty fuckin' kebab shop his uncle forced him to work at. A fuckin' kebab shop, bruv. Murdered right outside.

Fuck. Fuck. Fuck.

What the fuck man.

"What the fuck is going on, Hani? … I'm not telling Abid."

Hani avoids eye contact with me.

"Phone Mo. He'll tell Abid. Do it quickly before someone else fuckin' tells him, bruv."

"Fuck. You're right. But I don't even wanna tell Mohammed... This is all too fucked."

"You have to tell him. You have to tell him now."

I exhale deeply and notice that my legs are shaking.

Shaking from the shock of losing one of my brothers, I guess.

Shaking, 'cause I don't have a fuckin' clue what the fuck to do, for sure.

I'd never admit it to the other's, but Kamal and Izzat were the only guys in the crew I actually liked. The only guys I could stand. And now they are both dead. Fuck. Fuck this...

"Come on, bruv. You gotta do something." I wish he would shut up.

I know there's a good chance Abid hasn't heard about Ali just yet and its important he hears it from one of us first, and not the fuckin' cops or whatever.

My hands are shaky and I know this is not going to go well no matter what I do.

I pick up my mobile again and phone Mohammed, cradling the phone in my lap, not wanting to bring it to my cheek until I absolutely have to.

Mohammed's a good guy. Abid's golden boy. Where Abid's the voice of recklessness, Mohammed is the voice of reason, for sure. Fuckin' good guy. I picture him now, remembering a moment last week where he was laughing with Kamal about some shit they'd seen on the tube earlier that day. Laughing and having a good time. Fucks sake. I'll never see Kamal laugh again, what the fuck is going on? I'm scared, but I can't show it. Got to act tough.

I look down at my phone and realise that Mohammed's already answered.

"What?" a strong voice rings out from the mobile in my hands. I bring it to my cheek and the voice repeats "What do you want?"

I lick my lips and clear my throat, hesitating. Hani stares at me and then at the phone and then back at me, hurrying me along with his eyes.

I don't want to say it. I don't want to say it. I don't want to say it.… "Ali's been taken out," I blurt out, following this up quickly, suddenly desperate to keep talking so I don't have to hear Mohammed's reply, "He was found behind a bin in the carpark of his uncle's shop. His body was burnt. Set on fire."

There's a long pause at the end of the line. I wish I'd been cut off or lost connection, or could go back in time and not tell him, but the heavy breathing coming through the line tells me there is no going back. I look over at Hani and he stares back panicked and pale.

I get very nervous in these kinds of situations so keep talking. I blurt out "this is a war. Someone's after the crew. This is not just a coincidence. What do we do?"

"We need to tell Abid. Leave that to me."

Mohammed. Calm as fuck. As always.

I end the call.

"Hani, we gotta go, mate."

Hani nods and lights a cigarette as we make a move. The silent snake.

11 Istvánffy

Mohammed

Fuck all this shit. Why do I have to be the only one out on the street looking for these fuckin' sons of bitches who are killing us? Like I can search this whole fuckin' city by myself? While Abid that fuckin' pussy stays inside where it's warm and safe to "think things through in private." As if I couldn't possibly have anything useful to add to the conversation. Maybe *I* know exactly how to deal with this attack on us. Maybe *I* have a plan. What then, eh? What then, Abid? You fuckin' cunt. I'm not as stupid as you think. I know what you say about me behind my back.

"Yep, no problem," I'd said to him before I left. Fuck. What the fuck is wrong with me? Bowing down to him like a fuckin' pussy.

I spent the whole morning today driving around visiting anyone we know who might know anything about what the fuck is going on. My dealer in Whitechapel, a couple of fences I know in Woolwich, some friends and some, well less than friends, all of whom usually know who has beef with who. But of course, I found nothing. No one knows a fuckin' thing. What a load of shit.

One of them even suggested I get the fuck out of London for a bit. "Fuck off you little faggot", I told him, "I'm not a fuckin' pussy," but perhaps it's not a bad idea. The little cunt might have the right idea.

Parked in the carpark of BP in Shadwell, I look over out the passenger window of my BMW and watch as a pigeon tries his best to fuck another pigeon. The female pigeon flutters away and hops a half a metre away. The male rushes her again and pounces. This primal mating ritual continues and I find myself egging the male pigeon on in silence.

The female pigeon eventually flies off up onto a rooftop somewhere behind me and the male pigeon is left standing there, looking forlorn. I know how he feels. Rejected. I roll down my window, "fucking bitches, eh?" I say to him, as though my words of condolence will be understood.

The rejected pigeon flies away toward a rubbish bin and pecks around for scraps. I sigh. Life, eh?

Abid would never go for us leaving London for a bit. No chance. He's too stubborn.

I can't seem to shake this mood and I decide my only option is to go get high. Fuck this shit, hunting the streets, for what? As though I'm going to luckily fuckin' stumble across a gang of arseholes trying to kill us all.

I have to wonder if I'm being used as bait. But then that doesn't make any sense, someone would have to be following me. Following me around, watching me and trying to kill me? Nah, not possible.

I phone Abid to give him an update but he doesn't answer his phone.

Fuck it. I start the engine and drive back home. This is fucked. I want to get high, take a shit and then sleep.

Felix

Standing in my bathroom, leaning over the basin, water runs down my chin and splashes everywhere before it runs down the drain hole or hits the floor. It feels soothing against my cheeks.

Bach's Goldberg Variations, BMV 988 plays softly from the living room. I stare at my reflection in the mirror. Hair, jet black, blacker than black, my cheeks sunken, circles underneath my eyes hollowing out my face. My eyes themselves, appear so sad. So empty. What I am becoming? Some kind of monster?

No. No, Felix. You are a hero. A knight in shining armour. You are not some kind of monster, you are some kind of angel.

So why don't I feel that way? Why do I feel nothing?

Totally empty.

Not happy.

Not pleased with my efforts in life.

Not satisfied.

….

Only this recent adventure of killing has satisfied me.

Only the acts themselves. In the moment it's pure bliss.

The outcome, the… *now*, offers me nothing.

I'm glad for what I have accomplished thus far… but shouldn't I feel an overwhelming sense of gratification?

A sense of purpose?

Shouldn't I?

I sigh and reach for a large white towel to dry my face and hands.

From under the basin I remove a bottle of Antipodes Halo Skin-Brightening Facial Mud Mask and pour a small amount into my palm. Applying the mask becomes something of a metaphor for my actions. A mud mask. A mask of filth and negativity to be applied for a short time, then removed later, leaving you cleansed and refreshed. Anew. Yes, I am applying a muddy mask while I execute Abid and his crew. Once complete, I will remove the mask. Wash it off, down the drain and once again become cleansed. My soul will be cleansed.

I watch myself smile in the mirror in front of me, ignoring the fact that only my mouth smiles whilst my eyes remain as lifeless as pebbles.

I never really had many close friends throughout my life. At school I hung out with a group of people, but they were more my associates than my friends. We never really hung out outside of school. At home I always entertained myself. Lego, video games, books, my own imagination, whatever. I've just always enjoyed my own company better than the company of others. And that's not some ego thing, where I only think that I'm worthy of my own presence. No, I simply feel much more comfortable alone. Alone, I am free. In my world. Playing by *my* rules. No compromises having to be made for anyone else. I love it.

Tommy was my only true friend. Since he's been gone my world has become more and more… definitive. My vision more and more clear. I've successfully relinquished the need for comrades, companionship, the distractions of friends. I've become my own person. Purely Felix.

I've embraced the darkness, the emptiness. It's just been me and my thoughts for a very long time. And that's more than enough. Some people might say I've been perfecting my madness. I'd say I've been perfecting my clarity.

Moving back into the kitchen I take a can of Coke Zero from the fridge and seat myself on the cold leather sofa. I lean my head back and stare at the ceiling. Drifting into the music. Letting it wash over me, run through me, catch hold of my blood as it flows through my body and brings life to my weary limbs. As Bach's masterpiece crescendos so too do my spirits. I feel as though I'm no longer inside my body, as though I'm floating above it, outside the physical limitations of flesh. Simply, energy, hovering and rippling in time with the music. It is serene. This is what I live for. This feeling of endless possibility and calm. Nothing can offer me this, except for music. Not any material object, not the love of another human, nothing. Music is all I need.

Music.

And.

Killing.

All I want now is for Abid to suffer for what he did to my only friend and to all those other innocent people that he's hurt over the years. Every single one of them, dead or alive, deserve Abid's suffering. They deserve it.

And I'm the perfect one to deliver it.

It has to be someone like me.

I know that I'm different. One of these things is not like the others. Your average citizen could not do this, could not take a life. And I wouldn't want them to. Those affected by Abid have suffered enough. I must be the one to act on their behalf. I'm already a broken person. Who cares if I die? Look at me, I'm becoming increasingly hollow. A ghost of society. Soon, I may wither away into nothing. My reflection in the TV screen is that of an increasingly gaunt body suspended below a grinning skull.

As long as I've completed my task, I would gladly fade away. That would be perfectly fine. I'd gladly let the world fade to black knowing that I have left it a better place. That's a bloody good attitude to have, I think to myself. But not yet. I'm not finished yet.

Felix

Wednesday morning. 11:30am. 3 down. 3 to go, then Abid. Today is Qusay's day of reckoning.

Qusay, appears to be Abid's closest friend, despite Mohammed being Abid's right hand man, Abid and Qusay seem to be having the most conversations, the most chats. Most often breaking off from the group and wandering off together. I can tell they're close. This death will surely hurt Abid the most. I can only hope.

I'm not certain exactly where he'll be tonight, he's much less predictable than the others. Those first guys were the sitting ducks, almost always in the same places at the same times. Easy pickings, sure. Qusay? He'll be tricky. I'm going to have to follow him tonight. I'm going to have to take a big risk to track him down. I can almost bet that he'll go to Abid's though. Surely. With the execution of three of their friends, the whole gang must be in panic mode right now. Probably doing their best to band together and work out a little plan. I'll stake out Abid's place and wait for Qusay to show up. If not Qusay, then one of the brothers, Mohammed or Hani will turn up for sure. Otherwise, Abid will leave, I'll follow him and find at least one of them. It's risky, but there's nothing else I can do.

I feel a little faint as I stand and I notice my muscles are aching. Joints seem stiffer and I reflect on my health.

My appetite seems to be diminishing by the hour and I find myself, once again, having to remind myself to eat and drink. Food is becoming less and less tasteful and my interest in non-existent. This violence is hypnotic. *Hypnotic violence.* A great song title for my never-got-off-the-ground band, *The Blank Pages*... I'm feeding off the thrill of the kill.

The oats I prepare myself a few minutes later turn out lumpy and sticky. Like a bowl of baby vomit warmed up and sweetened with milk. I slice a banana over the top and stare down at the bowl of garnished baby sick with disgust. What's happening to me?

I lurch forwards over the kitchen bench as wave of nausea hits me. My head feels light and I panic, wondering if I'm about to faint. My hands are clenching the edges of the bench top and the knuckles are white, my hands. Jesus. Look at them. They are the hands of a skeleton. Bony and wrinkled. Like a withered old woman's. Worn. My previously delicate fingers now look completely foreign.

My heart shudders and thuds away inside my chest. Images of death flash before my eyes. A spiraling tornado of the deaths of both criminals and of myself. Spectacular. You could get lost in here. But I need to stop my thoughts from creating a destructive wasteland.

Voices haunt me from inside my head.

Grab hold of yourself Felix. You are stronger than this. You have purpose. You have a mission to complete.

A groan escapes me through clenched teeth and I stagger toward my bedroom. Sliding along the walls just to stay upright. Desperately seeking my bottle of Xanax, trying to remember where I put it. Desperate for anything except for this feeling.

The room sways. I don't know if that table over there is crooked, or if I'm the one who's crooked…

It's all too much to cope with.

Execution fantasies can be used as a coping mechanism.

A voice behind be whispers something dreadful.

I turn to see who it is, and I catch my reflection in the mirror inside my closet door. My lips are moving and I'm speaking all kinds of nasty things.

"This is all you will amount to, Felix."

"Your father wanted more for you than this."

"You could have been a successful architect. Started your own firm one day. Instead you chose to end your life prematurely."

"It is over for you. No going back now. You are finished."

"Just like your dead and rotting friend."

"Pathetic."

I watch myself as I convulse and let out a horrible moan and with all my will power clamp my mouth shut, willing the words to stop coming out. My mouth motors on behind the palms of my hands and my mind races across terrible thoughts for what seems like an eternity before finally easing off. I clench my jaw tight and breathe heavily through my nose, grasping desperately for thoughts any of happiness and of calm.

I need my music. I need my music. I need music.

On my bedside table sits my mobile, I lurch toward it and fumble the touchpad, teeth still clenched, mashing away with clumsy fingers until finally *Mozart's piano concerto #21* slowly pours out of the little speakers.

I drop the mobile onto my pillows, and with my last surge of energy I grab the little bottle of Xanax from the top drawer as I flop down on the bed. The darkness is coming. Like a blanket. Like a bucket of jet-black paint thrown over my face. Staring up at the ceiling, unable to move another muscle, Mozart invites me into a world of serenity, where nothing else matters. A world inhabited solely by me and by the music. A perfect world.

Two or three tablets slide down my throat and I don't remember opening the bottle.

I lean back into myself and let the music wash over me.

Mohammed

Abid, Hani, Qusay and I sit in a dingy corner of a backroom of a club near Brick Lane. When I say dingy, I mean dingy as fuck, bruv. Dust has mixed in with fuck-knows-what to become a heavy black grime festering along the skirting boards. The rusty tap over the stainless-steel sink behind us drips annoyingly. Empty cardboard storage boxes are scattered haphazardly about the place and I avoid touching the surface of the table in front of us so as to spare my jacket sleeves from becoming imprinted with years of grease stains. It's clear that this dingy part of the club is not used by anyone except for the bouncers who come here to play cards and fuck girls during their breaks. The air is thick, stale. I don't like it here, but I do my best to maintain my cool.

Abid's face is pale and he hasn't said a word since we all sat down.

I don't want to be the first to speak, so I stare over at Hani. He runs his hands through his greasy hair and breathes out deeply, his eyes avoid mine. I stare over to Qusay, he taps his fingers on the table top and glances up at me, raising his eyebrows. When we make eye-contact he nods his head and sits up straight in the little wooden chair. "What are we going to do?" he directs at Abid.

I glance over to Abid, and see the corner of his eye twitch.

"Revenge, bruv. What do you think? Revenge."

"Do we have any idea at all who's behind this? It's gotta be someone tryna' take over our turf, right? It's gotta be."

"It ain't *gotta be* nothin', bruv. Fuck sakes. Don't be jumpin' to fuckin' conclusions."

Qusay's face goes red and he shifts awkwardly in his seat.

Now that the silence has been broken I decide to speak up, "all we know for certain is that they are, like, fuckin' professionals. Everything is fucking clean. The cops can't even get any serious leads going." I'm nervous as fuck. "Our guys told us they spoke to a neighbour of Kamal's who saw a mailman in the area at the time, and the cops said the mail doesn't get delivered that early on his fucking street." I pause, surveying the room, all eyes are on me. Abid's are fierce. "Also, someone said they saw a guy acting proper suspect outside their window Tuesday morning, about the time Izzat was killed. Apparently, the guy didn't hang about for too long so they didn't call the cops."

This is shit we already know since the cops spoke to us all and my words add nothing to the conversation. Just noise. At this stage I'm just breaking up the agonising silence.

Hani jumps in, "those fucking bastards! When I get my hands on them…"

"Fuck, bruv. Calm yourself down, right?," Abid overrides him.

I continue on with my useless monologue, ignoring my brother's outburst, "so, these guys know what they are doing and they probably planned this for weeks. What I don't understand is why." I pause to let this sink in, "Let's think about this logically. If they started planning this a while ago - "

"How long ago?" Hani interrupts again, accusingly.

I stare him down, "I don't know, bruv, say, a few weeks ago, right? They would've had to have a reason back then. What did we do and to who, around, like, three weeks ago?"

"That's a fucked plan, bruv, how do you know it was exactly three weeks? Your whole idea relies on knowing when they started planning this shit. How the fuck can we know that?"

Hani was right, how the fuck could we know? I try to think of something appropriate to say. The room goes silent again. This time for too long.

"At least he's trying to think of something."

"Fuck off," I spit the words at Qusay. Little bitch. I don't need his help.

"This ain't fuckin' good! Stop your fuckin' bitchin'. All of you. We ain't got the fuckin' time for this shit. We need to stay focussed," Abid seethes with rage.

His chest rises and falls heavily, a bead of sweat runs from his temple. He doesn't notice and it drops onto his shirt collar. I see little broken capillaries in his nose which I've never noticed before. "Mo, go with Aziz and talk to his boys on the inside again, someone inside must know what's going on. Maybe someone we know well. Someone who thinks they are safe behind bars while their competition is taken out on the outside."

I nod.

Abid's eyes narrow in on me, he taps his index finger on the table top and leans toward me, "No fuckin' mistakes, bruv. I need a fuckin' answer. Aight?"

"You got it, bruv," I reply diligently.

Abid reaches into his coat pocket and pulls out a bag of coke. He starts racks up a line on the table and we all look away in a sign of respect as he fumbles with his bank card trying to cut it before he finally, messily, snorts it right off the table top. I make my way over to the sink to get him a glass of water, but he stands up moments after I do and marches over toward the door.

"Catch you later, give me a call if you find anything."

Abid yanks the door open and mumbles something to himself before slamming the door behind him, it bounces back and swings on its hinges.

Hani stands to speak once the coast is clear, "this is totally fucked. We don't even know who we're being attacked by and Abid's acting like we've got this shit all under control. Shouldn't we be going to ground? We're all fuckin' targets, bruv. All of us, eh."

"I don't know, bruv. I really don't. All I know is what Abid just ordered us to do. So, go do it. This is obviously not fuckin' random hits," I add, thoughtfully, "someone's coming after us, we're all targets, so watch your backs."

Qusay chimes in, "change up our routines, boys. These cunts have obviously worked us out. They know where and how to find us. No one stays home alone for the next few days, okay. We all crash at each other's places. Strength in numbers. Let them fuckers come at us if they want to."

Felix

Qusay lives in a council estate near Bethnal Green station. I've not managed to work out exactly which flat is his, but I've spotted him entering and exiting the place a few times and gotten the hang of his routine as best I can.

I make my way to his house at around 5pm on Wednesday afternoon. It's raining hard and my socks are already wet through my shoes from the short walk I took to pick up this hired car. Not cool. When I started following Qusay a few months back, I noticed that he often came home at around 6pm during week days. I'm guessing that's when his mother's making dinner and she probably insists he's home each day before he goes out later to get up to no good with the rest of those fucks he calls friends. I imagine in his mother's mind he's undoubtedly a 'good boy' working his 'normal job' during the day and then coming home for a family dinner before going out to work his 'part-time' job in the evenings. Typical.

I've no doubt this is what many parents think of their children involved in the gang violence which plagues this city and others. 'Oh, my boy would never do any of that! He's a sweet boy. He's too busy working all the time anyway.'

Yeah. Fucking. Right.

I know it's a long shot, but, I've really no other option here. I've never really landed on how I expect this exact execution will go down, there were always too many variables, but I'm hoping inspiration will come to me when I see him.

I have a hammer inside the laptop bag next to me on the passenger seat. Bought new, with cash, from a small hardware shop in Bow yesterday. Luckily, it's raining right now and a bit cold, so the leather gloves I'm wearing don't look out of place. Otherwise, I'd have waited another night for this.

The council estate Qusay lives is in way too exposed to views from the street and too busy for me to attempt to break in at night while he was sleeping. I've been passed a few times in the middle of the night and there is always something going on, always someone walking about or hanging around outside. Too many eyes.

The only way to properly get Qusay is to follow him. This 'going home for dinner' behaviour is his only discernible routine and I've no other choice than to use it. Ideally, if I can follow him far enough and strike him on his way, then I can circle back later and pick up this car and get the Hell of out here before anyone finds his body.

I'm disguised this evening in a pair of thick black-framed reading glasses, and a stick-on goatee that actually looks remarkable like the one Qusay has, now that I think of it. I'm also wearing a grey hoodie which I'll pull up over my head when I step out of the car. My hair is slicked right down and back, so it actually looks rather short. In this kind of weather, no one would recognise me from how I look day-to-day.

I've parked a few houses down from the flat where Qusay lives, but I can see the road clearly ahead of me where people walk down from the tube station, so there is no way I could miss him as long as I'm paying attention.

And attention is all I've got right now.

I roll down the window to smoke a cigarette and a moment of panic hits me.

This is fucking nuts. It's not hardly dark enough yet to make a proper move on him, and fuck, this is a busy street. No way could I *not* be spotted.

I quickly light a cigarette and smoke it through an inch of gap in the window. Droplets of rain bounce inside the window and I do my best to ignore them. After a few drags I'm calming down and I'm almost thinking clearly.

Despite how tempting it would be to just grab this heavy hammer when I see him, run up on him and start pounding on his face until his whole head caves into itself, the better option is to wait. Make sure he's in the flat, wait until he's had his dinner or whatever the fuck, and then hope like Hell he goes out again later. Then I can follow him and take him down when the opportunity presents itself.

As I sit here in the car chewing compulsively on Bubblemint Extra to keep my hungry stomach from eating itself, I wonder what Tommy and I would be doing this evening if he was still alive. Probably we'd be having a beer and talking about our days of work, I'd be making the usual complaints, too many ego's in the office, Donnie being his usual cunty self, too many arseholes on the streets. Then we'd play some PlayStation and cook some dinner. Just chilling.

I should feel sad about this now, reminiscing. But I don't have time to feel sad. Sadness is a luxury I can't allow myself to have right now. Right now, I need to focus on the moment.

There's only one thing that matters and that is taking down Qusay Hamza Zubeidi.

Times goes on, my music changes itself from Mozart to Slayer to Linkin Park to Michael Jackson as my various playlists run their course. The eclectic nature of the music echoing the wide-range of emotions I have riding all day. The calm, the rage, the pain, the pleasure, all climbing to the top of the heap at one point or another.

The clock ticks past 6pm and I must've seen over a thousand people walk past me in the last hour. Not one of them Qusay. Not one person even remotely resembling him walking into that estate.

He could be running late, sure, but I figure if he was going to be here this evening, he'd have arrived by now. Fuck. I've no choice but to give things a bit longer. Come on, you cunt.

I roll the window all the way down and smoke another cigarette as the rain eases a few minutes later, careful to keep the butt in the car so as not to leave a trace of my being here.

The clock passes 6:30pm and I'm now becoming desperate to pee. I'd been careful not drink any liquids since I last took a piss at about 3pm for this exact reason, but that's just how it goes.

I've got two options now. I can either wait it out here for a bit longer, in the hopes that Qusay does turn up, or I just bail now and come back tomorrow night.

The rational side of my brain tells me that this was a wild goose chase anyway and that if he isn't here by now, he won't be coming. The emotional side tells me that I have already invested the best part of a day in this stakeout operation and what harm would another couple of hours do?

My bladder pulses at me and I compromise, swearing under my breath.

I decide to stay until 7pm, then bounce. Fuck it.

7pm comes and I go.

12 Leonard

Abid

Debauchery.

The girl dances around my lap gracefully.

Like she's done a thousand times for a thousand men.

The machete I'm holding in my hand and pointing at her playfully doesn't seem to faze her at all. Either she trusts me implicitly, or she's so high on MDMA or whatever that she couldn't care any less. Either way, it doesn't really matter to me.

She arcs her little back and pokes her well-oiled tits out in front of her, running her hands across her tight stomach and slowly down between her legs. I feel myself becoming harder and harder.

"Come here, sweetheart."

This nameless body strides over toward me, the movement is all in her hips, emphasising each step like the professional that she is. Her heels are four inches high, metallic blue, to match her panties. The bra lying across my shoulder is also the same colour. Those panties must go, but the heels can stay.

The girl licks her lips slowly and then slides her left index finger inside her mouth, popping it out slowly, seductively. She slides the wet finger inside my mouth as she straddles my lap. I can feel my cock hammering against the inside of my trousers, desperate to be let out, like a little puppy jumping up and down at the door. She spots it and reaches down with her right hand to unzip me. I raise the machete and point the sharp tip at her head, right above her delicate little ear. She doesn't even blink as the blade is nudged against her skin.

She reaches inside my trousers, pushes my boxers down and lifts my cock out. The cool air of the room feels wonderful on my throbbing cock and her hand moves across it slowly.

"Take your panties off. I want to see it.'

She stands up and slowly slides them off, staring directly at me the whole time.

Her little pussy is perfectly waxed, only a thin strip of dark brown hair remains, like little bullet above her moist little hole.

That pussy glistens in the low lights of the room. Moist and fresh.

"Slide your fingers inside yourself."

I watch as she slowly penetrates herself with her index and middle finger, her eyes do not leave me as she does this. My cock throbs again and I realise I'm holding it, moving my hand up and down slowly. I won't last much longer.

Her fingers are removed and they come out dripping and sticky.

"I want to unload in your mouth."

The girl drops to her knees and creeps toward me like a lion stalking its prey. It's almost too much for a horny fucker like me to handle. I grip the machete hand in my hand, the cold power of death I wield getting me even harder.

She lets out a playful roar and tugs down my trousers. With big, doll-like green eyes she stares up at me innocently. I nod. She leans into my lap and takes my cock inside her warm little mouth. I feel her lips running up and down my shaft, tongue delicately licking me, she sucks gently and stares deep into my eyes, she knows I'm at the point of no return. I unload with the force of a shotgun, emptying myself inside this girl's mouth and then leaning back, satisfied. I lean over and pull my trousers back on as she stands up, wiping her mouth on the back of her hand. "Lovely, sweetheart."

"My pleasure," she giggles. She can't be much older than eighteen. As young as my little sister.

As I leave the club Mohammed phones me from a bad connection somewhere and during a painful stop-start conversation he begs me to tell the boys not to go to his uncle's wedding dinner tonight. Tells me that it's too dangerous. Tells me that he is a fuckin' pussy...

"I have all the protection I need," I tell him, "a fucking gun in my jeans and a machete in my fuckin' car."

"You can't bring that fuckin' gun to my uncle's wedding bruv, they have security on the door."

"Fuck off, you pussy. It's all good, eh? Don't get yourself scared, little bitch."

"Fuck, bruv..." Mohammed says, his voice trailing off.

"Let's just show up and make ourselves seen, bruv. We can't let people think we're fuckin' pussies hiding away. We're fuckin' tough, bruv. Fuckin' tough."

"Yeah..."

"Are you fuckin' tough? Or what?"

"Ye..."

"Then man the fuck up, bruv. Be staunch," I cut him off before he can reply. "I've been tough my whole fuckin' life. I'm not about to start hiding like a fuckin' rat. I'll take care of myself. These cunt's would be fuckin' mad to try and fuck with us at your uncle's thing. Do you know how many of our boys will be there?"

He says nothing and I wonder for a moment if he's hung up until I hear him breathing.

"There's plenty security there too, it's a fuckin' big party. Keep hunting for those bastards, Mo (I know he hates being called Mo), that's what I told you to do. Not to fuckin' harass me."

"Don't you care what's going on here?"

"Sure, I care, but with severe limits, bruv."

"We are all fuckin' target here. We shouldn't meet up in the same place," he pleads.

"Your connection is breaking up, Mo. I've got to go." I hang up and shake my head. That kid has a lot to fuckin' to learn. Paranoia will get you nowhere. We've had problems before. Usually isolated incidents, you know, someone gets pissed off, someone who doesn't know who we are, or worse, someone who does. And we've dealt with it every time. But, okay, I admit, it's never been anything like this. This is fuckin' big this time. But I can't let these boys see me scared.

The sun has already gone down across the city by the time I drive out of the club's car park. The sky is grey and it's windy as fuck. Miserable. Classic London Spring.

I'm not going to think about this shit anymore. I have an hour to kill before this fuckin' thing begins and I need to go get stoned before the boys arrive at mine so I can actually deal with their whinging.

Felix

Beautifully wrapped on the outside, yet something really grotesque on the inside. This is the thought which passes through my mind as I catch my reflection in a shop window shortly after arriving outside a community hall in Stamford Hill. I've cycled here, following Abid, Qusay, Mohammed and Hani here from Abid's place, with no real idea where we were all going, other than that it is obviously some kind of event, as all four are dressed in traditional thobes and little kufi skull caps. All four of them, right there in that little black car. Fuck, If I had a fucking grenade launcher or a submachine gun or something, I could finish this whole shit right here and now.

My plans to strike at Qusay on Wednesday night went to complete shit. Thinking about it I realise he probably changed his routine up, perhaps decided to stay somewhere else for a bit, which is a smart move. I've no other choice now but go back on the trail of these cunts and find another opportunity to strike. It's fucked up my whole schedule and set me back by at least two days. But I was prepared for this.

I can see from the number of vehicles arriving on the street and the endless swarm of mozzies making their way inside the hall, that whatever is happening this evening, this place is going to be packed. To be fair, the attendees are mostly older people, in varying states of preservation, but the few youths lurking about the place all look suspicious as Hell and it would be suicide to try to and follow Abid and his boys the inside of that hall. For a start I'm really not dressed for blending into the crowd here, I'm wearing a pair of black boots, dark grey jeans, a black t-shirt and a black pullover. I've disguised myself with a thin fake moustache. I tried to wear a fake beard, but it just looked wrong, too fake. Plus, between you and me, I couldn't bring myself to go that far once I saw myself in the mirror.

I'm not sure what my next move should be, I've got to think fast. Abid parks his car a bit further down the road and the four of them exit after a short while to make their way back up towards the hall. I immediately notice already their behaviour has changed. All four are looking around, checking over their shoulders, staring a bit longer at the people who walk past them. Suspicious of everyone. Paranoid as fuck. I have them shook.

I leave the Boris Bike leaning it up against a street sign on the opposite side of the road. I need to think quickly, I can't just lurk about outside and wait for them to come out, wait for one of them to peel off from the crowd... No.... They're expecting me to be out here, for sure. But on the other hand, I can't bloody well go inside that hall. That would be insane.

No... I need to be sensible.

The one thing I can be fairly certain of is that they will come back to this car once it's all over. When they do, I can't approach all four. That would be suicide. I need Qusay, or even Hani or Mohammed, to be separated from the rest. I can't afford to be outnumbered here. That's a risk I simply can't take.

I light a cigarette and take stock of the situation.

There are so many people around. For fucks sake. Perhaps this isn't the best idea. I wasn't expecting to follow these cunts into a fucking swarm of mozzies, all dressed in thobes and *"derka, derkaring"* about the place!

I survey the area, there are so, so many people here. So many Muslims and I look so obviously out of place. Fuck. I doubt I can get any of these guys on their own this evening. Forget it. I need to get out of here, this is not good. I know when to back off, I'm not one of those idiots who bang on about showing a 'can do' attitude about something he or she clearly 'can*not* do'. This situation, no 'attitude adjustment' will fix. I'll regroup and carry on.

I look down and watch as a cockroach scuttles along the side of the rubbish bin to my left. I lose myself in the moment and I feel a sudden rush of panic.

My heart feels cold and damp.

Something is very, very wrong.

The world around me feels like the cloudy, confusing horror of the final moments of a horrible nightmare.

As I instinctively look up, I come face to face with four angry Muslim guys glaring and pointing right at me from just across the street.

I look directly at Abid and he looks right back at me.

The whole world freezes except for the two of us.

Everything feels cold.

Everything feels damp.

In that very moment, completely caught off-guard, I've no doubt that the expression on my face confirms to all of them the awful truth. They are staring across the street at the guy who has killed three of their closest friends and was now coming after them too…

It all happens so quickly that I'm literally paralysed with fear for what seems like the longest single moment of my entire life. I'm a rabbit caught in headlights. Frozen. My mind is dissolving and my body is now doing its own thing. I feel myself gasping for air and I look down and see my hands shaking as they reach up to my throat. It's the reaction that confirms I've lost everything and my sudden glance toward the bicycle I've just parked up is enough to encourage these guys to scream out and begin their pursuit.

"Oi!" bellows out across the busy street. It's a violent exclamation and without a doubt, I am Fucked. "Get back here you fuckin' cunt!"

Basics instincts kick in. Adrenaline finally rushes through my bloodstream.

Fight or flight.

Fight? Or flight?

No. Only flight.

The bike is out of the question, I don't have time to fetch it.

Run, Felix.

Run for your fucking life.

Abid

The boys and I are cruising to this fuckin' family thing that Mohammed's uncle organised we've got to show our faces at. But we ain't stupid, we're armed up.

I've got a pistol tucked in my belt, and the boys all have blades on 'em. We ready for any mother fucker. And we'll keep rolling like this from now until we find whoever cunts have been killin' our boys. We ain't bitches.

I can tell Hani is a bit fuckin' scared and I know I've always given him a hard time, being the little bitch brother of our crew, but he's aight. He's earned his stripes, man. I probably should cut him some slack. "Hani," I say, looking in the rear-view mirror, "you been doing good, bruv. Steppin' up and shit." I don't really know what else to say. I say nothing else.

It seems to do the trick anyway. He smiles at me. I haven't seen him smile in a long time. We're cool.

The boys and I ride in mostly silence, listening to a bunch of rap tunes as we cruise through some pretty heavy traffic towards the event. I know what we are all thinking, this isn't how it's supposed to be. This isn't what we got into this game for. We're here to make some money, and do our thing bro. No one was supposed to get killed. Not like this anyway. Not like this. It wasn't supposed to be like this.

Staring at the red light as I wait for it to change to orange at an intersection, I have to admit, we all knew what we were getting into. This is not a game for boys, this is for men. And the risks were always there, we all know them. We all play this fuckin game, bruv.

Once we arrive I park my car and we all sit there for a bit. *50 Cent, Straight to the Bank* plays on.

"No one else is going to die," I say aloud.

No one responds, but I don't expect them to. I just want them to know.

We all get out and begin making our way towards the hall, as expected I spot about five or six people I recognise already, mostly friends of my parents and they nod at me as we walk past.

The mood is jovial, I suspect that only some of the people here actually know that Kamal, Izzat and Ali have been killed. And even those who know, probably wouldn't say anything to us anyway.

As we make our way towards the entrance, I get the sudden feeling that I'm being watched. You know that feeling, that really freaky feeling. Like, when you know that some unexpected eyes are on you, but you know that there's no way you could know that in any conventional sense. You can't see it, but you can *feel* it. Like a sudden cold breeze. Well, right now, I feel it and I know something's up.

The hair stands up on the back of my neck and instinctively I turn and look across the road and in a moment of total clarity I am faced with the fact that I know everything and I yet I know nothing, all at once.

A rush of connections are made in my brain between all the various bits and pieces, scraps, really, of information. In that one moment, my mind realises that I'm suddenly staring right into the face of the man who has killed three of my best friends and caused huge damage to my crew and my operations.

I know this is true but I don't know how exactly. All I can say is the stare in this gothic-looking white boy's scary fuckin' eyes tell me he wants me dead and that he is not here for anything else other than *me*.

Other things begin to make more sense - why we couldn't find an obvious gang or group of fuckers who were attacking us - why we were lost like sheep to a wolf in the night.

This was no street warfare.

No gang trying to muscle in on our turf.

No, we exhausted all possibilities we thought were reasonable. And we were *wrong*.

My mind races and plays out all kinds of scenarios in short order.

It was one fuckin' cunt all along.

Who the fuck is this guy? Some dude hired by someone? Nah, fuck that, bruv, no one we fuck with gonna hire a hitman. No way. He's gotta be part of someone's crew.

He's a fuckin' white boy and the only crew with white boys I know is the Blackwater Boys and they ain't got no fuckin' beef with us. They got their turf out west and we got ours. Those fuckers ain't got no fuckin' balls either so it for sure ain't them.

So, either this little fucker is with the Polish or, fuck - with the Russians - and if that's the case, this is way more serious than I thought.

But, no time for wondering who in the fuck this little cunt is. I need to get hold of him.

The boys notice I've stopped after a few more steps and they turn back to look at me and then quickly follow my gaze across the street. Out of the corner of my eye I see Mo turn to me and I hear him start to ask me something but I can't focus on anything right now except the surge of anger I boiling inside of me, bursting up in a tidal wave of hatred so quickly I almost feel as though I'm going to vomit rage all over place.

"FUCKING CUNT!" I hear someone yell. I think it's me, but I'm not certain. It doesn't matter anyway.

A car drives past in the street between us and snaps us and the little fucker and I out of our staring competition.

I feel myself moving forwards and the boys moving behind me. I reach for the pistol in my belt but I realise I can't take it out here - too many witnesses - including my mum, who is already here since this afternoon. No, I gotta be clever. This fuckin cunt is outnumbered anyway...

The boys ain't stupid and they keep their blades in their pockets too. At least for now.

The little white shit makes a break for it.

I can see the panic in his eyes as he hesitates for a moment before he gets his shit together and sprints off.

The boys and I rush across the street and a car angrily sounds its horn at us as it slams on its brakes. I don't even bother to look over at the driver. I'm on a mission.

This little cunt is fuckin' quick, I'll give him that. He dashes off like a lightning bolt. Quick, yes... But, so is Hani, who blazes past me and the boys and makes fuckin' good gains on the shithead up the street in front of us.

"This is the fucker, bruv," I hear someone say.

"He's fuckin' dead, bruv," I reply as we run.

I see the little cunt turn a corner and we lose sight of him for a moment, Hani is less than five seconds behind him though.

Five seconds, sure, but it's enough...

As the rest of us turn the corner we come across a shitty little park and I see Hani walking around in a circle scanning the bushes all around and the crowd of people making their way in and out of the park.

"Fuck, fuck," he shouts. Mothers with their children nearby glare at him for his language.

We jog up to him and he apologies to me for losing the guy.

Fuck. He can't have gotten far.

We split up. We comb the fuckin' place.

The trail goes cold as the sun goes down and we regroup near the park's northern entrance.

The little fucking cunt has escaped.

We don't return to the party, it doesn't matter anymore.

We now know who the fuck we are dealing with, at the very least. This is giant leap forward.

"Find out who the fuck this guy is. Immediately," I tell Mohammed and the boys.

For the first time in weeks I feel a long-forgotten sense of calm and safety. It may just be some fuckin' little white boy shit who runs like a fuckin' bitch, I tell myself. A little fuckin' white boy who got lucky.

For the first time in weeks, I sleep a proper sleep, drifting off as I fantasise about the nasty things I'm going to do to this little cunt when I get hold of him.

Today was a good day after all.

Felix

I can see him between the branches of the oak trees which hang down low around me, Abid the piece of shit mother fucker.

He's got me.

Fucked.

Totally.

Totally fucked.

This is all going wrong.

This isn't what I planned.

This isn't what I planned.

This isn't what I planned.

FUCK!

Doubt sets in. Why the fuck did I think following these cunts to this fuckin mozzie fest would be a smart idea? What the actual fuck was I thinking? I'm a fucking mad man. I must be. No other explanation. Felix, you are fucked. They'll be on you in seconds...

Everything is fucked.

My heart is thundering so hard my whole body vibrates with each horrific beat. Sweat pours out of my skin like the flood gates have just been opened on a salty dam. A river of thick sweat runs down my back. My skin feels as hot as frying pan, encasing and cooking my flesh, boiling my blood. Everything except the scene directly in front of me starts to dim. The field around me becomes overwhelmed with the darkness and fades away...

I'm convinced that clouds have covered the moon, then I blink and the stars are also gone, it's dark as death. I blink again and let out a sigh. It's pitch dark and silent.

The world tilts and I vomit on the grass in front of me, doing my best to muffle the sound with the sleeve of my coat before slumping forward into the mess of sick. A thick black swirl of dark and tornadoes smother my vision...

There is nothing but someone's rapid heartbeat and someone's heavy breathing.

Those words that flight attendant said to me on my way back to London rush back and resound in my mind, "we are going to experience some turbulence."

If only she knew how right she'd be...

13 Ludwig

Qusay

"I'm tellin' you, it's that fuckin' guy! I've seen this fuckin' cunt around loads. I can't think where, but I recognise his fuckin' face. That fuckin' little cock-suckin', cunt! It's him innit... What the fuck!" A huge wad of spit fires out of Abid's mouth as he shouts the last "fuck" and it catches on his chin and just hangs there like the last drop of water which can't seem to escape the faucet. If I mentioned it to him right now, he'd probably fuckin' stab me in the stomach with the machete he's waving around in his hand. He's lost it.

"Bruv, let's think straight," I say. Keeping one eye fixed on that blade and its proximity to my body, especially my vital organs.

"Fuck that'! And fuck you!" The wad of spit finally comes loose and splatters across the wooden floorboards at our feet. "Let's kill that cunt! Fuckin' kill that little CUNT!"

"Shit..." I don't know what to say right now. He's got himself all worked up again.

"You fuckin' said you'd seen some fuckin' cunt following you around a while ago. Reckoned he was just fuckin' faggot, but what did he look like?"

"I said, back when I noticed him, that he looked like an ordinary white boy, in his mid-twenties, smallish guy, not very tall. Probably your height. Black hair."

"Right, and that fits the fuckin' description of this cunt doesn't it?"

I stare back at him. He attempts to gauge my opinion and I make sure my face is blank. Generic. Giving nothing away. I told him about this guy on Tuesday, and he ignored it. But the last thing I want to do is give him an opportunity to blame me...

"Yeah, you said. A fuckin' white boy the same height as you, a little older than us? Wow, you think that narrows it down, bruv? Fuckinell. This fuckin' city is crawling with cunts just like that."

I say nothing and stare down at the glob of spit on the floor.

I'd spotted this cunt like a month ago, following me around Whitechapel, from Sainsbury's all the way to a friend's place in Bethnal Green. Cunt was definitely following me, watching me, but I didn't think too much of it, thought he wanted to mug me off, or probably, wanted to buy some coke or something.

I'd told Abid about it, only because Kamal said some fucker was following him from the gym a few days before that and we thought it was fuckin' weird, but then nothing came of it. The cunt following me had blonde hair, the cunt following Kamal had long brown hair. So fuckin' what? Abid ignored it, and now he's lashing out. Blaming us for not telling him shit we already told him. He only fuckin' cared after Kamal and Izzat and Ali.

Fuck, bruv...

Abid thinks it's a fuckin' conspiracy, but I'm not so sure. We can't be jumping to conclusions and hunting down some fuckin' civilian just on a suspicion. The pigs are watching us all the time. Especially since Kamal was hit. Our business has taken a fuckin' massive hit. We can't hardly fuckin' make a move. Can't deal our shit on the streets and can hardly move product. The pigs probably have us like, bugged or something too. But who knows?

And now this crazy cunt Abid wants to go take out some civilian that he doesn't even know who the fuck he is? No fuckin' way. I mean, it might be him. It might be. But, honestly, do we think that one little white boy has gone about and managed to kill a bunch of our crew? All by himself? No fuckin way, bruv. Impossible.

Abid's fucked off though, that's for sure. He's fixed in one of his temper tantrums, angry at the world and ready to bring it all shattering down around him. No matter what the consequences.

For context, we've never been the closest of friends, Abid and I. Abid's uncle knows my uncle and so Hani and I met him that way. Abid, he's a couple of years older than me and he was already boosting cars, snatching phones and raiding houses well before we met. I was probably just bored more than anything and looking for something to do. Next thing I knew I was right there with him, on the back of a moped, snatching iPhones from Chinese students in Stratford, and it all escalated from there. Hani followed suit and within a short while we were hanging with Abid and the boys.

Abid and I complement each other. Or at least we have for the most part. He has the power and the dominating presence to keep the boys in line. He is also fuckin' smart and he always knows the spots to be in, the places to be where the pigs won't. He has some kind of natural talent for it. We all respect him for that. But I have a better connection with the streets. I keep the guys working together, doing their jobs in unison. I keep them organised and functioning. Abid can be pretty brutal, so I like to think that I'm the one that's able to calm him down, provide some common sense when he loses his shit. Some of the guys we deal with out there, won't deal with Abid, he's too harsh, too stubborn, too much of a loose cannon. So, they only deal with me.

Abid is the leader we need. He is a master politician. He knows when to stab in the back, he knows when to kiss arse, he knows when to build alliances and he knows when to break them. His sense of timing is impeccable. But his sense of drama is his weakness and if anyone's going to react way over the top about anything, it's going to be Abid. Sometimes I can reign him in, sometimes I can't. Always a gamble.

Felix

I'm going to turn off the outside world. Close the curtains and switch off reality. I can't handle it right now. I need to think.

I need the nothingness.

I need the darkness…

Everything was so perfect. Everything was so good. My sweet revenge…

It was all in order. It was all in order and… and now the order is gone.

I've lost control.

I've lost control over the whole situation.

How did this happen?

I feel tears running across my cheeks, warming up against my hot flesh and itching the skin as the salt oozes into my pores. My chest heaves up and down. I know I should be feeling the tearing pain from exhausted lungs within me and the aching muscles in my legs, but I feel nothing of the sort. Not my hands as they run up and down the sides of my legs, not my nails as they frantically scratch at my skin, I feel nothing. Nothing but the warm tears as they ebb.

This is too much to cope with. My head feels like it's made of candyfloss with little pieces of my brain peeling away, oozing out of my ears, floating up, up towards the ceiling and away into dust.

I hear an awful sound start to rise around me. It's low and heavy at first, a hum that becomes a squeal. It rises and wild tones within it become clearer and clearer. The sound hits peak squeal and then it keeps going, flowing on into a nasty scream and then echoing out in a rage-filled moan. Hundreds of voices echo out in a cascading of howling.

I rise up in dread, terrified of the source of this sound, but realising as I do, that the horrific sound is coming from me.

Abid

At 5am this morning my mother was woken with a knock at the front door. Guess who the fuck it was? The fuckin' cops. Yet, again.

Now, these fuckers have been all up in our shit since Kamal was killed and, right, I get it, don't get me wrong, they gotta ask these questions, right? They gotta be like, "who do think did this to your bruv, blah, blah", but we ain't told them nothing and we ain't gonna tell them nothing. So, why the fuck do these cunts keep coming back?

Anyway, my mother got the knock at the door. 5am. Fuckbags. She got nothing to do with this shit, poor old woman. Her English ain't that good. She got cops asking where I am, where my boys are, what she knows about any troubles I've been having with other gangs etc... Man, what the fuck? Like she knows shit.

Anyway, she came to my room a few minutes later and woke me up. I'm fucked off enough at this point that she's waking me so early, right? But then she told me the cops are downstairs in the kitchen and I kicked off. "Don't let these fuckin' cops inside the house. Fuck!"

Now I don't ever swear or yell at my mum, bruv. But, honestly she should know better.

I tugged on some shorts and pulled a hoodie on before walking downstairs behind my mum who was already putting on a cup of tea for the two fuckin' cops standing by the sink writing all kinds of shit down in their fuckin' notebooks and making themselves at home.

Their smug faces grinned at me as I entered the kitchen. One black dude, one white dude. Two mark-brand mother fuckers.

Felix

I decide to risk going back to my flat. I have to. I can't live out here on the run.

I spent the last two nights in a random Airbnb in Camden that I had to book at the last minute. Too scared to go back home in case Abid and his fucks spotted me, in case they've somehow worked out who I am and where I live. Ugh.

Paranoia is paramount.

I know it's unlikely they would've worked it out so quick, but still, I really couldn't face this risk. And to be honest, I still really don't want to take this risk...But I know I have to. I need my things. I need a change of clothes. For fucks sake, I've been wearing the same Calvin Klein underwear, the same socks, the same everything for almost three days now.

Disgusting.

I am filth incarnate.

I've been sleeping nude (nude even when I was pacing up and down the hallway, tense and on the verge of a psychotic break), to preserve my clothes. I must have looked like a complete lunatic.

I only left this flat only twice, just to buy food from the corner shop, and that's it. Ridiculous, I know, but it's taken me two days to build the courage to step outside and head back home East.

Back into the wild, wild, East.

Fuck it, though. If this is how I'm going to die, so be it.

But I'm fucking getting back inside my flat and getting a change of clothes if it is the last fucking thing I do.

Two nights of suffering through vicious cycles of fear and paranoia, replaying the moment I was caught over and over in my head. Considering from every angle how I could have fucked up so badly after all the careful, precise planning. How could I just throw it all away like that? Now I need to sleep in my own bed... even if it's the last sleep I ever have.

I've been amateur. A complete fucking amateur. Months of preparation wasted in a whirlwind of stupidity.

For fucks sake.

I need to regroup myself.

I shouldn't have been so bold to just stand there across the street in the middle of the day watching them. Especially when they were obviously on highest guard. Their mates have just been murdered and they expect they are next. Durr. I was fucking retarded.

Jesus. H. Christ.

First things first, though. Sneak back into my flat. Even though none of them live that close to me, it's still too close for comfort and there are plenty of Muslims in the area who may be on the lookout for me. I just don't know…

Obviously, worst case scenario, Abid and his cunts have worked out where I live already and are staking the place out, waiting for me to show my face.

This is the real fear I have to face. I need my laptop and the files on these fucks. I have to scour everything I have on them and see if I can salvage anything from the remaining plans.

I have to get back on track.

Come on, Felix.

I'm not finished, until I'm finished.

Of course, I wait until dark to make my move.

I put on the *Combichrist* track *This is My Rifle* on repeat, for motivational purposes. Singing, under my breath, the lyric "we are the masters of our enemy, until there is no enemy", over and over again until I convince myself that I actually believe it.

An hour later and I'm nervously exiting a Central Line carriage at Mile End station.

I bought a baseball cap from a souvenir shop on the way. 'London' is embroidered on the front of a white cap in big red lettering.

I've pulled it down as low as I can have it without looking too suspicious. Which, to be honest, is not that far at all at this time of night. The only saving grace is that everyone looks suspect around here.

My nervous half-walk, half-jog to the flat takes place in record time. A group of black and Arab dudes hanging about in the shadows of a council estate carpark spot me, but they don't appear to be too interested and I reach my building entrance I'm wondering if I've even taken a single breath since I left the station.

When I enter my flat I waste no time in barricading the door, pulling the sofa from the middle of the living room into the hallway and jamming it right up against the door which I lock and bolt up, of course.

I pour myself a very strong vodka and tonic and then strip down, out my filthy clothes.

Next, standing naked in the living room, I turn on some music. *Vivaldi, Four Seasons – Spring*. A classic.

The vodka already feels good and I pour another, this time even stronger.

I feel safer here, at home. Despite being closer to danger, this is my turf. At least this little flat is my zone. My territory. I have my weapons here and if I have to make a stand, I could go down in here with one Hell of a fight.

This is a comforting thought.

I finish my second drink as *Spring* finishes and turns into *Summer*.

It's 10:58pm and I need to rest. Seriously. I need some proper sleep. In my own bed. I can wake up tomorrow and sort it all out.

My mind is knackered and my body is in complete zombie mode.

Vodka number three is in my hand as I crawl into bed.

I leave Vivaldi and his seasons playing in the living room on repeat. Fuck it.

I lie there in bed. Nervous and shivering, but calm. Too tired to deal with any more serious thoughts now.

If I had some plant, I would happily smoke the shit out of that right now. Just to get me right off to sleep. But, alas, I'll settle for knocking one out quickly. Grabbing my laptop in a haze I knock a lazy one out to a video of a woman in her fort fisting a young girl who doesn't look older than twenty. Good times. Yet, sad times.

I fall into one of those sleeps where your body doesn't hardly move the entire time. The heavy head, heavy body, comatose sleep.

I dream of watching myself in the back seat of a car speeding along a country road in the middle of the night. Trees outside rushing by. An endless blur of greens and browns and dry yellows. Infinite forest. I'm sitting there in the back, silent. Staring ahead. Expressionless.

The car races along, winding around the empty roads. Forest and the heat of a summer night fading. All seems serene.

Except.

Except, there is no one in the driver seat.

I'm the sole occupant of this car.

Sitting there in the backs seat, cruising around in this car with no driver.

The steering wheel shifts from side to side. Calmly. In tune with the music playing on the stereo just for me. Steering smoothly as though invisible hands hold it. But there's nothing there up front.

Just me. The passenger. Watching everything unfold.

The scene skips. From a birds' eye view I see myself lean back and close my eyes.

So totally relaxed.

The camera moves closer in to focus on my face.

The car windows are open now and the cold night air laps against my cheeks and sends my hair flapping around my ears violently.

Serene.

I look so calm.

Calm like I haven't been in forever.

As the dream ends, the car reaches a city and now from the birds' eye view I can see only the car from a fading distance. It cruises onwards. Driverless, but somehow, getting the passenger all the way to his destination.

Guiding him to places he never expected he would reach.

Is this divine intervention?

Or just a mental health problem?

Felix

Standing on the platform at South Kensington Station, I'm staring at the tracks beside me. Appreciating the rays of the sun as they glisten off the cold steel. It's beautiful.

I appreciate the precision with which these tracks have been laid. The way the steel lays there waiting for the unrelenting weight of the next train to glide gracefully on top of them reminds me of something from childhood that I can't quite define.... Nonetheless, it's a comforting sight. This represents order. It represents longevity and reminds me that long after I'm gone, long after Abid and his fuckin shitty boys are gone, this station and these perfect tracks will remain. Life goes on.

Only hopefully a little bit better for those who come next, due to what I've done. It's all I can hope for. Leave a better world behind...

A cold breeze touches my cheeks and the sun disappears behind the clouds. The beauty of the train tracks isn't lost at all, if anything it's made more dramatic.

I feel myself sighing out my nostrils and the music I'm listening to becomes a nuisance. I can't even hear the rhythm any longer it's become nothing more than loud screaming in my ears. This happens from time to time. Music, as much as it defines me, as much as it drives my mood and my energy, sometimes gets in the way of moments of just Felix, and the world around him. Felix, and nature. Felix, and his life in London.

I take my earphones out and stuff them into my pocket.

The platform is almost completely quiet.

The world is quiet.

The beauty of the whole scene is paramount. The wind picks up leaves from a tree nearby are blown across the platform past me and onto the tracks below.

Two humans are standing further down the platform behind me, staring down at their phones, but I'm otherwise all alone.

I stare at these newly blown leaves on the track as they rustle along between the sleepers and the steel. In the moment of bliss, a sudden urge, no, a temptation surfaces. The temptation to put an end to the eternal struggle. To just... sleep the final sleep. The Forever Sleep.

The serenity of the moment is swiftly disrupted as the rumbles and screeches of an approaching train sound out. But this is perfect, the heavy, aggressive train bearing down only adding to the totality of the drama. The sun flashes out from behind the clouds once more and I catch a glimpse of the sun shining off the train's cold steel. Glorious.

I close my eyes for a short moment and in that moment I rehearse a possible end. I rehearse the graceful movement I could make as I lay my body to rest and lay my soul down to sleep.

I stare at those beautiful tracks, at the exact spot I could fall into the Forever Sleep.

The tracks look so inviting. The end would be so swift. I lean in, eager. It's bliss...

The train approaches. Loud and masculine. Heavy and unforgiving.

The moment approaches and nothing else matters.

I stare on. The train is nothing but a growing blur in the corner of my eye.

I stare on at that sweet, sweet spot.

Staring into a coldness, so inviting...

They'll be coming for me, for sure. But, worse, they'll also be waiting for me to try and strike them again. Like a farmer lying in wait for the wolf to try and take another lamb.

Death's scythe is now sharpened and ready. I feel it poised above me. As if Death himself is shadowing me in everything I do, everywhere I go...

The moment fades. The train rushes past me, the brakes screeching as the driver hits them. A blur of carriages pass over top of the sweet, sweet spot.

Lucifer closes the gate again. He isn't ready for me yet.

I board the train, put my earphones back in and let the music feed me once again.

The time will come.

But that time is not right now.

Not yet

....

Roaming about later that day I stop and stare across the Thames back towards the CBD. Tall buildings stand out like weeds poking up from a garden. Sunlight shines bright from these glass behemoths and they sparkle. I don't know how many people live in this city, but finding me amongst them all would be a challenge for the entire police force, let alone for a group of stupid east London street thugs. I tell this to myself over and over until I start to believe it's true.

A small plane flies overhead, its engine battering the air and rumbling away. I finish my can of sugar-free Red Bull and toss it into the trash can beside the bench I've been sitting on. If only I could get a vantage point like the pilot must have, to be able to see the situation from afar. To once again find these thugs and watch them now, without them watching me. It was easy before, they had no idea I was watching, following, preparing, but now, they'll be wary of anyone who gets too close.

I panic as I hear a police siren from across the water, but it's coming from somewhere in the City. Not after me. I sigh and stretch my legs out.

Come on, Felix. Be confident.

I can't give up now. I either finish this, or I die trying. It's as simple as that. Fuck it. I've come this far. Those sweet train tracks aren't going anywhere.

The Forever Sleep is always beckoning...

It's 5:15pm and the sun is already beginning to set. I stand up and take a deep breath. The small plane overhead circles back around and rumbles past again. Write a report on your own insanity, Felix. Imagine doing that. Where would you even begin? Are you crazy? Are you talking to yourself right now? Which Felix is in control? Felix 1, Felix 2, Felix 'n'... ?

No. there is only one. It's not as simple as that.

You are not crazy.

You are a watcher, a planner, a hunter.

Soon you will strike the lambs again.

Jess

The History Channel is playing in the background. German soldiers are marching in perfect formation in front of a saluting Fuhrer. The volume is turned down to the point where any sounds from the TV are just a dull noise emanating from the corner of the room. No one knows why this is playing in the background, who turned the TV on or even how long it's been playing for.

How long have I been sitting here?

I look around over and Lynndie and Helen who sit around the table with me for a reply, but when I'm met with a blank stare from Helen and, well Lynndie looks like she's comatose and couldn't reply if she wanted to, I wonder if I actually spoke that question out loud or whether I just thought I did.

Moments later it doesn't matter anymore as I've completely forgotten what I was thinking about and am now totally engrossed in the belief that the laces on one of my boots has been tied on tighter than the other boot. And I wonder why it has taken me all day, all night, Hell, my whole life, to realise this?

But then, is it real?

I have no idea.

But the more I think of it, the more certain I'm going to be that my right boot is tighter than the other. The impulse to reach down and re-tie both sets of laces is strong. Only the drugs pulsing through my system are rendering my body slow and useless enough to stop me from doing so.

I light another cigarette and blow the smoke across the table. Helen racks up a line of Ket and snorts it before handing me the plate and the baggie.

"You okay?" someone asks me.

"Yep, all good."

"Huh?" Helen looks at me, expectantly. And now I'm wondering, wait, was it me that asked "you okay?" and I just fucking replied to myself? Who said what just now? I have no clue.

"Nothing," I reply. Just in case.

I snort another line of Ket and realise that my cigarette has now already burned itself out before I've even smoked any of it. The fingernail on my index finger is completely stained yellow from cigarettes and no matter how much I wash is, the stain doesn't come off. Like the fucking smoke has permeated into my cells. I look at it and it looks horrible. All I can think is that every non-smoker out there sees that finger when I'm out and about and judges the fuck out of me for it. I tell myself that I'm not the sort of person that cares, but let's be honest, no matter how much we pretend, no matter how much we try to convince ourselves that we don't care what other people think, we can't get away from it. Of course, we care. Of course, we're programmed to be self-conscious.

This sesh we're in the midst of started out of nothing. As the best ones usually do, I suppose. Lynndie lives with me here and Helen lives in Vauxhall with some of her friends. I mean, we all have class tomorrow, my first class is at 10am, no idea about the other girls, but I know they both need to be *somewhere* at *some point* tomorrow.

Anyway, Helen and I were out doing some shopping today and decided to come back to mine for a drink. Of course, Lynndie came home and joined in. Just happened to be that Lynndie had a couple of grams of Ket. Wednesday night, why not get on it?

So, god only knows how long ago we started on it, but realistically by now it's probably well after midnight.

I never used to be this... reckless? Is that the right word? Nor did Helen, she's sweet, but she just follows others, she is like a puppy, as terrible as that sounds. I love her to pieces, but I know that whatever I suggest, or whatever Lynndie suggests, Helen will agree. Whatever party, whatever location, whatever position etc...

Anyway, the Ket is setting in real good and I don't give a fuck about this chain of thought anymore.

Anyway, I wasn't always like this. Not until... well. Not until...

I sigh and lean into the goodness.

I take another cigarette from a packet on the table, no idea who's packet this is. Lynndie mumbles something in her spaced-out half-sleep state and I proceed to stand up. No idea why, it just seems like what I should do right now. This Ket is fucking great.

The Schutzstaffel march on and on behind a hunched over Lynndie and the scene cuts to footage of Germans shooting prisoners in front of a ditch already loaded with corpses and it's kind of surreal to think all this happened like, what, seventy years ago? I mean, this is what our grandparents were doing. My grandfather was a solider in the British army, okay he probably didn't do anything like this, but Helen's grandfather was in the German Army. And I know for a fact that he was a member of the 707th Infantry Division. Look them up. They were notorious...

I mean. Fuck. That is her fathers' father. And my mother's father, he was fighting against him. Like, to the death. To the end of everything. And now we all just carry on. Here is life. Here we are, 2011. Fuck it.

Anyway, this Ket is fucking great.

For some reason the anxiety that comes with drugs always hits me way quicker than most people. Like, with snow, for example, some people get that real bad come down, the real, low-low, a day or so later, where the suicidal thoughts and the depression begin to overwhelm. This is normal.

For me it always hits really quick. For example, I can do a few lines of snow and be happy as fuck. Supergirl as fuck. But within an hour or so, the anxiety will hit me. While I'm still high. Which, could be a blessing, I suppose? But I don't want that. I never get it days later. I always get it hours later.

Anyway, since... the incident. I've taken to the downers quite a bit though. I haven't been properly 'snowboarding' since last year. Now it's all about the alcohol, the weed, the Ket, the anti-depressants and the lovely painkillers. It's all about taking the rough edge off of life.

I wasn't always like this.

I look at Lynndie with her pretty head rolled back, now snoring away in the chair across from me. She's such a smart girl. Honestly, she 'gets it' if you know what I mean. But she's never had anyone to encourage her. Never had anyone to spur her on. And so, she became very average in terms of grades etc... never expecting enough out of life to motivate her to do become her best self.

She's clever, but she's also constantly seeking validation and attention from boys. And boys, the mother fuckers that they are, can smell this like a shark smells blood in the water.

And so, they take advantage. And so, her situation worsens.

I don't need to go into detail, you all know what I mean.

I love her to bits, she's like the sister I ever had and so I would do anything for her. But what this mostly means is just supporting the decisions she makes, no matter how much I agree or disagree with them.

We've known each other since high school and been through it all together. As a teenage girl, you have so many insecurities, so many worries, so much to consider. Does this makeup match my skin tone, or do I look like a big orange Oompa Loompa? Do I fit into this dress or do I have a muffin-top going on? Have I shaved my legs properly? What if I missed a patch? Even beyond that, what if my pussy tastes like dead fish? What happens if I go home with a guy and he's going down on me and he stops and looks at me and says "damn, you taste like rotten fish, what's wrong with you?" Christ almighty. That would kill me.

I envy men in many ways. They can literally do what they want, with basically no expectations or pressure, but us girls, we have to be perfect.

I light another cigarette and Helen also lights one. As she does, she moves herself over onto the sofa to lie down. Lynndie snores on... completely fucked.

I manage to get my body moving to find the remote and change the TV from this Nazi shite to something else. I settle on just a radio show, anything with some fucking music.

The Ket and all the alcohol take over. I feel lonely.

I am sad.

I am a sad girl.

I am a sad little girl.

The all-time sadness has found me yet again. I haven't been able to shake it for years. It is always lurking.

Tomorrow I need to hand in a report for university that I have spent the last two weeks writing. In my current Ket-brain state, I feel like every word I have written is complete shite and everything I've wrote is just a sad plagiarism of everyone else who came before me. But then, the alcohol tells me, 'who cares? So is everything. Nothing is unique. Everything is a reiteration of something else.'

I just want to finish this stupid degree and become a proper adult.

Helen is now asleep on the sofa and I light another cigarette. Lynndie has abandoned the world outside for her dreamland.

I get up and have a quick tactical vomit into my kitchen sink for good measure and then amble on down the hallway to my bed, cigarette in hand.

As I climb my drunken and drugged-up self into bed I wonder, stubbing the cigarette out into an empty coffee mug from yesterday, 'what the fuck am I supposed to be doing with my life?' Tommy was killed and I'm expected to just carry on? My brother gets murdered and they get away with it?

I pick up my drug box next to my bed and proceed roll myself a joint to get me to sleep.

Is this what life is supposed to be?

Felix

"Be cunning, and full of tricks, and your people will never be destroyed."

That is exactly how I feel right now. Thanks, Lord Frith, thanks, Richard Adams. I couldn't have put it better myself. Childhood memories come rushing back. Times of peace. Times of carefree play. I let out a long sigh and light a cigarette. Times long gone.

I cannot allow this to be my defeat. I mustn't give in and allow a simple detour from my plans to grind me to a halt. No, Felix. No. Think back to therapy. What did Dr Franks tell me? "Everything doesn't need to be perfect, there is no such thing as perfect. Perfection is a relative thing."

"Felix, you can rise above this. You are stronger than the situation you are faced with." I whisper to myself.

I let out a sigh through flared nostrils and press my fingers hard against my temples, trying my best to kill the pounding headache doing its best to drum my brain into a paste.

My fingers have gone white by the time I release them. My hands still look lifeless and aged. I do not feel at all like myself. I am truly losing it.

What do I do now?

Something stirs in from somewhere deep, driven by an instinctual drive to survive. I haven't eaten since yesterday, well over twenty-four hours now. I really should get up off this couch. I should rise up and regain my strength. I know it's the right thing to do.

But part of me can't.

That voice...

I failed.

I was so close and I was so foolish.

You'll never get to Abid now.

You are nothing Felix.

You have let your friends down.

Abid and his empire go on.

Your work has been nothing but a slap in the face to him. What a waste. You should be ashamed of yourself.

Thoughts of waste and hopelessness cascade over me. I pull the blanket back over my head.

I wake up some time later in a cold sweat, the blanket is strewn across the coffee table and the cream-coloured candles which usually sit on top have been knocked over on the floor to my right. My face feels sticky and my tongue dry. The only part of my body with any energy appears to be my eyes which dart around the room soaking in the scene and doing their best to help my brain recall how I came to be here.

For the first time in days I feel absolutely nothing. No pain. No sadness. No hopelessness. No joy. Just… regular. Nothing. Like a sheet of blank A4 paper. A clean slate. Without emotions. Just like a regular Londoner. I feel nothing.

What I do from here on is my choice.

I am in charge. This is where I begin again.

And, I want music. I *need* music.

I muster enough strength in my depleted muscles to reach to the table at my side and lift the stereo remote control. Rachmaninov is what I want, *Prelude op. 23 no. 5*. Bliss…

It's time to get my shit together.

I take a deep breath. I have two options and two only.

Option 1, I quit now. Call it a job half done, but a message sent nonetheless, and I leave it. Walk away. Get on with my life. Let Abid live and say fate decided it would be that way.

Option 2, I revise my plan and carry on. I've come this far. There's work I've left incomplete. Embrace the fact that nothing, absolutely nothing is over, until it is truly over.

Go out with a bang, Felix. Abid is still alive. And so are you. The game is not yet over.

"Felix," I say aloud, "do this. Finish it. You're still in charge here. You still have the upper hand. They don't know who you are or where you are or where you will strike next. You are still calling the shots."

I have to finish this. One way or another. I need to carry on. There are four names left on my list and all four of them will be taken down. My planning was not perfect. But perfection is a relative thing. I can be *perfectly* adaptable.

With renewed strength, I rise to my feet, my muscles aching and bones creaking from inactivity. I must've been lying on this couch wallowing in my own self-pity for over thirty-six hours now. Jesus. My head feels light on my shoulders and slowly the blood flows back to my hands and feet, bringing the rest of my body back to life. Rachmaninov plays on. I feel my heart pounding rhythmically. It's time to walk this off and get my head back in the game.

An hour later and without a clear sense of direction I march ahead. The menacing sounds of cars racing past on the damp asphalt the only distinguishable noise over the roar of the wind raging at me from the Thames. My footsteps are easily drowned out by the crashing waves and howling breeze.

Walking along the Thames path, on the north side of the river, appreciating the fuck out of my packet of cigarettes, I wonder how, throughout my life I've always seemed to envision an absolute masterpiece, but somehow it always swiftly materialised as a complete disaster. Am I doomed to fall short? Always? Over and over?

Moonlight shimmers on the water's surface, the light competing with that radiating out from a new apartment block somewhere further up along the water's edge. For a moment I think I see two people standing on the roof of the flat, staring down, directly at me, but my eyes must be playing tricks on me again.

I stop walking and stamp out my cigarette on the ground. Right. How could this go so wrong? I'd planned everything so well. Down to the last detail. Or so I thought... Jesus. If I got this one wrong, what else did I miss with Kamal, Izzat and Ali? Fuck. Fuck. Fuck. But I can't dwell on that. I need to progress. I need another way in. And I think I have it.

There is one blind spot in Abid's whole fucking structure. One thing he wouldn't expect at all and I've now exposed it. He'll be looking for me, for sure, of course. I'm a dead man walking, you might say. But, knowing the narrowminded nature of this shit head, I'm quite certain his guard will be completely down in regards to anyone else. To anyone else who is not me...

He'll be rejoicing and relieved that the people coming after him is not people at all but a lone person. Not a rival gang, or some other group, he'll now just be looking for one lone white boy. And that is what will bring him down.

I feel a renewed sense of energy and purpose. I feel something akin to hope.

I have a plan.

Oh yes, friends. I mean to find a partner. Someone with just as much hatred of these cunts as I have.

As for my original plan, I've lost the battle. Toss those plans out the window. I've been uncovered. I'm burnt. I'm done for. No disguise will be good enough now that they've spotted me, chased me down.

The only way forward is to take a massive risk and bring someone else into my plan.

It's a hugely risky move. By reaching out, it may mean I'm either basically handing myself into the police right away, or just as bad, brought down by that person's incompetence in the face of Abid and his boys, or any number of possibilities in between. But I have no choice. Time is of the essence and doing nothing, stopping now, is simply not an option.

I hear a sirens approaching me. I panic, ducking down behind a rubbish bin nearby. The siren wails out and draws nearer. Doubt washes back over me for a moment, as if in a hail mary attempt to bring me down the universe is throwing the kitchen sink at me. All sorts of odd thoughts flash through my brain as I huddle there. Visions rotate and change as though I'm looking through a View Master on LSD. A voice booms in my head and screams out with each turn of the View Master reel…

The Devil is a woman and I want to fuck her!

One man's manipulation is another man's teaching!

Incipient disaster!

Incipient disaster!

Let the lunatics out of the asylum for the day so they can roam about and terrorise the regular humans!

I want to see this through to the end!

I need to see this through to the end!

Incipient disaster!

Cats paws in makeup…

"What the fuck?" I hear myself mutter.

As the voice dies down, I hear myself repeating ominous words, "I'm finished…"

The siren wails its loudest, it's seconds away, then I see it and relief washes over me, a fire truck rushes by, the siren piercing my ears and in moments it's gone up around the corner. I sink back to the ground and take a deep breath. Control yourself, Felix. For fucks sake. For. Fucks. Sake. For the sake of fuck itself, control yourself.

I lay there for a moment. Weak. But planning.

I need an ally or at least an assistant, I don't care which, but I need to find them soon.

I know I can carry on. I know I can go back to the drawing board and work out a new plan. But I need to think this through now.

My mind is racing and my head is frantic with thoughts. Nothing seems to make sense right now. Every possibility I turn to seems impossible. So unattainable. It's overwhelming.

This is the problem. I had everything worked out. Every little facet thought through and every action carefully calculated. Yet, it all crumbled. In one fell swoop, the most well-structured and exact plan of my life was rendered impotent. Useless. Hopeless.

The three executions already carried out are pointless without completing the rest. Abid must die. This is all that matters. If I fail to kill Qusay, Hani and Mohammed, then so be it. But, Abid... Abid. Must. Die.

A lorry passes me at a considerable speed, the sound of it rumbling by snapping me back to the present. My surroundings rush back. A spray of water rises up from the wheels of the truck as it races along. I'm no longer along the waterfront, but standing near a large office building with only a smattering of lights in windows showing any signs of life. I've been walking without realising where I was going. The park behind this building has a path which leads directly to The Tank, a bar where Tommy and I used to snort meth and listen to electronic dance music back during University days. I pause for a moment and toy with the cigarette lighter in the pocket of my trench coat, this seems to have become some kind of compulsive thing for me.

The howling wind rushes past me again, biting at my ears and pulling at my hair. I let it bite and I let it pull.

No more hopelessness. It's not over yet. I either execute Abid, or I die trying. No. Grey. Zones.

Come on Felix, harden yourself the fuck up.

I know what to do. I have one option. She is my only hope.

Atop an overbearing government building the Union Jack flies high above and flaps in the wind violently.

With a clear sense of direction, I press ahead.

Mohammed

Qusay, goatee freshly trimmed, the light from the ceiling lamps overhead highlighting his impressive attention to detail. He probably spent an hour this morning in front of the mirror. Fucker. I know what Abid would say. Abid would say "you have better things to do with your time." He grins up at me from the seat he's taken at my dining table, a sly fucking grin, like a fat cat who just ate all the other cat's bowls of cream as well as his own. I wish I could wipe that fuckin' grin off his face… But, for a number of reasons, I don't. And, so, I have to deal with this shithead another way.

"Well, Mo boy, what's going on?"

'Mo boy?' This cunt thinks he can call me 'Mo boy' all of a sudden?

I bite my lip and breathe out through flared nostrils, moving to grab the back of the leather chair closest to me, leaning over it and staring at the floor. *Don't say anything, Mohammed.* Qusay's a good guy to be honest. Loyal. Hardworking. Easy to talk to. Smart. He'll do well if he just starts giving a flying fuck and paying the proper respect.

"Abid's going to be fuckin' furious," I say, mostly to myself.

"What am I going to tell him?"

"Well, if you know what's good for you, it won't be the truth."

"Fuck…"

"Yep, 'Fuck'. If Abid finds out we've had no fuckin' progress at all, he'll lose his fuckin' shit, bruv," I add.

"Why don't we tell him we're looking into it and we think we know what borough that fuckin' guy lives? You know, like, stall him?"

"You're a fucking idiot."

I laugh to myself for a minute, remembering one of Abid's famous remarks, he said something like, "there's no real fuckin' hope in this business anymore. No point in expecting intelligent behaviour with new boys you bring on board. All you can hope for is to get a bunch of lesser idiots around you each time."

Qusay sees me chuckle and the confusion on his face is paramount, especially when I quickly stop my smile and return it to a glare I direct right back at him.

"I need to make a phone call," Qusay half-asks, half-informs me.

"How long will you be?" I ask him.

"Not long"

"Not long? That doesn't exactly tell me how long..."

"Sure it does. It tells you I won't be long"

Fuckin' douche-bag.

"Alright fine. Just be quick, we aren't finished here. Arsehole."

"Fuck you."

"Uh huh."

Qusay disappears outside into the garden for close to ten minutes and while he's out there I sit and think through all this bullshit which is going on. All joking aside, this is some serious shit and we really need to get control of the situation before it spirals out of control.

I look out the kitchen window to the street outside, the sun is shining bright and the sky is clear of clouds. Some old couple are walking their dog, a

Doberman, along the footpath nearby and cyclists in full sports gear race past along the street. Music is playing from a neighbour's house nearby, something upbeat, but I can't quite make out what it is. The scene is peaceful. Idyllic. The way things should be.

But very different from the way things are right now…

As Qusay enters the house again, as I look at him and see nothing but stupidity and laziness. I get fired up, "listen you cunt, you know how this works, I'm the bigger dog here, and the bigger dog will always, until the end of time, tell the littler dog what to do. And I am telling you right now, to go and find out who the fuck is responsible for these murders. Someone out there knows something. Alright? Just go out there and get it fucking done. If you have to stand on a few toes to do it, then fucking stomp on them as hard as you can. You have a free pass from me."

"Right, boss," I'm on it, he replies, patronisingly.

"Don't…," I stare him right in the eye as I say this, "fuck this up, bruv… Do not fuck this up."

14 Niccolo

Felix

The clouds that have amassed in the sky looming overhead are thick and dark. Evil-looking twins of their happy, white, fluffy counterparts.

A heavy silence envelopes everything.

Thunder and all manner of drama is moments away. I can feel it. The tension is heavy.

Seconds later I almost shit myself as a fog horn starts sounding out repeatedly from a few blocks over and when I look around to see where the noise might be coming from, I notice that the streets all around me are suddenly empty. It's like something out of a horror film. All the humans have suddenly disappeared. Only it's the middle of the day, in the middle of London and the sun up there above us still shines behinds those clouds. I'm not dreaming.

The fog horn carries on and sounds out in short bursts. I continue to look around. A plastic shopping bag blows in the breeze a few metres ahead and then rises up to billow around erratically above me. There's not a soul in sight. The clouds cover the entire sky and thunder booms in the distance.

Then, just as suddenly as it began, the horn I mentioned stops sounding out.

I never get the chance to determine what the fuck it is that's fucking happening, as my attention is drawn to two groups of people I suddenly spot walking towards me. One along the path from behind and another has suddenly appeared across the street to my right. They are children with their parents and a group of tourists... Calmly strolling along as though they had been there all along. But they hadn't... They weren't anywhere to be seen just seconds ago... Creepy. Fucking creepy...

I keep moving. The scene swiftly returns to normality and there are now humans all around. I have no idea what to make of this, but I have to carry on.

The path from Baron's Court Station to Margravine Cemetery is busy as Hell this evening. People bump into me carelessly and my tolerance level for rudeness evaporates rather quickly, so I speed up to get through to cemetery before I lose it and end up hitting someone.

Earlier this afternoon I bought a gram of snow and spent the next half hour racking up thin little lines and snorting them with the tube part of a dismantled Parker pen while mentally rehearsing how I intend to convince Tommy's younger sister, Jessica, to help me get revenge on behalf of her brother.

It's a fucking long shot and to be honest, speaking to this girl could ruin it all.

It's already ruined, you useless fuck.

If she freaks out and goes to the police, I am fucked.

You're already fucked.

This is my only choice though. There isn't a single other person in this whole fucking city who would even consider helping me right now. Unless I was paying some fucking random gangsters to do my dirty work for me, I suppose. But

I don't have the money for that. Or the trust in anyone except myself... And now, possibly, hopefully, Jessica.

I know she attends Imperial College London, at the Charing Cross Hospital Campus and thanks to her posting a picture on Facebook about an hour ago I know she was in the cemetery with some friends studying. So, unless she's already gone, she must be around somewhere right now. Today is the day. I can only hope I don't miss her.

Sounds risky? Sounds desperate? Sure does... But something about Jessica tells me that at the very least she won't go to the police. No, at the very least she'll appreciate and understand what I've done.

Jess

The room is filled with hundreds of miniature neon-coloured elephants.

The bastards are fucking tiny, the size of rats and they're running all about the place. It's fucking mad. It's a miniature neon-swirled stampede in every direction.

I've been yelling at them to shoo, but they aren't listening, they obviously don't speak human, and when I realised this, I tried trumpeting out aloud in elephant-tongue at the fuckers, but that didn't work either. Rude little shits. They just keep running around, crashing into each other, bouncing off the walls and furniture.

So, I've taken to crushing them.

I started stomping on them with my bare feet and feeling the tiny monsters' squish between my toes in big bursts of neon juice is extremely pleasurable. I've crushed almost twenty of them so far, and I'm still stomping my way across the room.

I get a sudden rush of euphoria and pause for a moment. I notice something happening on the floor beside the sofa and I turn around and see the pools of neon juice melting together, rising up in a giant blob that keeps rising and rising. I stare on in awe as the blob begins morphing itself into shape. The blog begins morphing itself into a scantily-clad nine-year-old hooker.

"She's nine years old and look how she's dressed," I hear myself say to the remaining miniature elephants as they rampage around the living room floor at my feet.

I'm not sure how long I've been in this room or how long it has been since this tiny hooker arrived, but this concept is short-lived as my vision begins to blur again. The room is soon nothing more than a whirlwind of purple and orange and green and pink and yellow and blue.

It's out of control, but it's a happy place, and the nine-year-old hooker tells me she's giving up her trade and going back to school. I start to congratulate her on the decision, but the words don't make it out of my mouth and suddenly she's tiny, smaller even than the elephants and she rides off towards the hallway on the back of a fat bright-orange elephant with huge white tusks. They fade away, becoming smaller and smaller and more and more faint, eventually there is only a fog where they once were.

The remaining elephants start gathering in a line, side by side, along the edge of my sofa like pigeons on power line after you shoo them away. The orange ones begin to evaporate and disappear entirely. The purple ones all start expanding like balloons and I'm certain they're going to burst all over the place.

Jesus, I need to stop this.

I reach down and grab two miniature elephants in each fist and squeeze as hard as I can. They burst and neon purple elephant blood spurts out between my fingers. *Gross.* I wipe the purple goo on the back of my jeans and take a deep breath. I shout at the top of my lungs, "fuck off! Go on, go on, go on!"

Everything spins around me in a vicious tornado and suddenly all the little elephants are gone and the room is empty again. A deathly quiet fills the air. I feel strangely warm inside. Content. The madness is over and I feel as though I've saved the world again.

Jess, you are amazing.

I wonder if I'm now back to reality, looking around the room and scanning for signs of the extraordinary. Everything seems to be relatively normal. Ah yes, everything except the fact that the sofa has become a giant fruit bowl and the cushions are giant apples and giant pears. It looks so inviting though. I climb inside the fruit bowl and nestle my head underneath one of the oversized granny smiths.

A few hours later I wake up sitting on the toilet bowl. Once again trying to piece together my life in what is a regular, daily, sometimes bi-daily, emotional breakdown.

Ever since Tommy was killed, I've just... struggled.

I look at my watch and see that it's 10:15pm.

I sigh, get up and light a cigarette while I stare at my poor self in the mirror.

I spent half an hour yesterday arguing with the staff at Burger King over the lack of mayonnaise on my Whopper. I specifically asked for a double serve of mayonnaise and the burger had barely a spit of mayonnaise (or cum, or actual spit? or whatever they actually put in there) inside. Then when I decided I didn't want a Whopper any longer, I ordered a Triple Stack and the fucking child behind the counter told me they no longer served the Triple Stack, that it was a special, limited offer. For fucks sake. However, this greasy-faced boy told me, I could order a BBQ Bacon Double Cheeseburger with an extra slice of meat and cheese though, which is the exact same thing. And then when I agreed that this alternative was appropriate, the pimply-faced mother fucker behind the counter turned around and yelled out to the cooks in the back "Triple Stack!"

For. Fucks. Sake.

Seriously. Welcome to my life.

Why I'm remembering this right now amidst the receding haze of shroom-brain, I have no idea. My makeup is completely fucked. Bits of mascara all over my cheeks and nose, eyeliner smudged into my eyebrows and I'm not even sure how I've managed that.

Jess, get yourself together. Look at yourself. No wonder you're single.

I'm hungry as fuck and all I have to eat in the flat is a can of sliced peaches from like, Christmas three years ago. I haven't been to the supermarket in weeks.

If I could be bothered going out, I'd get some takeaways, but, I can't be bothered. And since I don't trust delivery guys, I won't order anything online, so what the fuck can I do?

Anyway, I've no fucking money with which to buy any food. I'd have to sell my blood or something… Jesus fucking Christ, that'd be an experience for the lucky son-of-a-bitch who got injected with it.

Hmmm.

That gives me an idea, what if I like, dried up and snorted my own blood? There's so much drugs floating about in my veins, I wonder if I'd get a second hit?

I ponder this for a while, sitting back down on that toilet.

My last memories of today are those of leaning against the wall of the bathroom and knowing that I am on the verge of sleep once more. I don't even think about fighting it.

I don't even care anymore.

Felix

I light a cigarette as I stand in the cemetery near the entrance closest to Baron's Court and look around to see where I should start looking first.

Music on. A full packet of cigarettes.

I start by making a clockwise circle around the grounds of the cemetery and every group of people I see sitting on the grass or standing in a circle get a long stare from me. I begin to wonder how long I'll have to search for, lurking about like a complete creep. But, Lucifer steps in and within a few minutes I don't have to worry about any of this.

After a short spell of being both disgusting and yet very interested in watching a homeless lady eat her dinner out of a rubbish bin about ten metres away from me, Jessica appears, like an angel. Out of nowhere.

There she is.

I see her walking along the western side of the cemetery talking with a group of friends. I'm trying to work out the dynamics here and I decide that two of her group are clearly a couple, for sure. But that leaves Jessica standing rather close to a tall black guy and I have to wonder if they are together. I'm hoping not, because that would make it much tougher to get her alone to discuss what I need to discuss, propose the madness that I need to propose, without raising too many questions.

Felix, you are a demon. Look at yourself. If her boyfriend sees you, he'll no doubt start asking all the kinds of questions that you want to avoid.

I need to approach her alone. This may not be the time. Fuck.

I fidget about with my hands in the pockets of my jeans. Nervously looping my thumb in and out of the belt loops. Fuck. This is not the right time, perhaps? I need to approach her when she's completely alone. Fuck.

Felix, don't panic.

As she gets closer, I glance back up and realise that she's more beautiful than I remember. That is for damn sure. Dark brown hair, brown eyes, athletic body, with legs to die for. If only I was her type... If only this was a parallel universe where I wasn't her older brother's nerdy best friend.

If only you weren't a sociopath, the voice in my head tells me. What an arsehole...

I've not seen Jessica since Tommy's funeral and we haven't spoken properly in over a year. She never really hung out with Tommy and I. Every now and then she would never visit our flat. Tommy would go see her every few months, but that was it.

I've known her for years, but never well enough. But I always felt there was something there. We always got along, were always drawn to each other when in the same room. I remember, every time we were at a party or any kind of event together, we'd always end up with each other, outside on the balcony smoking cigarettes, in the corner chatting, off on a little mission to the off-licence to buy more alcohol and more rigs... we'd always end up together.

I always wanted to get closer to her, but she was my best friends' sister, and an aloof character to boot. She was always just off doing her own thing. And yet here she is. And yet, now I need her more than I ever thought I would.

Tommy, I'm sorry.

I stare at her from across the cemetery, behind my dark sunglasses, from a distance (like a creeper, yes, I know, especially as it's getting dark now). I begin to wonder if I should approach her at all. She is so innocent. Look at her. A student. Studying medicine. To become a doctor. A nurse, or something? Something, for the better of humans, at the very least. Something useful. And here I am, Felix the fucked-up creep killer...

I should leave now. Leave her alone. This is my fight. My problem. I've fucked it all up. No going back. Why should I ruin her life too? It's not fair to implicate her.

Don't be a fucking wimp. You've come this far, Felix...

I should find another way. Surely. Come on Felix. Leave the poor girl alone. Look at her. She has her whole life ahead of her. And you want to risk that for your own selfish revenge? You piece of shit.

I watch her laugh and I look away quickly as she suddenly glances in my direction. It's obvious I was staring and I freeze, hesitating for an awkward moment. The awkwardness does not go unnoticed. She turns to her friend, touches her on the shoulder and a small conversation is had before the group disperse. The couple leave together and the black guy, with no signs of affection at all towards Jessica, waves goodbye and walks off in the opposite direction.

Uh oh. No going back now.

I'm not certain what move to make next. I feel uncomfortable and exposed. I want to turn and walk away. Perhaps I abandon this plan altogether? My thoughts are laced with panic and regret. A hundred opposing feelings begin to fight in my mind and I feel sick. I want to get away from here. This is not good.

The Sober Fear rises up.

I need to get out of this cemetery, away from Jessica, and decide what my next move will be.

Fuck this shit. I'm out.

As I move to turn around and walk away, I take one last glance in Jessica's direction and my heart skips a couple of beats when I see her striding directly towards me across the thick grass.

I'm not sure what's more concerning, the fact that I've been spotted so easily, or the fact that I'm quickly realising that I haven't actually thought through properly what I'm going to fucking say to her. Despite all my planning and rehearsing. All the obsessive-compulsive control. I haven't even planned what the fuck I'm going to say!

Fuck, fuck, Felix, come on.

I try to rehearse a few lines to get my message across as she approaches, but all of these words seem as real the Tooth Fairy or Santa Clause. Useless. Superficial. Obsolete. Obvious. What do I do?

She's probably fifteen meters away and I haven't a fucking clue what to do.

She makes me so nervous.

I turn to move and she smiles and raises her hand to wave at me.

Oh Lucifer, I'm fucked now.

I make eye contact with her and then quickly glance over her shoulder to make sure that her friends are long gone.

I raise my hand in reply and force a smile of my own.

Fuck.

I remove my sunglasses as a sign of respect and realise, embarrassingly, that it's actually not very sunny at all and I must have stood out like a sore thumb standing here in the corner of the cemetery dressed in black with dark sunglasses on a rather grey afternoon. What a fucking idiot.

"Felix," she announces, with a coy grin, "what are you up to, lurking about over here?"

I hesitate. She makes her way forward steadily to stand directly in front me.

"Were you stalking me?"

My brain stops working. No words come, no response. I stand there like a fucking mannequin. The answer is yes.

"You creeper," she adds, laughing. But I can see in her eyes that the question is very serious.

I have to play it cool.

"Yes, I've been stalking you online for a while now and I've recently begun escalating my depraved behaviour to stalk you in the real world," I reply, without much thought, wondering where my wit is taking me with this. I seem to have lost control of the words coming out of my mouth. At least I'm saying something, though?

"Right. Well you've done a great job of finding me here." She's smiling, but I can see the smile is becoming harder and harder to maintain. She's very suspicious. Rightly so.

A puppy with a large stick in its mouth runs past us casually and we both glance over at it, the puppy thankfully breaking the awkward moment and buying me precious seconds to decide how the fuck to handle this.

"Well, I knew you studied medicine here and then when I saw you post on Facebook that you were here studying I followed you and your friends into the cemetery here. Pretty simple really," I try to downplay the whole thing, but I'm getting increasingly nervous and she is clearly on to me…

Lucifer, Felix, why did you say that you saw the post on Facebook? Like a fucking loser? Oh, fuck, Felix… 'I followed you and your friends?!' Just leave now, mate, you are done. Fuckinell…

Jessica stares at me, confused and apprehensive.

I shut out the (obviously correct) voice in my head in a moment of sanity, take control of the situation and speak.

"Look, I um, I need to talk to you about something…" I stumble through the sentence, but I get there in the end. She just stares at me. I continue the stumble, "I, uh, need your help with something."

Why the fuck am I so nervous?

I look into her eyes and nothing else seems to matter.

"Well, go on? What is it?"

I take a deep breath, look around me to make sure no one is in eavesdropping range, "it's about your brother."

Jess

I've not seen Felix since Tommy's funeral and at the time, we barely spoke. In fact, I recall our conversation quite clearly. He walked over to me with an expressionless face, offered me a cigarette and I said, "How've you been?"

"Oh… terrible…" he'd replied, slowly, without emotion, looking through me rather than at me. He was like a ghost of himself. Fortunately, our conversation was broken up by someone approaching to pay their respects to my mother and I. Felix just, kind of, wandered off and I haven't seen him since then.

Until today.

I've always found him very interesting. Like a puzzle you are putting together but you know that you might be missing a bunch of pieces.

Felix found me, and told me he wanted to talk about Tommy. So, I was ready to listen.

We walk through the cemetery and Felix makes small talk about my studies and a band we both kind of like that has a concert coming up in Alexandra Palace, but while he's talking all I can think about is how random this all is and I'm beginning to wonder just what this is all about, but then suddenly Felix turns to me and his tone, posture and even the light behind his eyes changes.

Matter-of-factly, Felix looks right into my eyes, places his left hand on my shoulder and tells me that he has a plan to trap one of the guys who killed my brother. That the guys who killed Tommy sell snow in East London and that he has one of their mobile numbers and will use that to lure him into a trap.

He tells me he recognised them one night just recently. He saw one of them selling snow in Hackney and manged to get the number from the guy who bought the snow.

I look into Felix's eyes and I can see that he's not joking. This is not a weird prank he's playing on me (not that Felix is the prankster type), and I can tell that every word he says is true. And as I listen, I've no doubt he's right and that the guy he saw was indeed one of Tommy's killers. If Felix knows, then it's true.

We walk and talk. Felix outlines his plan and I am captivated by how thorough and matter-of-fact he is…

The plan is to arrange to buy some snow from one of them, for *me* to arrange this, so that Felix can get close enough to check that it is really them and then contact the police. That one guy will lead to the others and then once they are all arrested testify in court that those were the guys who killed Tommy.

All I can really think of to say is "that's quite a favour…"

I'm really not sure about the whole thing but I trust Felix, I've known him for a long time now. He's a good guy. He wouldn't put us in danger and I suppose he can't go to the police unless he's certain, right? Not if he has to explain that the way he found Tommy's killer was by arranging to buy drugs. He's gotta have everything nicely wrapped up.

A million thoughts race around my mind.

"Felix, umm, do you really think this is a good idea? Can't we just go to the police with his number? Give them all the details. Let them track him down?"

"It's fucking freezing out here. Let's go to the offie and buy a rum and coke..." he replies, ignoring my question altogether. Or perhaps he didn't hear me.

"Why don't you...?"

"Jessica, you know what I firmly believe, especially so, these days?"

"No, tell me..."

"That you need to go out there and grab life by the balls. Grab them and squeeze until you get what you want. Leave no prisoners. Get exactly what you want. Settle for nothing less. Nothing less... The only real thing worth losing is your life. Everything else can either be replaced, or bettered.

And wouldn't you want to die knowing that you'd given everything you had to achieving everything you wanted? That you'd taken advantage of every opportunity, every sign given to you from the universe, from God?"

It seems rather poetic to me and I guess he's right. To be honest, I'm not really in the mood for this kind of deep talk and I'm feeling overwhelmed by all of this. I just want to go home.

But, part of me also wants to help. I can see he's desperate. I can see it in his eyes. And, well, these mother fuckers killed my brother. They fucking *killed* my brother. God damn them.

A rage surges inside me and for a moment I can see myself helping here. Bringing these shits to justice. Felix looks as though he hasn't slept in days and he sways around as though his legs haven't hardly the energy to hold him up much longer.

I make a decision.

"Can we just meet this guy in a park or something? I don't know, like, wherever this kind of thing usually takes place." I realise I must sound kind of childish 'wherever this kind of thing usually takes place', oh dear...

"We'll just ask him to meet you somewhere *reasonably* public, so you'll feel safe. Obviously, I can't let him risk seeing me, in case he recognises me from when they boys spotted me the other night. But, Jessica, I'll obviously be close by. I'll be right there in case anything bad happens. But it won't... trust me. This is just a normal coke deal for this guy."

"Felix, I've wanted to say this for a long time, call me 'Jess', like everyone else. You are so formal. 'Jess'..."

Felix comes to life. I see the hope rise behind his eyes and I feel for him. I really do. I can see how much he must've struggled these last few months.

I, well, honestly, I've been distracting myself with drugs and alcohol and study and sex and sleeping and trying to convince myself every day that what will be will be and that eventually I'll get over it. But, it's not as simple as that, is it?

What these mother fuckers did to my brother...

Hell, what they did to Felix as well.

Fuck them.

Let them rot in prison.

And if I have to get my hands a little bit dirty to make this happen, so be it.

Felix

I am about to do something really fucking shitty.

Why? Because I am a selfish cunt. Why else? Because I am desperate. A desperate selfish cunt.

I won't put Jess in harm. I won't allow that. But I need her help, and I know she won't do what I really need of her, unless I force her into it. Unless I trick her. I don't want to be known as a sneaking fuckin' snake. But, when you back a wolf into a corner, he will do anything he can to save himself.

Jess, I'm sorry. I have no other choice.

Only Lucifer can judge me now.

15 Nicola

Qusay

I spent most of the morning in the gym today. Chest day, my favourite. Nothing quite like the feeling of building a solid chest up to press its way out of nice tight shirt. I suppose the ladies must feel the same way. Nothing like the feeling of a couple of solid tits doing their best to bust their way out of your top.

The training session didn't help though. Putting myself through the physical pain and exhaustion hasn't reduced my anger. I couldn't sweat it out. Sometimes, I think the only solution is to smoke it off and then fuck it off.

I let out a heavy sigh and have a moment of truth.

I really don't want to be involved in this shit right now, man. Its heavy. Fuckin' people are getting killed out there. So much fuckin' heat, bruv. It's not supposed to be like this.

Feeling like the cops after around every corner, like that killer is around every corner. Sirens all over the city. Fuck, bruv… Every time I hear one, Bruv, the fuckin' hair stands up on my neck.

Abid wants me to fuckin' go and try find that cunt. The little fuckin' cunt. Man…. I don't know where to fuckin' look. And what if this cunt gets at me first? He's still fuckin' out there, bruv. Fuck that shit. How the fuck am I supposed to sleep at night?

I look down and see that I'm wringing my hands together and my legs are trembling, shaking up and down. "Fuckinell, man, get hold of yourself," I whisper.

I run my knuckles down my torso, feeling my washboard abs through the thin fabric of my shirt. Damn, you are in great condition, bro, I think to myself. Don't waste it.

It's only a couple of blocks from the gym back to my place and I make the journey on foot in good time. As I approach home, I get an unwanted call from Abid that for some reason, like a loyal puppy, I answer. But in the moment Allah steps in and the signal cuts out and all I manage to hear is "Hey, Qusay, where..."

Standing there on the dark footpath, buses rushing by and sirens sounding out in the distance, so close to home, to comfort, I realise I really need a smoke before I can face calling Abid back. So, I dash down the road and across the yard quickly to my block before my phone rings again.

I've too much on my mind to act normal.

I fuckin' can't believe this shit. Who does this kind of shit? A fuckin' really pissed of gang would do it. That's the only fuckin' people who would have the balls, bruv. Not some fuckin' random lone white boy. It doesn't make sense...

I storm into my flat, drop my gym bag in the hallway carelessly and head straight to my bedroom to grab some weed.

Standing in the kitchen a few minutes later, smoking a joint, I see a bus full of people drive past down the street below and in that moment, I have a sudden urge to just pack up everything and get the fuck out of here.

I'm seriously considering this pathway when my phone vibrates again and I take a long puff on my joint before answering the call with a sigh.

"Abid," I say, without even looking to see who was calling.

"Answer your fuckin' phone, bruv! Where the fuck are you?"

"Having a smoke, bro!" I respond, a little too aggressively. Normally I wouldn't be so short with him, but now isn't the time to play nice.

"You haven't got time for a smoke, mate."

I say nothing, inhaling again and holding the smoke down in my lungs for as long as I can.

"Go see the black boys," he continues, "find out what they know, those boys always know what's going on in the neighbourhood. Always, bruv. Got it?"

"Right, boss."

"Good, as soon as you're done, come see me. I'll let you know where to find me."

"Alright."

Abid hangs up.

Fuckinell...

I'll do it. I mean, I've got no choice. But before that, I need to get some cash. Got to keep making money. Some guy messaged me while I was at the gym wanting a couple of baggies. I can drop this shit off to him in Kings Cross on my way to see the black boys in Holloway.

Stepping back outside a little while later, it's gotten pretty dark and a lot colder. This Spring sucks. I zip up my jacket and start making my way to my bike, hands in my pockets to keep them warm.

The black boys are the blacks we buy our coke in bulk from, they deal with the big dogs who actually bring the stuff in from wherever. The black boys are like the middle of the spider web around there. They know everyone who knows everyone and if this little fucker is acting on behalf of some gang, they'll know. If not, then it's just that one fucker. But, to be honest, that may be worse. One fucker that nobody fuckin' knows, in this fuckin' city, is a fuckin' nightmare. Better if it's some fuckin' gang we can hit back at, proper.

I reach the street where the customer told me to meet and it begins to rain. I text him to let him know I'm there but he doesn't text back. As I approach the entranceway to an old flat block, I feel a presence approaching me from behind, instinct kicks in and I reach for the blade tucked into the back of my trousers.

But as I spin around, heart racing and spittle flying from my mouth, poised to kill, I confronted with just some scrawny geek in a cheap suit who looks a lot more frightened of me than I am of him.

Fucking Hell

Calm yourself down, bruv. It's alright to be cautious, but you almost slashed a random civilian on his own front doorstep. Not a smart move, Qusay.

My breathing starts returning to normal and the dude, a fuckin' faggot by the sound of his voice, apologises to me and then walks on past. I stand there and watch as he opens the main door to the building with a security pass and follow in behind him. Moments later, in the lift, the dude eyes me up and down, even though I know I look good, it still makes me uncomfortable…. But only a little bit. It's nice to be admired.

"He's a fuckin' faggot", I whisper under my breath, not sure who I'm talking to. The guy next to me doesn't appear to hear me.

He exits the lift on the same floor as I do and that's a pain the arse. I'm here to do a deal and I definitely don't need civilians hanging about. Lucky for him, the fuckin' faggot moves off down the hallway and I breathe a sigh of relief. I can't shake this tense feeling and I need to get in and get out as soon as possible.

The corridor is a fuckin' disgrace, a cockroach scuttles along the skirting board and there's a pool of yellow liquid near the fire exit which looks like sugary piss. Fucking Hell. The sooner I get out of here, the better.

I knock on the customer's door, hoping to get this sorted quick as fuck. And almost in the same instant my phone begins to vibrate in my pocket.

But all of this is suddenly completely irrelevant.

I feel a sudden rush of dread washing over me like a cold bucket of ice.

Something is wrong.

Seriously wrong.

By the time my brain interprets what's happening, I know my body is already too many steps behind. My opportunity to react effectively has long since passed.

Everything in the scene around me pauses for a moment. Everything is crystal clear.

My blade has been removed from my belt, my face shoved hard up against the door and then it gives way and I'm spiralling forwards as the whole world gives way before me.

The world suddenly slows to a normal pace.

I make a clumsy, far too late, attempt to spin around and retrieve my knife, but I'm tumbling forwards, right onto the floor below. Right at someone's feet.

The world no longer feels familiar, even though at a glance I'm in a pretty standard room in a pretty standard flat. Suddenly it's a horrible playground of fear and confusion. My body can't seem to act fast enough, no matter how much I struggle, my limbs are not listening. If I was less scared, in less shock, I might have realised sooner that the blow from behind had stunned me. The thought flashes across my mind for a brief second, but all of this is just too much to consider right now. Too late anyway. All I want to do is escape this place, something is here is very, very wrong and instinct is telling me that I need to get myself away, get out of this room, as soon as possible. Don't even bother to fight. Just run.

The worlds blurs and I can't hear anything except for a high-pitched ringing in my ears, like that sound you hear when your mum's TV has been left on too long.

The threadbare carpet I see in front of my face is so close I can watch fragments of dust rising up from it as I inhale and exhale. It's disgusting and distracting and I need to focus on getting myself out of here.

I see the blur of what looks like a pair of worn out Converse All Stars ahead of me, blue canvas with mud caked on the white rubber tips. I can hear someone half-coughing, half-choking and I can only assume that it's me.

As my limbs slowly find some strength the room around me rushes back into perspective, the feeling is like that of being trapped in a wind tunnel. Only in this tunnel all the air is rushing away from me, whooshing past my ears. I hear voices through the stifling whoosh and I catch two words, "stop me."

I've no time to get to my feet before an incredible weight is on top of me, forcing me back down towards the floor, face-first into the carpet again. What is this on my back? A foot? A truck?

As my cheekbone thuds into the floor the impact gives me a moment of clarity. I recall my steps moments earlier and realise that I've been fuckin' targeted...

That guy in the fuckin' lift!

A get the cold sweats. But I'm not done yet. These bastards are not going to get me like they got the others.

"Hey, get off me you fuckers!" I try to yell, try to assert some authority, but the words I end up barely sputtering are, "help! Fucking help me! Please!"

A jarring pain roars in my side and my brain tells me that I've been kicked in the ribs as I've attempted once more to get to my feet. The pain is fuckin' awful but its overwhelmed by the fear I feel as I roll over backwards onto the floor, helpless and now fully exposed, like a mouse caught in the claws of a big fat cat. Confusion settles in and begins to override the last vestiges of confidence I thought I had. I wonder for a moment if this is the end.

Is this how I'll die?

I let out a groan and clutch my ribs involuntarily. You are such a fuckin' fool, Qusay. Fuck, bruv. Fuck, fuck, fuck. Words repeat in my head, echoing away of their own volition, telling me now how foolish I am. scolding me.

Shut up, shut up.

"Hey!" I try to scoot around on the floor, to make eye contact with this cunt, I can feel his presence close to me now, "get o-"

Then, all of a sudden, it doesn't matter anymore. A figure looms above me, menacingly. Two things resound in my mind. Blatantly obvious now.

One, no one is going to help me.

Two, this guy attacking me is going to kill me, if I do not kill him first.

Fight, Qusay! A voice inside my head commands, and I intend to obey. The guy's face is expressionless, the eyes empty and yet somehow inviting. He's a killer. I can tell. I've met enough of them to know one when I see them. It's all in the eyes.

I scramble backwards on the floor like a crab as best I can, not wanting to let him get too close before I can get to my feet.

Foolish.

It's amazing how one split second decision can change a life forever, or end one.

I should've just stood up.

....

He lunges down on top of me with all his weight.

I don't even feel him land.

What I do feel is a kind of serene relief as I realise that without doubt, I am now going to die.

My whole life. All my struggles. Everything, is about to be over.

It's a sweet, blissful moment which is over far too quickly. The bliss washed away by a searing sensation from just above my belly button, as though boiling water has been poured inside me. I look down, it's all I can do now.

My mind has betrayed me and given up resisting. My body has dumbly followed along.

A gloved hand holds a thick military style knife, the blade of which is embedded almost to the hand guard inside of my stomach. A dark red stain is forming around the entry point. My hard worked for abdominal muscles are useless and ruined.

I want my hands to reach out and shove this mother fucker off of me, but they've become useless artefacts belonging to a long-gone era of Qusay's strength. The tools of a great warrior who once was. The fittest, physically strongest of all of us, and look at me, helpless, on my back beneath a fuckin' skinny nerd.

I don't care what happens next.

My stomach feels warm and my head light. A combination reminiscent of a belly fresh full of a big meal followed by big fat joint. I go with it.

My head is lifted up and I feel like vomiting. There is a gloved wrist beside my eye, a face leaning in close to mine.

"Listen carefully, shit head," a voice says with incredible calm, "you are going to tell me where to find Abid, Mohammed and Hani and you are going to tell me quickly because I'm slowly pulling this knife back out of your stomach and faster I pull, the faster you bleed out."

I obviously don't respond because my head is quickly yanked up closer to his face. This time I can see rage burning in yellow eyes.

"Talk to me, you fuck!"

I don't think I say a word.

I don't think I even can.

He may be speaking to me, he may be slapping me around, stabbing me again, I'm not sure. The only thing I know for certain is that I don't care anymore.

The room blurs out of perspective for the last time.

The only thing left in my world is a fly-shit stained ceiling above me, a dusty threadbare carpet underneath me and the pleasant, oozing heat slowly spreading from my stomach towards my brain.

16 Nicolas

Felix

"Why are you vibrating like that?"

"I'm scared of you."

I consider this.

It's a fair point.

"You're scared because you're a smart girl," I pause for dramatic effect, "stay scared."

She ponders this for a while and I stare at her, hardly blinking. She stares at me and then at nothing in particular on the wall beside us.

"You never told me this was going to happen. You never... you never said this... you never told me this would happen." She keeps repeating shit like this and I just stare at her until she runs out of breath.

"Felix?"

"Yes?"

"What have you done? Why did you bring him to my home? You said we would find them *tomorrow*. And in *public*. Somewhere else! This was not the plan! You fuck..."

She's clenching and unclenching her fists and a vein is throbbing away on her forehead.

There's a long silence.

I don't do anything to help shorten it.

I let her reflect on the situation as Qusay's blood begins to coagulate on her carpet.

Time seems to stand still.

She unclenches her fists.

"I always wondered what it would be like," Jess admits, leaning back against the wall behind her. Her eyes escape me behind the shadows as her hair falls across her face.

Those are the only words said in this room for at least three full minutes. I'm not sure if she's talking about being betrayed by me, or about killing someone, or about something else, but I don't actually care, in any case.

After handing me a kitchen cloth to wipe the blood off my gloves and jacket, Jess sits down at her table in one of the worn out 70's style leather chairs, rusty silver studs running along the edge of cracked red leather, stainless steel frame, you know the ones, classics. Foam stuffing oozes out of the cracks in the leather, old flaky foam with all manner of grime accumulated and more accumulating still.

The body of Qusay lies in the next room on the living room floor. A giant fucking elephant in the room that we need really do need to address. A giant, dead, human fucking elephant.

"Well, that didn't go according to plan," I announce, lamely.

"You had a *plan*?" The cheeky bitch. She makes eye contact for a second then looks away.

Jess pulls a packet of cigarettes from the pocket of her robe and a lighter from the other. I stare on, my brain overloaded with considerations. Is this girl going to lose it in a minute and attack me? Why is she suddenly calm? Too calm…

Then, naturally, I start to panic.

Should I get out of here?

Should *I* run?

Should I kill her?

Too many considerations…

Too many possibilities…

I stare on.

The silence is heavy.

Jess finally lights her cigarette and takes a long drag, staring at the empty table in front of us. I hear a door slam shut in the hallway outside her flat.

"Sit down," she suggests, pointing to the seat in front of me.

I find myself sitting.

She shoves the packet of cigarettes towards me and the lighter. I stare at them on the table and take a deep breath.

Jess reaches over to her left, opens the refrigerator and pulls out two bottles of Kronenburg 1664. She removes the caps on both and plants one down in front of me with a thud.

"I just killed one of the cunts who killed your brother," I say. Not knowing why I continue to bother stating the obvious.

"Yup, you did… and I just watched you do it," she says, raising both eyebrows dramatically and then gulping half of her bottle of beer in one go.

"Don't you care?" I ask her, shocked and genuinely confused with her new found apathy.

"Sure, I care... but with severe limits," she replies with a shrug, continuing to stare at nothing in particular on the table. She scratches her neck and takes another sip of beer.

I don't get this girl, she is either really fucking insane or really fucking... no... actually, she's just insane. She has to be. She's a fucking weirdo... but I've known this for a long time, I suppose. No wonder I've always been drawn to her, I feel calm around her. Somewhat... disarmed. Fuck, that's a risky train of thought. Especially right now.

She burps and swallows the rest of her bottle of beer staring right at me.

Right into me.

This unnerves me, so I turn around and look over at Qusay's body, trying to decide what my next move will be. I'm surprised at the amount of blood pooling around his corpse and also the peacefulness of his expression. As though in his final moment, when his body finally let go of life, it found true happiness. Sheer ecstasy. I'm almost envious of him.

But it wasn't meant to happen this way. I wasn't supposed to have to do it this way.   I find myself biting my bottom lip and I quickly stop, composing myself. Hmm. I have to get out of here. I look over at Jess. The younger sister of my best mate. Something like regret begins to saturate my mind. Fuck. Fuck. Fuck. This situation is not ideal. It was somewhat hastily arranged and I feel ashamed to have had to obtain her assistance under such duress.

My heart feels cold and damp. I take two Xanax from my pocket and swallow them down, no water required.

I feel like showering, washing off all the bullshit. Not to mention I'm covered in blood stains, a change of clothes would be great... I need to get the fuck out of here and re-evaluate.

Jess seems to be handling herself well. Much better than expected.

What *did* I expect, though?

Her composure and quiet makes our current situation rather... unpredictable.

We continue to sit in silence only interrupted by Jess lighting another cigarette.

As the last flow of blood oozing from Qusay's corpse finally stops and then, coagulating, begins forming a skin, I turn my full attention to monitoring Jess's actions carefully.

She's wearing a pair of red Emily the Strange slippers which for some reason I hadn't noticed before. Her nails are painted black. Her dark eyes are inquisitive and mysterious. In any other circumstance I'd like this to be a date. She was my best friend's sister, but I've never had the chance to know her beyond that.

Her flat is a terrible mess. The colour scheme is absolutely fucked. Oranges clashing with browns, clashing with dark blues, strange, new colours of scum not yet known to humankind clashing with everything. Hideous. Countless surrealist cartoon posters cover the living room wall like Dali came in and vomited through the ceiling fan after eating anime stew. It's a mushroom-heads paradise.

Again, I feel calm around her though. A thought crosses my mind that she may actually keep quiet about this shit. She may actually be willing to help me. It's worth a shot. I don't want to have to threaten her, or kill her.

"I'm going to get rid of this body and you will never hear from or see me ever again."

This is only a half-truth.

"How do I know if I can trust you?" she asks.

She cannot trust me.

"I don't know, I guess you have no choice. You have to trust me."

She really shouldn't.

"Tell me the most fucked up thing you've done," she asks, dead-pan, "what do you fucking regret?"

It's a fucking bizarre thing to ask, but to be honest it's the kind of left-field question I'd probably find myself asking someone in a situation like this. It's a question where you can gauge a person not by what they say, but by the way they say it. I decide to tell the full truth, no hesitation, I have nothing to lose really, and I need her trust.

"When I was a teenager," I begin, "I once killed a litter of kittens and their mother which were living underneath my mother's house. I fed them bleach mixed with cat food and milk one day. For about three weeks after, the smell of death permeated through the floorboards in the living room and it was almost too much to take. My mother obviously noticed the stench, it was unavoidable, and she must've noticed the kittens and their mother were no longer hanging around under the house, but never she said a word... Never asked..."

Jess and I stare at each other, sussing one another out.

Jess blows cigarette smoke in my direction.

I blow some right back, the smoke mingling in the air between us and then evaporating away.

"Wow... That's... Um... Pretty honest of you..."

"Yeah. I'm a pretty honest guy..."

"...Are you?"

I pause., "nah..."

"Now, *that* is honest," she giggles and for the first-time smiles.

I smile back. We have a small moment.

I want to say something in this moment, but it's quickly interrupted as Qusay's mobile beeps from behind us. My heart skips a beat or three.

Jess looks over to Qusay's body, "are you going to check that? Could be useful for you..."

This fucking girl is a smart cookie.

I make my way over to Qusay's body, then holding the cigarette between my lips to free up my still-gloved hands, I rummage through his pockets for the phone.

Finding it in the inner pocket of his leather jacket, I see a message from 'Big A', which must be Abid. The message reads 'Where the fuck are you? I need to know what the black boys know. Meet me outside the Camden Lock Market in an hour.'

'Right bruv' I message back, imagining how Qusay might respond. This is a positive development. We may well be back on track.

I decide to take a chance and leave Jess with the corpse of Qusay for the time being. No real choice. I don't have time to get rid of it now. Plus, it will keep her from going out, running away, going to the police, whatever. She's well implicated now.

Felix you are a fucking prick.

It's close to four in the morning as I exit Jess's flat, blood wiped clean from my gloves and jacket, all the kitchen roll and tea towels we used to clean the blood have been set fire to in the sink, just to be safe. Jess didn't even blink I told her to do this, which makes me wonder what kind of life she's lived... But, I've no time to fantasise about Jess's life now, I have work to do. I need to find a car.

Abid

I don't know where the fuck Qusay has been for the last few hours, but I told him to get his arse here over an hour ago and I can't be fucked waiting anymore.

He ain't picking up his phone and he ain't replying to my messages. Well, fuck him then. I'm sick of this shit. If that fucker's ignoring me without a good fuckin' reason, bruv, fuck, he's gonna get it. We ain't got time for fuckin' around anymore.

I give Aziz a call and tell him not to bother coming to Camden. I thought I'd come to help Qusay speak to the black boys but, you know what, fuck it. I'll talk to the black boys myself tomorrow.

I bounce and drive back home.

Man, fuck Qusay. Takes a man to do this job. Send a boy to do a man's job? This is what happens.

Jess

When I was sixteen years old my grandma was killed in a car accident not far from our house.

It's interesting how much detail one can remember of a time of significant emotional distress. I remember the white t-shirt with the black dripping blood diamond print I was wearing that night, the black and all-white Converse All Stars with the scuffed toes I'd been meaning to replace for months but hadn't got around to, the little shaving cuts on the chin of the police officer who was waiting at my doorstep, the way his lips quivered as he told me my grandma had been killed. He had been first on the horrific scene. I remember the words having no impact when I first heard them. I just stood there and stared at him. At that moment words had no meaning and the world was suddenly and most definitely something entirely separate from me. In many ways it still is, I suppose.

Over the following few days, the shock of it had hit me like nothing had ever hit me before or perhaps ever will.

The overwhelming sensation of helplessness and anger, sensations of rage and fear, all of them battling it out in your mind for supremacy. The extremity of these sensations only those people who have had loved ones taken from them can understand. A Spin to Lose prize wheel of emotional suffering.

It became clear to me during the weeks following my grandma's death at the hands of that driver what a horrible place the world really is. How it really operates. It was a hit and run. The driver of the car was never found, never turned himself in. Never bothered to even stop and see if my grandma was okay when he t-boned her car and crushed the door panel through her spleen and took the side of her face off with the drivers' window. After a week or so, the police ended their investigation and that was that. No more grandma and no more innocence.

My eyes were opened. It made look at the world from a different perspective. So much death, so little care for one another.

I never really got past it at all. I never really accepted what had happened nor did I really want to. I just tuned out from being emotionally connected to people. If no one really cares out there in the world, why should I?

Qusay killed my brother, and now Qusay is dead himself. So what?

Law of jungle…

Felix

As I drive along the motorway, well over the speed limit, towards Erith, with pieces of an already decaying corpse in the boot and a meat cleaver on the passenger seat covered in all manner of irrefutable evidence relating to my complicity in murder, stoned out of my mind to make everything less intense, in the broad daylight of half-past noon, I still find myself perfectly distracted, sternly focussed on a lunatic driver ahead of me who is weaving in and out of traffic like a fucking lunatic. It's a nice distraction.

The guy must have a death wish or something, either that, or he's on the run from the cops for something equally as fucked up as I am. This has to be a good thing, though, right? With two of us death-rowers speeding down the motorway toward an inevitable end, this halves both our chances of being caught, surely. I've done this lunatic a favour if anything. And he's returned it. The cops aren't going to be looking for *two* maniacs on this stretch of motorway today. No chance. I push the pedal towards the floor and race ahead of a few cars to my right. In this situation the best position to be in is the lead lunatic.

As I gain ground on this nutcase he weaves in between two cars and one sounds its horn angrily at him as he races on ahead. I push the pedal down harder and beads of sweat run down my chest and settle somewhere on my stomach. The weed convinces me I can hear sirens behind me and the beads of sweat suddenly become a waterfall, my t-shirt becoming nothing more than a stylish towel. My palms follow the fun and games and my grip on the steering wheel starts to loosen. Fuck.

As I reach up to my fellow fruitcake he swerves into the lane to our left and I pull up beside him, victory and freedom get closer by the miles per hour. The sirens scream on (or do they?), the red and blue lights are surely moments from appearing in my rear-view mirror. I glance over to my left to make eye-contact and acknowledge my tag-team partner before I stab him in the back and sacrifice him to the law. But I spot something truly confusing.

Some man who is clearly disabled sits in the driver's seat. A fucking wheelchair is strapped to the roof, with one of those machines which moves it down to the driver's door so he can move access it. A blue badge permit is displayed clearly on the front windscreen and the guy is driving using the controls on his steering wheel. He looks focussed on the road, cool, calm and collected. He swerves around another car and almost clips the bonnet as he pulls back in front. We're going over 110mph, but this guy knows what he's doing. He doesn't even look over at me as I stare on at him. Then it dawns on me. This guy just doesn't give a fuck. He's already fucking disabled. What the fuck does he care if he has a car accident at these speeds? What does he have to lose?

I'm the one who's going down today. A torrent of sweat escapes my body. I'm surprised there is any left. The Fear starts setting in and voices start preaching to about me being gang-raped in prison every day for the next twenty-five years and how I'll probably never spend another day in the world free again.

This is your final day. Final minutes. Final moments. Etc..

If that's so, make them count Felix, make them count.

As the (probably non-existent) sirens wail on behind me I swerve recklessly towards the nearest exit ramp, crossing two lanes of traffic in the process and risking god only knows what kind of carnage. The retarded racer passes me by at breakneck speeds, eyes still glued on the road ahead, life still not worth more than the thrill of speed. Good for him... good for him. I salute him as he speeds out of sight.

The car bounces a little under me as I run over a road cone, or at least I hope it was a road cone, the meat cleaver on the passenger's seat next to me slides off and falls to the floor with a dense thud and once again my vision starts to become way too blurry for me to see much of anything clearly. My body is not coping. Peripheral vision is fading fast as the increased beating of my panicked heart exacerbates the drugs in my system and gives over control to The Fear. Old Man Fear is on the brink of complete victory over little baby Felix.

I slow down to what I hope are somewhat regular speeds as I exit the motorway and head off into the suburbs. As I continue on, I pull up alongside a fuel tanker which is hurtling along, looking big, shiny and menacing. Being in a car near a fuel tanker has scared the shit of me for as long as I can remember. I must have seen something fucking awful relating to fuel tankers and cars as a child. Probably on one of those 'Worlds Most Fucked Up Shit Caught On Tape' television shows. Jesus.

I really want to slow and let the tanker move on to a safe distance up ahead, but the sirens still ring in my ears and I'm still waiting for those the flashing lights to catch up to me. Fuck. Fuck. Fuck.

By now my clothes have become damp coverings resembling nothing more than a wet blanket papier-mâchéd to my skin with sweat. Disgusting.

Blow up the Outside World is playing quietly on the stereo and it seems rather inappropriate at this point in time, although since I can't risk moving my slimy hands off the steering wheel to switch the radio station I find myself singing along half-heartedly and nodding my head to the tune.

The fuel tanker and I both approach an intersection and when his indicators start flashing to the right I naturally switch mine to the left and fortunately the light turns green a moment later. Death and I part ways for the moment, he drives his tanker off and I cruise deeper into the unknown. Relief washes over me but I wonder where the Hell I am. Clearly the suburbs, but definitely not the good neighbourhood of this borough.

The streets are lined with rubbish, broken television sets and old mattresses. Fucking, perfect. Pairs of children's shoes have been flung up over the power lines down the main street. Lucfier. This is either fucking perfect setting for what I need to do, or the fucking worst thing which has ever happened to me today. I drive on, unsure.

Expectedly, the suburban streets are relatively quiet and the sirens fade, their wail seems to be coming from a few blocks over now. The cops have lost my trail. For the moment... I have some time. A few moments to catch my breath and have some thoughts. Hopefully logical ones...

I pull up and park opposite a small shopping centre, take a deep breath and let it out slowly. The man inside my head is plotting something bad, I can feel it. He is lurking about in my mind.

Move quickly, Felix. Move!

I start the engine and cruise slowly into the car park of the shopping centre just as a group of six or seven black gangsters exit the convenience store at the end of the row of shops. They're all wearing bandanas and looking pissed off. Looking for trouble. This is the last thing I need, but for some reason they only give the stoned, nervous-sweat-drenched, bush-man-looking (I admit it), mother fucker in the beat up old Toyota with his eyes fixed on her rear-view mirror, a fleeting glance as they walk past me, waddling off to rape and pillage, as gangsters do.

The streets seem otherwise deserted and the shops in front of me empty and run-down. Where the fuck is everyone? The sirens are still threatening from afar although I feel as though the cops have lost their way. I need to get rid of this corpse right now. I look down at the cleaver on the floor of the passenger seat and remember that Jess said it was a gift from her sister when she got her own flat. She was pissed that I used it to hack up Qusay's body, but, needs must.

With increasingly foggy vision and a throbbing pain in my back I scout the area for a good place to offload my cargo. I just have to dump and run before I have a full-blown panic attack and someone calls an ambulance.

Behind the liquor store I spot a burnt-out car parked in the corner rusting away alongside at least two motorcycles and a refrigerator. This seems like the suitable location to dispose of a rotting corpse in the ghetto and I slowly move the car around behind the liquor store, careful not to attract any attention.

Scanning the area to see if I'm being watched, I convince myself that the place is truly deserted and in any case, the row of shitty shops provide full cover from the road.

"Best make it quick and get the fucking Hell out of here," I whisper to myself. Why I don't know. But it seems to help.

I pull up next to the burnt-out car and take a few deep breaths. In for seven seconds, out for ten. In for seven seconds, out for ten. I need to make this quick.

I wish I had more weed on me. Fuckinell.

I get out and make my walk to the boot. One last glance around and I'm satisfied that I am completely alone. I lean over and with one hand lift up the already ajar boot of the burnt-out Audi, fortunately it's almost empty. This is a good start.

Without second thought I pop the boot of my car and reach inside for the black rubbish bags of corpse bits, grabbing bags of what used to be some fucker who killed my best friend and them over the crest of the boot. The adrenaline coursing through my body seems to provide me with the strength I need. I grit my teeth, forgetting how heavy these bags were and with some difficulty I manage to drag the torso over the side boot and a shot-struggle later, I dump it into the burnt-out boot next to me. The other bags are less trouble and before I know it, he's all tucked up inside a new boot. I grab the cleaver from the passengers side and toss that in the burnt-out boot too. Then I douse the whole area in bleach, as well as the boot of my own car and then toss the bleach bottle over behind a rusting motorbike.

Taking off the disposable gloves I find my hands are shaking and the sirens wail again like clockwork. Cockroaches scuttle past my feet, and I'm not sure if they're real or not. But I suppose it doesn't actually matter anyway. I feel like vomiting everywhere. I'm so deep in this now, no turning back.

I stare down at the scene in front of me. I try to make light of it all. "One boot to another. No harm done." I whisper to myself. The next moment I slam both boots shut and march straight back to the driver's seat. It is done. Time to get the fuck out of here.

Part of me knows, just knows, that no-one has seen me. That I may well have gotten away with this. If I can just make a clean exit now.

The sirens fade.

As I drive around the front of the deserted shopping centre I make eye contact with a proper Essex skank involved in some kind of confrontation with the cashier inside a small off-licence.

Turning back to the cashier, the skank scowls and raises her arms aggressively, "Oy! Where's the fucking exit?" she yells at the cashier.

The poor Indian cashier winces as though she's in pain and then points to the wide-open exit metres from where the skank is standing.

"For fucks sake!" the chav-bitch, all Adidas tracksuits and pinned back ponytails, yells out, storming outside throwing her arms up in air and shrugging her shoulders. This girl is wild.

She walks towards me with a glare on her face which suggests that I just get the Hell away from this shit. You don't belong here Felix. Just go.

The Fear makes one last attempt to get hold of me.

All I ever wanted was to be happy... but whenever happiness showed it face, I shunned it... why? I guess I'll never know. Something internal? Something instinctual? I have no explanation for my natural rejection of everything I really needed in life when it was presented to me. All the good things. Instead I was drawn like a magnet to the most fucked-up things I could. The craziest bitches, the worst jobs. The worst decisions. The worst situations. Just like this.

17 Nikolai

Felix

"Umm, what are you doing here?" Jess asks me, her head rolling about, clearly drunk. A blend of rum and beer wafting off her hot breath. Her clothes stinking of cigarettes.

"I was just in the neighbourhood."

"Really?"

"Yeah, right, I just fucking love hanging out in the ghetto," I reply, jokingly, rolling my eyes, but remaining otherwise expressionless.

"Smart arse."

"Come on, I need your help. Can we talk?"

"I've ... umm. Had a couple of drinks…

"What, a couple in the last five minutes? Plus a few more before that? Look at you. You're a wreck."

"Piss off. How'd you find me anyway?"

"I just need to ask you something…"

"Well, go on."

She takes another swig of her beer and leans forward over the table, tilting her head and looking up at me with raised eyebrows, taunting me.

She's absolutely gorgeous, I have to admit. In other circumstances I may think about making a move here. But this is pretty much, one-hundred percent, *not* the right time for that kind of behaviour.

She spots me checking out her boobs and she feigns disappointment in me.

"Come on, Jess. We can't talk here. You know why," I plead.

"Ohhhh, so this is about, ummm, that thing that we did?"

I grit my teeth. This is not the most isolated of tables and the pub definitely isn't loud enough right now to drown out our conversation properly.

I move over to her, lift her up under her right arm, frogmarch style and with my free hand I pick up her beer and down the rest of the pint.

"Oi! Fuckinell," she protests, but she's drunk and she does little to stop me.

I walk her outside into the carpark and she stumbles along. I have to be careful that I don't look as though I'm abducting her or something. Even though, obviously that's exactly what I'm doing. I just hope I strike the right balance between the concerned boyfriend taking his drunk girlfriend home and, well, just a creeper dragging a girl out of there like some kind of predator.

"Get in the car, I bought you a milkshake."

"What flavour is it?"

"Strawberry."

She stares at me, unsure.

"It's pink. Come on," I motion to the passenger seat.

"You trying to lure this little girl into your car old man?" She says this a little too loudly and although she's trying to be cute, I can't risk catching attention from strangers right now.

"You must be, what? Twenty-one, twenty-two? I'm twenty-five? Get with the program, love."

She takes the milkshake, which I bought for myself but then did too much snow and now don't want.

"I hate this fucking milkshake. God damn it!" She yells, but still taking another slurp with a revolted expression.

"Then why are you still drinking it?" I ask.

"I just fucking hate it okay?"

"This is the worst conversation I've had in a long time. Get in."

She slumps herself down in the passenger seat, pouting, still drinking the thick shake. She doesn't put her seatbelt on, but I don't care. I slam the door and walk around to the driver's side.

Despite being a little bitch tonight, there's something about Jess which intrigues me. Yes, there's the obvious sexual attraction, to be sure. But, it's more than that. Beyond that. She's... different. Unusual. Exactly what I'm drawn to. The calm and matter-of-fact way she dealt with the aftermath of me killing Qusay right in front of her, was impressive to say the least. She's a rare one.

I can't think of the appropriate words to describe her and it frustrates me. But all I can say is, Jess is a bit like me. We're both missing something. We've both seen and done too much. More than we should've. We're both a little... detached.

How do I know? I just do.

I can see it in her eyes.

She moves with grace, like a lioness and she's cunning and clever, like a fox, but scratch the surface and she's as cold as a shark. She's a rare creature.

I can trust her.

I know I can trust her because she thinks just like I do.

As we pull away from the curb, I look over at her sucking away on that disgusting milkshake and although I don't want to, I find myself thinking 'I'll probably kill her too at the end of this. Just to tidy things up.'

"I promise you I'll come for you," I tell her. I don't know where the words come from as I didn't intend to say it. I look over at her hesitantly. She nods in silence.

Jess

"Fuck... it feels like we've been sitting here for hours..."

"It's been seventeen minutes, you drunk bitch... now sober up. Fucking Hell. What's the matter with you?" he growls back me.

I look over at Felix and I see that he's trying *not* to check me out. He's trying too hard. It kind of turns me off a little bit. He should be more assertive. 'Be a man,' I want to say to him. 'Grab me around the waist and pull me in, feel my breasts press against your chest. You know you want to,' that kind of stuff. But, I don't, of course. I'm no slut. Instead I decide I'm bored with the whole situation and want to go home, so, I better find out what the fuck he wants.

"Go on. What do you want to talk about? You got rid of that... problem... now let's just forget about it, okay?"

"It isn't as simple as that."

"I'm pretty sure that it is."

"There are a bunch more of these cunts out there, and they're looking for me right now. Seriously. I'm fucked if they catch me. And you know what? Now *you're* fucked too."

A light switches on in my brain. A very sobering light.

The fucking cunt, son-of-a-bitch, arsehole.

The rage rises inside of me.

"You absolute, fucking cunt," I slap him across the face and I see spittle flying out of my mouth and landing on his cheek and I'm kind of proud of myself for getting a good connection on the slap. A nice 'whop' sound rings out as my fingers slap his cheek.

"Ow! What the fuck?" he grabs his face and leans back away from me.

He knows he deserves it though, I can see it in his eyes, half expecting that was coming.

"You fucking planned this whole thing didn't you? You fucking cunt. Bringing that mother fucker to my flat?"

He doesn't reply. He just stares at the back of his hand, inspecting his manicure.

"You can be a real arsehole, you know?"

"Yep. I know..."

"You planned this. You cunt. You fucking planned to bring this fucker into my flat and kill him in front of me."

He sits there in silence. Clearing his throat as though to say something, but he doesn't, he just stares at his fucking fingernails.

"Look, I think you need to..." I start.

"Hold it. Unless the next words out of your mouth are going to be, 'be more awesome', I suggest you don't say them."

The smug bastard.

"You aren't even taking this seriously!" I yell at him.

"I have... almost... no idea, what you're talking about right now... but it sounds... intense..."

I know he is trying to lighten the situation with jokes, but I can't deal. "Fuck you. I'm leaving. Don't you dare ever come near me again."

"I'm trying take the edge off a very intense situation here. Relax."

He looks over at me with a wry smile and I slap him again. He doesn't even try to stop me this time and while it's not a very good slap, I still make him cry out and grab his cheek again.

"Ugh. I hate you, Felix!"

"You can hate me all you like, but there's really no changing things. If you tell anyone about this, we'll both go straight to prison. There is no way you'll convince a jury that you were forced into this. Hell, you helped me chop up his corpse, bag it up and load it into the car. You cleaned up the flat, destroyed all the evidence. If anything, it would be *me* who could pretend that you coerced me into helping *you* get revenge for the death of your brother."

I hear myself mumbling something in complete indifference and from then on, I just sit there in silence.

I pull out a packet of cigarettes, give one to Felix, take one for myself and he lights them both with a silver Zippo.

Felix starts the engine and turns on some music to break the now heavy silence. He chooses *Muse, Map of the Problematique*. His sense of drama never seems to dull.

It starts raining and this take the edge off too. I'm all numb and if I were a guy, I'd say that Felix 'had me by the balls' right now. He's an absolute demon, and yet if I were him, if that were *me* in his position, I'd do exactly the same fucking thing.

Hani

It's raining outside and the three of us are sitting in Abid's car in the carpark of the gym in Mile End. We're here for a workout, but none of us are really in the mood for it. Qusay has now gone missing and since we found out this morning, Abid hasn't spoken a word. I've never seen him like this before. He's beyond angry. Beyond it. He's in another zone right now. He's sitting there seething, his breath whistling through his nostrils.

I'm scared of what he might do. I want to ask Mo what he thinks, but I can't seem to catch a moment alone with him. I decide to send him a message on WhatsApp and hope that Abid notice.

I reach into my jacket pocket and see my hands shaking as I lift my mobile out. I send Mo a quick message 'wat do we do bout Abid?'

He replies shortly after from the front seat 'Jst leave hm. Lts c wat he sez wen hes ready.'

I look over at Abid and catch his reflection the rear-view mirror. Nothing but rage.

Fuck.

Man, this shit is just out of control. I don't even want to be part of this anymore. These are Mo's friends, bruv. His *boys*. I hang because they're cool, but shit, I ain't up for being fuckin' stabbed or some shit, bruv. Nah.

I'm considering just telling Mo that I'm out, that I just want to fuckin' chill for a while. This is not my fuckin' mess, bruv. Fuck this. But I know it's hopeless. The boys won't let me leave. No chance. Abid is fuckin' psycho, that's for sure. He fuckin scares all of us. Mo is definitely scared of him. I used to see him as cool, like a fuckin' tough guy, you know? Like a fuckin' badarse, no-one could touch him. But now, after his boys, shit, my boys too I guess, have been fuckin' taken out, he's changed. We've seen the real side of him. And, bruv, its fuckin' scary. I feel like this cunt would do anything right now to get his hands on that white boy. Anything. He'd sacrifice his own mum, bruv. Shit, he'd sacrifice any of us sitting in this car right now, for sure.

It's all he cares about now. Finding that fuckin' white boy and tearing him into pieces.

There's gotta be a way I can get out of this. Some way I can be real fuckin' busy in the next couple weeks. But I can't think of nuffin. So here I am. Feeling like I'm waiting to be fuckin' killed, bruv.

Abid opens the car door and the cold breeze that rushes in is refreshing. I look over to Mo, who senses me looking, but doesn't look back. He opens his door and steps outside. I can tell he's torn, as much as I am. I need to talk to him alone.

Jess

I'm lying on the couch in my flat. The grey mink blanket that my mother gave me for Christmas is wrapped around my legs. I look out the window and guess it must be well past midnight. Fuck. That means I slept through the alarm. Classic fucking mistake Jess. You stupid girl. Fuck. Don't you realise that you are in danger here? What if someone followed you? What it those Muslim boys come looking for their friend? You're all alone here. They'll rape you. They'll torture you.

Silly, little girl.

I can feel my muscles are completely numb. I embrace a deep yawn and I can feel the muscles in my jaw tense up then relax swiftly. Peacefully.

Sleep beckons.

Again.

Sleep this all away, Jess.

I.................. just need to remember to set an alarm.

I pick up my mobile with the last strength I have left and hit the pre-set alarm for three hours from now. I pull the thick mink blanket back over myself and nestle into worn-out white couch facing the blank television screen. My head sags. My chin hits my chest. Time to rest a little. I close my heavy eyes.

.....

I wake sometime later. Music is playing from my laptop in the living room and for a moment I think that someone else must be here. I panic.

Is someone else here?

No, don't be absurd. *You* turned that on. Stupid girl.

"Days before you came..."

My head feels incredibly heavy and I worry that I'll vomit. But I don't. Champion.

I feel like death. Death warmed up. Microwaved death…

My head hurts and I need to shower.

Jesus, I need to wash the makeup from my eyes, I need to shave my fucking legs and wash my hair.

"Jess, you are a fucking mess. A disgrace," I'm whispering so the walls don't hear me.

I lean over the side of the couch expecting to find a bottle of water that a sensible version of Jess would've left beside the bed. But I'm sadly (yet, expectedly) disappointed. Sensible Jess was obviously overwhelmed by drunken Jess.

I try to remember how I got here.

I remember being at some bar.

I remember those fucking ugly guys staring at me from the corner of the bar all night.

I remember the bar tender offering to 'buy me a cab' when he finished his shift (I know what that means), and then I don't recall much else….

Oh.

Fucking.

Wait.

A God Damned minute.

Felix…

That shit sucking mother fucking prick.

He found me.

And, oh God, what did say?

"Murder?" "Complicit?" "Get rid of a body?" "Now you're as guilty as me?"

Oh, my fucking God.

I dry wretch over the side of the bed. Wishing I could vomiting properly, but I haven't eaten anything in… I don't even know… so my body has nothing to give.

Fuck.

Jess… what is wrong with you?

Did I fuck him???

Jess, did you fuck him?

Fuck.

I don't even know…

I struggle for a moment wondering, half expecting that vampire-looking cunt to ooze himself out of the corridor from my bedroom any second with that big fucking constant grin on his face like he fucking knows everything. Like he's got every single fucking person worked out in his head.

That.

Fucking.

Cunt…

He doesn't appear.

This is a small consolation.

What the fuck happened last night?

I remember being at the supermarket. I was buying some coffee and razors, I think. And then what? Then I made my way home?

Come on, Jess. No, you didn't.

You went to a pub. You went to a fucking pub to get drunk.

And do you know why?

Because yesterday, a person was fucking murdered in your flat.

In this very fucking room.

In this very fucking room. A human was killed. His blood was all over the rug that used to be on the floor just there. And now? There is no rug. Why? Because you had to throw it away, because it got too soaked with blood oozing out of the human that was killed right in this very fucking room.

Oh God. My thoughts are not my friends.

I need to shower.

I need to wash my makeup off.

I pick myself up slowly from the couch and as I rub my tired eyes I see the dead, dry mascara rubbing off on the back of my hand like little spiders legs.

Jess, you are a mess.

A few minutes later I stand in the shower wondering what the next logical move actually is.

The water is sobering.

I tidy myself up. Shave, exfoliate, wash my hair, sit on the floor on the shower and think.

Felix. That fucking cunt.

He's trapped me in this. He really has, I'm now an accomplice. He's right, I just as guilty as him.

Those fuckers killed my brother. He deserved it.

God. No, that isn't a good reason.

I turn the shower off and stand there for a moment looking at myself in the steamy mirror, dripping.

You are a bad girl, Jess. A real bad girl.

Go to the police, a voice inside my head instructs, girls don't go to prison. Girls are victims. Do it.

Do it.

The rational part of my brain tells me that this is nonsense, ignore it. That would be suicide.

I'm in real trouble here.

Felix fucking lied to me.

I want out of this whole situation. Tommy was killed, yes. But that doesn't make another killing right. It doesn't.

Two wrongs don't make a right. Do they?

What would my mother say?

This is not who I am.

No more of this. Stay away from Felix.

I say this to myself in the mirror, "no more, Jess. Look at you. You have your whole life ahead of you. Get away from all of this. Run."

I'm convinced.

I stand in my bedroom, wrapped in my towel staring into my wardrobe for what seems like forever. Eventually the sun starts to come up. By the time I'm finished sitting my hair has dried itself.

I've changed my mind. I will help him. I want this.

Classic Jess.

Felix

A world of pain. A world of hatred.

Every morning I wake, wondering why. Why, Lucifer, have you condemned me. Why have you tortured me with these things we call feelings.

Awful things really.

Make a man weak, if he's not careful enough to avoid them…

I remember Tommy's face.

His laugh.

Shit, the times we laughed. Drunk, stoned, snowboarding, whatever. We laughed.

University… fuck… playing poker at his flat. Drinking vodka and playing for real money. We thought we were kings. Lords of the underworld.

We were kids. Nothing more.

I miss your face, Tommy. I miss being happy, brother.

And, now?

Emptiness.

Horror.

You were like a beacon in the fog. A light in the darkness, Tommy. I miss you.

I won't let these people get away with ending your life. I simply won't.

Your life meant more than that, mate.

I'm sorry I've dragged Jess into this mess. But I promise you that I'll keep her safe. I promise you I'll look after her until the day I die.

Which may be sooner than we think...

18 Sergei

Mohammed

It's Sunday night and I'm making my way home from the gym. I'm walking since Hani is borrowing my car. I decide to stop and buy some food at a pretty decent chicken shop on the way. It's fucking cold outside despite being pumped up from lifting weights. I recognise a few local boys outside the shop and we talk some shit before I head in. The old woman in the shop mumbles something to me and I don't even bother to try and work out what she said. I place my order, throw a tenner on the counter and wait.

I put my headphones back on and jam some beats while messing about on my phone. I get a feeling that something is not quite right, like. Something is just a bit off, but I reckon I'm probably just low on blood sugars like my trainer says, so I think nothing of it.

I get my food and start eating it as I walk, making my way around Victoria Park, up towards home. It's been raining and I try to avoid stepping in the puddles so I don't get my kicks dirty, but to be honest, they already fucked. I've my music playing and I'm otherwise not really paying too much attention to what is going on around me, but I suddenly feel very uncomfortable. Like, legit, somethings up.

I finish my food and throw the box away. I could just be overreacting, but the feeling is getting stronger and I turn the volume down on my music to hear things a bit better.

I hear no footsteps or any sounds of another person out there in the darkness, and for some reason, this makes me feel even more uncomfortable, as though the sound of some stranger following me would actually be better.

I take my headphones off entirely and stuff them into my gym bag. Something feels messed up. I suddenly feel like a helpless child again, scared and alone in the dark. But then, I think to myself, get your shit together, bruv, you a grown arse man.

I walk along the canal edge and the only sounds I hear are those of my own footsteps and my increasingly agitated heartbeat.

"Get a hold of yourself, bruv," I say to myself.

I try to think happy thoughts. Remind myself that I'm a scary looking mother fucker that no one would mess with, surely? *Nothing to worry about. Nothing to worry about. No one would dare fuck with you, bruv!*

The night is cold.

The night is full of danger.

I am not safe. I am not a man. I am in danger. I am a child.

The killer is behind me.

A sound escapes me, a horrible noise, as though my brain is desperate to speak but my mouth doesn't want to.

When you run. When you truly flee, you move yourself with one thing in mind and one thing only. Staying alive. Nothing else matters. It's such a primitive emotion that I think it's rarely felt by people in this day and age. It's a feeling which can only be described by the rush of pure adrenaline which flows throughout and takes hold of your body. Like an animal. Like a reptile.

Run. Move. Go. Go. Go. Do not stop.

My muscles tense. My cheeks become as tight as vacuum packed meat. I hear my heart beating like a fuckin' dragon is inside my chest trying to break its way out. But, I don't feel it. I feel only the rush. The fuckin' rush, bruv, like a fuckin line of the best coke you've ever done. Running through your head. A bull in a fuckin' china shop, or whatever they say. Incredible.

The ground below me is nothing. A blur of greys and blacks and dark greens. Nothing.

The danger accelerates me.

It's exciting. A rush. I forget for a moment why I'm running at all, I just enjoy the moment. This is fantastic. The wind in my face.

Yes.

Yes.

But the human body is not designed to operate at such a level for too long. It simply can't. It's a short-term drug released to assist us in escaping a life-threatening moment. One simply can't operate on this level continuously. The body won't cope. Eventually you'll stop. Either by choice, or by the failure of your body to carry on. If you reach the point of the latter, you know you're in severe danger. You're almost certainly a dead man.

If you have the will there will come a point at which fight mode will override flight mode and you must stop running, take stock of your situation and be prepared to fight. You have to make a choice, continue running and hope for the best, risk dying a coward, stabbed in the back, not even giving yourself a chance to fight, or, you can turn around and make a stand.

Before your body gives up and makes the choice for you, in these instances, you have to make a decision.

I made the wrong one.

Felix

Now, sometimes fate plays right into your hands, does it not?

Tonight, I decided that I'd take a drive to clear my head. I hire a car, and cruise my way around East London.

I have no idea how next to strike at these fuckers. My perfect plans have been totally ruined by bad luck and bad choices. Abid wasn't there in Camden that night last week. Did, I miss him? Was he actually there, but I just didn't see him? Did he see me? Did he know I was coming? Was this planned? Was my text response 'Right, Bruv?' the wrong response? Was that not something Qusay would say? Shit, I don't know…

I need to work out a new way in. A better way forward. I know only where these fuckers live. I have nothing else to go on.

The perfect plans of mice and men. Is that how the saying goes?

I have nothing. Jess has disappeared on me, she won't respond to any of my calls or messages. Probably for the best, I've caused her enough harm. It's safer for her to stay away.

I'm not finished with this mission though. Not hardly. While there's breath left in me, I'll do whatever I can to bring harm to Abid and the rest of these cunts. I'm in too deep now. No going back.

Driving helps me think.

I roll the windows down and turn up the music, I'm not even paying attention to what it is, it's just noise at this stage. I'm running out of money, that's for sure. Not working for the last four months has left me relying on my savings to survive. And those are running slim now. I probably have about a month, perhaps two months left before I'm broke. The prospect of me getting a job again seems now so remote. So, unlike the new me. Felix, working in an office? Working a 9-6 job again? No way. No going back now. I'd rather be dead.

I hardly remember even being that guy I was last year. Hell, just a few months ago. He seems like such a different person. A ghostly memory of who I've become.

For what I have done, regardless of the reasons why, no one, no one in Hell, would allow me to avoid prison time. No chance. And if I got put in prison, I'd be killed for sure. No doubt about it. A white boy who goes on a serial killing spree against a gang of Muslims. Hell, in this day and age, I'd be surprised if they didn't give me the firing squad.

I drive around Victoria Park. From the Stepney Green end up to Cassland Road and then down.

My thoughts disperse and I realise the music has stopped. I reach over and put Mozart on the stereo as I drive. It makes me calmer.

But I am no longer a calm person.

I had everything planned. Down to the last stab.

But now it's all gone to shit.

Why did I expect any different?

The best laid plans of mice and men.

That's it.

I wonder if it's all over for me.

After a while the music playing shuffles to Evanescence. And it's too sad for me to deal with right now. I turn it off and just cruise in silence. Listening to the sound of the engine hum in the night.

I need to find a way to finish this. Even if it means going down in the blaze of glory.

I drive down Grove Road, wondering if I could actually find that Bon Jovi song on my phone, without pulling the car over and searching for it on YouTube.

I cruise on, wondering… and then I stop.

I almost slam on the fucking brakes and scream out. It can't be real. No. Fucking Way

I must be hallucinating. I slow down and rub my eyes as though I can rub away what is across the road from me. I open them again and low and behold. What do we have here? Mohammed Hussein, stuffing his face with chicken and chips, strolling along without a care in the world.

"Come, on…" I say to myself, this is too good to be true.

I slow down and pull over up ahead of him, waiting for him to walk past me on the other side of the street. I can see my blood pulsing in the veins on the backs of my hands I grip the steering wheel tight. I try not to be too obvious about it, but I can hardly help myself.

Lucifer's ball's. It really is him. He passes by and my heart skips more than a few beats.

Well, well, well. I'm not going to let this opportunity go by.

Felix

"Let's get that knife involved."

"Allah, help me. Allahu Akbar."

He sounds concerned.

His voice cracks as he speaks and his lips begin to tremble.

But I'm not finished yet and he is nowhere near as concerned as he should be.

"Allah told me, you're leaving here," I begin, "your time has come to join him. He asked me to deliver you to him. It's a beautiful honour. I thought you desert people 'lived' for death?"

The mess in front of me starts to sob.

"This is happening, so just deal with it." There is nothing else I can say, really.

Tonight, is a good night.

I lean in and start to play.

...

The sight of his suffering and the cruelty that I was inflicting upon him only encouraged my actions. I was devoid of almost any emotion. A sudden feeling of something like regret and a questioning of what I was doing rose to the surface for just a heartbeat. No long enough for me to do anything less more flinch, to hesitate for a second or two, then carry on having my fun.

In that moment I felt totally alive and yet, I felt nothing else. Not happiness. Not relief. I only felt a sense of raw, animalistic, compulsion. Even still, it was a feeling that was wholly cold and completely empty. Devoid of anything *real*. For a fleeting moment alone, I regretted everything including what my hands in front of me were doing to the creature beneath me. Then, just as swiftly, the moment was gone.

And so was any last shred of humanity that I had clung to over the last few weeks. It was bliss. And it was the death of Felix, as a human, much more than it was the death of another…

I stand tall over the mess beneath me now. A hot steam rises up from it in the cold night. I breathe it in and smell the fresh fragrance of death wafting into my nostrils. There is so much blood you can taste it in the air. It hangs around in a heavy metallic mist.

Pure.

Glorious.

If I believed in such things, I might say I was right now breathing in the soul of Mohammed. But I know this isn't true, so, I just breathe the salty heat.

This is by far the most gruesome thing I have ever borne witness to with my own eyes. I have bits of what I guess are brains in between my fingers and from the waist down I'm soaked through with blood. My jeans will never be the same again. My socks are wet inside my boots with blood and sweat…. I've no idea how this *one* mother fucker had so much blood…

Rather incredibly my shirt seems only to have a little blood spray on it. My face feels a bit itchy which suggests to me that there is blood spray on my face as well.

For a brief moment the itchiness of the blood and the warm dampness of my jeans reminds me of something from childhood, but I don't have time to dwell on that right now.

I drop the pair of scissors I have in my hand into the lap of the what's left of the creature in front of me and feel myself smile.

Fuck, that felt good...

I'm not sure what came over me in that moment, but I just let loose.

You needed that...

I bask in the satisfaction for a few moments longer, enjoying the silence and beauty of it all.

The night is quiet. I have no doubt that his screams, although short-lasting before I removed his tongue and he passed out, would've attracted unwanted attention from nearby residents. I hear no sirens approaching, but I know it's a good idea to get the fuck out of here as soon as possible.

Given the circumstances, I've made no plans to dispose of the body. Well, now I have to say, the bits of body... I have no choice but to leave them here. It's a fucking mess, and it will be a horrific thing to come across, but I have little choice. This was rather spontaneous and I've no other options.

For certain I've left DNA around the crime scene, my spittle, my own blood (probably), my sweat and possibly tears of joy. I don't even know. I don't even care anymore.

I wipe brain bits off of my hands on the grass nearby and with one last look back at the bloody mess that was once a human, I turn and walk briskly off to the darkest edge of the park.

I leave the knife and scissors at the scene, it won't matter anyhow. The clock is ticking for me. I have precious hours now to finish this. The net is undoubtedly closing in.

A few steps from the edge of the park I hear a siren wailing in the distance.

As disgusting as it is, I know, I dive into the canal, I need to wash this shit off me. The cold water feels wonderful. I feel nothing else.

Felix

Sometimes, I wonder I really do. Is this what my life was meant to be?

Was I designed from the day I was conceived, to go on a rampage? To kill?

To not care?

To be a ruthless animal?

Surely not.

Surely not.

I never imagined this life for myself when I was growing up. This was not it.

And what do I do when this is all over? Huh? What do I do then? Do I try to just assimilate back into normal life? Honestly, is that what I do? Pretend that Felix, is and always was, just a *normal* dude? "No problems here, mate." All thumbs up, smiles, shaking babies and kissing hands, all that?"

No, sir.

No fuckin, way.

I can't do that, Jesus.

I could never live that life again. I couldn't go on like that. Pretending like everything was okay. I'd be constantly looking over my shoulder. Wondering when the cold hands of the law were going to descend upon me. Lock me away and label as a monster for all eternity.

No chance.

A scary thought crossed my mind as I woke up today, *what happens if it all ends here?*

What happens if the police bust trough my front door tonight, shouting, pointing guns, game over? What would happen? What would I really have achieved? Partial revenge against a gang of fucking cunts? A failed mission?

No doubt partial revenge is better than none at all, but honestly, a job unfinished is like fucking without cumming. It's far too much of a tease.

Although, despite it all, I feel like my climax is still on the horizon, but I'm not quite hitting the spot yet.

The most liberating feeling is accepting that I have nothing left to lose now. Perhaps Felix wasn't supposed to live forever. He wasn't born to get old. He was born to be a signal, a light in the darkness to others. He was born to shine bright. For a short time, not a long time.

And that is exactly what he'll do.

Felix. You mother fucker. You must do this. Even if you are remembered only for a moment. You will go down in the history books, and one way, your legacy will be held up as a glowing example for others.

Felix stood his ground.

Felix got revenge.

Go out there and finish this.

One way or another.

You die in the process, you are a martyr, you live, you are a hero.

Do it.

Jess

Tonight, I decided that I'd leave London for a while. I have to. This shit is all too much.

I mean, two nights ago, I fucking watched as a man was slaughtered in front of me. Right here in this room. Right here in my fucking living room!

And then, like the obedient little bitch that I am. I fucking helped cleaned up the God damned mess. Fuck, Jess. For fucks sake.

Jess. Come on. You have your whole life ahead. And look what you've done. Please go to the police...

The voice in my head fades away.

Decisions have to be made.

I walk to the bus stop near my flat and wait for the next bus to arrive.

Where would I go?

I look around for clues. What is the universe telling me that I should do?

A not bad looking guy sitting in the bus stop shelter is checking out my butt and for a moment I consider just turning around, asking him to take me home and distract me from all of this. Protect me.

I feel so, very vulnerable.

I can't turn to my friends. I can't tell them what I have done.

I feel tears on my cheeks.

I don't wipe them away.

The world should see this.

I feel the end of my life within reach. And although it scares me. It also seems right. As though part of me realises that people like me are the outliers. We are anomalies that shouldn't exist. Not in the perfect world. And so the world will always find ways to wipe us out and fix its little mistakes.

We are broken.

Something is wrong with us.

Tommy's death triggered me in a way that, I think, was unique to me. Other people experience similar horrors. Similar terror and similar pain. Yet, they do not go about planning to kill one of the guys that did it.

Planning and then carrying out murder? Other people just don't do that.

Yet.... Felix... You, did...

You not only accepted this pathway. You jumped for it. You sought it out.

And now here you are.

You have killed.

You, Felix, have killed someone.

Jesus. Christ. That is such an inconceivable concept to so many people. And yet, you... you just embraced it like it was a just another footstep as you walk up that hill.

I stand there for a moment, waiting for some kind of sign, a realisation or something, in my mind. Like, an explanation, 'why?' 'why me?'

The silence in my mind is deafening.

I walk away from the bus stop and light a cigarette. My destination? The off-licence.

I know I'm messed up. I know it. But, what can I do?

Only embrace it.

19 Václav

Jess

"Get the fuck out of my way... fucking pigeon."

Right now, I'm marching through the West End. I got off the train at Green Park, walked past The Palace, down The Mall, through to Trafalgar Square and now here I am in the Square dealing hundreds of mother fucking pigeons scooting about at my feet.

I don't want to hurt these little bastards, but you could very easily convince me that they want me to hurt them... Playing a game of 'how close can you get to Jess's boot before jumping out of the way.'

I did a bit of Ket on the train and now I'm fucking feeling this shit like you wouldn't believe. It's coming on hard. This doesn't help with the joint I smoked on the walk to the train station and now I realise that either the Ket or the weed would've been enough.

I slow down my walking and I realise I have actually already stopped. God knows how long I have been standing here actually... people are just walking around me, going about their business.

Well, okay, Jess. Time to move, you're going to start looking suspicious here.

I watch as a couple with a new born baby in a pram fawn over the creature, touching its cheeks to see how warm it is, tucking its little blanket in at the sides, arguing with each other in an attempt to 'out-love' the other. It's a disturbing scene that I cannot relate to in the slightest and for some reason, feel queasy and know that I have to get out of here. I have to get away from all these people.

The next thing I notice is that my fingers are starting to swell up. I have a silver snake ring on my right-hand ring finger that my mother gave me many years ago. I try to pull it off and it gets stuck.

I take a deep breath, try not to panic and remind myself that this stress is probably mostly in my head anyway. I need to cool down so I walk into the Tesco on the corner of Trafalgar Square and within (what seems like, but probably was a lot longer) thirty seconds, I panic, forgetting why I'm in here at all, and feeling as though every single customer in this busy store (why is this such a small store when it gets so fucking busy?!) are staring at me, judging me. And then The Fear tells me that someone has definitely phoned the police and even though I have no drugs on me, somehow The Fear convinces me that either way, I'm fucked.

I move back out the door as quickly as I can I then get myself across the street to the Waterstones book store which to me seems like a safe and calm location where I can gather myself before attempting to decide why I'm even out in the public right now anyway. Ideas which I most certainly forgot long before I even got off the train.

Once inside Waterstones, I have a sudden urge to sit down and it becomes obvious to me that this bookstore is not like the library I'd imagined in my mind. If anything, it's just as loud and intimidating as the world outside, with huge dark bookshelves looming over me, heavy and the contents completely foreign to me. Like the books themselves are judging the state of me.

I feel a noise escaping my mouth and realise, as I notice that my lips are totally dry and cracked and I feel one of them split open as the groan escapes. No one around me seems to notice anything out of the ordinary and I move forward towards a stack of cooking books with Gordan Ramsey's face plastered all over the front of them.

At that moment I have an overwhelming urge to piss, shit, vomit and sleep, and I can't decide which one is real. Possibly all four. And I look down at my hands to see if they are still swollen but I forget to do this the moment I look down and so I just stare at the table in front of me and then at my boots and back at the table. I hear words escape my lips, but to be honest, they are probably still just in my head, "man. Is this table crooked? Or am I crooked?"

Fuuuuuck. That is a great question.

What the fuck am I doing here?

I'm terrified and I look at the books in front of me and despite Gordon Ramsey's smiling skull on the cover I can see the torture in his eyes. They eyes don't lie. They can't. The restless rage I see in his eyes mimics my own and the feeling of warmth, the feeling of comfort that rises in me in that moment brings me back to life and I know that I'm not alone. We share a moment, Gordon and I.

Sometime later I've made my way home, the drugs have all worn off and I've been crying for some reason, the split in my lip keeps closing up and reopening and it stings when salty tears run across it.

All I want to do is sleep.

As I walk towards the entrance to my block of flats, that unrelenting cunt, Felix, is sitting on the ground outside smoking a cigarette and staring right at me with those yellow eyes of his that I just can't deal with. Despite how hypnotising they are, I see the same torture in his eyes as I see in mine, the same restless rage, but this doesn't comfort me. Felix's restless rage has taken him too far.

Staring at him from a distance, I know in that moment that he is lost. Utterly lost.

But... I need him.

And he needs me.

If we are going to be lost, we'll be lost together...

Any shadow of doubt or fear of what we've done or going to do subsides and I decide that the one thing I must make sure of, is that *my* restless rage doesn't leave me as eternally lost as Felix has become. Felix has lost his humanity. I can't give it back to him, but I can protect what is left of mine.

Felix stands up when I approach and we both move to say something, but in the moment that we pause to let the other speak, we realise there is actually nothing to say at all.

Felix

It's a cold Friday evening and I know that time is running out for me to finish all of this. To take down Abid and the rest of those cunts before the inevitable happens. Either I get caught by the police or, worse, by Abid himself and said cunts. It may be only a matter of fucking time.

With that in mind, I decide a sesh is in order. I decide that right now, with no clear fucking idea how I'm going to pick up the pieces of this train wreck, that the only way to clear my head is to fill it with enough drugs and alcohol that they squeeze out all other thoughts.

Distraction calls to me.

I buy more snow, I say more, because it would seem as though I've been buying so much recently that even I've lost control of the situation. I have eight grams sitting in my drug box at home and yet in my pocket now as I make my way over to Jess's place is another four grams.

I reflect on this relinquishment of control over what used to be such a controlled aspect of my life.

Felix, you are changing.

I don't feel good or bad about this change taking place. I feel nothing, only as though this is just who I am now. Whatever is left of me.

On the way over to Jess's, I buy a small bottle of cheap and nasty vodka from Sainsbury's for £6.50 which may seem like a bargain but in reality, I'm probably just drinking turpentine or something equally as nasty with vodka flavouring. Nonetheless, it gets the job done and within a short while I'm drunk and the weight of the world seems to escape from my body. I'm hit with the glorious out-of-body sensation of release that we all feel with alcohol.

Within a short while I'm back at Jess's place in Kings Cross and I press the buzzer for her flat but no one answers. I try one more time and then decide she mustn't be home. Undeterred and for some reason very confident that she will return home this evening, I decide to wait. Fuck it, I have nothing else to do and nowhere else to be. Sitting here is probably safer than being at my own flat anyway…

I don't have to wait too long. Four cigarettes, a listen to *Mozart's 40ᵗʰ symphony in G minor* and his *9ᵗʰ symphony in C (Allegro Molto)* and then she arrives. She's wearing black combat boots with white laces and I wonder for a moment why I haven't thought to put white laces on my own.

As Jess approaches she looks at me as though she was expecting me to be there and I look at her as if to say, 'I always keep my promises.' I know she understands why I'm here and we walk inside in silence.

Once inside I immediately walk over to her laptop which is sitting on the writing desk in the corner of her living room with the big Bose speakers on either side.

"What's your password?"

"Why do you want my password?"

"I'm going to put some music on."

"NeedlesandPins, both the 'n' and the 'p' in capitals."

I put on some Marilyn Manson, something that I'm pretty sure we can both appreciate, *I Want To Kill You Like They Do In The Movies*, a great track that seems both cheesy and yet perfect for our current situation. Jess pours us both a drink and we stand in her kitchen near the open window to smoke.

I stand next to her and catch a whiff of her perfume, I've either not been this close to her before, or I've just not noticed it. It's lovely, delicate, yet strong, familiar, yet mysterious, and when those I hear those words come to me in my head, I realise they are describing Jess precisely. She is all of those things and still so much more.

She stares off into the darkness while I stare at her.

I've never thought about it before, but she reminds me so much of myself. For a start we look like we could be brother and sister, a thought, which for some twisted reason, probably something to do with my childhood that my subconscious has repressed, turns me on…

Her hair is long and dark, almost black like mine, but hers has a soft amber glow to it that I'm jealous of. Her eyes are just like mine, black in the darkness, but when the light hits them, they look like pools of honey melting in the hot sun. She's basically the same height as me, which means when I look into those eyes of hers, we are staring directly… into each other's souls.

She turns to me and I think to myself, perhaps we really are siblings, separated at birth. Two damaged individuals trying to make our way amongst all the regular humans on this planet, sometimes successfully convincing them that we too are human… but, mostly failing to do so.

We don't need words to explain this understanding. As I look into her eyes, I know that she knows. I know that she feels the same way.

Marilyn Manson is still playing the background from the other end of the flat, shuffling through his entire catalogue of songs, entire catalogue of emotions. A catalogue that seems so obviously written for the both of us. Just for Felix and Jess.

Just A Car Crash Away, plays on and Jess suggests we move back to the living room and bring our drinks. I pick up the bottle of whiskey from the bench as well as the bottle of Coke Zero and Jess takes a couple of Kronenburg's from the fridge.

In her living room we sit on the floor next to her coffee table and rack up a couple more lines of snow. I do the racking and she tells me that the lines I've made are huge. To me they're perfectly normal and I remind myself that I have indeed become a snow junkie, a professional snowboarder, as it were. So I say nothing and cut those lines in half, into what I would call 'baby lines,' lines for children, but these are apparently acceptable to Jess and we do one each.

Everywhere I go the snow follows me.

We drink some more and when our eyes meet, I lose myself completely.

The always confident and stoic Felix is suddenly like a small, innocent child who meets Santa for the first time, incredibly nervous and choking on every possible word that might want to escape his lips. I can't think of the right words to say. There's so much I want to say, and yet everything seems foolish and unnecessary. Even the important things seem pointless, as though those melting honey eyes staring back at me already know every single word I will say, every single thought I could possibly muster.

I'm helpless and exposed.

And then a sudden compulsion to open myself overrides everything. In that moment when our eyes lock, I can see the same confusion and rush of emotions hitting her as well. We're both in the same boat. We're both, fucked.

These words that I would never, ever, have let slip out of my lips before escape, "you make me so nervous, Jess, I ...."

"Don't know what to say... "

"Yeah."

"I feel the same way."

"I feel like a child, so nervous and I just can't create words to describe what I'm thinking."

"You don't have to. I can see it your eyes."

A wave of relief washes across me.

"Jess, I've never met anyone in my life at all like you. You're something else."

"You're the same, why can't I get you off my mind? I've known you for a long time, you were always there, Tommy's friend. I'd always would see you and we would have small conversations, but… but.."

"Nothing like this…"

"No."

"We never opened this door."

"I never imagined it."

"There was always something," I admit to her, reflecting on all the times we'd met previously, always a connection there which even Tommy used to joke about. "Oh, your little girlfriend's coming to the party tonight," he'd taunt me, when he knew his sister would be there. I'd brush him off and play cool, still not knowing for sure what the connection was that other people could clearly see. I tell her everything.

People around us could see it, and yet we ignored it, as best we could. But we both knew…

Sitting here on the floor of Jess's living room, I can see exactly what they all saw. The chemistry is unmistakable. Like a nuclear reactor boiling away all this time. A nuclear reactor that we have just lifted the lid on.

No going back now…

We do another baby line each and smoke another cigarette. Jess changes the music to Deftones and the way that we both feel music resonate with us is so powerful. The way we both communicate through music is astonishing. I've never met anyone who understands and feels music the same way I do.

Deathblow, plays on, oozing out of the speakers and I reach over and touch her cheek.

In that moment I feel like life has given me hope. A hope that has been always out of reach, like a racing dog chasing a rabbit that it never gets. Always close, but never quite. Until now. When my fingers touch her skin, it's warm and soft, yet cold and hard at the same time, and I just don't… I just don't know what the fuck is going on…

Our eyes meet and, in that moment, I know that that I have never understood anymore one more, never *loved* anyone, never cared for anyone more than myself ever, but I know that I would die for her. She deserves it. Jess deserves all of it.

Without another thought, we begin sharing our deepest darkest thoughts and secrets. Things which neither of us have ever shared with another soul. Its therapeutic and even the most horrible, scariest parts of my soul I expose, and she exposes hers right back.

A conversation which would terrify most people becomes to us the most natural pouring out of our own souls that we've ever experienced. We talk for hours, days, who knows?

Experiences from our childhoods right up until now, everything, trauma, emotional, physical, sexual, all of it pours out. We drink, we snort, we smoke, we listen. The more we talk, the more time seems to stop moving and to speed up at the same time. Nothing matters anymore except the two beings in this very room and the connection they feel with one another.

Not a single word of our current situation is spoken. The situation we have to deal with is entirely secondary to just us, right now. This is for future Felix and Jess to deal with.

Jess tells me things that would shock most people and I tell her things that anyone sane would run from. And yet all it does it spur us on. All we feel is a need to open ourselves, like opening our veins to let the other suck the bad blood right out.

Two vampire siblings, reunited in life after a lifetime of separation. We joke that Satan must be our father.

The more we talk, the deeper we dive, the more the joke is exposed as the irrefutable truth.

We are not like the others, Felix and Jess, we are something else...

Something else entirely...

Whether you believe in such things or not, we discuss our astrological signs. Felix, your humble narrator, is a Taurus, Jess, your narrator's dark angel, is a Scorpio.

We do more snow, smoke more and pour another glass of whiskey.

Jess's mother, it turns out is a guru on such aspects and Jess sends a text message to her mother for some feedback on the two of us. Almost immediately she hits us back with commentary that is both shocking and yet not at all surprising.

Jess reads out the message from her mother, as she translates from Italian to English.

"When a Taurus and a Scorpio come together, it is nothing if not intense, which can manifest in either a positive way or a negative way, or both. Taurus and Scorpio are opposite signs in the Zodiac, giving them a special, intricate connection."

This seems about right to me, thinking of the way this girl makes me feel. I sit there and admire Jess as she reads.

Jess carries on, her eyes opening wide as she reads the message, "they can combine to make an extremely powerful whole, each's strengths balancing out the other's weaknesses. Their sexual attraction is incomparable."

My thoughts race back to depravity and I imagine doing all manner of debaucherous things to Jess right here on this floor. Jess takes a break and waits for the next message to come through from her mother, who I'm very surprised is like, right here with us right now, giving us this information. We smoke another cigarette or two (time has no meaning anymore) and then the next message pops in.

I rack us up some more baby lines.

Jess clears her beautiful throat and reads on.

"A very intense blend. Taurus and Scorpio combined form the basis of all real relationships, love and passion."

We stop there. The reality of what we are hearing is too much for either of us to deal with. Neither Felix nor Jess was ready for any of this and we both look at each other and sigh.

"Woah," is the only thing I can muster.

"Yep... cigarette?" Jess replies.

Absolutely.

We smoke in silence. Now finding ourselves sitting on the kitchen bench with the back door wide open to the cool night air to let the smoke out and let the night in.

All concept of time, of reality, of the things we have done, the killing, the seriousness, of what we've done over these last weeks is totally irrelevant.

I wonder to myself how this could have happened between us.

No answers come to me...

For a brief moment I glimpse the sadness in her eyes that exposes how she feels about what she has done. The regret, the pain and the self-loathing. She is tormented and aching.

I recognise it. I understand it. But I don't feel it myself...

I don't feel these things anymore. No longer can I put myself in another person's boots, as it were. Whatever remnants of empathy I had are now long gone. Killing another human, apparently has this effect on humans.

Jess is sad and confused. She is feeling this right now, in this moment.

I've lived in that same moment, feeling those feelings, for what seems like forever now. Endless sadness and confusion.

I understand.

Yet, I do nothing to subdue this emotion. I want her to feel it too.

I lean in and take the back of her head with my right hand, pulling her beautiful, tortured face towards mine. Our amber eyes meet, and all words and thoughts are no longer relevant. In that moment all pain is taken away, all fear is gone, all wrongs are righted and the tilting world washing against us both becomes balanced.

I kiss her and she kisses me back.

The nuclear bomb that we've had locked away for all this time goes off.

Nothing else matters.

Jess is the one. The only one that truly understands.

We are broken creatures.

We are lost children.

We are siblings.

We are brother and sister.

We are Satan's children.

Nothing can keep us from each other. Nothing at all.

From now on, nothing.

Words escape me again without my control, "I'll be beside you forever. In life and in death. Always."

"Always," she replies, her soul wide open and blending with mine.

We both know it's a match made in Hell, and we both accept it.

The sun is coming up and our soundtrack plays on. *The Last Day On Earth*.

'Hope that we die holding hands, always.'

As I stand up and take her by the hand, leading her into the bedroom the last words she says is "this place is death."

Jess

We awake the next afternoon with a renewed sense of purpose.

Without a word spoken we kiss and we both know that together, we're going to finish this. Together we're going to end this. One way or another. Felix gets up to make us coffee while I lie there content with myself that this is the right decision.

"Let's get that bastard Abid, and end this," he pronounces from my kitchen.

"Let's," I reply. I want to say more, but there really is nothing to say.

Felix has taken me to a place in my mind that I thought only existed in the movies. He is like... like the answer... the like *answer*... if that makes sense?

It scares me that he is so incredibly just like me.

It makes me wonder how he could actually be real.

For a moment I consider the possibility that I've gone completely mental. That I've lost it. That since Tommy died, I've went off the rails. And now here I am imagining things.

Is Felix even really here?

Did any of this actually happen?

Why do I feel as though someone, *as though Felix*, is inside my mind?

Come on, Jess... get it together. He just a guy. Right?

But, no... No, he is not.

He is something *else*.

I watch him closely as he returns with two coffee mugs in hand. He's naked except for his black and white Calvin Klein boxers that he slipped back on when he left the room. He's lean and muscular. He looks after his body. Abdominal muscles and that 'v' shape that forms around the groin area... his long black hair is messy and wild. I've never seen it like this before. So messy. He's never let me see him in this state. I'm sure he never lets people see him... imperfect. And I love it.

Right now, he looks like a fallen angel. Which is totally fitting.

Like a perfect angel cast out of Heaven. Much like Satan himself.

Felix was such a regular guy. Just a regular dude. One of the millions out there.

And yet, look at him now... you wouldn't even guess he was the same nerdy architect boy we all knew back then...

He has evolved. He has become his true self.

An angry little machine.

A perfect killing machine.

He hands me my coffee carefully and then climbs into bed next to me.

Once again, sober now, both of us look at each other and are lost for words.

But words seem so pointless, and we both understand this.

I'm nervous and yet, so is he.

He leans over and pulls my head onto his chest.

We lie there in silence.

I have never felt so at home, so protected, so certain and yet so scared at the same time.

20 Vasily

Felix

You are never too young to die in style. Ever.

I realise that this may be my last day on earth. But, Hell, every day could actually be our last when we really think about it. The bus coming towards us that we don't see when crossing the road, the misstep we make on the train platform, that drunk driver who crashes into us on the motorway. Hell, even that slip we have in the shower that breaks our necks. Anything. Absolutely anything at all. Fatal accidents occur all the time. Last year, the police recorded one-thousand eight-hundred and fifty deaths by accidents on the roads alone, that is five people per day on average. Five fucking deaths a day, just on the roads.

With death staring us in the face constantly, why would any of us risk an ordinary, lame death? Why would we not pursue a proper, memorable, *epic* death? If you have the option of going out falling down the stairs in your underwear, cracking your skull open and shitting your pants, or on the other hand going out swan-diving off the top of the Empire State Building, which would you prefer? How would you like your death to be remembered?

Death is around every corner. We can either choose to try and outrun it, or we can turn around, face it and take control. The choice is ours.

Embrace this simple control.

I stare out the window of my flat and watch as a couple with a baby stroller pause to cover up the baby as it begins to rain. The mother struggles with the buttons and the father flinches, seemingly about to lean in to help, but then he simply stands there, pulling out his mobile and staring at the screen, totally ambivalent.

The rain begins to pelt down loud and I turn my music up to hear it better out over the drops pounding on the windows.

Elisabetta de Gambarini - Pieces Op.2, 1748. Such an old-fashioned piece. It floods me with feelings of what must have been such a simple, proper time in human history. Men were men, women were women and if crossed another person, you were struck down for it, accordingly.

I wonder, have things ever been this fair in the history of humanity? Have things every really been proper and honest? I'd say, probably not. We've probably never had a time when things were fair. Never honestly fair. We just reimagine history to suit ourselves.

To be honest, I don't know if humans have it in them to be fair. We are at our cores, fucking animals. And animals do not, by and large, play fair. They play to win. Survival of the fittest reigns supreme.

This is what we do.

It's what we have always done.

The moment that a human has an opportunity to exert some influence over another human, be it psychological, or by physical force, it would seem as though that opportunity is irresistible to us, and must be taken up. We must influence that person. And we convince ourselves, it's for their own good, right? We, the dominant ones, know best.

And so, the circle of life goes on and on.

But, I like to imagine a time when things were more simple.

When justice was served.

When sweet justice was served on a sour plate.

One can always dream, right?

An hour later, I buy two grams of snow from my dealer, J (they're all called J, aren't they?), who kindly delivers right to my flat. And I spend the next hour racking up little lines and snorting them through the tube part of a dismantled parker pen, while I mentally rehearse how I'm going to take down Abid and his remaining cohorts, ideally without being killed in the process. Mozart's fortieth symphony is playing in the background, loud enough that I cannot hear the razor blade in my fingers tapping away on the plate in right front of me.

Part of me just wants this whole thing to be over, just to wipe them out and be done with it. The rest of me knows that I still need to be tactical, precise. Do not rush this, Felix. Act with care. Do not rush this, Felix. Act with care. I type those words out on my laptop over and over until the screen blurs and the words are filled with so many typos the sentence is lost.

It is time to move.

Felix

Abid's house in Hackney.

I have no other choice now but to strike him at home.

He is always there, Friday nights. This is where is hangs. Like clockwork.

I don't know if it some Islamic thing, or whatever, but Abid is always home on a Friday night for dinner.

And sometimes his boys are there too.

I never wanted to step into the hornet's nest. But, now… fuck it. I'm heading in.

Everything is back on track.

To a degree.

And while I don't have time to work out a proper execution plan like I did before, I don't really care anymore. I just want to go at these mother fuckers with everything I've got, and if I die in the process, so be it.

No matter what happens from here on out, I can be certain I won't go down without at least scarring these mother fuckers for life in the process.

The 'best result', you might ask? The best result is that I take all of these fuckers down in one final action inside that house. Catching them all off guard and ending Abid's life while he stares right into my eyes, knowing exactly why I'm doing what I'm doing to him.

Worst result? Obviously worth asking at this point… Worst case, I go at them and Abid and his last remaining band of cunts take me down like a fucking child and kill me in the most gruesome fashion they can conjure at the time.

But you know what, my beautiful audience? In either situation, your humble friend Felix gets his sweet relief.

I just don't care anymore.

As I told you all, the 9 to 6 work life, becoming the family man, getting married, raising children etc… that life was never for me. I tried for so long to make it so…. I wanted to be like everyone else. But, I just couldn't. That was never me.

I know I've done right. I know I've done the world good by removing those shithead cunts from this planet so far. I know that if God exists, he will accept me and my actions as righteous. As good for humanity.

I have no fear of this.

Killing in the name of righteousness is not only acceptable, it is encouraged.

Felix, you are good man.

Felix, you are a lost soul.

"No," I say aloud, shaking such thoughts away. "Do not doubt yourself, man."

I go to my bedroom and lay out my favourite clothing on the end of the bed. The best of everything I own.

My death uniform.

I've accepted the finality of what I will do next.

This is a suicide mission.

It is unplanned and totally rogue.

But that is exactly how I feel it should be…

Even if I kill Abid and whoever happens to be with him, there's no chance that I will escape the police. They'll find me eventually.

And Felix… you were not designed, not created to be confined to prison or whatever would come next.

No, you are a free spirit.

You must end your own life if the authorities are going to capture you.

"Obviously," I say to the voice in my head.

I've known this since the beginning.

No going back.

I'm in too deep.

21 Wolfgang

Felix

It ends.

I shouldn't go in there. I should stay the fuck away. I should cut my losses and run. I should quit while I'm ahead. I should stay the fuck out of there. But life is full of *should's*. So, fuck it.

What's worse than death?

Life forever.

Getting old, falling apart, both physically and mentally? Awful. If I die tonight, I'm more than happy to say goodbye to this hopeless place we call Earth. Who really wants that?

You?

No… of course you don't…. None of us do…

I finish my cigarette and snap myself back into the scene I've created.

I can see Abid's car parked in the driveway and I hear loud, angry voices coming from inside the house. Voices which sound remarkably like those of Abid and his cronies.

I stand across the road, under the leafless skeleton of a plane tree and ponder. Prepare.

I listen to one last track, to get myself in the right mood. To set the scene. *Lux Aeterna*, a beautiful, deep, dark track which perfectly encapsulates the significance of the coming moments.

This is it.

I don't even care what happens to me from here on out to be fair. This is both liberating and empowering.

The most confidence inspiring and motivational thing I can think to myself right now, is that whilst those cunts inside that house want to live and are afraid of death... I, on the other hand *want* to die and have now become more afraid of living.

My advantage over them is supreme.

I've never felt such complete relief. Such complete freedom.

When you approach a situation from the perspective of being already dead, nothing else, absolutely nothing else matters. Nothing can stop you and nothing should.

Make your life mean something.

Make it life mean anything.

Make your life remembered... long after you are gone. No matter what it takes... It's all we have...

Alright everyone, fuck it. Time to move.

I'm not sure who exactly is in that house right now, but I know for certain that at the very least, Abid is in there. If I can take him down, my mission will be accomplished and I can die a satisfied man.

I take the SOG Seal Pup Elite out of its sheath and take a moment to admire the beauty of this knife.This is considered one of the most user-friendly military issue knives in the marketplace. And despite is being a on the more expensive side of the knife spectrum, one of the still the most commonly available in London. The clip point blade moves the tip closer to the centre line for improved piercing-style cuts. In addition, the partially serrated edge offers the benefits of both straight and serrated edges in one blade. Given that the weight of the knife is perfectly balanced, a stabbing thrust glides almost effortlessly through the air.

The light from the living room window shines off the blade as I turn it around in my hand.

The end is now.

I knock on that front door and feel nothing but happiness and satisfaction.

I hear Abid speaking. The door creaks open and I move inside.

Abid

"Listen. The system is rigged. It's all set against us. Call it what you want, bruv, it's fucked. Its fucked so that when someone's winning, someone else is always losing. It's always been that way and it always will. Someone always has to be the bad guy. The world needs villains. I don't mind being the baddest of them all. I'm good at it. It's fucked, bruv. We all just animals. And, we'll fuck it."

Someone knocks and interrupts my speech.

I get up to answer the door.

Felix

You mother fucker. That's where people like you have it all wrong. Thinking your necessary. Thinking you're serving some purpose. You are nothing. The world could only ever be a better place without your kind it.

Everything you do has a completely selfish motive. You are no better than animals. And I know you might love to hear that, that might give you a hard-on hearing, but to me, to most people, acting like a fucking animal is beneath us.

You are no more useful to us, to the world, than a fucking pile of rubbish. All we want is to see it gone. No. value. At. All.

You are bottom-feeders of the worst order.

We don't need you here, in our communities, in our faces. We don't want you. So why are you here? All you do is take, take, take from us, and what do we get in return? Fear and intimidation.

You are worthless.

This is why the police investigation into the deaths of Kamal, Izzat, Ali, Qusay and Mohamed have been lacklustre at best.

The end begins now.

Abid

You know what you are, cunt? A complete fuckin psychopath and a complete fuckin idiot. The worst combination of all.

I think this to myself as I watch the white boy approach. Yet no words are spoken. No words are needed.

Felix

And I know that I'm fucked.

This is the end, beautiful friends.

Any thoughts of hope are dreadfully absent. But if there's one thing I should remember right now, it's that I should be dangerous even in defeat.

I've only one opportunity here to finish this. One moment, and I must take it now. Before Aziz can reach me. I can see him in the corner of my eye, lurking.

My heart pounds and that stabbing, choking sensation begins to take hold. I shrug it off as best I can. No time for that now, body, I know that I've abused and taken advantage of you too much over the years. This isn't the time for reminders. This isn't the time to fail me.

Abid reaches for the Glock on laying on the floor beside the couch and dive onto him, desperate to stop him. We wrestle for a brief moment, his hot breath washing over my face. I'm using every possible muscle in my body to fight with him, to hold him back, Aziz begins moving towards us. Abid moves around to face me and this is my moment, his torso is exposed, I snatch the SOG Seal Pup Elite combat knife from the floor beside us and thrust it into his chest, aiming as close to his heart as possible, but given the angle I'm working from, I'm not sure if I get the right spot.

The blade pops through his chest well enough though and he squeals in pain. I stare at the entry point waiting for the blood to start seeping through, but it always takes slightly longer than you think. I pull the blade back out and he falls back and crawls away, holding the wound.

Before I have a chance to catch my breath Aziz is on me, grabbing me by the shoulders and throwing me backwards onto the hard floor.

I don't even see his fist coming as it connects right in my face, my jaw feels like it's suddenly no longer part of my head. The knife falls out of my hand and Abid yells to Aziz to get back, I know exactly what this means.

Instinctively I rise to my feet, I'm dazed, but most certainly not confused.

A cockroach scuttles past my boot and I think to myself, guns don't kill people, boredom kills people... It's an odd thought to have right now and I don't know where it's come from.

I watch his finger as he squeezes the trigger. The skin stretching across his finger and wrinkling in slow motion as it tightens. I see the slide moving backwards and a moment of utter serenity washes over me and for the first time in my life, I'm not afraid of anything.

The back of my throat feels warm, verging on hot and also very doughy, then I realise it's because its quickly filling with hot blood, some of which is trickling down my back between my shoulder blades.

I suppose he's shot me in my neck and the bullet has gone right through. Impressive.

I feel no pain.

This is most confusing.

I just feel calm. Warm and calm. All of this niceness centred in my throat. Like a warm mother's womb. If I could wrap my whole body into a tiny ball, small enough to fit inside my own throat, I would comfortably live there until the end of days.

I watch as Abid drops to his knees, the gun falling hard on the floor beside him. Blood oozing from his chest and creating a beautiful dark wet patch on his shirt.

Everything is in slow motion, everything exaggerated.

I got him good enough after all.

I can't move a muscle. I just stare. Felix the mannequin.

Abid clutches his chest and I watch his eyes roll back in his head. There is a lot of blood oozing through his hoodie now. It's making a beautiful stain, all that blood. Too much. Too much for a human to lose. I'm satisfied as I see his body go limp.

As I breathe out in relief a small spray of the hot blood flies out of my mouth, hitting my lips landing on my chin. I switch off from this reality and let my mind float on the soft waves of *Beethoven's Moonlight Sonata* as the warmness spreads throughout my body.

I know, I know, I am dramatic, I warned you of this. But I want to greet the endless sleep with a soundtrack befitting me, befitting Felix.

I feel nothing but the warmth in my throat and the lightness of my mind as I reach into the darkness towards the endless sleep.

I imagine my body lying there on that floor, smiling. Content.

Beethoven plays on. The room is overcome with its melody.

It's all in my mind.

And the music is lifting me away from this place.

Retribution has been fulfilled and so has my purpose on this planet. My place in history is secured.

....

In the distance I hear sirens and as I prepare to breathe my very last breath, welcoming the forever sleep now, I see Aziz scampering out the door. Whatever... fuck it...

Moments later I'm floating up, weightless, forever upwards.

This is a death worthy of a hero.

I have nothing else to offer this world.

A voice calls out to my body below.

A sweet voice.

It's the enchanting, melodic voice of a Siren. Of a demon sister. A daughter of Satan.

Everything is hideous and painful.

And yet her voice calls to me....

Everything is beautiful.

"All the world will be your enemy, Prince of a Thousand enemies. And when they catch you, they will kill you. But first they must catch you; digger, listener, runner, Prince with the swift warning. Be cunning, and full of tricks, and your people will never be destroyed."

Printed in Great Britain
by Amazon